Entertaining Mr Pepys

Deborah Swift

W F HOWES LTD

This large print edition published in 2019 by
W F Howes Ltd
Unit 5, St George's House, Rearsby Business Park,
Gaddesby Lane, Rearsby, Leicester LE7 4YH

1 3 5 7 9 10 8 6 4 2

First published in the United Kingdom in 2019
by Accent Press Ltd

A CIP catalogue record for this book is available
from the British Library

ISBN 978 1 52887 854 8

Typeset by Palimpsest Book Production Limited,
Falkirk, Stirlingshire

Printed and bound by
ational in the UK

For John, who plays a part in all my stories

~ ACT ONE ~

1659

'O Heavens! How wretched have you made the state of Women . . . you make us subject to our Parents humours, when Maids; when married, to our Husband's wills; and yet in either State such your Decrees, you plant in us a will to disobey.'

Otrante in *Flora's Vagaries*, a play by
Richard Rhodes, 1664

CHAPTER 1

London, March 1659

When someone is in love, they turn inside out. The man you think you know is gone, and a new shining man appears. A man that is the opposite of everything he was before. So it was with Bird's father. Instead of his sober lawyer's doublet, he took to wearing lace-tipped cravats, flapping coats in the Indian style, and the worst sin of all, curling his hair with clay curlers. It made him look like a Royalist, and the curls, with his balding pate, made him look ridiculous.

Bird had tried, she really had, for her father's sake, to like Dorcas.

But Dorcas wanted to own Bird's father, and was busy fencing him around with her opinions. And Dorcas had plenty of those. Bird shouldn't wear this colour petticoat, or that height of shoe. She shouldn't play this sort of music, or read that kind of book. According to Dorcas, nearly everything was 'unsuitable'.

So now, they had found Bird a suitable match.

She paced the tiled hall, dressed in her Sunday suit of lilac watered silk, her skirts swishing as she twisted at each turn. Behind that door was her future; her freedom. Twenty years old, and she was ready to burst out of this life and into another.

Inside the chamber, the hum of men's voices was too low for her to hear.

'Shall I . . .?' Sukey, her pale-faced lady's maid, reached for the door handle.

Bird pulled her back. 'Wait!' She held up both her hands with the fingers crossed.

Silently, Sukey shook her head, but made the same gesture back. Neither smiled. Both knew it was far too serious a business for smiling. The dream of what lay beyond the door couldn't be spoken. The fairy-tale knight was too ridiculous an idea for a grown woman, and yet somehow that hope still clung . . .

Bird took Sukey's hands and squeezed them, something Dorcas disapproved of. Her voice echoed in Bird's head: *Never touch the servants.*

Sukey squeezed back, her expression grave, and mouthed, 'good luck,' turning the handle and swinging the door wide.

A deep breath. Bird sailed through the open door, eyes immediately searching out the stranger standing before the ornate oak fireplace.

'Mature,' her father had said.

She stopped, mid-step. He was old. At a guess, a good ten or even fifteen years older than she. Thirty? Thirty-five?

4

At once, everything within her seemed to be mired in quicksand, sinking. A glance was enough to see his clothes were dark and a little too tight, skimpy even, and the knees of his breeches rubbed thin with wear. A wiry body, and nervous, restless eyes that alighted everywhere but on her, and the wary stance of a dog that had strayed into someone else's territory.

It was then she realised that love doesn't just blind. It renders everything irrelevant except the one object of its affections. Her father had lied. There was nothing in the least handsome or well-favoured about Mr Knepp.

Bird paused, balanced on tiptoes, as if she were about to cross a physical line into the room, hoping somehow that time might re-spool, and she might find herself back outside the parlour door.

'Mary Elizabeth,' her father said, using her formal name and beckoning her in.

Bird curtseyed as was polite, and drew herself back to upright. She was robbed of words. That Father could have thought Mr Knepp a suitable match had pole-axed her. She stole a glance behind her, where Sukey, still hovering by the door, was rigid, eyes fixed on the newcomer.

'Miss Carpenter.' Mr Knepp made a brief nod of acknowledgement in her direction, as one hand unbuttoned and re-buttoned his coat.

Should she speak? She had no idea what to say. She had the impression that she'd somehow stepped into the wrong room. She cast desperately about the chamber, hoping her father would break the awkward tension.

'Mr Knepp's livery business is one of the busiest in London,' Father said, his hand plucking at the curls of his careful coiffure. As if the business made up for everything. 'Farringdon and Knepp's, Hackney and Horse Hire and Livery.'

'It's not a bad little business,' Mr Knepp replied. 'Pays its way.'

Bird was still taking this in. Horse hire. Well, at least she could ride. She heard little of her father's pleasantries until he turned towards her again, 'And her height suits you very well, you being . . .' Her father stopped and waved his hands vaguely.

Short. She'd be taller than him, in pattens.

'Can she manage a budget; staff, and so forth?' Mr Knepp barely even looked at her.

Bird stepped forward, 'I do all my father's tallies, and I—'

'Oh yes. And she can do wonders with pastry,' Father said, cutting her off as usual.

Wonders with pastry. She clamped her mouth shut. What an inane recommendation, as if she had no sensible virtues at all.

Father turned to face her and mouthed, 'He's a good prospect.' Their guest saw it and turned away, as Bird felt her face flame. Aloud, Father said, 'What do you think, eh?'

As if she could answer! With him standing right there. She quelled her seething emotion.

'Speak up,' her father prompted.

6

No words came. She knew what Father wanted. If she was to accept this man, the unspoken tension that plagued their house, the icy sharpness between Bird and Father's new wife, Dorcas, would be gone. He would be able to breathe easily again. He was eager for his life of unrestrained passion, and Bird wanted to please him, but . . . this man? Still, she hesitated, but knew it would be grossly impolite, and beneath her schooling and upbringing, to reject the man openly.

'Did you have far to come, Mr Knepp?' she said, finally managing a conversation.

'Smithfield,' he replied. 'Near St Bartholomew's.'

She nodded. Her head bobbed up and down foolishly as she sought for something else to say. In the ensuing silence Mr Knepp gripped his hat in front of his chest as she grew hotter and more flushed, uncertain where to look without catching his eye. She searched her mind for something positive. He had nice hair, she thought. Good, thick hair. It was the only thing she could see to recommend him. At the same time, the thought came that she didn't want to be Mrs Knepp. Bird Knepp. The name sounded sharp; ridiculous. But of course he wouldn't call her by her mother's over-familiar nickname, he'd call her Mary Elizabeth, as Dorcas did.

A rustle of taffeta. As if summoned by her thoughts, Dorcas stepped forward from the open door. She was a pale, buxom woman, laced tight into her bodice, so her white chest bulged over it, reminding Bird of milk boiling over a pan. Her pale curls were stiff with sugar water, and her prominent, over-innocent eyes made her appear like a small lap-dog. Bird stepped out of her path, glad of the diversion.

'Is the deal not settled yet?' A fan tapped impatiently against Dorcas's thigh. 'Another five, Joshua dear?'

Bird turned to her Father. The conversation seemed to have jumped ahead without her. Five what? She couldn't really think Father needed persuading? Surely it was she who needed to be persuaded?

'I suppose we could.' Her father beamed and placed his hand on Dorcas's arm in a gesture of doting affection that instantly shut Bird out. She watched the hand move from the arm and downwards. It lingered over Dorcas's rump before it dropped away.

'Thirty-five guineas,' Dorcas whispered, nudging him.

At the sound of this enormous sum, Sukey let out a little gasp. Dorcas turned, made an impatient shooing gesture, and Sukey scurried out.

'Very acceptable.' Mr Knepp's voice was firm. 'I'll take her.' As if he were buying a joint of beef. He did not even look at Bird, but reached out a hand to her father, who clasped his arm to pump the hand up and down.

'Best not to wait too long,' Dorcas said. 'A June wedding. What do you think, Mary Elizabeth?'

She couldn't think. Her opinion seemed to be too late. She just kept staring at the man who was to be her husband.

'June then,' Dorcas said.

As her father prepared to go up to bed that night, she caught him by the arm. 'Father, I've been thinking . . . Mr Knepp is not . . . I mean, I don't think—'

'It's a good match,' her father said firmly. 'You are very fortunate he picked you out.' As if he had not offered him an incentive at all.

'But is he like us? I mean he seems . . .' She struggled to find the words. 'Father, have you seen where Mr Knepp lives? Tell me about his house. I'm anxious to know more about it. Is it in a fashionable part of town?'

'Farringdon and Knepp's is a big place; just off Smithfield. Close to the city walls and the fleshmarket.' He shook her off; tried to dismiss it, knowing what she meant beneath the words of the question.

'And who, pray, is Mr Farringdon?'

'Oh, he's deceased. Mr Knepp used to be the junior partner, but of course he's in charge now. And a good thing too; Farringdon was a good tradesman in the old King's day, but he'd let it all slide; he was eighty you know, when he died.'

'Have you dined there, Father? How many servants does he have?'

A pause. He twisted the button on his cuff. 'Of

course I have.' His eyes slid away to the window. 'Though I didn't see everywhere, just the parlour. There seemed to be a great many men in the yard.'

'But what about his other interests; does he like music, or play? Has he many books? He didn't have much to say to me, and he doesn't seem the sort of man to—'

'Tush. What a question! You know I always want what's best for you. How many books he has doesn't matter one whit. One can always buy books.'

'It matters to me,' she said. She went over to the spinet in the corner, put a finger on a key, and heard its plaintive twang. The note made him turn. 'Is there nobody else?' She held his gaze.

Up until now, her father's authority had been absolute. And to stay in the house, where she had become unwelcome, with the overbearing Dorcas quashing her every move, was plainly unthinkable. As the note died to silence, for an instant the whole dilemma was laid bare before them; her father's guilt and regret, her own reluctance, and the impossibility of the whole situation.

Her father was the first to brush it all away. 'Come, Bird, he's an excellent prospect; the man's got a thriving business. Up and coming, they say, up and coming.' He flapped an impatient hand at her, turned to go upstairs. 'And you are getting no younger. It's time you were settled. You can make a success of it, I'm sure.'

'But he seems, I mean . . . it seems a rough sort of trade, horse-hiring.'

'Nothing wrong with good honest labour. You'll gct used to it,' hc said gruffly. But she heard the regret in the words; that like a sudden shaft of sun coming from behind clouds, he'd seen for a moment what it meant to her.

'Father, I'm not sure I will be able to find affection for him.'

'Whoever marries for fancy?' Silence, before he made a small cough in his throat to cover the irony of this fact.

'I mean I can't—'

He opened his mouth, about to say something, and hope flared, but then; 'Joshua?' The call was sharp, proprietorial. Dorcas appeared at the top of the stairs in her nightgown, her hair loose and hanging. 'It's late. Aren't you coming up?'

The tender moment was gone. Father shrugged and, like a dog to its master, hurried up the stairs. She watched him stumble on the top step and fall into Dorcas, who stifled a laugh and hauled him back to standing. 'Naughty boy!' she said.

The bedroom door shut with a click and laughter drifted from behind it. Laughter that squeezed the breath from Bird's heart.

CHAPTER 2

June 1659

Bird had expected a simple wedding, and the wedding service was short, the church naked of decoration as was the Puritan way, even though by then Richard Cromwell, the Protector's son, had resigned his feeble grip on the country. He was still living at the Palace of Whitehall though, and the uncertainty of what was to come next meant the mood in London was austere, with a general feeling of malaise.

In St David's Church, the exchange of vows was hurried, the congregation a blur. Another wedding party was shivering outside the door when the newly married Mr and Mrs Knepp came out. Who'd have an English summer, thought Bird. June, and the wind was cold enough to cut.

'Stroke of good fortune, wasn't it, that the parson could manage to accommodate us at such short notice?' Dorcas said to Bird's father, as he helped Bird into the carriage, where her domed trunk of clothing was already stacked next to the driver.

Her new husband had sent an impressive coach

and four to fetch them home from church, but the thing was open-topped. She rubbed her goose-pimpled arms, as Father passed Mr Knepp the iron-bound dower box, patting it with a benevolent smile. Mr Knepp gave a curt nod, and stowed it on the floor.

Bird pressed down her blowing skirts and held tight to her hat, her hair whipping around her face. The carriage creaked and tilted as her new husband got in opposite her. She couldn't believe it had come to this; that she was actually married, and her stomach lurched as she realised it was done. Irrevocable.

Father reached over the door and took her hand, and kneaded it, and opened his mouth ready to speak, but the horses were matched chestnuts that pranced in their traces, and the pock-faced boy who was driving couldn't hold them back. With a jolt, they lurched into motion. Bird was thrown back against the seat, and could not even wave. The horses were wild with the wind, and everyone had to leap out of their way.

Mr Knepp swayed on his seat opposite, the dower box wedged between his feet. He gripped the door easily with one hand as if riding a runaway coach were an everyday occurrence. Finally the horses slowed as the traffic queued for the city walls. He was more smartly dressed than before, she would say that for him. He wore a dark suit with a single row of buttons up the front of the vest, and breeches of serviceable black moleskin,

13

but his dark demeanour made her green summer gown seem frivolous and over-fussy. Bird's stomach heaved. She was already nervous, and the wind had messed her hair, made her dishevelled before Mr Knepp. *Christopher.* His name felt strange on her lips. He hadn't called to see her since they had become betrothed, though he had sent apologies twice, and it had bothered her, his lack of interest. But Father had reassured her, saying summer was the busiest time for the horse-hire business, and the engagement had been short.

'He sought you out,' Father said. 'He asked me about my daughter last time I hired a horse, and I told him how pretty you were. Did you not see him looking last time we hired a carriage from him?'

She didn't remember. Nothing about Mr Knepp would have drawn her eye. But her father had told her this over and over in the last few weeks, and it had mollified her somewhat, to think Mr Knepp had been so smitten, and she imagined he would tell her how pretty she was, and how much he wanted her. Perhaps it would be pleasant to be worshipped that way, and she would grow fond of him. In any case, she looked forward to escaping Father and Dorcas. She had made a point of always pausing before entering the parlour lest she find them both unlaced. She was shamed seeing her father's hands roaming over Dorcas's neck and chest.

Her mother had borne this from her father over

14

and over. The women coming and going like carriages. Father did what he wanted as if it was his right, and Mother could do nothing about it. Her protestations got weaker and weaker over the years. Father was impervious to the wringing of Mother's pale hands, to her face blotched pink with humiliation. He did what he wanted, no matter the cost to her. No words made a difference; he denied it all, even when the evidence was such that any fool could see he was philandering. In the end Mother wasted to nothing, seeming to die of silence. They said it was the wasting sickness, of the chest, though Bird suspected it was a broken heart. When Mother was gone, there was nobody left to protest about his ever-changing liaisons. Was Dorcas different? Would she change him, and put an end to his dallying ways? She doubted it.

Bird took a deep breath, fanned her face with her hand to cool her feelings, and focussed on the passing view. She must not turn into her mother. She refused to fade away. She had always felt that there was a much bigger person inside her, bursting to get out, if only someone would give her the chance.

'These are fine horses,' she said brightly, smiling at her new husband, determined to make the best of it.

'So you think you know something about horses then?' he asked. His expression held a slight sneer.

'No,' she said, flummoxed. 'I mean, not a great

deal, but—' He was already looking away out of the carriage.

Chastened, and unaware what she'd done to offend him, she looked down again into her lap, where the nosegay of wild marjoram and purple comfrey was ragged and broken by the wind. Her stomach was even worse now, filled with a hollow sense of disbelief. This wasn't what she'd imagined.

'Will we be having our marriage feast at home?' she asked, trying again to get his attention.

He turned his head slowly. 'No feast. Your father didn't pay for one.'

She took in the accusation in his tone, and her hands tightened on the seat. No feast? Even a proper farewell to her father had been snatched away.

Out through the crenellated archway at Newgate, and at last the horses could find passage through the traffic. Ahead of them a herd of cattle swayed their rumps on their way to the slaughterhouses. The men behind them goaded them on with switches. One of them had a little bull-calf following, and the cut of a switch drew blood from its flank. The sign at the end of the street read, Cowe Lane, and shortly afterwards the horses turned under another arch to a big cobbled yard surrounded by stabling. She turned to look back at the larger building that must be the house, which spanned the passageway into the yard – a house that had probably once been a tavern, built over the arch of the bridge. Above were a pair of narrow shuttered windows with a round one, like an eye, in the centre.

As they clattered through, the horses' heads poked from the stables as if to see who was arriving, and several rough-looking stable lads appeared and gawped at her.

'Say nothing, d'you hear?' Mr Knepp shouted to them.

They stood back as he got down, the dower box crushed against his chest.

'Take these horses and get them fed and watered, and the carriage cleaned up. It's going out for hire again at four.' He turned to Bird, gestured impatiently with his free arm. 'Get down, we haven't got all day.'

But it's our wedding day.

The thought came and went like smoke as two boys grabbed the reins of the leading horses. She scrambled down.

'What about my trunk?' Bird said, anxious she might never see it again.

'Purler,' Mr Knepp shouted. An emaciated boy in half-mast breeches who was sweeping the dung from behind them, stopped and stared. 'Bring my wife's trunk into the house.' The lad put a hand across his mouth to stifle a giggle.

'This way,' Mr Knepp said, and set off ahead of her towards the house.

It was so unlike what she had imagined that Bird could only follow, dumbstruck.

17

The entrance to the house was dark and smelt of horseflesh and old leather. A collie dog whined and came to her wagging its tail. She knelt down to pat its silky head, and it licked her hand. At least that was some kind of a welcome. She ruffled its ears and the whole of its backside shook back and forth with pleasure.

A grey-haired man with a pinched-out face and pointed beard appeared at the door. The dog slunk away back into the yard. 'She's here, then,' he said to Mr Knepp. His voice had a nasal quality.

'This is Mr Grinstead, who minds the office. Grinstead, my wife.'

'A pleasure, Mr Grinstead,' she said.

Grinstead gave a brief nod, but then held up some papers. 'I've had a look at the bills of sale for Northampton.' He sniffed and wiped his nose with a grey kerchief before continuing, 'That matching pair of greys. They sold for fifteen guineas at Derby, but they're two years older now. We might get them for ten. And Baxendale says Viner's got his eye on them.'

'Hell's teeth.' Her husband swiped the papers out of his hand and examined them.

Grinstead gave a shrug. 'Can't you get someone to nobble them?'

'Bloody Viner. I didn't know he was going. He'll bid me up again, blast him.' Mr Knepp turned sharply to Bird. 'I've got work to do,' he said. 'There's provisions in the back kitchen. I'll be in at six bells for something to eat.' And he was out of the door, with Mr Grinstead gesticulating at his elbow.

Bird watched them stride across the yard. Her husband still had her dower box and Grinstead's papers clamped to his chest. The house behind her was silent.

She swallowed the urge to cry. She was a grown woman, not a babe, and her husband was busy, that was all. He'd be in later to make a fuss of her. She'd better look lively, and see what she was to be mistress of.

Taking a deep breath, she pushed open the door into the parlour and navigated around the table in the dark, inhaling a smell of soot. Throwing open all the downstairs shutters, she revealed a large but echoing chamber, panelled in dark, grimy wood, its ceiling stained yellow with tobacco smoke. No ornaments graced the walls, but a faded print of a horse race hung unevenly over the fireplace, and a blackened hunting horn dangled from a beam. She shivered as a draught blew through the door – the fire grate was broken and there were no fire irons.

My Lord, but it certainly lacks a woman's touch, she thought.

No maidservants in the kitchen either. She coughed as the smell of damp caught the back of her nose. A fire would need lighting here if anyone was to cook. A quick glance into the copper in the scullery revealed chipped earthenware bowls and filthy trenchers floating in a scum of grease.

On the kitchen table was a packet of barley, some onions and leeks, and a brown paper package leaking blood. Her knees started to shake.

The shock. It must be the shock. Her thoughts tumbled over each other. She wanted to go home, back to this morning to her warm chamber, back to the moment when she had slid on her new silk stockings tied with a blue riband, back to before she was married, before she wore this wedding band. She pulled at it, but it wouldn't budge. He had skimped on the gold. Or had thought her smaller. Either way, it was there for good.

It was then that she thought of her father.

He *knew*, she thought. He knew exactly what she was coming to, and he had said nothing on purpose. How could he do this? To his own daughter?

Angrily, she strode into the gloomy passage. She'd better see the whole house.

Up the narrow creaking stairs to a set of low-doored rooms above the archway. Again bare walls; not a shelf, not a book, not even a news-sheet. Two rooms, each with a heap of tangled, unmade bedding. Hooks on the wall held coats and caps, and a single basin and ewer stood on the window ledge. She would have no privacy, she realised, not with the stable men so nearby.

From up here she could see into the yard, but there was no sign of Mr Knepp. Three solid-looking gentlemen were hiring horses, the stable-boys helping them mount. She watched them clatter from the yard with a kind of envy, before going into the next room, the one with the round window.

This must be Mr Knepp's bedchamber. The sight of the bed made her cover her mouth. It was a wooden bed frame with no drapery at all. No pillows, just a plain sheet and some rough striped blankets. She went a bit closer. They were horse-blankets, she could swear it.

He hadn't bothered to make any kind of welcome for his new bride. A kind of horror drained her anger.

A rattling noise on the roof made her start and glance at the window where stripes of rain dashed against the greenish glass. Heavy footsteps on the stairs, and two lads blundered through the door with her trunk swinging between them, the corners bumping into the door jamb. They dumped it with a crash in the middle of the floor.

'Thank you,' she said, summoning a semblance of control and dignity. 'I'm Mrs Knepp.' The name sounded odd to her ears, as if she'd aged overnight. 'And you are?'

'We know who you are, Missus.' The taller one, his pale face pocked like porridge, hair sticking damply to his forehead, wiped a hand over his wet face. 'That short-arse's Nipper and I'm Dobbsy. Stable lads,' he said. 'Pleased to meetcha.'

'Pleased to meetcha,' echoed Nipper. He was stunted, with a head that looked too big for his scrawny body and freckles. 'Can you cook?'

'Well enough,' she said. 'Though you should wait to speak until you're spoken to.'

A moment's pause. 'Thought you'd need to know,' Dobbsy said, jutting out his chin in defiance, 'there's eight of us live here in the yard and Master said as how we'd get a good dinner once you got here.'

She did not react, though inside her heart sank. 'Eight?'

'Eight that live in. Two coachmen, two grooms, two runners and us. And then there's Mr Grinstead but he don't live in.'

'Are there no indoor staff?'

'We all work in the yard. It's hungry work, mucking out,' Nipper said.

'No cook, or housemaid?'

'Only Livvy who comes days to do the brewing. There was a cook, but she's gone, now you're here. Master gave her the heave-ho.'

'You may go,' she said, hoping this was the right way to dismiss them. It seemed to be, as they shuffled off and she heard them go out of the front and the door bang after them. A phrase of her mother's came to mind: *She's married beneath her.*

She stooped to her trunk and opened the lid, but hastily shut it again. She couldn't unpack. Not here. She'd glimpsed her brand new cotton lawn nightgown embroidered with rosebuds and ribbon, where it lay on the top of the pristine white linens and her best gowns. She knew every item in that trunk, and she could not imagine any of them in this house. In fact she wanted to protect them from it, as if its very air might sully what was within.

With heavy feet she went back downstairs. She could leave now. But then she thought of her father and a tightness drew around her throat. He'd done this on purpose. She simply couldn't bring herself to go back home to Lombard Street.

Her mother's voice came back to her: *Humour him, Bird dear. It's always less trouble in the long run.*

He'd been so desperate to get rid of her, he'd sent her to *this*. The thought burned like sulphur. She couldn't bear to see his face, this night, of all nights. Perhaps Mr Knepp was just unused to women, or unsure how to treat a lady. Perhaps he would be kind, and be glad she was here, and she could clean this place up, if he was willing. She had plenty of energy, and given time, she could make things comfortable and pretty. Hadn't she always said she enjoyed a challenge? She'd give it one night.

By six o'clock she had mended the fire and made a passable stew with the beef, leeks and barley that had been left out for her. She'd scrubbed the worst of the dirt from wherever she could, and afterwards washed herself, just up to the elbows; there was no time for more.

Humming a tune to herself, she lit candles to dispel the gloom, but paused as the bells of St Bartholomew's clanged the hour. Her stomach gave a somersault. Eight people, Dobbsy had said, and her new husband too. And she, the only woman. She wiped her hands again and again, licking her dry lips, waiting. It was a torture. The quarter bells went by, and then the half. She kept hurrying over to the stew to stir it, with her palms already sweating. Foolish to have it ready before they came, the bottom would be burned.

Should she fetch them? What should she do?

Finally she hurried out into the yard. The rain flattened her springy hair to her scalp. Not a sign of anyone. A light glowed in the stable door across the yard, and laughter. She steeled herself and made a dash for its cover, hunched against the rain. Over the top of the half-door she made out men round a rough plank table, cards in their hands, a leather-jack jug of ale set on a barrel. The lanterns hung from the rafters reflected glints from the piles of coins next to the upturned decks. There was no sign of Grinstead, which was a relief. He'd set her teeth on edge.

'Supper's ready,' she said, over the slash of the rain.

They turned, startled. She had the impression they'd forgotten she existed.

'We'll finish this round first,' Mr Knepp said, not looking up from his cards.

Damn him. 'It'll spoil if you leave it too long, husband,' she said.

Sniggers from the stable-boys which were silenced by a look from Mr Knepp.

'I said, we'll be in when we're done.'

There was nothing for it but to walk away.

★   ★   ★

They came when she wasn't ready, and caught her staring at herself in the back window, trying to fix her ruined hair. *Your father likes me to look nice when he comes in*, her mother used to say.

'Good evening, everyone,' she said, determined to make a good impression.

Mumbled greetings and stares. The men sat, and fished their eating knives from their pockets, and all eyes were fixed on her hot face as she doled out the stew. Reluctantly they put the knives away and picked up the spoons she'd left out. Their expressions showed their disappointment with the meal.

They were wiping their bread around their bowls before she was even half-way through hers, and had to endure the stares as she lifted the spoon to her lips. She felt her face begin to perspire.

'Looks like we might have to wait all night,' Mr Knepp said, gesturing towards her. He waved to the men. 'You go. Tell the landlord at the Tap and Bucket I'll see him tomorrow. I've one or two things to deal with before we ride to Northampton.'

The men sniggered. 'Give her one for us,' Dobbsy said, grinning.

'Mind your mouth,' Mr Knepp said. 'Now get out of here.' Scraping of stools and clatter of boots. Finally the door banged shut and they were alone. Bird forced herself to spoon down her meal, aiming for dignity but quelling the urge to run after them.

Mr Knepp stood and went to a shelf to take

down a box of tobacco. He lit his pipe without speaking and exhaled a thick stream of smoke. She smiled at him, inviting conversation, grappling for normality.

'Right, Mrs Knepp,' he said, fixing her with cold eyes, 'these are the rules. One. No visitors without my say-so. Two. Dinner on the table at noon, and supper on the table at six. You don't need to be here when we eat. You can eat before or after us, I don't care which.'

He paused to suck on his pipe, and she grabbed the moment to protest, 'But I thought we'd eat together, as a—'

'Three.' He raised his voice over her. 'I'm not to be interrupted when I'm working with the horses. Women are in the way in the yard. You'll work in the tack room cleaning the harness, and in the house. And you've to keep out of sight of the men; I don't want them getting ideas.'

She nodded, and the disappointment was curiously numbing. She hardened herself. This was not to be a marriage of affection; that much was obvious. It was to be a marriage of convenience – his. But if that was the case, the further away from him she was, the better, and in one way, it was a relief.

'Very well,' she said, feigning calmness. 'But I'm sure you will agree that if I'm to lodge here, the house needs some refurbishment.'

'It suits me perfectly well as it is.'

His stubbornness brought out her own. 'The fire

grate needs repair, and at home we had a drape on the door to keep out the draught. You would be more comfortable sitting here in the evenings if we did the same.'

'Perhaps. But there are more urgent repairs in the yard that need doing first.'

She took a deep breath and got to her feet. 'You had a larger than average dowry from my father, and I'm sure he'd want you to ensure my comfort.'

He stood and tapped out the plug of tobacco on the trencher before him where it sank into the remains of the stew. 'You're an expense. That's what the dowry's for. A wife is an expense, like a horse.'

'Then why did you marry me?'

He thought a moment. 'Other men my age are wed, and having sons. In time, I'll need an heir to take over my business.'

He held her gaze, raised his eyebrows, and the thought hung between them, unspeakable.

When she woke next morning it was to the stink of horsehair and an empty bed. She listened for any sound, but could only hear the clop of hooves in the yard and the squabbling of sparrows on the midden by the window. She hobbled to the wash-bowl, limbs stiff and cold.

She kicked her trunk viciously as she passed and her bare white toes stung. She was Mrs Knepp now, and no mistake. She should have left. Should have run. Why hadn't she? Because she'd been too polite, that's why. Mother had brought her up to

27

be polite and well-mannered, even to servants. Why, she had befriended all the servants at home, no matter how lowly.

She'd thought Knepp would see reason, if she was nice. She'd thought he'd stop, if she was nice, and asked him politely.

'It has to be done,' he'd said. 'We must needs consummate it.'

Even at the last moment, when she had winced with pain, she thought he'd stop. How naive. She'd thought if she pleased him, he'd like her, and she wanted him to like her. Even *him*. Why must she always want to be liked? She shrank with self-loathing.

At the wash-bowl she scrubbed everywhere, then balled up her stained nightdress and pushed it under the mattress. It couldn't go back in the trunk with her other clothes and she didn't want to look at it ever again. The wedding gown she pushed out of sight under the bed. It was contaminated by thoughts of *him*. She dressed in a hurry in practical clothes and went down to the parlour, in search of food, but found there was no left-over bread in the crock. The fire was lit though. Had *he* done it? She couldn't say his name; she didn't want to think of him.

A clanking noise from the direction of the back scullery made her curious. She went through the scullery and opened another door to the smell of hot ale and a woman's back leaning over a steaming copper. A brewhouse.

'Oh!' The girl turned, eyes wide.

Bird's eyes flared in the same way. The girl was a blackamoor, with the darkest skin she'd ever seen.

'I'm Mrs Kncpp,' Bird said. 'The new—'

'I know.' The girl bobbed half a curtsey. Black hair frizzed from under her cap. 'They told me you'd come. I'm Livvy, the daily. Have been, since last July.' Her voice had a slight accent.

Bird felt a rush of relief. The sensible words of a servant, even this one, made normality possible. 'Oh, Livvy, I'm so glad to see you!'

Livvy backed away, frowning, holding the wooden paddle in her hands.

She'd been too familiar, Bird realised. She took on a more formal tone, 'Do you do all the brewing?'

'Yes, but this copper's broke.' She prodded it. 'It's leaking, see. Things'll be different though now you're here, won't they? We'll get sorted, won't we?'

'It might take me a while to settle in, get used to things. You can carry on with your duties though, just as usual.'

'It'd make it more easy-like, with a new copper,' Livvy insisted. 'The men get through so much ale. Then I could fix the fires and such quicker.'

'What else do you do, Livvy?'

'Must I tell you everything?'

'Yes, please. If I hear it from you, we'll all understand each other.'

Livvy held out a pale-palmed hand to tick off on her fingers, 'Fetch the fat from the slaughterhouse, melt it down to make saddle soap, boot

29

dubbin, tallow for candles, hoof oil. Fetch linseed, boil it, skim it, bottle it. Clean the boots, collect the horsehair from the combs, take it to Jakes the upholsterer—'

'No maid's duties in the house?'

'Fires. I have to do those. For the brewing and the cooking. But Cook's gone now you've come. And I do the wash. Sheets and linens, the men's shirts. All them straw stuffings, the mattress and bolsters, I have to do, when harvest comes and we've new straw. I done that twice, last year. Soon be time again. And before, I used to lay out cold meats for supper, if there were any, but Master said you'd do that now.' Seeing Bird's expression, she bridled. 'It's a lot. All that, and I only get fourpence a week. Haven't had no raise since I came. Not no tip, nor nothing. 'Spect it's cos I'm black. Stable lads get tips all the time and they're—'

Behind Bird, a voice cut in, 'Talking won't brew beer.'

Livvy ducked her head, rolled up her sleeves, and turned back to stirring the barrel.

'That's better,' Mr Knepp said. 'Mrs Knepp can come with me.' He strode off, and Bird did her best to appear like the lady of the house as she followed, head ducked against the increasing drizzle.

In the cold light of the day, the yard was a pitifully ramshackle affair. It was in fact two yards, with about thirty stable doors. The cobbles, though, were damp but clean. As she passed, a battered

30

coach and four was just leaving; its occupants looked like tradesmen, in aprons and caps.

Mr Knepp turned into a long, low white-washed building with bridles dangling from pegs, rows of trestles bearing saddles, and a stall housing a gig with a broken wheel.

'Out of the way!' He pulled her back.

Dobbsy staggered in past them, under the weight of a wet saddle, the bridle hung over his shoulder. The pungent stink of horse-sweat came with him.

'She can do this one, first,' Dobbsy said, dumping it on one of the long trestles. 'Stable lads are glad to be rid of it, I can tell you. They'd rather be with the horses.'

Mr Knepp pointed to a bucket filled with cloths and brushes. 'Everything you need's in there. Wash first, then dubbin, then a polish with that saddle soap. It needs to look like these others when you're done.'

'Very well,' she said, attempting to stay calm. She'd never cleaned anything like this in her life. Servants had done everything at home. But it didn't look too hard; after all, when she was younger, she'd done her father's riding boots sometimes to please him.

'I'm travelling to Northampton today to the horse fair,' Mr Knepp announced. 'I'll be gone overnight.'

She was taken aback. 'But what—?'

He didn't let her finish. 'You'll need to feed the men, and clean the day's tackle.'

'I'll need money then,' she said.

'Grinstead will give you money for the week. The office is above the tack room.'

There was no time to think because every time she was about to finish one set of harness, another batch arrived. Sometimes the girths were full of sweat and the stirrups filthy. She had placed an old sack over her knee to protect her skirts, but her white cuffs were soon dark with grime. Half-way through the morning she heard Knepp's voice shouting instructions and then he appeared at the tack-room door. He eyed the row of dirty saddles waiting to be cleaned.

'You'll have to work quicker than that in future,' he said. 'You can finish now. Keep to the house whilst I'm away. I don't want you distracting folk in the yard. And don't go showing yourself in town.'

Covertly, from the window, she watched her new husband fondle a big bay's nose, then spring astride with a well-practised vault. He grasped the reins and gave them a flick before touching his heels to the horse's ribs. He'd shown the horse more affection than her. It gave her a kind of despair. Two of the runners rode with him, and as they clattered away under the archway, she felt her shoulders drop in relief. Perhaps if he was away a lot, she'd survive it. Some inbuilt pride or stubbornness inside her made her baulk at the idea of confessing the dreadfulness of her situation to anyone else.

As soon as their hoof beats died away, she headed

up to the office, a cupboard-like room up a narrow set of stairs. The room smelt of cough linctus even though it was summer. Grinstead looked up from a chapbook as she came in and thrust it hurriedly under the desk. She spotted only a few words before it was whipped out of sight: *Secrets in Physick and Chirurgery*.

'My husband says you have my allowance,' she said pleasantly.

'Ah yes.' Grinstead cleared his throat and bent over a coffer between his chair and the wall and unlocked it. Shielding it so she couldn't see inside, he brought out a small bag onto the table. Prising open the neck, he tipped out a few coins. 'You'll need to sign for it,' he said.

'Sign? Why?'

'It all has to go through the books, Mr Knepp says.'

'That seems ridiculous. The household expenses are nothing to do with the business.'

'Then you don't know Mr Knepp. Everything's to do with the business, as far as he's concerned. Here.' Grinstead passed her a quill and waved a hand at the inkwell. 'Two shilling, he said.' He turned a ledger to face her and pushed it across the desk.

'I'm not doing this every day,' she said, dipping the pen in the ink. 'Can't you give me the whole week's at once?'

'That is the whole week's.' A self-satisfied smile played over his lips.

She paused, the signature half-done. 'Then there's been a mistake. I can't feed everyone for that. There's barely enough bread for the men's dinner. You must've misunderstood—'

'He said you'd kick up a fuss. But I'm to let you have that and no more.'

She placed the pen firmly on the desk and with a sudden swoop grabbed for the rest of the purse.

Grinstead's hand shot out and covered hers, pinning it to the table. 'Now then, Mrs Knepp. Be reasonable.'

'Reasonable? Feeding ten of us on two shilling a week? What about the money from my dowry? I saw him bring that over to the office. Surely—'

Grinstead dragged the purse across the table into his lap. 'That? It's spoken for. It'll be well-spent, never fear. Your husband knows horse flesh and he'll invest it wisely. He'll buy well at Northampton and it'll make you money in the end.'

'He's using my dowry to buy horses?'

'Best thing he could do with it. Count the pennies and the pounds look after themselves, is his motto, and it's working. This time last year he had only six nags, and now look at him. Twenty, he has now.'

'But it's impossible. As soon as he gets back, I'll speak to him.'

'You can do that. Even a pretty face won't get Knepp to spend money. Not unless it's got four legs and can be hired out.'

*   *   *

34

Bird screwed up her face as she walked across the yard, imitating Grinstead's pursed lips and nasal voice. 'Now then, Mrs Knepp, be reasonable.' She squeezed the coins in her palm until the nails dug in. 'I'll give him reasonable.'

He'd said to keep away from the yard, so ignoring the mounting pile of filthy saddlery in the tack room gave her great pleasure. Instead, defying his orders, she fetched her cloak, took Livvy as chaperone, and went to the market in Cheapside. With the two shillings, to Livvy's evident discomfort, they bought sheets and bolsters and new blankets for the bed. It was the least she deserved, Bird thought, after enduring last night. The house was her empire, and she would bring civilisation to Farringdon and Knepp's. That's what women did. *Men need our gentility*, her mother had taught her. Perhaps she could show Mr Knepp a better way to behave, a more gentlemanly way to do things. When she returned, she sent Livvy up to make up the bed because she couldn't bear to look at it herself.

'What shall I do with this?' Livvy came to her in the kitchen with the stained nightdress in her arms.

'Get rid of it,' Bird said.

'But it's a good one. Got lace at the collar and all.'

'I never want to see it again.'

Livvy's broad face broke into a dazzling smile. 'You mean I can keep—'

'Just get it out of my sight.'

In the afternoon Bird went back to Mr Grinstead.

35

She planted her hands on the table. 'I've spent the money, so if you want feeding this day, you'd better open that chest.'

'I beg your pardon?' He blinked his pale, red-rimmed eyes at her.

'I'm not prepared to live in a hovel, even if he is. The men ate the rest of the bread at noon. If the men are to have their supper, I need two more shillings to buy herrings.'

'Mrs Knepp, I'm under strict instructions—'

'Then I shall tell the men you wouldn't give me enough to feed them.'

'Do that.' His expression had taken on a righteous look. 'I warned him you'd cost him, but he wouldn't listen. I've always followed my orders to the letter, and I don't intend to disobey them now. Especially not on the say-so of Joshua Carpenter's daughter.'

'My father has nothing to do with this.'

'He wanted you off his hands. That sly Dorcas Dalton had her claws into him, and he was that hot for her, he was like a dog on heat.'

The sting hit her deep in the chest. 'You know nothing about it.'

'Wrong. I was the one who told Mr Knepp your father was offering thirty guineas to anyone who'd take his daughter off his hands. We laughed at him; thought you'd probably be pig-ugly. Mr Knepp wasn't keen; couldn't think what use he'd have for a wife. Then he heard Viner's missus had a baby on the way, and he started to warm to it a bit more. Knepp can't bear it if Viner's got one up on him, and of course it helps that you're the daughter of a lawyer, someone of good standing, with a dowry put by. He thought about it a long while, though.' He smiled. 'Guess he should have thought on it a bit longer.'

The humiliation burned inside but she didn't let it show. How could her father have done that? Virtually held her up for auction to the highest bidder?

'Are you going to give me the money?' she asked.

'No,' he said.

'Then so be it.' She simply turned and walked out. She wasn't beaten yet.

At six o'clock she heard the bells go and the clatter of feet in the yard. She'd laid the table just as the night before, but had taken a better dress from her trunk. Now she laced herself into her stiff corset as if it was armour, and put on a starched white coif and neckerchief. She was ready for them. She thought of the old Queen Elizabeth and how she could command whole armies, and pulled herself up straighter.

The men came in and sat down noisily and expectantly before their empty bowls and trenchers.

'Gentlemen,' she said regally, holding up her hand for quiet. 'I am afraid there's no supper today.'

The men shuffled and looked to each other. Was she jesting?

'My sincere apologies, but my husband didn't

leave enough money to buy fish, and Mr Grinstead, in his wisdom, refuses to advance me more coin from the coffers.'

'But we always have supper,' Dobbsy said. 'Livvy does it.'

'Livvy is busy with other duties. And besides, there was no money to buy food. With my husband away, I cannot buy provisions with fresh air. If you wish to change this state of affairs and get your dinner tomorrow, I suggest you talk to Mr Grinstead.'

An outcry of complaints. Some of the men stood. The atmosphere turned dark.

'He said it would be better when she came,' the greasy-haired coachman with a bulbous nose turned to address the table. 'And it's worse already. I told him not to do it. We were fine before.'

'Hindle's right. I don't see why we should have to pay for our supper, we never have before,' a gangling groom in threadbare breeches grumbled.

'Is there no bread at all?' Hindle stepped towards her – close enough for her to see the open pores on his nose.

She stood her ground. 'You ate it at dinner. If you want to eat tonight, you'll have to go elsewhere, and pay for it yourselves.'

'Now look here,' he grabbed her by the arm.

'I'll go and look in the pantry,' Nipper said hurriedly.

'Be my guest,' she said, twisting free. 'There's nothing there. You finished it at dinner time. And

I'll thank you to keep your hands to yourself, Mr Hindle, or Mr Knepp will hear of it when he returns.'

'Leave her alone, Mr Hindle,' Nipper said. '"Taint her fault.'

'You should have told us before,' Hindle said, his face sour.

'When? I wasn't to know Grinstead would be so unreasonable. And you were all busy in the yard.'

'I'm going to talk to Grinstead first thing tomorrow,' Hindle said.

'And I'm not working here if we don't get fed,' Dobbsy grumbled.

One by one the men shambled out of the door.

Bird wiped her hands down her dress. She was shaking with the effort of keeping calm. The first round of this particular battle had gone to her. But she knew it wasn't over. Grinstead would have trouble on his hands in the morning, and he'd know exactly who to blame.

CHAPTER 3

Bird and Livvy spent the morning on tenter-hooks, cleaning the house. She heard the sound of shouting outside; raised voices complaining about the lack of a coach for hire. Grinstead's placatory grovelling made her shoulders tense, but she did her best to ignore it. Bird scrubbed and polished until her arms ached. She'd show Mr Knepp how a gentleman should live. To hide the commotion in the yard, she sang as she wiped the mantel.

'Oh the cuckoo is a pretty bird, she sings as she flies,
She brings us good tidings and tells us no lies.'

'Is that you singing, Mistress?' Livvy appeared at the top of the stairs.

In answer, Bird sang the next few lines,

'A-walking, a-talking, a-walking was I,
To meet my true lover, he'll come by and by—'

She stopped abruptly and pulled a face. 'So I don't know how I've managed to end up here, scared to death for when he comes home.'

'Don't stop,' Livvy said. 'I can't sing a note. Never feel like singing, me. But you've a lovely voice. I couldn't believe it was you; it don't sound like you're big enough.'

'Why?'

'Because it's deep and sounds like honey. I mean . . . it's so nice to listen to.'

'I used to sing all the time at home. We had a spinet, and I used to play and sing, and my father used to play the cittern.' She screwed up the cloth in her hands. 'That was my favourite when I was a child. "The Cuckoo". Mother used to call me "Birdy" because I sang it so often, and then it got shortened to Bird.'

'Suits you. You're sort of sprightly, and you've got that habit of putting your head on one side, like a bird.' Livvy clapped her hand over her mouth. 'Sorry, Mistress, didn't mean nothing. Didn't meant to be impert'nent.'

'It's all right, Livvy. Maybe if I flap hard enough I'll fly!' She flapped the cloth up and down.

'Eh, Mistress, you should sing more.'

'When I've something to sing about.'

Livvy shook her head long and slow. 'I know what you mean.'

She was just about to sing again when the door burst open. Grinstead's wild expression made her move to put the table between them.

'Do you know what you've done?' he asked, jutting his chin towards her.

'I'd thank you to knock, Mr Grinstead.'

'You've ruined him. Four of our workers have

41

gone and there's no-one to see to the morning's hires.'

'And why is that my fault?'

'You didn't feed them. They've gone to work for Viner.'

'No, Mr Grinstead. *You* didn't feed them. You are the one responsible because you were the one holding the purse strings, and you denied me.'

'I gave you two shillings and you wasted it. That money was for the men's food.'

'That money was my allowance from Mr Knepp. I'm in charge of the household expenses. It is up to me to decide how it is spent.'

'You foolish woman. He'll kill me.'

'It is a problem of your own making.'

'What am I to do? There are men waiting who booked a coach and no men to drive it.'

'Drive it yourself then.'

He shot her a look of such venom it could have peeled the paint from the walls. Moments later the door slammed and shuddered in its frame.

Livvy crept out from the scullery. 'Oh, Mistress,' she said in horrified delight. 'You'll be for it now. You don't know what Master's like. He's a temper fit to skin a cat.' She clapped a hand over her mouth. 'Beg pardon, Mistress, I didn't mean nothing by it.'

Half an hour later the door flew open to startle them again.

This time, Grinstead threw a purse onto the table where it landed with a thud. 'There. Go and buy provisions. It's a shameful wife who would let her husband and his men go without supper.'

'I told you to knock, Mr Grinstead. I won't have you walking in here any time you feel like it.'

'Damn you.'

Twenty minutes later she had persuaded a reluctant Livvy to accompany her to the market again. The weather had cleared and blue skies were visible under the scudding clouds as they hurried out under the arch, down Cowe Lane and over towards the fleshmarket. Bird had never seen a sight like it, herds of cattle and sheep and pigs, and the stench! She put her hands over her nose, but it did little to help.

'Stand back, Mrs Knepp,' Livvy said, pulling her out of the way of a flock of geese being whipped up the street by two be-smocked farmers, 'That's unless you want to be someone's supper.' Her laugh was a deep chortle.

They passed the slaughterhouses close to the Thames, which were oddly silent after the noise of the market, but the tang of blood in their noses was unmistakeable and made Bird shudder.

Livvy showed her where the bakery was on Gifford Street, and a butcher where they could buy a brace of rabbit. 'I can't face beef after seeing all those cows,' Bird said.

Livvy carried the basket, and Bird began to feel more like her old self.

'What'll Master say when he finds out I've done

none of his work?' Livvy paused in the middle of the road.

'I don't know. Let me deal with him.'

'You're not what I was expecting.'

'What were you expecting?'

Livvy's eyes were troubled. 'Best not to say, Mistress.'

'Go on, you've started now.'

'Well, I thought you'd be . . . well, you're a lady. Not ordinary folk like Grinstead's wife.'

'How can you tell?'

'It's how you are. Your voice. Everything.'

'Good. Because it's the only weapon I have.'

'Why?'

'People are intimidated if they think someone is higher class than they are. It makes them nervous.'

'Is that what gives you the courage to argue with Mr Grinstead?'

'No. Something about him just rubs me the wrong way.'

Livvy grinned at her. 'You and most everyone else in the yard.'

Christopher Knepp slid out of the saddle, and rubbed his aching thighs. Behind him, the groom followed with the new horses on leading reins. They weren't worth what he'd paid for them, and he knew it. Viner had bid him up, as he knew he would. Self-satisfied jerk of a man. Now he was stuck with the two grey geldings, and they'd hardly have earned aught before they were too old and had to be put down. He watched them trot into the yard. Fine animals, too, but expensive. Even now, he found it hard to divorce his love of horses from the whole economic difficulty of making them pay.

He supposed he'd better go inside and see that new wife of his, though he didn't know what he could say to her; she was so much younger than him. He'd imagined a meek, compliant sort of girl, not this self-sufficient, self-contained creature with flashing eyes, who looked down her nose at him. But he'd needed her dowry to dig himself out of the hole he was in. He handed his saddle to Dobbsy and braved the house. The kitchen was empty; the fire cold in the grate.

'Mary Elizabeth?' he shouted.

No answer. He called again, louder.

Nothing. His back ached, and he longed for someone to draw him a hot bath. Long rides in the summer heat tired him out. Not that he'd let anybody see. He made his way into the yard and up the stairs to the office.

'Have you seen Mrs Knepp?' he asked casually.

Grinstead sat back in his chair. 'You married a wrong 'un, there,' Grinstead said, sucking in his breath. 'There was no supper for the men last night. The yard's been in chaos. Some of the men have gone to Viner.'

'What?'

He could barely take in what Grinstead was saying. He'd only been away one day, and things were already out of control. He suppressed his anger; mustn't let Grinstead see him rattled.

He crossed the yard and strode up the stairs into the bedchamber, seething all the while. Money was so tight, and he had creditors breathing down his neck. Marriage was supposed to ease his troubles, not compound them.

He ripped off his sweaty stock and cast it down on the bed. Mary Elizabeth's trunk caught his eye. He flicked it open with a boot.

What met his eyes was a pool of lace and silk. Coloured taffeta, dainty gloves. The sort of thing Arabella used to wear. The thought of her made him almost double over. Her face swam into his mind; her slightly crooked smile, her arched eyebrows over questioning eyes. He'd thought that pain had gone, but it still incapacitated him, like a tourniquet tightening in his heart. Why was it still so painful? Why wouldn't it let him go?

He groaned and picked out one of the gloves, laid it on his palm. So small, the hand that would fit this. He remembered the touch of Arabella's hand, how he had raised it to his lips—

He threw it down on the floor. Mary Elizabeth was not Arabella. On the day he married Mary Elizabeth Carpenter, he realised she could never be Arabella. How had he thought she could? He was saddled with her now, and she would never love him. He was vile and unloveable. And something in him made him want to be more so.

He couldn't bear it, the sight of the clean linen,

all the little lady's things that made him feel so inadequate. He dragged the trunk to the fireplace and pulled out a flimsy lace-edged shift and stuffed it into the sooty fireplace. Striking a flint, he lit the tinder and blew on it. A moment later he thrust the flaming ball into the heart of the white linen.

At the market, Bird and Livvy bought a spray of roses for the table, as well as vegetables and a supply of millet for thickening soup.

The sundial on the side wall showed just after two when they arrived back, cheerful and dusty, with their baskets of provisions. Two new horses' heads poked out of the stable doors opposite the house; greys with white muzzles.

'Look.' Livvy pointed to them. 'Two more. Master must be back already,' she said, her expression suddenly wary.

But Bird barely heard. Her attention was caught by the house. Smoke billowed from one of the house chimneys. And the door to the house was ajar.

Livvy shook her head. 'Master's not got that fire going right.'

Bird speeded her step. 'It's not the kitchen. It's the bedroom. Look.'

Livvy gazed up at the smoking chimneystack. 'In the daytime?'

The two of them set off at a run. Through the hall, up the stairs.

A blaze roared in the fireplace, and a bundle of something was stuffed in there so tight it was blocking the chimney. Coughing, Bird rushed over to try to unblock it.

It was a big bundle of clothing. She prodded the poker into the flaming mass to dislodge it, and something fell out. It was a pair of stays, smouldering at the edges, like the embroidered ones she wore in her best . . . Oh no. Not that.

Frantically she tried to drag them out with the fire tongs, but the more she pulled them out the faster they burned.

'What's to do, Mrs Knepp?' Livvy shouted, trying to pull her away.

Bird dragged out a skirt of silvered silk, the one she'd worn for a recital of music only last year, and threw it down on the flagstones, stamping at it. But it was no use, the cloth was scorched and ragged, the edges aflame.

It was hopeless. The fire was well-alight. In the flames she saw the charred remains of her velvet reticule with the ivory clasp, the black skeleton of her fringed Chinese sunshade. Everything was ruined.

She turned away from the fire to see Knepp leaning against the door. Livvy immediately darted away down the stairs.

'Leave it,' Knepp said in a tone that brooked no argument.

'What . . . what have you done?' Bird could barely get the words out. One hand still clenched the tongs.

'Grinstead says you spent money that wasn't yours. So you will pay for it.'

She took a step forward, waving the tongs aloft. 'But my things. You've ruined them. They were *mine*, do you hear?'

He wrenched the tongs away in a single motion, and cast them down with a clatter. 'You are my wife. Your things are mine now. To dispose of as I see fit.'

'But what will I wear?'

'You should have thought of that before you spent my money on extravagances. And you won't need them. We don't need fancy sheets here, or fancy gowns. We work for a living. I thought I made that clear.'

'You had no right.'

He approached her slowly. 'The rules are very simple. And yet it seems you are unable to understand them. My yard has lost a day's business. My coachmen have left me with a queue of angry clients. Ted Viner is laughing at us. And according to Grinstead, you are the cause of it with your airs and graces. So, there'll be no more airs and graces in this yard.'

'What's left in my trunk?'

'Nothing.'

'You burnt it all?'

His eyes slid guiltily away from her. 'I left you the trunk. You should be grateful.'

Two hours later she stood outside her father's house in Lombard Street. She had walked all the way, as she would not ask that man for a carriage, and besides, she had no luggage. Only the clothes she stood in. She'd flung open the lid of the trunk, not believing for one moment it would be completely empty, thinking she'd find her shifts, or her calf-skin prayer book remaining. But no. He'd burned everything. All except the green summer wedding dress which he hadn't seen because it was still stuffed under the bed out of sight. This she had put on.

She rapped hard at her father's door to give herself confidence. She would tell Father she was coming home. It felt odd to wait at his door, when so often she had just barged through without even seeing it. Now, on the doorstep, she couldn't help but notice the pristine paintwork, the strange gargoyle-like face of the knocker glaring at her over its mouthful of ring. The key to her father's house had been in her purse which was now somewhere in the embers of Knepp's fire. It gave her a weird sense of dislocation to be locked on the outside of this door; a door she'd never once given a thought to before.

After what seemed an age, Sukey opened up, with a broom in her hand. 'Oh! Sorry, Miss Bird, we weren't expecting you. How lovely.'

'I'm so glad to be home, Sukey,' Bird said, embracing her. She would never go back to Knepp's Yard.

It was good to be called Bird again. Knepp hadn't used her name at all. Mary Elizabeth was a mouthful, and her father sometimes used to call her Betty, but she couldn't imagine Knepp calling her that, or Bird. She pushed her way past Sukey and into the front parlour, but stopped dead.

The furniture was covered in dust-sheets and two men were hanging new leather panels on the walls, whilst a pot of stinking glue was boiling on the fire. She took a few more steps forward and her heels echoed on bare boards. The rushes had all been removed. And where was the Turkey carpet that used to grace the big wall? She swivelled on the spot. There it was; rolled up under the window.

'Where's Father?' she asked.

Sukey shifted uncomfortably back and forth. 'Upstairs somewhere, with Mistress.'

Bird hurtled up the stairs, not waiting to be announced, and into her old bed-chamber. It was empty. The bed had gone, and her clothes chest, and the curtains removed from the windows.

A panic assailed her.

She shot through to her father's chamber. He used to see his clients there sometimes, but today he was sitting on the cushioned chair by the window, with Dorcas on his knee. His face was flushed and rosy and he looked happier than she had seen him in years.

'What are you doing to my chamber?' she blurted.

'Daughter!' His face burned red. 'Why didn't you let us know you were coming? But that's delightful. You can be the first to hear our news.'

51

Dorcas slid down, frowning. She assumed an air of superiority before throwing Bird a sidelong glance of triumph.

'Where've you put my bed?' Bird said. 'And what are those men doing in the parlour?'

'Alterations. You'll join us for refreshments, won't you? Where's Christopher? Downstairs?'

'He's not here. Father; it was quite impossible. I can't stay with—'

'Dorcas is with child. Isn't that marvellous?' He clapped his hands together.

'But you've only been married a month, how can she possibly—?'

'Never mind that now, I'm so proud of her. Give us both a kiss now, won't you, my daughter?' Bird couldn't take it in. In a daze, she embraced her father and gave a dry kiss to Dorcas's cheek.

'But you're too old to be . . .' she started, before realising how rude that sounded.

'I'm fit as a flea,' her father said, 'thanks to Dorcas here. And I'm not old at all! I'll beg you to mind your manners, *Mrs Knepp*.' He laughed, emphasising her new name. 'When my son arrives, your chamber will be the nursery, and a place for the wet nurse to sleep. We're re-styling it.'

A son. It was as if she'd been kicked. All men wanted was to make small versions of themselves. Women were simply the means to do it.

'It could be a girl,' she said.

Dorcas pressed her lips together in an angry line. 'My family always bear boys.'

'What happened to that beautiful old panelling in the parlour?' Bird asked, remembering how proud her mother was of its sheen.

'It had to go,' Dorcas said, 'and Joshua agreed, didn't you, dear? It was so dark and old-fashioned.'

'I liked it,' Bird said.

'You would,' Dorcas said acidly.

'Father, where did you put my things? The clothes that were left, my books and music?'

'Those old things? The rag and bone man took them,' Dorcas said. 'I think there are still a few bits and pieces by the back door. We didn't think you wanted them any more. Ask Sukey if they've gone yet.'

She wanted to run and look, but her father laid a soothing hand on her arm. 'After all, you had no more use for them, did you? Not now you're married, and living in that fine big house. They were filling the chamber, weren't they, Dorcie dear?'

'But it's not a fine house, Father. You know perfectly well it's not. Did you think I would not notice? It's dark and empty and—'

'Needs a woman's touch, that's all.' He never let her finish; must always speak over her. Bird swallowed her words. It was hopeless. Her father was determined not to let anything spoil his joy. A drowning sensation made her breath shallow. Dorcas was putting her 'woman's touch' on her family home, eliminating her father's former life, and by doing it, claiming it for her own. It was clear enough to Bird she would never be able to come back here.

She turned to go downstairs, and her father hurried after her. 'Now you're here, Dorcas will bring refreshment.' It was an order. He pulled out a shrouded chair, and bade her sit. 'You look well, my dear,' her father said. 'That gown suits you.'

'It's just as well, as it's my only one. He burned the rest.' She wanted to shock him.

Her father stood and moved away from her; he seemed unsure whether it was a jest, or whether to believe her. He stared at the fireplace as if he could see the answer.

At that moment, Dorcas arrived with spiced ale, and in the resulting bustle her father neatly brushed the problem aside and resumed his talk about the alterations.

Bird could barely breathe. Why was she being so polite? Why couldn't she stand up for herself? She didn't want Dorcas to know how much she'd been hurt, that's why. For what seemed like eternity she sipped scalding spiced ale, as Dorcas told her how much better it would be when the wallpaper was finished, and how she planned to remove the spinet and replace it with a bigger table for her friends to play cards. The thought made Bird want to weep.

As soon as she'd drained the ale she went to the back door to search out her belongings. The maidservant, Sukey, appeared behind her carrying a pail full of coal for the kitchen fire.

'Father said some of my things might still be here,' Bird said, 'by the back door.'

'Oh.' Sukey twisted her fingers in her apron. 'I'm so sorry, miss. The servants took what you didn't want. And the rest's outside in the yard. Mistress put them out; she said they were in the way.'

Bird pulled open the door to see a heap thrust higgledy-piggledy into a basket against the buttery wall. There was nothing left of any value there, she could see that, and it was soaked with rain. A broken fan, an old flannel nightdress that had been eaten by moths, some shoes that were too split to be re-soled, the old collar from her kitten that had become a cat and finally died of old age. She picked through the debris until she came to the heap of damp paper at the bottom. She dragged it out. Sheet music; and still legible! She remembered copying this, note by note, and the tune that still danced through her head. The papers were blurred and spotted but she straightened it into a neat pile.

'Sir says, do you want me to call you a carriage?' Sukey asked, poking her head out again.

Obviously Father couldn't wait for her to go. 'No. It's all right, Sukey, I'll walk.'

'Did you want those papers?' Sukey said. 'It's not my fault. There were more, but Mistress said to use them for the fire.'

'You weren't to know.'

'Shall I put them in a basket for you?'

'No. I can carry them. I'm going now anyway.' Pride made her sound casual.

'If you're sure . . . I miss you, miss. It's not the

same now you've gone. I can't seem to do aught right for the new mistress.'

'I miss you too, Sukey.'

'Shall I tell Master you're leaving?'

But Bird shook her head, and half-walked, half-ran up the street, clutching the bundle of sheet music to her chest. As long as she had the music. Nothing else mattered. It was only when she reached St Paul's Church that she paused. She needed to think.

She sat down on a gravestone off to the side of the path and stared at the cluster of barefoot beggars accosting passers-by for alms. A woman of her own age, dressed in a ragged oversized man's doublet and filthy skirt, pawed at every man's arm as they went through the portal. Her matted hair looked as though it might be crawling with lice. No man paid her any attention. That could be me, she thought. If I had no husband to support me, and nowhere to go. Marriage was a kind of rich woman's whoredom, she realised. You gave yourself to buy bed and board if you had no employment. She had imagined a polite, solicitous marriage of manners, like her mother and father's. One where the difficulties were ignored under a veneer of good manners. She had not imagined a marriage like her own could exist.

'What yer looking at?' the woman challenged Bird through broken teeth.

'Nothing.'

'Got a token to spare, Missus?' The tone changed to a wheedling one.

Bird shook her head and moved away, walking around the new portico on the West front where the jackdaws kept up a constant jabber from the crannies and crevices. On the opposite side of the street she saw another attractive young woman proposition the men as they passed, heading to St Paul's Walk. Close up, she was older and heavily powdered and patched, and dressed in a low-cut orange gown. A whore. Every single man stopped, she noticed, and looked the woman up and down, before shaking a head and moving on.

'How's about it, maid?'

Bird jerked to attention.

A bearded man, stinking of rough ale and sweat, caught her by the shoulder.

'No.' She flinched and twisted away.

'Come on.' A hand thrust into her bodice.

Without thinking she punched him hard in the throat.

He staggered back and let go. But already a knife was in his hands, and he was coming at her.

She jumped to her feet and ran. His footsteps soon receded; he was too drunk to follow her, but she did not want to take the chance to stop or look behind. Twenty minutes later she was panting inside the gateway to Knepp's yard.

Knepp was there, loosening a girth on a big bay hunter. He gave her a cursory glance. 'Your father throw you out, did he?'

The humiliation was like a gouge in her chest.

When she didn't answer, he said, 'Thought so. Well, if you want to stay here, there'll be no more gallivanting and you'd best earn your keep.'

CHAPTER 4

Axe Yard, London, 1st January, 1660

Elisabeth Pepys hurried ahead of her husband, Samuel, angry that the visit to his relatives had taken so long. To make matters worse, Samuel's cold was heavier and he'd been sniffing and snorting like a pig the whole afternoon. He paused beside her for another resounding blow into his damp ball of kerchief, so Elisabeth tutted in disgust, and speeded her step. She got the key to the house ready in her hand and glanced back, to see Jane, the long, lanky, maid hurrying after her, the appropriate few steps behind.

Axe Yard was gloomy and there were few lights in the neighbouring windows, so Elisabeth navigated the icy cobblestones by feel, one hand on the cold wall, glad she knew the way so intimately. With a practised touch she found the keyhole and let herself in through the door, hurrying up the stairs into the ice-cold parlour, where she banged the shutters closed.

'Brr. My blood will freeze!' She grabbed the poker and thrust it towards Jane. Jane obliged, and prodded at the dead, grey embers in the hearth.

'I knew it would be out,' Elisabeth said. 'Samuel just wouldn't stop talking. We were *hours*. After that sermon too. *C'était interminable*. Far too long, don't you agree?'

'Yes, Mistress. Too long.' Jane crouched close to the grate and blew on the ash settled there.

'And Samuel's father needs someone to look after him. Have you ever seen such fingernails? Long and yellow like . . . like claws! And I'll swear he hasn't been shaved properly for weeks. His beard was all matted.' She shuddered. Her husband could turn into exactly this, indeed she saw the signs of it already; the jowls, the bulging eyes. How terrible to grow old and turn into that puttering, vague old man, with no decent conversation. 'And his wife! What is she thinking, to leave his stockings in such a state? One big hole. And giving us that poxy ale in chipped cups?'

'What indeed, Mistress. I'll soon get this fire mended, never fear.' Jane scraped at the ash pan and began to stack sticks on the grate.

Elisabeth ignored her, and sank into a chair clutching her stomach. 'My stomach, it is still cramping,' she said. 'Hurts like the very devil.'

'I'll make a fennel infusion,' Jane said soothingly, 'soon as I get this fire lit.'

Elisabeth watched Jane place the coals very precisely, before puffing energetically at it with the bellows until a meagre flame appeared.

'There!' Jane slapped her hands down her skirts with satisfaction. 'Now, you just stay where you are, and I'll get to the kitchen and fetch your drink.'

What was taking Samuel so long? Dawdling again probably, looking into everyone's windows.

Elisabeth shivered again, disconsolate. It was ugly, this room, and lacking in comfort. The English style was dark and heavy, as if the more solid the wood was, the longer it would last. She longed for something French, something light and fragile, with sinuous curves, arabesques and gilded fleurs-de-lys. A chandelier with shimmering crystal. She glared at the shutters, wishing for airy louvres opening onto leafy boulevards, instead of these clumsy blocks of wood to keep out the cold and fog. Why had she come back to him, to these five rooms in a damp garret? She should have had the courage to go back to France. But she knew a woman with no husband was a woman who did not exist. Either that, or she would be branded a whore. She was 'Mrs Pepys', an appendage to him, like his periwig.

She pulled off her hat and doubled over as a spasm of pain hit her again. Her cramps were a reminder, as if she needed one, that she had her terms again and no child would be coming. Samuel hadn't been able to mask his disappointment, and the fact he could not, that his stupid face was so transparent, made her even angrier.

How had it happened? Their romance, which

had been sweet and luscious, like a ripe peach, had gradually gone over and festered into this rotten, mouldering thing.

Just then, the door opened and there he was, a fatuous smile on his face.

'I thought you'd got lost.'

'I went to check the coal store, see how much was left. You must tell Jane to use less coal, she's far too extravagant.' He moved to stand before the fire with his backside nearly in the hearth.

'Have a care,' Elisabeth said. 'Those breeches will catch light, stupid great things.'

'I thought you liked them. You did yesterday. Wide legs are quite the thing; everyone at court's wearing these petticoat breeches.'

'Only fops and fools.'

'Like our new king, you mean?'

Elisabeth ignored him. 'You're blocking my heat.'

Samuel moved away reluctantly. 'What's for supper?'

'Cold turkey again, I suppose. Ask Jane.'

He trotted off to the kitchen. How could he still be hungry? He'd only just dined at his father's. His stomach probably ruled the Navy too; ships could be sinking, sailors dying of dysentery, but if Samuel was hungry, they would have to wait.

A few minutes later he returned, clutching a greasy turkey leg and a platter of bread. 'Do you want some?'

'Ugh. *Non*. I've turkey coming out of my ears.'

'Could be why you never listen.' He laughed,

pleased at his little joke. 'That's Christmas for you. We weren't to know my father would give us turkey pie too. Aren't you going to take off your cloak?'

'When I can't see my breath before me, perhaps.'

'You seem out of sorts, my dear. What is it?'

How could she explain? That she felt swindled. That marriage was supposed to be the pinnacle of a woman's life; a sacrament full of romance, and mystery. Her life wasn't supposed to be this. Stomach cramps, and an ugly house, and a husband with greasy fingers and a blocked-up nose.

'Come on, wife, take cheer.'

'It's nothing, just my monthlies.'

'Is that all?' He approached, reached out to her with a greasy hand.

'You need a napkin,' she said, giving him a look designed to wither him to nothing, and moving away to prod the poker into the fire again to coax it to more heat. Samuel merely smiled. It made her feel guilty. She knew she was snappish and awkward. She turned to stand the poker in the coal bucket, to find him still staring at her, at a loss. A moment passed where his complete incomprehension played across his features, where he tried to speak again, but could think of no words to say.

We have nothing to say to each other, she thought. We can't seem to get underneath the surface to anything real; we are like actors playing a role. Except they can go home from the theatre, when their play ends.

The door opened. 'Shall I put the warmer in your bed now, Mistress?'

'Yes do, unless you want to warm it yourself, eh Jane?' As usual, Samuel could not resist the ribald jest.

Elisabeth, still poking distractedly at the fire, made a strangled noise, half-moan and half-cry. She turned to see Jane blushing, in embarrassed silence. Then she closed her eyes and wondered how many wives had killed their husbands with a poker just like the one she gripped in her hand.

CHAPTER 5

Farringdon and Knepp's, Smithfield, four years later, August 1664

Bird stopped by the stable door where a big chestnut gelding had his nose stuck over, hoping for more fodder.

'Any more oats?' she said, impersonating the horse in a gruff cockney accent.

'Sorry, Vulcan, but you've had your ration,' she replied in her own voice.

'How's a fella supposed to pull a coach 'n' four when all you give me is chaff?'

'Never mind,' she said. 'Just be grateful you're not a human. You have a carefree life.'

The horse blew out through its nostrils and she blew back. She wouldn't admit it, but she was wary of the bigger horses. Giving them voices helped to give her courage when she had to feed or water them.

She crossed the sunshine and shadow of the yard and drew a bucket of water from the pump. It sloshed against her skirts as she hurried to the tack room. Grateful for cool water, she dunked the bridle bits into the bucket and rattled them about before she sat down on a stool to survey the day's cleaning.

As she began wiping the grime off a saddle, she caught sight of Knepp passing the window, deep in urgent conversation with Grinstead. Knepp. Livvy had told her she'd never heard anyone call him Christopher. Good. The name Knepp suited him; snappish and curt. She watched them go by with the usual impassive loathing, wincing as she heard her husband swear to Grinstead in words that should have burned her ears.

Years she'd been here, and no closer now to getting out. She'd worked hard enough for an opportunity but it never came knocking. She'd learnt to appreciate small things, like the occasional sunny day, the smell of clean leather, the welcome twist of tea given by a happy customer, and Livvy. Compared to Livvy, she was lucky, she could see that; servants had so little time to call their own. Knepp kept her clothed, and fed, and as long as she kept busy, life was bearable. But was it sinful to yearn for more than this, once in a while?

She knew every item of harness now by name. The surcingle, the whiffletree, the breeching strap, the crupper. The terrets, the shaft-tugs, the blinders. She rubbed the inside of the saddle harder to remove the grease, one eye on the men. They controlled the purse, and every little thing had to be itemised in her weekly accounts.

Thank God she had no children. The dutiful once-a-week poke on a Friday remained fruitless, as she'd intended it to be. She fitted a lime-skin tight inside every week, as Livvy had told her to do. 'Slave-woman's secret,' she'd said. Knepp'd never be able to see in there, thank the Lord. Though in the winter, when limes were scarce, Bird had to make do with a sponge soaked in lemon juice.

She paused in her cleaning. He blamed her for their lack of children of course. Shouted, and beat her and called her useless. If she disobeyed him, he found small ways to hurt her; like banning Fetch, the collie, her sad-eyed friend, from the house. She responded to Knepp's advances with icy disdain, which only enraged him the more. Still, she'd get out of Smithfield one day, and a baby would make everything much more awkward.

A few moments later she saw him mount up and trot out of the yard. She dumped the saddle and shouted out of the door to Grinstead, 'Will he be in for dinner?'

Grinstead glared. 'No. He's all riled up because he's just heard that Ted Viner's expanding. And he can't do anything about it today because he's got to go to his brother James's. A letter came; James's had a bad fall from a horse.'

She retreated back into the gloom, fished the horse-bits from the scummy water and dried them. He husband was obsessed with Viner. Everything Viner had, he had to have. According to Knepp,

67

Viner's yard took all the best clients even though his own horses were just as good. As far as she could see, the difference was, Viner was pleasant and jovial, and didn't give the impression it was a nuisance to supply the customer with a horse.

How typical of her husband, not to tell her where he was going. His brother lived way out in Essex, at least a day's ride. So he'd be away overnight. It must be urgent, because he rarely did that; he didn't like leaving anyone else in charge. She closed her eyes a moment, relieved.

He wouldn't be inspecting this tack either. She hurried through it all with a sense of urgency, running the traces of the carriage through her cloth with practised speed. She might even be able to get away from the stables for a few hours. The day suddenly stretched ahead, golden.

As soon as she'd finished she went to find Livvy. Knepp didn't like her to be familiar with the servants or to have friends. He had put a stop to her cultivating the friendship of other wives by forbidding other women in the yard, and he never let her go abroad if he could help it. At first it had felt odd to confide in Livvy. Her black skin reminded her constantly that they were not alike, and she had only ever seen slaves and servants that looked like her. But as time passed, and she was the only woman Bird saw enough of to befriend, she had got used to it, and now they were easy with each other.

Livvy was boiling linseed in the kitchen, a hot,

sweet stink that hung like glue in her throat. The white froth on the pan had to be stirred constantly if it wasn't to boil over or stick.

'He's gone out then?' Livvy's face shone in the heat.

'Overnight. Can you believe it!'

'Well that's mighty good. Guess when the cat's away, the mice can—'

'Get out of this hell-hole for once.'

Livvy laughed. 'You'll have to wait while I make up this mash,' she said. 'I feel sorry for the horses if they don't get fed. What about Grinstead?'

'He's a bad tooth as well as that constant cold. If Knepp's away I'll wager he'll do nothing but read about physick and cures for his imaginary ailments until it's time to go home. And I bet you a ha'penny he'll light a fire and burn coal even in this heat.'

'They say there's a new play on at the King's,' Livvy said, grinning. 'Wouldn't mind seeing that. Starts at three o'clock.'

'I've never been to the theatre. Can we really?'

'You're the mistress. You decide. But if we go together, they'll let me in. Don't like us darkies going in alone. Got to be with someone, a mistress or master, or pay a bribe.'

Bird served dinner early and chivvied the men out, so she and Livvy could race through the clearing away and pot washing. Upstairs in the bedchamber she opened her trunk and pulled out the dress she'd arrived in. With arm-twisting, Knepp had bought her two other suits – one a dark blue for church and the other the serviceable working skirt and bodice she was stripping off now, a heavy felted wool in a shade she could only call dung. The bodice fastened at the front, close, with no room for a stomacher or any fancy trimming, and in this weather it was always too hot.

She pulled it off, flapped it to get some air, and slipped on the green skirt over her chemise. She was still as slim as on her wedding day; if anything, slimmer from all the labour. The embroidered stomacher fit neatly and pushed up her chest. It hurt, turning back into a lady, even in an out-of-mode dress like this. Five years married. How had it gone so fast? She didn't like to dwell on it now, how she'd got here, how she appeared to be stuck in this place, like a fly to flypaper. She did her best, twisting and turning, to pull the back-lacing taut enough, then pushed her feet into the tight-fitting shoes. Heavens above, she used to wear these uncomfortable things every day.

The theatre. Even the word conjured up colour and music and forbidden pleasure. She had never been. For most of her childhood it had been banned as something wicked, so now it exerted a fascination akin to a fairy tale. Since the playhouses had re-opened, she had seen their flysheets stuck to the city walls, but only heard about them from Livvy. But now she was to set foot in one, and she wanted to look pretty for once, and be fit to be seen. She pinched her cheeks to make them rosier, twisted her braid of thick wavy hair into a knot.

'Mistress?' Livvy's voice rose up from below.

'Coming,' she called.

No sign of Grinstead. Running awkwardly in her tight shoes, Bird stumbled after Livvy, under the archway and out into the hot dust of the street. Livvy pulled her along by the arm, anxious that they should be able to get a good place to sit on the benches in the gallery. What Livvy called 'the pit' would be 'too rough for a lady the likes of you'. The sun beat down on Bird's shoulders as she wove through the crowd. A carriage rattling past made her flatten herself to the walls. What if Knepp returned early?

'I don't think I want to . . . I mean, I don't think this is a good idea.'

'You soft molly. We're nearly there. Come *on*.' Livvy grabbed Bird by the arm and dragged her forward into a knot of people rammed into the tight alleyway between Catherine Street and Bridges Street. Hurrying, they dodged around the posts that held up the overhanging jetties. Each one was plastered with a handbill of the current play, stuck over the torn remnants of previous productions.

'Look!' Bird said. 'It's called *Flora's Vagaries*.'

'What's a vagary?' Livvy asked, screwing up her forehead.

'It's when you do something sudden and peculiar. Like a whim or a caprice.'

'Oh.' Livvy didn't look any the wiser. 'What's "caprice"?'

Bird didn't reply, and instead Livvy tugged her through the crowds.

'Let's hope they'll play us some lively tunes,' Livvy said, breathlessly.

'Music? It will have music?'

''Course it will.' Livvy was dismissive. 'They've eight viol men here, from the King's own court players.'

Bird felt her heart beat faster in her chest. Except for the cries of street traders, she hadn't heard music for years. Only her own singing, and recently it had sounded so sad that she'd vowed never to do it again.

She didn't know if she could bear it. 'Wait!' She caught Livvy by the shoulder.

'What? We'll be late.'

At Livvy's impatience, she closed her mouth. Out here, odd as it was, Livvy was definitely in charge. She followed her inside to where the smell of hot people was almost overpowering; a mixture of sweat, hot cloth and the clove and aniseed of pomanders.

The prices had gone up since Livvy last came. 'It's robbery,' Livvy grumbled. 'We can't afford that. Let's go home.'

'No,' Bird said, opening her purse, 'Not now you've got me here. Seize the day.' It was a shilling for a seat in the far reaches of the upper gallery. Bird handed over two shillings, knowing

72

it should have bought meat for the men in the yard.

'Is that tonight's supper money?' Livvy asked.

'Don't ask.' Brass tokens in her hand, she led the way up the creaking oak stairs, with Livvy following hard on her heels.

She handed the tokens to a woman dressed in a bodice cut so low it showed half her nipples. Bird averted her eyes. Once in the gallery she squashed in next to another grey-haired couple, edging up to make room for Livvy on the bench. More and more people kept arriving until she had to clamp her elbows to her sides. It was already packed even with a half-hour to go.

She peered over the head of the man in front, whose long hair was tied up in a ragged pigtail. Livvy told her the theatre had once been a tennis court, so it was a long rectangle with a jutting stage at one end, and a big decorated arch above. Before it hung six chandeliers on chains, each with twelve candles. They were already dripping, and had to be lowered down to be trimmed even before the play began.

A sharp rap. Two more. And then the sweet sound of viols soared up from the back of the stage, a curtain on a wire was rattled away, and there were the musicians, on a platform above the stage. The notes tugged inside her, delicate as a spider-web, then a strong surge of strings like the sea. Bird almost wept.

'Good, isn't it?' Livvy elbowed her, but then

73

stopped when she saw the people next to them staring.

Bird couldn't even speak. She was hooked like a fish. The heroine, Otrante, was a woman caught between her desire for freedom and her love for her father. The pain of it echoed deep in Bird's heart. But there was no lover for Bird like the handsome Francisco strutting on stage. No-one with whom *she* could elope. This was just a story, and she was wedded to Knepp. That was real life.

But she watched how the women manipulated the men, how they talked back, and how they schemed and plotted. That women should be shown to do these things openly shocked her.

'Flora and Otrante, they're not played by boys, are they?' she asked Livvy at the end of the second act as they trooped downstairs to take a breath of air.

Livvy laughed, hanging over the stairwell, 'Ha! Haven't you heard, Mistress? New king's set a fashion for it, and Mr Killigrew's set up a school for stage jades.'

'But who are they, these women?'

'Just women.'

'They behave like ladies, but I can't believe any real lady would be so brazen! They look the gentlemen in the audience right in the eye, even the wealthy young blades and the aristocrats in the boxes. Where do these women come from?'

'Anywhere. Nell says she'll get to wear the clothes

of countesses for her roles. A counterfeit countess, she'll be, so she says.'

'Who's Nell?'

'Just a friend. Nell and her sister were brought up in Coal Yard Alley where I live. My landlady runs the wash-house, and when Nell's ma was busy with her gentleman customers, I minded them both. Rose is the eldest, but Nell's a little jack-in-the-box.'

'Is she . . .? I mean, is she like you?'

'Is she black, you mean? No. Not her. I reckon you could count the blacks in London on your fingers. Nell's in what Killigrew calls his "nursery" now, training to tread the boards. Pish. I wouldn't want it, even if they'd let me. Ha! Couldn't learn me all those lines. And Rose says Killigrew's a dirty old dog, too.'

But Bird was fascinated. She plied Livvy with questions, until Livvy grew impatient.

'Look, I don't know all the fal-de-rols. You'll have to talk to Nell. She'll be with Rose and the other orange girls down below, and they can't talk when they're working or Mrs Meggs'd have their tongues ripped out by the roots. But we can try to catch her later, after the play.'

'I'd like to meet her,' Bird said. The words did not give away the frisson of excitement that shot up her spine. When the bell was rung and they all crushed back up the stairs for Act Three, she peered over the balcony and could see the orange girls going along the rows with their baskets. Their

75

breasts were exposed like the token collector, in a way that made her blush. Was one of them Nell?

A lively jig struck up, and under the candles, the women on stage sparkled and glowed, as they danced in their rustling gowns. Good heavens, they were showing their ankles, and they were only a few feet from men's eyes. The men yelled for more, and the ladies refused, but smiling, full of good humour. Banter went back and forth between the audience and the stage as the woman playing Flora strutted and flounced provocatively before the painted background.

I could do that, Bird thought. The notion was like a flame that made her eyes widen, and pitched her further forward to the edge of her seat. Just at that point, the woman playing Otrante burst into song. Her voice was piercingly loud but off-key.

Bird winced. And I could sing that better too, she thought.

The rest of the play passed in gales of laughter. As the action became more frenetic and the plot more convoluted, the audience roared and howled. At the end Bird found herself on her feet, whooping like a fish-maid, amid the clapping, stamping crowd, unable to tear her eyes from the stage.

Livvy eyed her with consternation on her stolid features. 'You all right, Mistress?'

'It's just . . . can we try and talk to your friend?'

'Nell? Go on then.' She dragged Bird to the stairwell. 'Downstairs.' The surge of people carried them down and would have taken them into the street, but for Livvy's sharp elbows nudging the advancing tide aside.

A fussily dressed woman in blue, with a disgruntled face said, 'Pardon *me*,' and stood in their path in a way that meant they had to pause, and press themselves against the wall.

'Can you see your friend?' Bird asked, peering over people's heads.

'She's over there,' Livvy said, pushing past a man who lost his footing, lurching so he bumped into Bird, squashing her up against the wall.

'Oh! I do beg your pardon,' the man said, looking down into her face with an amused expression, but showing no desire to move. His lively brown eyes stayed on hers.

Bird was too startled to respond, but ducked her head to escape.

The man levered himself away from her by pushing on the wall, still blocking her path with one velvet-clad arm. 'Not hurt, I hope?'

'Not at all, sir. It was our fault,' Bird said, regaining her composure. 'We're trying to get into the playhouse, not out.'

'Ah. A woman after my own heart. One can never have enough of the theatre.'

'It was foolish,' Bird confessed. 'We should have waited until everyone came out.'

'Have you left something within? I'm always forgetting my gloves.'

She laughed. 'No, we came from the gallery above. We are looking for one of the orange girls.'

'Then let me escort you,' the man said. 'The name's Pepys. Samuel Pepys.' He had a pleasant melodious voice, and his clothes marked him as a merchant or better.

'Mrs Knepp,' she said, and curtseyed.

He hooked his arm into hers, and miraculously, the way through became clear. Just as they emerged from the corridor, a plaintive voice cut through the hubbub.

'Samuel!'

Her companion stopped dead as if hauled by an invisible string. Bird turned to see the fussily dressed woman in blue, hands on hips, fixedly watching them. The man sheepishly let go of her arm.

'I'm sorry,' he said, and his complicit expression seemed genuinely apologetic. 'My wife.'

Bird nodded to the wife, who was openly glaring, and curtseyed to the gentleman as a farewell, and walked towards where Livvy was waiting, propping herself against one of the empty benches. When she turned back to look, the man called Samuel was still watching her. He gave an elaborate mock bow, and winked once, before his wife latched onto his arm and pulled him away, whispering into his ear furiously, with much gesturing towards them.

'Who was that?' Livvy asked.

'I don't know. Peeps, he said, but I might not have heard him right. He nearly tripped over me. He was apologising.' She was still smiling. For it was strange – that brief conversation had made her feel something. For a moment, she was the woman she'd been before. A gentleman had escorted her as if she was someone to be proud of. He'd treated her like a lady; like she existed. It was a long time since she had the feeling that she mattered at all.

Livvy was frowning. 'Watch out. Some men come to the theatre just to grab themselves a bit of petticoat.'

'He wasn't like that,' Bird said. 'He was a gentleman. And besides, he was with his wife.'

Livvy snorted. 'You think that make a difference? Let's find Rose and Nell.'

They hurried over to the front of the stage, where there was a set of steps, and a group of orange girls were counting out money into piles.

'What do you want?' A large elderly woman with a soft, wobbling jaw stood up, her ragged shawl tied tightly across her ample bosom. Her manner was aggressive. 'I've told you before; we're not taking on any more sellers.'

'Beg pardon, but I just wanted a word with Rose and Nell,' Livvy said.

'Wait outside then. You've no business loitering in here. They'll be done in a few minutes.'

'But—'

'Be off!' The woman made a sudden lunge and raised a fleshy hand as if she'd slap her.

'Take no notice of Mrs Meggs!' came a shrill voice. 'I'm all done and counted. Just give me a minute to fetch my cloak.'

'That's Nell,' Livvy said.

'But she's so young,' Bird said. She watched the child run up the steps onto the stage and disappear behind a painted column.

'She's fourteen. And Rose is seventeen. They're like my younger sisters. I earned a bit extra of a night minding them whilst their mother worked.'

Bird was taken aback. She'd thought to be dealing with mature women, like the ones on stage. These were just girls. If girls this age could do this, then so could she. Seeing the world lit up on stage had awoken her to a tempting possibility.

Just then, Nell appeared beside them. She was certainly appealing, and Bird could see she'd do well on the stage. She had an expressive face with a wide forehead and mischievous tawny eyes. She seemed inordinately pleased to see Livvy.

Livvy kissed her on both cheeks. 'How goes it, Nelly?'

'Blind me, it's hard work. I have to remember so much, and I need eyes in the back of my head to dodge that old goat Killigrew. He's a right randy animal.'

'Is there no-one who can look out for you?'

'Hart's all right. He distracts Killigrew for me sometimes. It makes me laugh. I can look after myself, so I don't need Hart. But it's like a game, all three of us chasing round the chamber, with Hart looking hangdog like this . . .' she pouted and rounded her shoulders, '. . . and Killigrew running after me, panting.' She panted and stuck out her tongue. The image was comical and Bird couldn't suppress her laughter at Nell's antics.

'Who's this?' Nell tossed her head towards Bird.

'My mistress, Mrs Knepp, from Farringdon and Knepp's.'

'Oh. Do beg pardon, Missus.' Nell looked her up and down, wide-eyed. 'Didn't know we had royalty here.'

'Mistress wants to know about the theatre.'

'Why? What d'ye want to know?'

'How you get to be on the stage. I mean, how they decide who to take.'

Nell was puzzled. 'You just sell oranges, and if you banter enough and stick out your chest, Killigrew asks you up to his chamber. It's up to you then, if you know what I mean.'

Bird understood but chose to ignore it. 'How does he know if you can do it? Act a part, I mean?'

'Think he cares? Not a whit. So long as you're bold and can catch men's eyes. But you need a good pair of pincers.'

'Pincers?'

Nell hoisted her skirts and did a jig. 'Legs. Killigrew likes you in breeches so they can see your bum. They're getting Etheredge to write another play where the girl dresses as a man.'

'Will you be in it, Nell?' Livvy asked, as they made their way out through the stage door into daylight.

''Course. I hope it's short and funny. Can't stand them tragedies.' She pulled a mournful face, 'Die,

die, and thrice die!' She mimed slitting her own throat. She leant back against the wall of the alley. 'Worst thing is, I can't read. Barely anyhows. I have to get someone else to read me the lines. I 'member most all of them, though. No-one seems to mind much, as long as they're nearly right. I make it up in rehearsal and get everyone laughing. They're talking about having a play that's all women. No men in it at all. Can you imagine that? I asked our Rose if she wanted to be in it, but she turned up her nose. She says she don't like being on display, but I said to her, you'll like it once you catch the eye of a fine duke. But she wasn't having any of it, she just wants to stay as a dresser and sell oranges. Can't get the other girls interested either. They're afraid of Killigrew.'

'He wouldn't scare me.' Bird stepped forward out of the shadow of the overhang. 'I'd like to try it; being in a play.' Nell's eyes widened at Bird's words.

'She's jesting,' Livvy said hastily.

'No, I mean it. Let me try. I can be in the play. Killigrew can't be worse than Knepp. I'd even sell oranges if I had to.'

'Don't be foolish, Mistress,' Livvy said, her expression shocked. 'Acting's for whores.'

Nell bristled with indignation. 'Hey!'

'No good making a fuss, Nell, you know I'm right.'

Nell grinned. 'Better a rich whore than a poor beggar, eh Livvy?'

'You're mad, Mistress,' Livvy said. 'What would Mr Knepp say?'

'He'd forbid it. Of course he would. But I've spent years worrying about that, and I always swore that if a chance came, I'd take it. The worst he can do is kill me, so I'll risk it. If I had my own living somehow, I could leave him. And I can sing, and I like doing voices. I can do this; I know I can.'

'Leave him?' Livvy and Nell exchanged glances.

'Killigrew might not have you,' Nell said. 'It depends if he takes a fancy to you.'

'When can I see him?' Bird insisted. 'Tell him I'll be in his play.'

'Should I ask him?' Nell asked Livvy. 'She's a lady. Just hark at her voice! Why would she want to join the likes of us?'

'It's turned her head,' Livvy said in a whisper. 'All those women giving lip on stage. She'll change her mind once she sleeps on it.'

Bird turned to Livvy. 'I'm set on it, I tell you. Soon as I saw those women on stage I knew I could do it. And I can read, too.' She put a hand on Nell's arm. 'I could help you – help you learn your lines.'

Nell shook herself free. 'I don't need no help.' She flounced away. After a moment's thought she turned. 'If you really mean it, then I expect you'll have to come and see Killigrew.'

'Soon?' Bird asked.

'I'll see what he says. If he agrees, then I'll get him to send a note when you've to come.' Nell turned to Livvy. 'She's crazed, your mistress.' She laughed. 'But then she'll probably do right well with us other fools at the King's.'

Just then her sister Rose came out of the side door and Nell ran over to link arms. After a brief farewell they left for their lodgings at the theatre nursery.

Livvy waved at their retreating backs, before turning to Bird. 'You've lost your wits,' Livvy said.

'Or maybe I've just found them.'

'What's come over you? You've turned bedlam. The master will do for you, if he ever finds out where you were.'

'I'll make an excuse. Say I was sickening. You'll tell him so, won't you?'

Livvy's mouth worked, but then she nodded uncertainly. 'All right. Yes, Mistress.'

With a flash of insight, she realised Livvy had agreed only to keep her position. The lines between them had become blurred.

'You won't really join the King's Playhouse, will you?' Livvy asked.

'Have you a better idea? I've learnt no skill, just cleaning saddlery. And I'll never get away from Knepp unless I can support myself. I hate him. He seems to bear the whole female population some sort of grudge. Just the look of him makes my insides curdle.'

'He's not as bad as Grinstead,' Livvy said. 'Imagine having him!' They shuddered and giggled.

'It's still early,' Livvy said. 'Let's walk the long way home.'

'I've a better idea,' Bird said. 'Let's go down Cheapside. If I'm to be in the theatre, I'd better see what's fashionable.' She said this with a bravura she didn't feel, and strode on down the road. Already Livvy's words had sobered her and she was beginning to regret the idea. Knepp would never allow her to do anything like that. But a woman could dream, couldn't she? She turned to see Livvy standing uncertainly where she'd left her. 'Come on.'

Livvy was mulish. 'I wish I'd never brought you to the theatre.'

Bird stopped. 'Don't say that.'

'If he finds out you plan to see Killigrew, he'll think it's my fault.'

'He won't find out. Not until I've tried. Nell was right, let's cross one hurdle at a time. Killigrew might turn me down.'

Cheapside bustled with well-dressed women, and young bucks swaggering in strange flapping breeches. The players had been wearing these skirt-like monstrosities on stage, but she'd thought them just gaudy costuming. The fashion for wigs was everywhere, and every man seemed to have long flowing curls. At Farringdon and Knepp's they served the occasional fashionable man, but it was mostly tradesmen, and none of the workers at the yard sported such impractical apparel.

Bird passed down the street as if in a foreign country. To think, she used to be brought here by her mother for her new hats, or to buy cloth for new suits. She'd hardly come here at all since marrying Knepp. Now young King Charles was on the throne, everything was impossibly shiny and glossy; carriages lined the road, with servants in gold-braided livery waiting alongside, and new shops had opened, all with ostentatious signage. She supposed it was the influence of the French, for the young king had been exiled to France. The signs had the appearance of being French, with curly, hard-to-read lettering, and gilded decoration. She said the names out loud. 'Bormann – Ladies Bootmaker', 'Jones the Furrier, Sables, Muffs and Tippets', 'Farine's *Parfumerie*'.

And the prices. She stopped, transfixed by the tempting row of tiny glass-stoppered bottles in the *parfumier*'s shop. One small vial of perfume cost more than her housekeeping for three months. It was staggering.

A shopkeeper moved, as if gliding, to greet them at the open door.

'Would you like to sample one, Mistress?'

'No, thank you. Not today.' How could people afford this? She turned to Livvy, 'Let's go back,' she said.

She swivelled around abruptly and set off walking briskly in the direction of St Bartholomew's and Smithfield. She was both jealous and angry. She'd forgotten how much the city revolved around money, the trading of gold, the lending and borrowing. It was obscene, this ostentation.

It made her recall stories of the excesses of Rome, just before the fall, when people were so rich they ate twice and vomited the second meal into the *vomitorium*. For once she felt a glimmer of sympathy for her husband; he worked all hours, breathing in the smell of blood and shit from the slaughter-houses, desperate to claw his way up to be the best hiring yard in the city.

They turned down the Shambles towards Newgate and stood to one side as a well-dressed man and woman pulled themselves away from the shop window they'd been staring at, and came up the street towards them. They took up a lot of space, because the woman's skirt must have been made of two dozen yards of material. The couple strolled, taking their time, as Bird and Livvy waited to pass. Behind them, a maid laboured under a large number of bags and packages, pulling a small boy by the hand. The man was portly, his over-hanging stomach upholstered in an embroidered waistcoat under a long coat in the new fashion. Under his hat hung an extravagantly curled wig. There was something about him . . . Her eyes locked on his familiar leaning gait. Only now did she realise who it was. Her father.

A hot flush of bitterness came to her cheeks. She couldn't get out of his way. A meeting was inevit-able. Defiant, she stepped into the middle of the thoroughfare and into his path.

'Father.'

Shock made his eyes wide; he hadn't expected

to see her. And now they were liquid with guilt. 'Ah. Bird. We were thinking to call on you.'

'Were you? Next year perhaps?'

'We've been . . . well, you can see, Dorcas is confined again.'

Confined? An odd word for someone who was clearly out shopping in the most expensive part of London. 'It's been a few years, Father.'

She remembered the day she told him Knepp had burned her belongings. But no more was said about it. Maybe Father thought she had said it just to goad him. But he hid from it, the possible glitch in his smooth-running life. He didn't enquire further, or call at Knepp's to see if his daughter needed any help.

Curse him, she thought. She was too proud and too angry to ask or expect anything from him. It didn't help that Dorcas viewed every other woman, even a daughter, as competition, and her father was too weak to say no to her.

'You could have visited us.' Her father raised his chin in a familiar, petulant gesture.

How dare he? He'd condemned her to a pauper's life, and yet he still expected her to pay calls to him. 'There is very little time for anything else at Farringdon and Knepp's but work,' she said, 'as you well know.'

A big sigh from Dorcas. 'Come on, Joshua. I'm getting tired. My legs ache like the devil, and I want to get to Unthank's before they close.'

The unfamiliar maid was leaning against a wall,

blowing air up from the corner of her mouth to cool her forehead. What had happened to Sukey? Had Dorcas got tired of her? The boy kicked the wall petulantly with a boot. She saw Livvy smile at him, but he ignored her.

Dorcas moved the boy away from Bird and Livvy as if they were contaminated. She was dressed immaculately in forest green silk, which made Bird's gown appear shabby and insipid, and she sported a fashionably low-cut bodice with swathes of gold point edging the neck and sleeves. Her belly had an obvious swell under the voluminous fabric.

'We'll visit soon,' her father announced.

How could he say that, when they both knew he wouldn't? He found Knepp's embarrassing. It confronted him with the reality of what he'd sold her into, and he didn't want to see.

'I'm always there, Father,' Bird said. 'Any day will do.'

He planted his hands on her shoulders intending to kiss her on the cheeks, but she stiffened and leant away. So instead he just shook her slightly, with an air of regret.

It made her want to strike him.

The three of them moved off up the street. 'Who was that lady?' she heard the boy say.

As Bird walked home, she was silent, as the hate for her father increased like a burning coal. After her mother died, she'd done everything for him. Then snap! As soon as Dorcas had flashed her eyes at him, everything else was forgotten.

'Was that gentleman your father?' Livvy eventually asked her.

'Not any more,' Bird said. 'And he's not a gentleman.'

When she got into bed that night she couldn't help hoping that Knepp's brother would need him a few more days. Or even better, that Knepp had met with a ruthless highwayman on the way home, and was lying in a ditch with a musket ball in the chest. Then she cursed herself for such wicked thoughts. Even if he were dead, she couldn't go home. Her father didn't want her and she didn't know where home was any more. But the magic of the theatre still had hold of her, and would not let her go. She re-lived the rustle of expectation as the stage curtain swished open, and saw in her mind's eye the animated presence of the women on the stage. She wanted their life; the life that looked as if something richer than blood flowed in their veins. Partly it was the colour – the deep claret of the curtain, the women in their lavenders and blues, the ethereal glow of candlelight on the gold-painted arch over the stage. And the tunes. The jigs went around in her head and wouldn't stop.

It called her, with a pull that seemed to come from deep in her chest.

CHAPTER 6

In the bookbinder's in Galley Street underneath the racks of hanging leather, and the shelves of twine, sixteen-year-old Stefan Woolmer hunched his shoulders over the desk and scribbled furiously.

'Father Bernard, I didn't catch that. Would you slow down a little?'

The old priest ignored him, deep in his own memories, his rheumy blue eyes far away, looking into some dark distant past.

The quill was growing soft and furry, and Stefan had trouble controlling the flow of ink. But he was determined to scratch down the words as they flowed from the priest's tongue. His father had made him promise it before he died; under threat of hell and damnation, to keep the Catholic faith and to find Father Bernard and get him to write down the Jesuit history.

His memories of his father were fraught with emotion, and scribing wasn't exactly his choice of occupation for his leisure time. Still, he thought, Father Bernard had been good to him, so he supposed he owed him this much.

Of course he had been only a child when his father had died, and he hadn't realised the importance of a Jesuit history. But now, after five long years of stops and starts, the old man was actually prepared to give him his memoirs, and his vow to his father needled at his conscience like a biting flea.

'So Southwell took over the Jesuit finances from Weston?' Stefan prompted.

'No, no, no.' A sigh, as if Stefan was stupid. 'Father Garnet assumed all the financial responsibilities after Weston's arrest.'

'When was that?'

'Fifteen eighty-five? No, eighty-six, I think. Well before your time, son.' Father Bernard sucked in his breath through his few remaining teeth. 'He took control of both the mission and its finances until . . . well, until they executed him.' He paused a moment, tightened his lips. 'Before you ask, 1606.'

'I've always been fascinated by Garnet.' Stefan paused, shook his aching arm.

Father Bernard shook his head in a gesture of impatience. 'He's not the only priest that defied the king, you know.'

'I know, but—'

'You're taken in by the glamour. You young folk are all the same. The nonsense in the broadsheets and pamphlets. His notoriety. But it was bad for our Faith. It drew attention to us in a way that made things difficult.'

'Then let's write about it!' Stefan was eager. 'What's the point of writing this "history", if we don't tell it as it was?'

Father Bernard raised his eyes to the heavens again, pursing his mouth so his face creased in folds like an old parchment. 'The purpose of the history is not to tell the truth. Every history tells the truth only of its own time, don't you know anything? Henry More's so-called history of the Jesuits should have told you that.'

'But isn't that why we're writing it? To correct misinformation?'

'That was so when we started. But since the death of Father General Nickel, we Jesuits have no strong leader. The Jansenists will want to take advantage and denounce us all as heretics, and we mustn't let that happen.'

Stefan had no idea who the Jansenists were. 'Well, what's changed?'

Another sigh. 'We're writing it now because we need a new Catholic history. One in English, not Latin. One that doesn't look so threatening to the new king, and one that no longer paints the secular clergy as spies and liars. If we want the Jesuit mission in England to survive, we have to make ourselves appear to be more accommodating. Of course, having Catherine of Braganza as queen helps but—'

'Hush! I think I heard the door.' Stefan scraped the papers into a pile and thrust them under the hinged lid of the writing slope.

'Hoy?' A deep melodious voice came from below.

'Just coming,' Father Bernard called. He pulled a brown twill apron around his waist and tugged a woollen cap over his aging pate. Not that he was dressed as a priest in any case, but Stefan understood – it was better to look the way people expected a bookbinder to look.

Father Bernard struggled down the stairs a step at a time, wincing because of his aguey hip, and disappeared into the shop below. Stefan heard snatches of a conversation about leather embossing, but was interrupted as the bells went for three o'clock.

Zounds, that time already! Stefan picked up his cloak and hat, and buckled on his rapier. He must hurry if he was to get to the theatre; time had galloped on.

He'd remember his part, though, no trouble. He'd been a player ever since he had come to London when he was only a boy. Eleven years old, he'd been, and green as they come. The money, pittance though it was, helped pay Father Bernard for his keep. But it was only a small part this time, and it worried him, the way the theatre was going. He used to have the pick of the female roles, but not now. Not since real women had taken the king's fancy. Some damn-fool idea of the French. For a while it hadn't caught, but now there was no ousting the women, and he was stuck in-between – not old enough for big male parts, and too old to play boys.

'This way, my Lord. I pray you will find our hospitality to your liking,' he muttered, rehearsing the lines. Servants were all he got now, and extra bodies to make up the armies. But he was 'doubling'; playing three different servants in different hats, and Killigrew would have him strung up by his bootlaces if he knew he hadn't looked at the script all day. He was supposed to be studying it now, but at least he'd finally got something useful out of Father Bernard, and his father's spectre stopped its heckling.

Hurriedly, Stefan checked the room to make sure anything associated with the Mission was under lock and key. Catholics were still not tolerated, even in this city of whores, crooks and rebels.

He re-buttoned his doublet and smoothed back his long, fair hair before going downstairs. At the last moment he spotted an imported Catholic missal and tucked it behind the other books on the shelf. It was a forty-shilling fine for buying, selling or importing Catholic books.

When he finally got to the bottom of the stairs, the man who was engaging Father Bernard's attention looked up at him in surprise.

'Stefan? What are you doing here?' Charles Hart, one of the actor-managers from the theatre looked him up and down. Large, barrel-chested, and undeniably handsome for his forty-some years, it was hard to believe he'd ever been famous for his women's roles.

Stefan was powerless to stop the heat rising to

his face. 'I've been studying,' he said. 'I lodge here. In Fa . . . Mr Bernard's upstairs room. It's quiet there.'

'So you know each other?' Father Bernard asked.

'This is Mr Hart,' Stefan said. 'He's one of the managers, where I work at the playhouse. And an actor.'

'Ah. That explains why you want this play bound.' Father Bernard waved a sheaf of paper aloft. 'Is it something you are performing?'

'No.' Hart tried to look modest. 'It's just a little play I've written. *Cerbillus*.'

Stefan was surprised. He didn't know Hart fancied himself as a playwright.

Father Bernard screwed up his eyes to look at the papers. 'How interesting. What's it about?' he asked.

Hart's face lit up with enthusiasm. 'It's set in ancient Greece, but it's really an allegory about Catholics plotting to bring down the state. The lead villain is a pagan priest called Cerbillus. He and his men instigate a civil war, and then they engineer the killing of the emperor. Just like the Catholics hoped to destabilise England by killing our good king's father, Charles the First. It's all a pagan, that's to say popish, plot to weaken the state. But of course there's my hero Alexander, who arranges to bring back the emperor's exiled son, and scupper the pagan takeover. I'm hoping to stage it, if Killigrew can find us the finances. I'm sure the king will love it.'

96

Stefan stole a glance at Father Bernard who had paled.

'What about the queen?' Father Bernard asked. 'She's from Spain, perhaps she'll be offended?'

Hart waved a hand dismissively. 'She rarely comes to the theatre. And she's a foreigner. She won't understand the allusion anyway.'

'It sounds like a fine play,' Stefan said, willing Father Bernard to show some enthusiasm, but Father Bernard was too busy wrestling with his painful conscience to add his seal of approval.

'When will the bound edition be ready?' Hart asked.

'Well . . . I should think by next Tuesday,' Father Bernard said, eyeing the papers with distaste.

'And you've no need to collect it, Mr Hart,' Stefan said, thinking quickly. 'I can bring it to the playhouse when it's ready.'

Father Bernard shot him a look of relief.

'That's good of you, boy.' Hart slapped him on the shoulder. 'You must run a good house, Mr Bernard,' Hart said, turning to him. 'We couldn't persuade young Stefan to lodge in the actor's house, not even to be closer to the orange girls.'

Especially not to be closer to the orange girls, thought Stefan, but he laughed along anyway.

'I'll walk with you sir, if you're going there now,' Stefan said.

'Splendid.' Hart opened the door and gestured Stefan through. Once he was on his way down the street he glanced back just once, and saw Father

Bernard on the doorstep, staring after them with a worried expression.

Poor devil, thought Stefan. If they find out what he is, they'll kill him. But then the thought instantly sobered him, for it was followed by another hot on its heels. *If they ever find out what I am, they'll hang me too.*

Waking after her night at the theatre, Bird peered from the window into the dismal yard, and it took only a few moments for cold reality to set in. In the daylight, Bird felt the full weight of what she'd done. Too late now, though; she'd have to hope nobody had noticed her absence.

When she got down to the tack room, the recalcitrance of the grooms was sobering.

'The master told us you weren't to go out,' Dobbsy said. 'But the harness and the tack were still filthy this morning.'

'And you weren't in the harness room yesterday,' Nipper said.

What had happened to the two young boys who'd been so full of life? Now in a few short years, what stood before her were hard young men, schooled in the art of grumbling and apt to use fists if they didn't get what they wanted. They'd moved on to be drivers, and two other young lads were learning the ropes in the yard by mucking out and grooming.

'I am mistress here,' she said. 'And I just . . . I just had to get out.'

They gazed at her blankly. She realised that in their view, mistress or not, she was like a servant, only there to do what the men decided. Of course they knew what Knepp was like, but they didn't think it their place to comment. She was a woman, and beneath their notice. Even as lads they had that slight air of superiority that came with their sex. She thought back to the women on the stage, how outspoken they had been, how ready to riposte, how full of wit and verve.

Livvy stopped to pass a few words with her on the way back with the linseed to the kitchen.

'Thank you for introducing me to Nell,' Bird said. 'I hope something will come of it.'

Livvy made a doubtful shrug. 'I know you don't like *him*, but you could be worse off. He works hard to give these men work. Nell only does it 'cause she's no proper family and it's that or starve.'

They had taken to calling Knepp *him*.

'I was at home all day yesterday, if they ask. I was ill, remember?'

Livvy nodded but looked uncomfortable.

Knepp clattered into the yard at lunchtime, with the two runners trotting behind. Two impossibly young stable lads doffed their caps and hurried to help, as he slid off.

King of the Castle, Bird thought bitterly.

She turned back to the cleaning, trying to catch up with herself, knowing it wouldn't be two shakes before someone told him about last night. She was practised at the tack, though she still hated the stink of horse grease on her hands. Today though, her stomach was full of knots. She faced the door with the saddle tree before her so she'd have some warning.

After half an hour Knepp still hadn't appeared and she relaxed, upturned the saddle on her knees and settled into the rhythm of the brush as it swooped back and forth over the padded lining. Someone had forgotten to put a blanket on the horse first, and the saddle was full of gingery horsehair.

When he spoke from the door it made her startle. 'You've been shirking again.'

She stood up straight away, defiant. 'Not shirking,' she said, knowing instantly what he was referring to. 'I was unwell.'

'You seem well enough now.' He was tapping a switch against his palm.

'It was just a chill to the stomach,' she said.

'Is that so? Then how come Livvy tells me you had a bad head?'

'It was both,' she said, scrabbling for an answer.

'Liar.' He was across the cobbled space in an instant, a fist connected with her cheek, and in her haste to step away, she fell backwards over the stool and crashed to the ground, hitting her head on the cobbled ground.

She heard the whistle of the switch as it came down, and felt its sting on her arm, but she rolled over, letting her stays and skirts take the worst of the beating. By the time she sat up to examine the damage, Knepp had gone. She rubbed her head, wincing at the egg-shaped bump already tender beneath her fingers. She'd been stupid. She should have arranged a better story with Livvy. It was her own fault, but the resentment still burned in her that she must endure his thrashing. She recalled the shock of the first time he'd used a switch on her, like one of his damned horses. Now she'd got used to it. She stood up, brushed down her skirts, swallowed down the humiliation, and picked up a pail to collect clean water. Nothing could be done. It was the way life was, and she'd learned to live with it.

Not content with applying the switch, Knepp would make her pay, she knew; he'd do something to hurt her. He'd always been adept at finding out exactly what would hurt her the most, and using that against her. Withdrawing her housekeeping money, or stopping Grinstead from loaning her the *Gazette*. Last time she'd displeased him, she had come home to find her music shredded and scattered around the parlour.

On woolly legs she finished the morning's work. Her hands were unsteady, and even polishing made her stomach heave. She saw the looks of the stable men, who must have known what happened, and it shamed her to see their eyes slide away from her red cheek.

It was to be eggs and bread for dinner, with apples and ale. Around noon, she crossed the yard to the house unsteadily, still seeing floaters at the corners of her vision.

When she got to the parlour it was to find that the table hadn't been laid, and there was no sign of Livvy.

'Livvy?' she put her head into the brewhouse, but there was no sign of her.

'Have you seen Livvy?' she asked one of the stable-lads.

A voice from behind her. 'She's gone. And she won't be coming back.' When she turned, Knepp's expression was one of smug satisfaction.

Her reserve crumbled. 'Why? Why cut off your nose to spite your face? She's worked here six years. How will you manage in the yard without her to fetch and carry for you?'

'Plenty of lads can fetch or carry. I've two young lads who'll be glad to do it, and for less.'

'But she needed the work.'

'You should have thought of that. She lied to me.'

'She didn't! You don't know—'

'You told her to lie,' he cut in. 'Grinstead was on his way to get a tooth pulled and saw you queueing together to go into the theatre. The theatre! No respectable wife would choose that bull's pizzle over hard work. You imagine you're a fine lady, do you? With nothing better to do? I see you haven't enough to occupy you, so Livvy has gone, and you will do her work of brewing the ale and laying the fires.' With that he turned his attention to two customers who had entered the yard.

Poor Livvy. What would she think of her? It was her fault she'd lost her employment. And with Livvy gone, who would she talk to, who would she share confidences with?

In the upstairs office, Knepp stared, unseeing, at the lines of figures in Grinstead's account ledgers. Grinstead was out, and he wanted to have a few minutes to see how the figures added up, without Grinstead coughing all over him. But he kept seeing the shock in Mary Elizabeth's eyes when he had punched her. The business with his wife had unsettled him. He'd meant to just give her a birching. His heart was still pounding and he put a hand to the front of his waistcoat to still it. Where did all that anger come from? He shouldn't have hit her so hard. It was a man's duty to chastise his wife, but he hadn't meant to lose control, for her to crack her head like that. But she shouldn't have disobeyed him, and now it was he who looked like the villain, when it was all her wilfulness that was at fault.

The theatre. Trust her to go there. It was so bloody public. She couldn't have chosen a worst place to make a fool of him. House of rakes and whores, all prattling nonsense and lies to the empty heads of the aristocracy; people like the Viners. For a moment, Knepp pictured himself in a box, with a well-dressed Mary Elizabeth on his arm. He imagined Arabella Viner looking up at him from below, wishing she'd chosen him instead of Viner.

103

All fantasy. He leant on the table a moment and closed his eyes to banish Arabella's face, and forced his attention back to the ledgers. He flipped the pages and ran his finger down last month's columns for profit and loss. Worse than he thought. He'd paid for a horse doctor to come to one of his best horses, Vulcan, who had trodden on a nail and the foot had festered. The horse didn't recover and he'd had to put it out of its misery.

He always did the despatching himself. It was not a task he wanted to assign to anyone else, because he knew how painful it was. The sight of a horse's deep brown trusting eyes when you lifted the pistol; well, it always pierced him. Somehow the horse always knew, and the liquid eyes would be full of reproach.

Now he had the bills for the horse doctor, and the tannery who'd taken the dead beast away, and no matched pair for hiring his best carriage. He shut the book. If things didn't improve, he'd be heading for debtor's prison. And now to add to all his woes, there was his mother to contend with. One more extra expense he hadn't bargained for.

CHAPTER 7

Bird threw herself into the work. Better not to think. Better to just get on with it. When things had calmed down, she would try to find an hour or two to find out where Livvy had gone and apologise to her. She'd make it up to her somehow; she couldn't bear the idea there might be bad feeling between them.

By the time supper was finished, she could barely stagger to clear the platters. Partly it was that her face throbbed where Knepp had hit it, and partly it was that the extra work of lugging coal buckets and barrelling the ale had taken its toll on her already aching muscles. But to show weakness might give Knepp satisfaction, so she refused to buckle.

'Sit down,' he said, re-appearing in the parlour when he'd finished his after-supper pipe with the men. She saw him glance at her swollen cheek, then look away.

She sat, warily, wondering what was coming.

'Tomorrow my mother will be arriving. You will make sure she is comfortable and has all she needs.'

Bird blinked. This was not what she had expected; she'd thought he wanted more recriminations over the theatre. She pulled herself upright. 'How long will she stay?'

'A month or two. She's seventy-two. My brother fell off his horse and both legs are broken. He always did ride too fast. My sister-in-law cannot care for them both, so Mother has to come here. She'll be able to advise you, and tell you how things should be done.'

She didn't need anyone's advice. But, another woman! Her heart lifted. 'Which chamber will she take?'

'Mr Hindle will see to sorting out where she will sleep. There need be no change to our arrangements.' In other words, they would sleep in separate chambers, except for the once a week coupling. Thank God. She tried not to show the relief on her face.

That night she put a cold compress on her cheek and by the next day the swelling had gone down, leaving only a faint bruise. She hoped Mrs Knepp's eyesight was poor, or she'd guess Bird had displeased her son.

Whilst she was clearing the breakfast platters, Dobbsy arrived with a curtain rail and hammer and nails. He started to unload the plate cupboard of dishes and cups, and stack them on the table.

'What are you doing?' she asked.

'Mr Knepp's orders. I'm to make up sleeping quarters for old Mrs Knepp.'

'In here?'

'I've to move this cupboard out of the alcove and stand it over there.' He pointed. 'By all accounts Widow Knepp's got gout and often she can't get upstairs, so this is the best we can do.'

'Not in here,' Bird protested. 'She can't sleep in here. Not when I have all the meals to do, and the—' She was at a loss. She would lose her privacy. Knepp's mother would be there in the corner, watching her every move. 'Is there nowhere else?'

'Master's orders.'

By lunchtime, the slatted box bed was in place and a curtain pinned across it. Bird had been told Mrs Knepp would bring her mattress with her, but she would need to supply bedlinen. Grinstead brought her a pouch with two shillings and told her to go and buy sheets and a bolster cover, and a decent blanket. She bit back a retort. More than they'd thought to do for her when she arrived, she thought.

Once on the street, she called in to the butchers. 'Any news of Livvy Black?' she asked Mr Bull.

'Gone to work for Viner's,' he said continuing to slice up a side of lamb with a cleaver. He paused, sucked his teeth, then said, 'Says she'll never work for Knepp's again. And she used to speak so highly of you.'

'I know. My husband dismissed her.'

'You treated her shamefully, she said. Stood by, and never spoke up for her.'

'Mr Knepp . . . well, he's a difficult man.'

107

'Aye. Well, Livvy'll not cross your doorstep again. Can't say as I blame her. She's owed a sennight's wage and no way of getting it now. She sends any spare money home to her mother, you know. She's got a little brother too young for service.'

Bird was chastened. She hadn't even known that, not the most basic fact about her friend. 'Where does her mother live?'

'Abroad somewhere. Barbary? Africy? Where she comes from, I guess.'

'I'll go to Viner's and talk to her. I'll try to get her the wages she's owed somehow. But there's no time today, I'm expecting my husband's mother this afternoon. If Livvy comes in again, tell her I'm sorry, and I was asking after her.'

'Don't think it will make any difference. Work's work, and hard to come by, especially for a woman like her.' He lifted the cleaver to the block again.

Bird had to be content with that. When she got back from the linen draper's a cart stood by, with two hauliers already unloading things into the parlour. Six dusty trunks and valises were piled on the flags before the hearth, and four hat-boxes thrown onto the table. Black garments of a fusty appearance teetered in a pile on a chair.

How many bags did the woman need? Bird's heart fell at the invasion of her space. She had never met Knepp's mother, because a previous attack of gout meant she'd been unable to travel for the wedding. What sort of a woman was she?

She examined the clothes and trunks for clues. Everything was old and worn. But perhaps that was to be expected from an old woman who never went anywhere. Maybe she'd be able to win her over, and use her influence to persuade Knepp to be more reasonable.

And having another woman in the house might be a help. She could shell peas, or chop vegetables even if she couldn't walk far. She was just thinking this when the mattress was dumped at her feet. An old and stained bag of straw and feathers, it stank, and looked so foul that Bird begged them to put it on the bed box straight away.

She covered it up with clean linen, and had a hand on a trunk ready to drag it to a more convenient place when a woman's voice in the yard made her hurry to the door.

'No! I'll take that.' There was nothing in the least frail about the voice. 'And take your cap off, Christopher. You're not a servant.' It was a voice of authority, and surprisingly, a voice of class.

Mrs Knepp was already out of the carriage and clutching a bamboo cage in one hand. She flapped an impatient hand at Dobbsy, who retreated.

'Your arm, Christopher,' she instructed.

Knepp obliged, and she hobbled towards the door, leaning heavily against him, her stick tapping on the cobbles. The cage swung at her side, and inside, two canaries flustered and squeaked.

'Let me,' Bird said, rushing forwards to take the cage.

'No. I'll carry them.' Knepp's mother stopped, and looked up at Bird through narrowed eyes.

Knepp paused. 'This is Mary Elizabeth, Mother.'

Bird attempted a smile. So he actually knew her proper name. It was the first time she'd heard him use it since he'd said the words, 'I take thee, Mary Elizabeth.'

'It's a pleasure to meet you, Mrs Knepp,' she said, stepping forward.

'So you're the wife.' A nod was all the greeting she offered. She whispered something to her son which sounded like, 'No sign of a babe yet?'

Knepp shook his head.

Bird tightened her lips and ushered them inside. Mrs Knepp glanced around the parlour and sighed. 'She should have taken this in hand.'

The words bit into her; Bird suddenly saw what she must see; the spartan room, the worn furniture, the lack of comfort. Even though she'd polished everything until it shone, there was no disguising the lack of money.

Knepp lowered his mother into the moth-eaten cushion on the chair near the hearth, and put his cap back on. 'She'll show you where you're to sleep, Mother,' he said, back to addressing Bird in his usual way. 'Make yourself at home. I have to be getting back to the yard. I'll see you later.'

'Embrace your mama then.'

Knepp leant over to peck her on the cheek, and Mrs Knepp ruffled his hair as if he were a small boy.

When he'd gone, Bird had a chance to get a good look at his mother. 'I'll make you a drink, Mrs Knepp,' Bird said. As she warmed the ale and filled the jug, she stole a few glances at her new companion. The family resemblance was marked; the same slightly overhanging brow, and expression of watchfulness. Her thick wiry hair sprung low on the forehead in the same way, but was grey where Knepp's was black.

As Bird worked, Mrs Knepp rubbed her top lip over and over with a crooked finger, as if trying to erase an invisible moustache, or decide what to say. The cage of birds on the table kept up a constant frantic cheeping. Bird knew better than to speak first. She'd leave it to Mrs Knepp.

Bird placed a cup of warm ale before her.

'Is it fresh?' Mrs Knepp asked.

'Brewed it myself this morning.'

'It has to be fresh. My stomach can't abide old ale.' She drank a few sips and then frowned and left it untouched. 'You don't need to stand about, girl. You can unpack my things for me and put them away. Take the keys.' She un-clipped a bunch of keys from her waist and threw them towards Bird. 'Start there.' She pointed at the biggest trunk.

Bird stooped to put the biggest key in the lock and heaved open the lid. A smell of old fur, stale lavender and camphor hit the back of her nose.

'Careful now,' Mrs Knepp snapped. 'Don't just pull it out. Unwrap everything slowly.'

Bird felt in the folds of the rabbit-skin cloak,

111

and found it was full of pewter plates, dishes and cutlery. She unloaded it all onto the table. Where would it go? There wasn't enough cupboard space for all this. And another worse thought – this wasn't just a few things for a few weeks' stay. It looked like she was moving in.

She shook the rabbit skin cloak and took it towards the door.

'Where're you taking that?'

'Just to air it a little, Mrs Knepp. I'll hang it in the yard.'

'Don't let it get damp. I can't abide damp. It makes my bones ache.'

Outside she found a gate to hang the cloak over, and took in gulps of fresh air. Already she had taken a dislike to Mrs Knepp, and the thought of having her in the house for longer than one night made her spirits sag.

'Come on, Bird,' she said to herself. 'She's an old lady. Be agreeable to her, and she'll soon come round.'

When she went back inside it was to see that Mrs Knepp was out of her seat and was peering inside the sideboard. Clearly there was not as much wrong with her legs as Bird had been told.

'They'll go in here, my things,' she said. 'You'll have to move those other platters out.'

'Beg pardon, Mrs Knepp, I can't. I need those every day for the men's meals. But don't worry, I'll find a good place for yours where they'll be safe.'

'My pewter should go in here. It's valuable. Christopher will agree with me.'

'Why don't you sit down, and let me unpack the rest.'

'I'm not an invalid, you know.'

'But you must be tired, after your long journey.'

'Don't tell me what to do.'

Bird turned away and began to unpack the rest of Mrs Knepp's belongings in icy silence. There was no sound from behind her, so presumably Mrs Knepp was still standing, despite her bad legs.

More household goods emerged. A dented brass warming pan, burnt-bottomed cooking pots, a set of greasy candlesticks, a porringer and a quantity of rather thin and darned linen. There was even a trunk full of faded rugs and mildewed cushions, and another of what appeared to be mourning clothes. As she opened the last, an inlaid marquetry box, she caught a glimpse of white before the stick landed with a thwack on her shoulder.

'Close that up again,' Mrs Knepp said. 'That's my business.'

Bird closed her eyes tight and slammed the lid. Partly, she was relieved. She didn't want to handle any more of these things. Despite Mrs Knepp's imperious manner, they were all filthy, shabby and well-used.

She'd just shut the lid when there was a rap on the door. Bird jumped, and the canaries flustered and twittered in their cage. She was unused to callers. Despite her urging them not to, everyone at the yard just walked in.

'Answer it then,' Mrs Knepp said.

At the door a messenger passed her a note. She was about to run up to the office with it when she saw it was addressed to *Mrs C Knepp*.

'What's that?'

'A letter for you,' Bird said. 'They must know you're here.' She passed it over.

Mrs Knepp gave it a cursory glance. '*Mrs C Knepp*.' She tutted. '"C". I'm "R" Knepp, girl. Christopher's father was Roland. It's for you.'

Usually Livvy collected up the mail and took it to the office. No letter had ever come for her, though she always hoped her father might write.

Puzzled, she fetched a knife from the drawer and slit open the string that bound the letter together.

Mrs Knepp, I would be pleased to hear you read for me at 2 o'clock on Thursday.

Send a reply to confirm. On the day, please be punctual. The audition fee is two shillings.

Thomas Killigrew

She felt the flush of excitement rush to her head, before she realised that first, Mrs Knepp was here now, and it would be hard to get away, and second, that she didn't have two shillings. Nell had never mentioned a fee.

'Who's it from?'

'Just the laundry bill.'

'Does the thought of the laundry always make you blush?'

114

'I'm not blushing. It's just warm in here.'

Mrs Knepp's sharp tone had been a warning. Bird folded the letter back up and pushed it awkwardly into the hanging pocket in her skirts. Be calm, she told herself.

Mrs Knepp frowned at her. 'I'll tell Christopher you had the laundry bill,' she said, scrutinising Bird's face.

'No need,' she said, face still hot with emotion, 'I'll tell him myself.'

The next day she carried out her household tasks with old Mrs Knepp observing her, like one of the gargoyles on St Paul's. She had a criticism about everything, from her baking of the bread to the way Bird mopped the flagstone floor. She never once offered any sort of help, but kept up a running commentary about how it should be done until Bird longed to throw the pail of suds over her head.

After the men had been in for their mid-day meal, she made an excuse and said she must go out to buy more onions and a joint of meat if they were to eat that night. She didn't need onions, but she did need two shillings. She untied her waist-apron and pushed her thick brown hair under a coif.

'If Mr Knepp wants to know where I am, tell him I've gone to the market,' she said.

'You can fetch me some bird-seed then,' Mrs Knepp said. 'Millet if you can get it. And get some greens. Cabbage.'

'What are their names, your birds?'

'Bodkin and Thimble. Thimble's the smaller one. But you're not to go near them. Leave their feeding to me.'

'I'll put it on my list.' She opened a drawer and took out paper and a lead to write with.

'Don't be long. No gallivanting or dawdling. I might need help to get to the closet. And don't forget the seed, now.'

Bird finished writing and stuffed extra paper and lead in her pocket.

As she went out she glanced behind. Mrs Knepp did not smile or wave, just stared, as if she were an exhibit in a glass case.

Every time she went out from under the arch she felt a lightness, as if a yoke had been lifted from her shoulders, and now the sensation was even more intense. The sky was a soft pale blue; the clouds mere wisps. The street smelled of dust and hot cobbles, and the faint smell of sweating horse. The letter from Killigrew hovered in her thoughts. It was her chance, her way of escape. She paused just outside the gate to lean against a wall and write a polite reply.

To; Mr Thomas Killigrew

Thank you for your invitation to read for you on Thursday at the King's Playhouse. I will be there prompt, at two bells.

Mary Elizabeth Knepp

At the end of the street a bunch of link boys loitered, waiting for work, so she sacrificed a farthing from her housekeeping money and sent one of them with the message.

She turned left then, and hurried up the road towards the city centre. After about a half-mile she came to a cross-roads and turned in past the stone mounting-block into a wide sweeping drive. Over the biggest arched doorway was a dark green painted sign, with gold lettering, and a silhouette of a sedan. 'Edward Viner – High Class Coaches, Carriages and Horses for Hire. Sedans a Speciality'. On the opposite wall was another sign, 'Travel in Comfort with Viner's'. And one that made her pause to read it twice; 'Clean Lodgings for Gentle-Folk and Travellers from the North. 6d a Night'.

Oh no. Viner's were taking in lodgers. Whatever Viner did, Knepp would want to do the same. She could see the advantage – you could rest a night, do your business in London, then hire a horse or carriage to return home. But she also knew that hospitality was not Knepp's strong suit, and they had not a single chamber good enough for paying guests.

She sighed. Viner understood his market, whereas Knepp seemed oblivious to it. Against a hitching rail stood several well-muscled horses with polished gleaming coats and tails plaited into intricate knots. Everything was so immaculately tidy it made her eyes hurt.

'Yes?' A lad in dark-green-and-gold livery approached her.

'I'm looking for Livvy Black. Does she work here?'

'Yes. But she's busy in the lodging rooms above the yard.'

'Will you tell her Mrs Knepp's here to see her.'

'Mrs Knepp? Of Farringdon and Knepp's near the fleshmarket?'

'Yes, that's me.'

He backed away. 'I'll have to ask. I'll fetch Mr Viner.'

'No need to do that. I just want a word with Livvy.'

'Is there a problem, Mason?' A burly be-whiskered man cut briskly between them.

'No, sir.' Mason almost clicked his heels.

Viner was well-dressed in a navy top-coat and embroidered vest; he rubbed his hands together and smiled politely at them both, his eyes small as raisins.

'This is Mrs Knepp,' Mason said. 'She wants to see Livvy.'

The genial smile was replaced by a frown. 'That won't be possible.'

'I'm happy to wait.'

'Not on my premises. If he's sent you to get her back, she won't come. The pay is twice what your husband gave her.'

'He didn't send me, I came because—'

He held up his hand. 'My customers tell me your husband quotes one price, then charges another. We only do honest business here, Mrs Knepp, so if I were you, I'd cease wasting my time. Livvy will be well-paid, with a day off on Sunday to do her Christian duty. You can tell Knepp the honest prosper, and the Lord God punishes thieves and rogues.'

He was right, but she wished he didn't look quite so self-satisfied about it.

There was nothing to do but go. 'I'm sorry you are too small-minded to hear me out, Mr Viner. It seems your reputation for customer service is somewhat over-rated.'

As soon as she was off his premises she walked around the back searching for another way in. By the back wall was a small alley right next to the dung heap, with a wooden plank door set into the wall. She pushed the door open and found herself in a narrow thoroughfare with doors either side, and what looked to be a hayloft above. She passed the fodder room, with its lidded corn barrels and sacks of meal, and pushed open the door on the opposite side to reveal a boot room with highly polished boots on rows of wooden trees.

A noise outside made her turn. She shouldn't be caught here, not when Viner had told her to leave. She pulled the door open again with a finger and was in time to see a groom going down the alley lugging two wooden pails of water. She slipped out behind him and was relieved to see him enter the next stall, which housed the fodder room, and she could smell it, the boiling of hoof oil and linseed.

Set in the wall was a set of wooden treads to the

rooms above. Bird tiptoed up. Hearing a noise from one of the rooms, Bird pushed open the door and Livvy turned, a striped bolster pressed to her chest. Her face broke into a smile, but it was immediately replaced by a guarded grimmer expression, 'What do you want?' She shoved the bolster into its cover and pummelled at it.

'I came to bring my apologies. I know I made you lie to him, and it cost you your employment.'

'So?'

'Well, I just wanted there to be no hard feelings between us.'

'Is that all?' She flung the bolster onto the bed, and bundled up the dirty bedding. 'You think it can be mended just with words?'

'Well, I thought—'

'You didn't bring my wages then? What I'm owed?'

'I can't speak to Knepp. You know he never listens. But I promise you'll get it back. I'm to audition for the King's Players. A note from Killigrew came today. I thought you'd like to know, and when I get my player's purse, you'll be the first person I pay.'

Livvy stopped what she was doing then, dropped the bundle on the floor. 'He won't let you do it, you know he won't. It was' . . . she searched for words . . . 'big fool idea.' She grabbed a second bolster.

'It's too late. Nell's arranged it. It's tomorrow.'

Livvy shook her head. 'Killigrew, he might not like you.'

'I know. But I can't leave Knepp unless I have employment.'

Livvy paused then with the bolster held to her chest. 'You'd do that? Leave him?' She made an explosive 'pouf'. 'He kill you first.'

'I'm going to try. What's to lose?' Bird raised her hands in a shrug.

'You be a bold one, no mistaking.'

'What's it like? Working here?'

'Better than with you.'

Bird took the blow.

Livvy saw, and relented. 'Mr Viner treats us like he's in the pulpit, and we're the sinners. And I don't trust him. He looks at me too long when he thinks I don't see. But the wages are fair and the work's easier.' She shook the bolster into its case. 'It's a different sort of customer; gentlemen, you know? Prospects might be better. I'm after being wed, so I can keep my own house. Make my own beds, not someone else's. Maybe open my own brewhouse. But mighty hard, being a darkie. I look like a slave and no-one wants slave for wife.'

'I'm sorry. I didn't mean to lose you your position. I wish you luck, Livvy.'

She softened. 'I'm glad you came. You my friend. Never had no mistress friend before.'

'I miss you, Livvy.'

Her mouth worked and she was silent. After a moment she said, 'Come back tomorrow and tell me how it was with Killigrew. Watch him though; Rose says he's got hands with a will of their own.'

121

'Don't worry. After Knepp, he'll be a babe-in-arms.'

'His arms is what I'm worried about.' Livvy unfastened a drawstring bag from her waist and drew out a small wizened object. 'Here, take this. My lucky hare's foot.'

'If you're sure . . .?'

'Never fails. Kept me safe right across the ocean, and waves high as a house. And I hope you get away from Knepp. I heard Ted Viner tell Missus he's wanting to take over Knepp's yard by the time the winter season begins. Says it's in a good position for travellers from all over the north-west.'

'Knepp won't sell.'

'That's what Mrs Viner said. But Viner just laughed. "There's ways of squeezing him out," he said.'

Bird dashed into the seed merchant, bought a bag of millet, and queued for vegetables, fidgeting restlessly from foot to foot, knowing she had taken far longer than she'd intended.

When she got back a brand new carriage was blocking the entrance to the yard.

That's not one of ours, Bird thought. It's too new. But it was right outside the door, which was standing open, with two junior stable lads lurking on the threshold.

'What's going on?' she asked.

'Doctor's here,' one of them said. 'Dobbs fetched him.'

She hurried through to see a tableau of people clustered around the alcove in the parlour, her husband, Dobbs, and Grinstead, plus two strangers.

'Where've you been?' Knepp's face was drawn with anger.

'To the market. What's happened?' She dumped the basket on the table and took off her hat.

'My mother fell, and lay here for more than an hour with nobody to help her, that's what,' Knepp said.

'Is she all right?'

'Dobbs found her.' He glared at her accusingly.

Dobbs nodded, 'Shouting for help, she was. It was good fortune I was passing the window.'

'You should have been here,' Knepp said.

'I went for provisions,' Bird protested. 'I always go on a Wednesday.'

'It interrupted my work,' Knepp said. 'I had to send Dobbs out to fetch Hopkins the physician.'

Over in the alcove, a grey-haired man in a pair of pince-nez was gesturing to his boy-servant to open up his bag. Grinstead was hovering over them.

'What does the doctor say?' she asked.

Grinstead sniffed. 'He bled her, but she's still in pain.'

'Where? She was fine when I left her. Let me see.' She approached the bed and the doctor reluctantly moved aside. 'Mrs Knepp, where does it hurt?'

Mrs Knepp groaned. 'Everywhere.' She was supine on the trestle bed, her arm over the covers before her. Her skin was grey, wrinkled as paper, and covered in writhing black leeches, where presumably the physician was trying to bleed her.

Bird suppressed her revulsion. 'What happened? Were you taken ill?'

Mrs Knepp opened her eyes again. They were surprisingly alert. 'I needed a drink,' she said in a quavering voice, unlike her previous imperious tones, 'and there was nobody here.' She threw a look of appeal to Knepp, who hurried back to her bedside. 'When I tried to get up from my chair and fetch a glass, I fell in a dead faint. And then I couldn't stand. My legs wouldn't hold me.'

'Now, now,' Knepp said stroking her forehead. 'Don't try to talk. Save your strength.'

Bird stepped away to give them room. 'It's probably just the upheaval of moving,' she said to Grinstead. 'Too much heat and movement. Now she's been bled, she'll soon be right.'

'I don't want to cause any trouble,' Mrs Knepp said.

'You are not causing trouble,' Knepp said firmly.

The doctor plucked off the leeches one by one, scraped them into a jar and corked it up. As he bandaged the bony arm, he said, 'Is there someone who can sit with her?'

'Yes, she will,' Knepp said, indicating Bird with a jerk of his head. He patted his mother's arm. 'She'll sit with you until you feel stronger.' She smiled back up at him. 'But best to stay in bed a few more days; we can't be too careful.'

A few more days? Bird's shoulders slumped. She

was already planning in her head how she might get away for a few hours to read for Mr Killigrew, and now this to add to the difficulty.

The doctor fastened the bandage with a catchpin and stood up. 'Her humours will be better balanced now. I'll give you a script for some physic; a wine tonic should thin the blood. She'll need strengthening food, and plenty of peace and quiet, and make sure the fire is always lit, it will drive away the overheated humours.'

'Are you sure the heat's necessary?' Mrs Knepp said, lifting her head. Her brow was already perspiring. 'It seems wasteful. It's August after all.'

'It's essential,' the doctor said, frowning at her, at the same time as Knepp said, 'Don't worry, Mother. We can bear the expense. Now lie back down and take your ease.'

The doctor packed his jar of leeches into his leather holdall, took out a nib and ink and scrawled out a bill.

Knepp blanched and swallowed as he read it. 'You'd better come up to the office. Grinstead, take Dr Hopkins and settle up.' He glared at Bird. 'Don't leave her on her own again, hear me?'

Knepp led the way out. The doctor gave her a brief bow as he passed, his boy-servant traipsing behind him lugging his bag. The other men followed behind, Grinstead pressing at the doctor's shoulder. She caught the words, 'I wonder if you could take a look at my chest, sir,' as he passed. The entourage reminded Bird of the King's procession.

When the door closed behind them, and Bird turned back to the bed it was to see Mrs Knepp already sitting up.

'He's no use, that physician,' she said. 'I tried to tell him, my constitution's too weak for bleeding, but he wouldn't listen.'

'Are you feeling better?'

'A little.'

'Good. I'll light the fire then.'

'It's quite hot enough. Does he want to burn me alive?'

'If my husband says it's to be lit, then it's to be lit. Or I'll suffer the consequences.'

'What's that supposed to mean?'

'Nothing. Just rest. And let me get on with it.' She shut the curtain on the bed with a rattle. In the corner, the birds cheeped listlessly. Sorry for them, she emptied some millet into the cage, and gave them a lid of water.

She'd just have to hope Mrs Knepp recovered quickly.

Dawn had barely tinged the sky when Bird heard her name from below.

'Mary Elizabeth! Mary Elizabeth!' Mrs Knepp was calling.

She hesitated a few minutes to see if Knepp would stir from the room across the hall.

The call again, 'Mary Elizabeth!'

Bird hurried down. 'What is it?'

'I need your arm,' Mrs Knepp said, 'to get to the closet.'

'Why not use the chamber pot? It's nearer.'

'Can't. My legs won't bend that far.'

Bird helped the old woman out of bed. Without her clothes she was kindling-thin, the cotton night-dress clinging to her shrunken frame.

'Pass me my stick.' The look in her eyes was still intimidating. She was a woman used to being in control, just like her son.

When the business was done Bird helped her back into bed, and started to draw the curtain across.

'No,' Mrs Knepp said, fixing her with a pin-sharp look, 'My curtain will stay open.'

A few moments later Knepp appeared, in his shirt sleeves, looping his belt around his breeches. 'Better, Mother?'

'A little. But still not myself, dear. Another day abed, I fear.'

'Where's the bread, wife?' Knepp complained, 'You're late with it again.'

Bird hurried to the pantry to fetch bread, cheeses and meat for the men's breakfast.

'You can bring your saddlery work in here today. Keep my mother company.'

'In here?' Bird didn't like the idea of dirty saddlery being in her clean parlour. Somehow bringing his world into hers offended her.

'Dobbs will bring some saddle trees and a pail of water.'

★　★　★

127

By the middle of the day, Bird was tired of turning circles in her head. The appointment with Killigrew grew in her thoughts like a fungus. She couldn't keep it away. If she was to go out and Knepp found out, it would be a beating or worse. She was wanting to do something impossible, she knew that, like wanting to become queen, or for the Thames to turn to ink. Yet the thought stuck in her head and would not let go.

She couldn't decide if Mrs Knepp was really ill, or whether it was just an excuse to have Bird run after her. Every few minutes she would need something – a drink, or to be passed another shawl, or for the pillow to be straightened.

Bird did her work silently, aware of Mrs Knepp's watching presence in the corner. Every so often one of the stable lads would bring her another dirty saddle, and she'd set to work with the cold water and scrubbing brush. If she could get out for an hour, she could keep the two o'clock appointment. Once the midday meal was served, perhaps Mrs Knepp would sleep, and she'd be able to risk it.

She made a heavy soup of leek and beans with ground lettuce, served with bread and dripping. Lettuce was supposed to aid sleep, that's what her mother used to say. She served Mrs Knepp first, on a tray on her lap. Whatever the ailment was, it didn't seem to affect her appetite. She ate heartily, and Bird began to wonder where on earth she put it all in that skinny stomach. Once the men had been fed and gone back to work, she was gratified to hear snores coming from the bed in the alcove. Quickly she shot up the stairs and struggled out of her work skirts and into her green dress; the one she'd worn to be wed. Better look respectable, even if it was old-fashioned. She piled up her hair and skewered it under her hat with pins.

As she stood up she saw that there was a pile of books on the table near the bed. She didn't know Knepp had any interest in reading because he always forbade her news-sheets or books. She creaked open the top leather-bound book. *Psalms*. In the front of the book was an inscription, *Christopher Henry Knepp, Royal Latin School, Buckingham. Scholar's Prize 1639.*

She guessed he was thirty-five years old now, so according to her calculations he would have been ten years old then. So he was better educated than she thought. What had made him turn his back on it all?

The book beneath was even more puzzling. *Leviathan or The Matter, Forme and Power of a Common-Wealth Ecclesiasticall and Civil*. She'd never heard of it. But flipping through, she found it a dense, almost incomprehensible treatise of power and government. The thought that Knepp might even read something like this filled her with wondering.

A peal of bells. The half-hour after one.

Hurriedly, she put the books back and crossed her fingers in a silent salute to herself. With any

129

luck, Mrs Knepp would sleep a couple of hours, and she'd be back before anyone noticed she was gone.

Downstairs on tiptoes, clinging to the banister. She crept to the door and grasped the door handle.

'Where are you going?'

She almost shot out of her shoes. The woman was awake.

'I won't be long. We need . . . some more flour for tomorrow's bread.'

'You got flour yesterday,' Mrs Knepp said. 'I saw you unpack it from the basket. And you've changed your clothes.'

'It's not just flour,' she said improvising, 'your son's very concerned for your health. He asked me if I'd pick up your wine tonic from the physician.'

'When will you be back?'

'I won't be long. Just half an hour.' She glanced at the wall-mounted sundial through the window, saw the finger of shadow had crept round.

'You're leaving me on my own.'

'Only for a few minutes.'

'Well, I need to use the closet again.'

Bird gritted her teeth and helped her out of the bed. The thin cold arm, the reddened knobbled toes on the dark flagged floor. The woman was moving even more slowly than she had before, deliberately taking her time.

When she tried to settle her back into bed, Mrs Knepp said, 'If you're going, you can bring more sawdust for the canaries' cage.'

'Yes, yes. I'll get some sawdust from the stables later. Now settle down.'

'I need another blanket.' Now she was sure Mrs Knepp was delaying her on purpose, for only earlier hadn't she complained vociferously about the heat?

She almost threw the blanket onto the bed, grabbed her basket from the table.

'I'm not sure you should go just now,' Mrs Knepp said, her voice becoming feeble. 'I'm not feeling so well.'

'In that case, the tonic will do you good,' Bird said briskly, already turning the door handle. 'You sleep, and I'll be back before you know it.'

With that, she hurried out of the door. She hadn't got a script for the tonic from her husband but had no intention of stopping now. It was ten to two and she was going to be late. '*Be punctual*,' Killigrew had said.

The summer heat beat down on her shoulders as she ran down Duck Lane, and through Alders Gate into the city, with one hand clutched to her hat, the other clinging on to her basket. On Paternoster Row, she came across a great crowd of people celebrating. One of the men grasped her by both arms and tried to jig her round in a crazy dance.

'Let me go!' she cried, wrestling herself away. From their excited talk, she gathered that some-where on the other side of the ocean, New Amsterdam had been ceded to the English and

131

now was to be named New York after the Duke of York. A whole city could change just like that, but she was still stuck with Christopher Knepp.

Down the road she ran, towards the bridge over the Fleet, a stitch in her side making her clutch her ribs.

Clang. Clang. The two o'clock bells rang out over the city, and she was still a half-mile away from the theatre.

She put on an extra spurt, panting, the stink of the Fleet like rough tweed in her nostrils, until finally the theatre came into view. There was a crush of carts and carriages on Catherine Street, so she had to hop from foot to foot waiting to cross. Spotting a gap in the traffic she made a dash for it, leaping out of the way of a horse and cart and missing it by a whisker. As she landed, her boot skidded from under her and in an instant she was flat on her back. She scrambled up and out of the road, yelping as her foot landed on the cobbled road. A slick of horse dung showed the mark where her heel had slipped.

She hobbled to the side of the street and leant up against a wall which was plastered with peeling papers, for the new play. She pictured Killigrew waiting down the road at the King's. Gingerly she put her full weight onto her left foot, but immediately withdrew it. A sharp pain shot up to the knee from her ankle.

She paused a moment, nauseous. She'd have to go forward or back. And both would be slow and painful. She took a deep shuddering breath and steeled herself before doggedly limping in the direction of the King's Playhouse. There was something wrong with the ankle. She cursed it, that it should let her down now. A hundred yards. She could do it, if she went slowly and leant against the wall.

Gone two bells now, and they might not even see her, but she had to try.

It was Livvy's half-day, and she hurried up Lambeth Hill, hitching her skirts out of the soil in the street, her boots kicking up puffs of dust as she went. At the Sign of the Hourglass, she pushed her way through the door, amid a gust of hot wind. The Frenchman, M'sieur Hubert, gave her a cursory glance before his attention returned to his desk, where a watch had been dismembered amid a row of small gold parts. He was a small, scanty-haired man, with pale, heavy-lidded eyes, but he smiled politely when he saw her, because they had an arrangement, and recognised each other as fellow-foreigners in this city.

'A moment, please,' he said, pushing his wispy, wheat-coloured hair out of his eyes. He stayed seated, for he had an affliction of the leg that made him lame.

She nodded and waited, enjoying the quiet which was punctuated only by the whispered tick of the watches.

M'sieur Hubert fumbled in a desk drawer. 'She's

regular as my clocks, this mother,' he said, passing her a square folded paper, tied and sealed with string. 'She write every month, eh?'

'She promised she would, now I have enough to pay for the reading and writing of them.'

Hubert nodded, but then took out another watch and turned his back to give her some privacy. Livvy held up the parchment with both hands, examining the writing. A rush of warmth and joy. It was indeed from her mother, as she knew it would be. For who else would ever write to her? She had never learnt to read, except her name, which she could recognise by the two upturned 'V's in the middle of it, yet this little ritual had to be done each time before she handed it back to M'sieur Hubert to read it out.

Painstakingly, piece by piece, he placed the tiny watch parts to one side so he could lay the letter out flat. As he slit the seal and string with a penknife, flakes of brown wax dropped on the desk. He brushed them away with his long thin fingers.

Livvy fidgeted, plucking at her apron, waiting for him to begin. The moment reminded her of church, of waiting to hear the words from the pulpit, and the whispered tick of the timepieces made the silence even more intense. None of the watches were on display, because they'd be too vulnerable to street thieves, but they ticked from the drawers and cupboards that stood around the walls, as if time itself had been locked away.

The only visible timepieces were four large long-case clocks.

M'sieur Hubert mouthed the Dutch words on the paper, his forehead creased in concentration. A letter from her mother came to her, through him, every month; rain, sleet or snow. Safer to send it to him than to her employers, who had no idea where she came from. Her black face marked her as foreign, but nobody had ever asked her about her home country. They made assumptions based on her black skin, and she did not bother to enlighten them.

'What does she say?' She moved around the desk to read over his shoulder, but the words meant nothing; just dancing shapes on paper. She clung to the back of his chair. 'How's business?' she asked him.

'Hmm? Oh, can't complain. Now then, let's see. I'll read what I can and you must correct. '*Mijn livee, Livvy, anstig veel mensen zijn in ons huis aan de pest gestorven.*'

M'sieur Hubert looked up, twisting around to see her reaction.

Livvy translated, 'She says they've lost many in their house to the plague. Go on, don't stop.'

'*Te veel begrafenissen. Maar met Jan gaat het goed. Hij is een aardige, kalme jongen, en onze meester en zijn vrouw hebben het overleefd. Ik hoop dat de pest nooit de zee zal oversteken naar Londen en dat jij in goede gezondheid verkeert.*'

'My brother's a good boy. And so he is! And

135

now she's hoping it's not in London, and I'm well. What else?' Her mother could write, but only very basic things. She imagined her mother's broad, shiny face, her pillowy lips drawn together, as she decided how to best use the few words before her scribe grew too impatient to carry on. Her words always sounded like she was dictating, not speaking in her flowing chuckle of Dutch patois. She imagined her handing over her hard-won coin to the scribe who could read and write, and would be prepared to write these few precious words to her daughter.

'Stop breathing in my neck,' M'sieur said.

'Down my neck,' Livvy corrected, moving back to look at his face.

He tutted. 'I am supposed to be the clever one, *n'est-ce pas*?' But his chiding was without rancour.

'Tell me the rest.'

M'sieur carried on reading the Dutch, his voice measuring out the words slowly.

'She says my brother is still well, though in Antwerp the plague is bad. And the fruit tree I planted still survives and grows stronger.'

He smiled. '*Hij herinnert mij iedere dag aan jou. Mamma*. It reminds her of you. That is all. Then she has made her sign. Here, you can see.' He pushed the letter towards her.

Reverently, she bent over it, and stroked her mother's untidy signature with a forefinger. The upright H, the curved D. 'But I must reply, to tell her I'm well.'

She folded it again and pushed it down her stays, feeling the warmth of her mother's good wishes pressed against her heart. It made her ache. It always did, that she could not press herself into those comforting arms; that she might never be able to feel that embrace again. No household ever wanted two black servants. One was a novelty, as long as he was a small boy, but two it seemed, made the householder look as if he liked negroes, which was not to be borne. At least not in Holland, so her mother had reluctantly sent her to London, arranged for her to work her passage with an English planter's wife. But the wife caught chill on board ship, and died shortly after. Now Livvy had no means of returning. Not unless she was to marry a rich merchant adventurer with a taste for black servants, and the chance of that was about the same as finding a gold sovereign in St Giles. When the letters came, she missed her family with a love so fierce it was almost rage.

She took a long ragged breath, swallowed salt water.

'There,' he said, gaze full of sympathy. 'At least you have someone who loves you.'

She nodded. She was grateful for his ability to read and keep his mouth dumb about these letters, just as she did for him. He had a little Dutch, which made it easier, but he never commented on her mother's words, or Livvy's letters back.

'Shall we write that reply?'

Livvy spoke slow, each Dutch syllable clear as

he wrote it down. 'I am well. I am a servant now to Mr Viner on Cradle Alley. It is a good position. The plague is here, but no more than usual', finishing with; '*I miss you. Uw Livvy.*' I miss you. Your Livvy.

'In English? *I miss you* in English?'

'The Dutch will make me cry.'

'Maybe French would be better? *Tu me manques.*' He blotted the paper and handed it to her to make her sign. She picked up his nib and made her mark, drawing the straight lines in the pattern she knew; L.I.V.V.Y and then adding the upright cross as a sign of faith.

'*Très bien,*' he said. Together they sealed it and tied it up, ready to go to the King's Post on Poultry Street.

'So, have you something for me?' Livvy asked.

He stood and limped over, his wasted leg dragging, and unlocked a cupboard embedded in the wall. Probably once it had been used for provisions, as it had a perforated grill in the wooden doors, but now it was stacked with untidy bunches of pamphlets, bundles of paper, and leather-bound books, their names written along the edges of the pages.

He pulled down some books onto the desk as he searched. They landed on the watch parts he had put to one side so carefully. Livvy picked up one of the books to move it out of the way and opened it to show a picture of a bearded man on one side with some heavy flagstones in his arms, and, judging by his strange sugar-cone hat, what could be the pope on the other. They flanked Mary-Mother-of-God, with a fat baby hovering above on sculpted eagle-wings. All white people. It was obviously something religious. Livvy flicked through the pages to look at the pictures. Not a single person like her.

She lost interest and closed the book just as he limped back to the table with a weighty parcel, already wrapped in a dirty, stained cloth. She guessed it was another book, as usual. 'Where to, this time?' she asked.

'Mr Bernard, the bookbinder on St Dunstan's Lane.'

'I know it. He has the hides hanging outside. The usual message?'

'Yes, just "from a friend", and if—'

'Yes, yes. If anyone asks me, I didn't get it from you. I'm to say I can't read and I found it washed-up on the shore and was taking it to sell it at the fleamarket.' She tucked it under her arm. 'There seems to be a mighty lot of books washed up, there, don't there?'

Monsieur Hubert smiled.

CHAPTER 8

In the King's playhouse rehearsal chamber, Stefan tilted back in his chair, stretched out his stringy legs in their pale-coloured hose, and leant back against the wall, script in his hand. He lowered his head to squint at it, for it was covered in crossings out and was difficult to decipher. He sighed; another small part, so his pay would be down again.

'What's the line after, "Verily I do"?' he asked old Will Wintershall, one of the assembled actors. 'Is that me, or is it Don Roderigo?'

'You, ducks,' Mrs Corey said, lowering her ample bottom into the mock medieval throne that was next to Will's chair. She took a moment to strike a flint and light her pipe. 'Though I don't suppose it will make much difference. This play of Dryden's drones on and on like a leaky pipe. Never read such foolishness in my life. How am I supposed to bring life to this? Julia's an empty-headed turkey.' She sucked and released a stream of smoke. 'I'm surprised Killigrew took it on; he's usually got more sense. It'll flop I tell you, just like his last.'

'Don't say that, Mrs Corey,' Stefan said. 'We're still learning the blasted thing.'

'I've hardly got any decent lines, and I can't see how it's supposed to be funny,' Will said. 'Where does Dryden get them from? They get more goosey each year.'

'He's got no sense of humour,' Mrs Corey said. 'He fancies himself as a poet, that's why it's so long-winded. But he's a bootlicker, if you ask me. I was in Herringman's bookshop last week, and under the counter they've got a copy of Dryden's poems in praise of . . . guess who . . .?'

'Go on, who?' Stefan asked.

'Only an elegy to our great Lord and Protector Cromwell, that's who.'

'No!' Mohun, who was lounging in the window seat, slapped his thighs and grinned in scandalised glee.

Mrs Corey waved her pipe, 'And now he's the king's lapdog and he's writing this dross where the women are all behaving like simpletons. I can't believe any woman would fall for a bonehead like Gonsalvo, the way he's written it.'

'Good thing it's Hart playing Gonsalvo. It makes it at least vaguely believable.'

'Even Hart's handsome face won't help that script. It's got three women in it, that's the only reason he took it. He wants more women on stage,' old Will Wintershall said. 'More women means more backsides on benches, so Killigrew asked Dryden to write something with more skirt. He

141

turned down Hart's play for this rot. I ask you, what's the world coming to?'

'And that's not all,' Mohun said. 'Killigrew's writing one himself now – and it's *all* women. What the devil shall we do when the whole business is taken over by a horde of scolding women?'

'Hey!' Mrs Corey leapt up and slapped him playfully across the beard with her script. 'Less of that! We've been kept out of the profession long enough, and it'll soon level out. Theatre's supposed to reflect the world, and there can't be a world with no women in it, can there?'

'Or one with no men in it,' Mohun retorted.

'Don't see why not,' Peg Hughes said, looking up from her script. 'It'd be a better one.'

'It'd die out, my lovely,' Mohun said, winking.

The door to the rehearsal chamber swung open and Killigrew rushed in; a stooping figure with his thin brown hair tucked under a beaver hat, 'Smells like a bear pit in here,' he said, wafting the smoke with the sleeve of his robe.

'We've been hard at it,' Mohun said, twiddling his long curls around his fingers, and showing no sign of moving from his perch by the window.

'Know it all then?' he asked, picking up Mrs Corey's script from the floor.

'Enough to get it on the boards,' Mohun said lazily.

Killigrew peered down his long nose at the script in his hands. 'What time is it? Did anyone hear the last bell?'

'I heard it strike the two about fifteen minutes since,' Stefan said.

'Then she's late. There's a woman coming in to read for me. She's untrained, but she might do for Angelina.'

'Untrained?' Mrs Corey raised her eyebrows to heaven.

Stefan returned her look of disgust. He'd been a long time working out how to convey every female mannerism, how to be more womanly than a woman, by the use of small gestures, by the slight raised tone of his voice, and by the subtle use of his eyes. He'd been doing it since he was a lad of eleven. Now all that work was to be wasted. But he couldn't openly object. He could see that the women in his company would make short work of him, if he did. But he could not help resenting how his profile had shrunk, from lead player, to walk-on spear carrier.

'I'll train her,' Killigrew said, 'like young Nelly Gwynne. At least this one can read. So she'll be able to learn by heart without assistance. That's if she ever gets here. First rule of the theatre; be on time. Stefan, go and see if she's waiting at the stage door.'

Stefan frowned. So he was to be a lackey now, was he? It wasn't fair. He sighed and went down the rickety stairs and out into the bright light of the street. There was nobody there. Maybe the woman wouldn't come.

When he got back, the play was in rehearsal.

'No?' Killigrew asked, script in hand.

Stefan shook his head.

'Bloody woman, wasting my time like that. And we need someone mature. Nell and Elizabeth are too young for Angelina. I need someone older. And reliable.'

'Shall I stand in for her, sir?' Stefan asked.

'I suppose so,' Killigrew said. 'Someone had better read it.'

Stefan gave the reading his whole attention. He was fluent, and knew how to milk the audience's emotion. On course he knew it was hopeless, that Killigrew would never allow him to take a woman's part again. Not just because it was undoubtedly more realistic, but also because it gave Killigrew a position of power from which he could 'choose' women on the basis of how favourable they proved to his advances.

But he threw himself into the performance, and the rest of the actors played up to meet him. The play suddenly had meaning and drama.

At the end, Killigrew turned to him, 'Good try, Stefan,' he said quietly. 'But you're back to the messenger tomorrow.'

Stefan closed his eyes a moment, the full weight of his disappointment crashing down on his shoulders, before he threw down his script and stormed from the room. The humiliation cut through his armour like a knife. As he shot out into the street the door cannoned into a young woman. She gave a screech of pain, and leant down to rub her ankle.

144

'Bloody stupid place to stand,' he snapped. 'You'll get knocked over.'

'Is this the playhouse door?' she asked urgently. Her eyes were dark in a white face. 'Is Mr Killigrew still there?'

Light dawned. 'Oh. Are you that woman that was to read for him?'

'Yes, two o'clock. But I got held up because my ankle . . . I mean I—'

'You're late.' He gave her a quick assessing look. Glossy brown hair, large generous mouth, expressive eyes with a haunted look. He despised her already; she was just the sort Killigrew might like. Except she was late, and for an actor a late appearance was always a sin. 'He's in rehearsal,' he said. 'He won't see you now.'

The woman's face became hollow in an instant and she slumped back against the wall.

To hide his conscience Stefan dipped his head and hurried off, leaving her standing there. When he was further down the street he glanced back to see her still dithering on the doorstep, one hand propped on the wall. Women in the theatre; it seemed like women in the priesthood, unnatural.

What would he do when there were no more roles for men like him? The stage was in his blood, as if the greasepaint were on the inside, not the outside. It had always been to him a holy calling, the only way men could transform or become gods. Men created worlds on stage just the way God created worlds on the earth. It was the only world where a person like him could breathe.

He would have to learn to take on men's roles. And for that, he would need to become a different kind of man altogether.

Bird gazed after the departing back of the skinny young man who had looked at her with such disdain. He had been quite definite that Mr Killigrew wouldn't see her. Yet had she gone through all that pain and effort for nothing? She bent over to feel her ankle, and found it was hot to the touch and beginning to swell. She stood up again and knocked firmly at the door. No-one answered. She was here now, so taking her courage in both hands, she pushed her way into the dark corridor. When she tried the door, the passage to the theatre itself was locked, but there were stairs up, from where she could hear voices declaiming in passionate argument. The eloquent, mannered tone of it told her that it wasn't a real argument, but acting.

She clung to the banister and hauled her way up the stairs, wincing each time she had to put weight on her painful foot. The panelling was scuffed and scraped by sword hilts and boots. At the top, the voices sounded louder and the argument fiercer. The door was slightly ajar, so she peered around the edge. Two men and a woman were in a fight; the man had the woman around the waist and the other man was trying to prise her away. The woman was wearing breeches and hose, and a lawn shirt that was almost transparent and left little to the imagination. Bird pushed the door gently for a better view, but it creaked loudly and the actors stopped speaking and everyone's eyes swivelled towards her.

Immediately her face flamed. She stepped inside the chamber, amid what seemed to be a crowd of staring eyes, and took a deep breath. 'I'm looking for Mr Killigrew.' When nobody replied, she spoke up in a loud, clear voice. 'I'm Mrs Knepp. I'm to read for him.'

A sigh. 'Not now!' A man with thin brown hair and a receding chin, and dressed in an eastern-style robe, leapt up and flapped towards her. 'You missed your chance. Latecomers are no use to me. We run on a tight schedule. And now you have the gall to interrupt my rehearsal!' He batted at her with his sleeve. 'Out, I say!'

'I'm sorry I was late, I hurt my ankle and—'

'Out.' He pushed her on the shoulders and forced her back through the door where she gasped with the pain of landing on her bad foot. The door banged shut after her. Laughter from behind the door.

She felt like kicking it, except she couldn't stand on one leg. She closed her eyes a moment to gather herself. What she really wanted – the world of colour and poetry and music – was all on the other side of that door. She felt in her pocket, brought out Livvy's lucky hare's foot, pressed it to her forehead.

It was now or never.

She opened her mouth and began to sing, '*Oh the cuckoo is a pretty bird, she sings as she flies.*'

The stairwell was like a soundbox for her voice, making it soar and float, swirling up into the rafters where cobwebs trembled in the draught. Her volume increased, but the door remained shut. She added all the trills and decoration she could, and then finished the song with one last long plaintive note.

There was silence.

The door did not open. Drained, she lowered one foot onto the stair and with eyes blurred with tears, began the long, painful, hobbling descent to the bottom.

Behind her, raised voices argued from behind the door. They've begun the rehearsal again, she thought.

'Mrs Knepp!'

She turned. The door was open, letting light into the hall.

'I find I have a half-hour to spare after all,' Killigrew called down. 'If you will come to my chamber, I will hear you now.'

'I'll come. But I need help to get there. I've hurt my ankle.'

CHAPTER 9

O h, the indignity of being carried! Bird had to suffer being manhandled by Hart, the strongest actor, who had persuaded a reluctant and limp Mohun to carry her between them to Killigrew's chamber. Killigrew led the way, then fussed like a hen over a chick, insisting she elevate her foot onto a cushion. Mohun reluctantly went to fetch Jenkinson, the bone setter.

Killigrew's chamber was a dark, cupboard-like closet full of shelved manuscripts. A human skull leered from a gap in the papers, and a breastplate hung off the door amongst a selection of star-spangled cloaks and costumes hanging from hooks. By the window was a globe of the discovered world, similar to one in her father's chamber.

A momentary vision of her father turning his globe, in his tidy office, gave her a grim smile. What would he think if he could see her now? Killigrew's desk was the opposite of Father's – a great unwieldy thing laden with papers held down by a pot of cows-foot glue, and a wooden dagger stuck in a lump of plaster. Killigrew scrabbled about, dislodging papers and shunting aside books until he found what he wanted.

'Here,' he said. 'Let's see if you can speak as well as you sing.'

He handed her a dog-eared copy of *Twelfth Night* by Mr Shakespeare, open at the place where a woman called Viola, who was dressed as a man, was realising that the Duchess had fallen in love with her. It was a strange little speech, but he had her read it aloud from the script, and then repeat it, with this inflection here, and that lowering of the voice there, and this part in a whisper, and that part in a shout.

All the time, he kept saying, 'Good, good.'

His approval warmed her more than anything else. Knepp hadn't spoken a soft word to her since they were wed.

She grew more confident, as the lines grew familiar. 'I could do better,' she confessed, 'if I could pace a little, but my ankle . . .'

'Let me see it.' Though Killigrew lifted her skirts higher than was necessary with his long bony fingers, he treated her with solicitous concern. 'Good legs,' he said, but dropped her skirts hurriedly as the door creaked open and Dr Jenkinson arrived, a stooping figure in black.

The doctor squeezed and prodded, and harrumphed, then pronounced the injury to be a mere sprain, which of course did not make it hurt the less, but gave Bird some reassurance. After strapping it firmly with a calico bandage, he held

150

out his hand for payment, and Killigrew took out his purse and paid him.

Embarrassed, she tried to stand, but lost her balance and had to sit again. 'I'll pay you back,' she said.

'You certainly will. I'll make sure you work like the devil.'

'You mean you'll take me?'

'You show a little promise, yes. But it's raw. But you have good legs, and with a little extra training, well, we'll see.'

When she came out of Killigrew's chambers next to the theatre, she was cock-a-hoop. A queue of carriages were depositing merchants and their wives to wait for the theatre to open.

'*Viner's Horses and Carriages*', she read. A crest was emblazoned on the side of each one. Killigrew had given her money to take a carriage home, saying he would deduct the cost from her wages, but she did not dare take one of Viner's.

Killigrew had seemed taken with her enthusiasm and told her there'd be a part for her soon. Lusetta, he'd said, in a play he'd written called *Thomaso*, and something else in a play called *The Silent Woman*, but she didn't like the sound of that one so much. No money until it was on though, and it wasn't scheduled for another month. But oh, how marvellous! She was to be a player. At the same time, the thought of Knepp's reaction gave her a queasy feeling of dread in the pit of her stomach.

Limping, she raised a hand to summon a sedan carried by two bearers. She swayed through the streets of Smithfield, her ankle throbbing mercilessly as if it were clamped in a hot vice.

Nearly six o'clock and no supper made, and Mrs Knepp had been alone for hours.

But inside she was elated. She was to be trained, and the thought gave her a smidgeon of confidence to face Knepp, though her stomach still swooped whenever she thought of it.

The sedan made its stately way through the city towards Smithfield. As she grew closer she couldn't help but notice handbills plastered on every loose fence, and every pillar and post. '*Ted Viner's*,' she read, '*Finest Hired Horses in London.*' There was a woodcut of a gentleman on a fine steed on each one to draw the attention.

Right in our territory, she thought. She wondered if Knepp had seen these. As they travelled, it seemed the numbers were increasing the closer she got to home. They approached the hiring yard and she instructed the bearers to turn in. Her arrival brought out almost all the stable lads to stare, along with Knepp. A clunk and jolt as the sedan was set down.

Bird stepped through the narrow door of the sedan, groaning as she put her full weight on her ankle, which promptly collapsed beneath her.

'What's this?' Knepp asked, as she tried to stand, hopping in an undignified manner.

'I hurt my ankle,' she said, 'that's why I was out for so long.'

'Where have you been?' Not an iota of sympathy warmed his features. 'You left my mother alone all afternoon.'

A cough from behind her. The two bearers still needed to be tipped. Knepp shoved a hand into his pocket and thrust the coin at the front bearer, and the contraption moved off. Now it had gone she felt even more alone and vulnerable.

'You hired a sedan. A sedan, when I have a horse hire business. What will it look like?'

'No, I didn't pay—'

'Get indoors,' he said.

'I need to lean on you,' she said, gritting her teeth with the pain.

'Dobbs,' he called. 'Help her indoors.'

Dobbs scowled, but came and wrapped an arm around her waist so she could have his support. She glimpsed Mrs Knepp's face at the window. When they got into the parlour Knepp dismissed Dobbs as soon as she had been dumped onto a chair. She suspected Mrs Knepp had been up but had climbed back into bed as soon as they entered the door.

'Where in hell's name have you been?' Knepp said. 'I told you to stay here.'

'Have you seen the posters from Viner?' she gasped, to distract him. 'They're everywhere, even right outside our door.'

As she predicted, the mention of Viner's name made him pay attention. 'What posters from Viner?'

'There are notices pinned everywhere about his

153

hire business. Butchers Hall Lane, Duck Street. There's even one on the corner of Cowe Lane.'

'He wouldn't dare. Not outside my premises.'

'Go and see for yourself.'

She saw the battle go on in his face – should he stay to chastise her more, or should he go and see these notices she talked of? But Viner won, as she knew he would, and Knepp turned on his heel, slamming the door as he went.

'Foolish girl. What did you do?' Mrs Knepp demanded.

'I slipped in some horse dung. It's sprained, but now it's swollen to the size of a tree trunk. A bone-setter fixed it for me, though.'

Mrs Knepp hauled herself out of bed again and came around the front of the chair.

'Let me look at it then.'

Bird hitched her skirt and Mrs Knepp peered at the dressing, then pressed it. 'It's nothing, that. Rest will cure it.' She looked up. 'You shouldn't have been gone so long. Christopher's got a temper like his father, though he's not as . . . as erratic. You must learn to live with it. You can learn to live with anything, if you put your mind to it. Best advice I can give you is to stay silent. If you argue back it enrages them more. You have to keep your head down though, not go courting trouble. Where've you been?'

'Just to the market.'

'You don't get trussed up like a Christmas goose to go to the market.'

Bird dug in her heels. 'I went to the market, like I said.'

Mrs Knepp squinted at her with an unbelieving expression.

'Have you been to Viner's yard? Grinstead tells me that the black maid you were so fond of, Libby is it? That she's gone there.'

'Livvy. And I'm glad for her. She's better off there.'

'Well, beggars can't be choosers. What's it like, Viner's?'

'Nothing like here.'

'Better than here, you mean?' Mrs Knepp sat down opposite her.

'Put it this way. If I were to hire a horse – if ever, then I'd go there.'

'What would it take to make my son's yard better than Viner's?'

Bird laughed. 'Money. Everything here's falling to pieces. And something to make it look pleasing; a nice sign, men in a tidy livery who doff their caps to welcome the customers. Particularly the women.' She leant down to examine her ankle, which was aching again. 'I'll need to fetch a cold compress.'

'Is there no money?' Mrs Knepp persisted. 'I thought he married you because you brought a good bride price with you.'

She ignored the insult. 'He spent it on horses years ago. He thinks it's only the horses that matter. He can't see that it's the whole appearance of the place, the whole miserable, uncared-for look that puts the customers off.'

'I'll talk to him about—'

The door burst open and Knepp was in front of Bird in two strides. He thrust a bunch of screwed-up paper at her, which she had no option but to take. 'He won't get away with his damn notices on my patch.' It was as if it was her fault. 'I'll fight back.'

'Let me see.' Mrs Knepp took the ball of paper and smoothed one of the handbills out, lowering her face close to the print to see. 'We could do this. A bit of print and paper is nothing. But to stay ahead we need to be cleverer than him,' Mrs Knepp said. 'Anyone can put up a few bills. We need to get word out to the quality customers, not these butchers and meat men.'

'Let's not get too fancy, Mother. It's butchers and meat men that are my main source of income.'

'Then we need to think again. They're not the men with the money. It's people with leisure we need, not working men.'

'And I know how you can get the word out.' Bird said. 'I tried to talk to Mr Killigrew, to get Knepp's a contract. So I went to the theatre – to see who goes there.'

They turned to look at her, with matching expressions of disbelief.

'Mr Killigrew runs the theatre. It's where the king goes with his courtiers, and all the ladies-in-waiting. I know it's not what we're used to, but that's the custom we need. Aristocracy. Wealthy merchants. People with more coin to splash.'

'You expect me to take advice from you? You don't know one end of a horse from another.'

'But I know people,' she said. 'Viner has carriages sitting outside the Exchange painted with his livery. Anyone going to or from the Exchange to buy anything sees his name, and he gets most of his business that way. And he's started to take customers to the theatre. We need to stop him, get your livery out by the theatres. The Maypole in the Strand is too far for people to walk to hire a hackney, and this yard is closer to the places of entertainment than his. You could have carriages waiting outside the King's with your name painted on it, like Viner has.'

'I'm not saying she's right, Christopher,' Mrs Knepp said. 'But no harm in—'

'There's no room on Bridges Street for carriages.'

'No,' Bird said. 'But there's room on Catherine Street. Where the men load and unload the scenery. I sought permission from Killigrew for our hackneys to draw up there. He wants more people to get to the theatre, so I said you could bring them from the city.'

'You dared to try negotiate business without telling me? What nonsense is this? I don't know this man, Killigrew. And I want nothing to do with the players. They're just a bunch of braying dogs.'

'I did it for us. To try to advance us.' His sceptical look made her hurry on. 'I talked to him, and he was willing to do a deal with you.'

'You? How? Don't be absurd.'

Mrs Knepp heaved herself to her feet and put a hand on his shoulder. 'Wait, son, hear what she has to say.'

Bird took a deep breath. 'No, not with me. With you, of course. He wanted you to make a deal, but it was a cock-eyed idea, and I told him we couldn't accept it. Such a shame.'

Now she had his undivided attention.

'Why not? What did he offer?'

'He needs more women, and he wants my services in the theatre.' There. It was out.

Mrs Knepp stared down at her, agape.

'What?' Knepp's voice was dangerously low. 'How does he know you? If you've been . . .' He stepped towards her as if he might strike her where she sat.

She braced her shoulders. 'I went to see him to see if Knepp's could have sole right to trade by the stage door. But he'll only do it if you let me play for him at the theatre. Of course, I said that was impossible, and you'd never permit it.' She braced herself for a blow.

It did not come. His eyes narrowed in suspicion. 'Why would he want such as you for the stage?'

She was floundering. 'Not just me. He needs more women players, for small parts, servants and such, and for fetching and carrying behind the scenes.' She improvised, seeing the scepticism in his face. 'Sort of . . . serving women on and off the stage.'

'Sounds ridiculous. What a foolish way to run a business, through bartering for staff.'

'That's what I told him. Of course I said it was unthinkable, that you'd never agree.'

'Quite right, too.' Mrs Knepp said. 'Women in the theatre. Outlandish. It's no profession for a lady.'

'It's a pity we can't find a way to negotiate something else, though, because Killigrew seemed to think that to have our carriages there would increase our trade tenfold.'

Now Knepp's face took on an intent expression. 'Is Killigrew's theatre better than the Duke's?' Knepp asked.

'He's more profitable, and of course it being the King's players, it attracts all the courtiers and ladies-in-waiting, and the crowd from Whitehall. The king himself, often.'

The tenfold increase in trade had hooked him, as she knew it would.

'The king,' Mrs Knepp said, a dreamy look in her eyes.

'There may be something in it,' Knepp said. 'But not this foolish serving-woman idea. I'll talk to this Killigrew, see if we can't come to some other more sensible arrangement.'

Had she been too bold? Such a ruse could easily backfire. Knepp had sensed some sort of trickery, she could see by his face. What would he do if he found out she'd read for him already? Still, it was worth the risk. She would have to get to Killigrew before Knepp, though, and spin him a tale.

CHAPTER 10

After witnessing her gasps and groans at breakfast, Knepp agreed she could go to the apothecary for some pain relief for her ankle. Without it, she said, she'd be unable to see to Mrs Knepp, or carry water for the horses. Dobbs was to drive her to town as he went to collect a customer, and collect her again after he'd dropped off his passenger. The apothecary was three streets away from the theatre, and Bird limped there as quickly as she could, finding support against the walls as she went.

The rehearsal room rang with the clash of metal as Hart and Mohun practised their stage fight. Bird hobbled warily through, dodging their flashing swords, as she headed to Killigrew's closet. Today Killigrew was wearing a Chinese-type hat of embroidered silk, despite the heat, probably to hide the fact he was balding. Bird leant forward over his untidy desk.

'What is it, Mrs Knepp?' Killigrew said. 'Is your ankle worse?'

'No, it's much better, thanking you. The strapping is working.'

'But you are not to rehearse until next Friday.'

'I know. But I had to see you. You know my husband has a horse-hire and hackney-carriage business?'

'Hmm? So?'

'Well, I thought how useful it would be to have theatre transport right here on Drury Lane. So my husband is going to call on you to try to persuade you to give him sole use of the road for his carriages. Catherine Street, where they dock the scenery. And you will, won't you? It would serve you well, that townfolk could be brought right to the door.'

'I don't know, I hadn't thought—'

'And when my husband comes, you must tell him he can't have sole use unless I go on the stage. On this you must insist.'

'Why so?' She had his full attention now.

'For the very reason that he'll forbid me to be a player, unless he gets something from it.'

'And you have seen fit to use me as your bargaining tool, is that it?' His eyes sparkled with amusement.

'No, sir. But life will go much smoother for me if you agree.'

'And what will I get from this bargain, my songbird?'

'You'll get a player who works harder than anyone else in the company, and will sing her heart out for less than three shilling a week.'

'It seems to me I'm the loser in this, and you and your jockey husband are the winners.'

'Don't see it like that, Mr Killigrew! See it as a

transaction that benefits us all. I get to be a player, my husband gets more custom, and you get a happy audience who will come here even in the rain.'

'You say he doesn't want you to be a player. Will he cause me trouble?'

'If he does, I'm sure you can deal with him.' She gave him her most coquettish grin. 'But you must insist that no other bargain is possible. If he wants the trade, I must be free to be a player. I told him that it was just small parts, so you could reassure him of that.'

Killigrew sighed. 'Why are you women so much more trouble than the men?'

The next morning Knepp announced he was going to call in at the King's Playhouse on Drury Lane.

'I've had second thoughts,' Mrs Knepp said. 'I don't want a player for a daughter-in-law. How would we stand the shame?'

'Don't fret,' he said. 'No wife of mine will be associated with such a low profession.'

Bird spent the morning tight with anticipation and fear. When Knepp returned he was bad-tempered, and shouted insults at the stable-boys to make them hurry.

'He would not agree then?' she dared to ask.

'The man's a prancing coxcomb. It was a damn fool idea. Killigrew won't see sense. We could not agree.' And he loped away, towards Grinstead and the office.

Bird sagged. The dream was over then. Her ruse

had failed, and the world of greasepaint and candlelight was still to be kept tantalisingly out of her reach.

Dinner was a morose affair, with Knepp calling for everyone to eat in silence. As she looked around the table, the Knepps seemed to be the worst type of Puritans; miserable, sombre and dark. Bird was clearing away the platters when her eye was caught by a smart new carriage arriving in the yard. It was one of the new glazed four-poster *coraches* pulled by four matching bays. The whole equipage gleamed in the morning sun. She knew straightaway it wasn't one of her husband's for, as her chapped hands testified, she'd cleaned the harness for them all.

'What is it?' Mrs Knepp asked, as Bird stared motionless out of the window.

'I don't know. A visitor.'

Mrs Knepp hobbled over to peer through the window beside her. Bird watched the coachman dismount and open the carriage. The burly figure who climbed out was familiar. 'It's Viner.'

'That scoundrel who runs the other yard? Let's see.'

They watched Viner smooth down his coat, and speak to the stable-lad who was looking enviously at the polished coats of the horses. The lad tugged his cap and hurried off, presumably to fetch Knepp.

'He's changed, Viner,' Mrs Knepp said. 'He used to be a fit lad. Cunning though. He'd sell his own grandmother if he thought it would turn a profit.'

'You know him?'

'Oh yes. I know him all right, though I wouldn't have recognised him now. Not seen him for years. What does he want, coming here?' Mrs Knepp's voice was loud in her ear.

'I don't know, but I'll go and see.' Livvy's words came back to her; that Viner wanted to take over Knepp's yard.

By the time she got outside, the coach was surrounded by Knepp's men, all gawping at the shiny paintwork and fine metal undercarriage.

Ted Viner spotted her immediately and approached. 'Ah. Mrs Knepp. A fine morning, eh? Is your husband here?'

'I'm sure he will be here directly. A boy went to fetch him. In the meantime, you may wish to ask your man to move the carriage. It is blocking our entrance.'

'My business will not take long.'

'Nevertheless, please ask your man to move along.'

He made no move, but his glance travelled around the yard. She guessed he was counting the stable doors. 'Mrs Knepp,' he said, returning his attention to her, 'if you fetch your husband, it will be out of your way quicker.'

She was about to protest again when Knepp arrived, flanked by Dobbs and Nipper. She was immediately struck by how down-at-heel her husband appeared in comparison to Viner, but also that he caused a prickle of aggression in the air around him.

164

She had no love whatsoever for Knepp, yet his unkempt and slovenly appearance offended her pride. Her husband had two days stubble where Viner was smooth-shaven. Knepp's breeches were filthy with a sheen of horse-grease, and a ragged sleeveless jerkin hung open over a grubby shirt, with the sleeves rolled up to show his brawny arms.

'Yes?'

Facing him, Ted Viner puffed out his chest like a plump, sleek pigeon. 'I heard you might be interested in selling.'

'Where d'you hear that?' Knepp said.

'The corn merchant. And the hay merchant. You've debts everywhere. They all say you can't keep going. You owe too much. Brent the blacksmith gives you a month, at most.'

Bird heard her own sharp intake of breath. She'd no idea it was that bad.

'The man's a liar.' Knepp's face was impassive, but she saw him clench his fingers and knew he was rattled.

'I'll make you an offer,' Viner said. 'Fifty guineas to include the premises and all the livestock. You could get out of London. I've heard there's plague in this vicinity; it could be the best move you ever make. Just think about it.'

Knepp stepped forward, too close to Viner. 'I've thought about it and the answer's no. Now get your filthy animals out of my yard.'

'You're more of a fool than I thought.' Viner stepped back. Obviously unwilling to concede ground, he said, 'But I'll tell you what, I'll give you until next week. How's that for Christian charity? After that, my offer will be gone.'

'A week?' Knepp replied, scathing. 'I don't need a single minute. I'd never sell to a knave like you, not if you were the last man on earth.'

'Then you'll be in debtor's clink within a month. Don't come bleating to me then.'

'We'll see who's bleating. I have a new contract with the King's Theatre, and the king himself. We'll soon see who's buying who.'

Now it was Viner's turn to look disconcerted. He laughed uncertainly. 'What are you saying?'

'I'm saying, get your conveyance out of my yard before I set my lads on you.'

Dobbs and Nipper moved forward on the balls of their feet, fists up.

Viner backed away, trying to maintain dignity, but Dobbs pursued him until he cowered against the side of the coach. 'Don't you threaten mc,' he shouted, his cheeks flaring scarlet, 'or I'll get the constable to pay you a visit.' His coachman, sensing trouble, scurried to open the door.

'Gah! Get on!' Knepp ran at the horses so they leapt and shied, leaving Viner hanging half-in and half-out of the carriage door in an undignified sprawl. The collie dog, Fetch, sprang after it with his teeth bared, hackles bristling, mimicking his master's aggression. The coachman cursed and hauled on the reins to maintain control, trying to turn the horses in the narrow space.

Finally they burst out of the gate with Fetch barking and growling, running at the horses' heels.

Bird hesitated in the yard.

'What are you staring at?' Knepp cast her a cold look.

'Is he right? Do you owe money?'

'No more than most. I've invested. It's what tradesmen do. Things will turn around.'

'But did you mean it? About the theatre?'

'You're a whore anyway. I might as well make money out of you.'

She sucked in her breath, but kept her voice calm. 'Admit it; you care not a fig what I do. And this yard's been failing right from the very beginning. You just wanted my dowry to buy horses, and had to put up with the fact I came with it.'

'More fool me. You've done nothing but cause me grief ever since.'

'It's not about me. You're doing this to impress Viner. Why do you hate him so much?'

'I'd like to see his puffed-up face when I take the king or the Lady Castlemaine in one of our carriages. And I suppose having a whore for a wife is the price I pay.'

'You mean, you'll agree to Killigrew's terms?'

'It'll be better than having you whining under my feet all day.' And with that, he strode away, leaving Bird standing in the yard transfixed.

She brought out Livvy's hare's foot and kissed it. *Please let him not change his mind*, she prayed.

~ ACT TWO ~

They are as crafty with an old play, as bawds with old faces; the one puts on a new fresh colour, the other a new face and name. They practise a strange order, for most commonly the wisest man is the fool.

Donald Lupton – *On Players: London and the Countrey Carbonadoed,* 1632

CHAPTER 11

August 1664

Finally it was agreed; Knepp told Killigrew that on no account was his wife to have a speaking part on stage, and with this Bird had to be content. Knepp had the idea fixed in his mind now, and it was as if it was his own idea, and he had arranged it all. From this, Bird suspected his debts were deeper than she'd thought.

Of course old Mrs Knepp was outraged by the idea that Bird should be employed in the theatre. She tried arguing, and she tried wheedling, as she didn't want to be left alone all day. Knepp was not inclined to spend the money, but non-stop complaints from his mother made him relent, and a fourteen-year-old scrap of a girl called Anis was engaged to keep Mrs Knepp company. Anis seemed to only know two words – *Yes, Madam* – and that suited Mrs Knepp very well.

The first day Bird arrived at the theatre she had barely removed her cloak when Killigrew breezed in, with the youth she had met at the theatre door in tow. She recognised the youth's long blond hair and sharp, discontented features straightaway, and it didn't take much insight to tell he did not look pleased to see her.

'This is Stefan,' Killigrew said. 'He will go through the lines with you.'

'Lines? I thought I was not to go on stage?'

'No speaking part, your husband said. And this has no words.' He winked.

'Epicene,' Stefan said. 'I've played it before.'

'Oh. Is it . . . is it a man's part?'

'Yes.' Stefan said, scowling. 'But Tom has decided, in his infinite wisdom, that this time it should be played by a woman. Always keen on getting his money's worth, aren't you, Tom?'

The bitterness in his tone made Killigrew suck in his lips. 'Now then, Stefan, you know Epicene is a woman for nearly the whole blasted play. She's only revealed as a man in the last act.'

'But that's the whole nub of it! That the audience have been fooled. You'll ruin the revelation. How can she play the man? Just look at her.'

They both stared fixedly at Bird's chest, so she was forced to look down at her feet.

'Hmm. We'll bandage her. And she hardly speaks,' Killigrew said. 'It will give Mrs Knepp a chance to get a feel for the stage.'

'Yes,' Stefan said. 'I daresay she has never set foot on one before.' He threw Killigrew a look and then thrust the script at her, and without thinking, she took it.

172

'Mark me,' Killigrew said, 'she'll be a sensation in breeches. I take it your ankle is better?'

'Yes, sir. Doesn't hurt at all, now.'

'Good, good. Now, Stefan, sit down with Mrs Knepp and go through the lines. I want to see at least two scenes learnt by the end of the day.'

By this time, more actors had arrived and were watching her with curiosity as they threw off cloaks and hats and greeted each other with effusive kisses. The men joshed in educated tones, and were expensively dressed in silks and satins, worn with a louche air of abandon. The women stared at her with assessing eyes, their faces white with ceruse, and peppered with black patches. It was intimidating, this gaudily apparelled group, all rowsey in hats with feathers, and ears that twinkled with stones that were too big to be anything but glass. Next to them she felt horribly drab.

Hot with shame and embarrassment, Bird sat down and took refuge in the script. *Epicene, or The Silent Woman*, she read. A quick leaf through the pages showed she had little dialogue, and that for the most part she was to be dumb. All the same, she knew Knepp would be annoyed at this bending of his rules.

Stefan did not sit. 'Why are you sitting down? It's no use sitting,' he said, gesturing her to stand up again. 'For this part, it is all in the body language. I'll have to show you.' He made it sound like a chore. 'I'll play the old man, Morose, who

173

hates noise, and your task is to prove you are the perfect silent woman, understand?'

She understood only too well. She had spent most of her life trying to perfect that role, first for her father and now for Knepp. And it grated even more to be told what to do by this surly boy who was barely old enough to shave. Still, this was her chance to make her mark, and she was going to make the most of it.

'Now, you need to react only with your eyes for this part, and blow out your mouth in disgust . . . so . . .' Stefan demonstrated. In another corner, two more actors were reciting their lines, and Bird struggled to hear Stefan's instructions. Her eyes kept drifting to where William Wintershall and the handsome Mr Hart were rehearsing some sort of duel, and she was keenly aware that the other women were still watching her, like cats watching a mouse.

'Aren't you listening?' Stefan's voice broke into her thoughts.

'Yes, oh yes, I am. It's just, it's so very noisy.'

He sighed. 'It's always like this. You'll have to learn to love it. The audience will be twice as noisy and distracting as them. Now show me how you react when I say my line.'

She took up a posture and imitated Stefan exactly. He looked displeased. 'Too much posturing. And you don't look submissive enough. Do it again.'

The women in the corner laughed behind their

hands and whispered. Bird's face burned hotter. So the morning continued, with Stefan snapping at her. Despite the fact it was a comedy, not a single laugh had passed her lips. Nevertheless, she gritted her teeth and smiled, and did everything asked of her.

By the afternoon she was waning, and her head throbbed. She asked Stefan politely if she might take a breath of air. They had not stopped to dine, and he seemed intent on getting to the end of the play in one day.

'You'll need more stamina than this if you're to survive a night on the boards,' he said.

'Never fear, I have plenty of stamina. And I will work hard. A few moments fresh air is all I ask.'

'A quarter bell,' he said, 'at most. I have my own part to learn as well, haven't I? I can't spend all my time with you.'

She closed her eyes to blot out his disgruntled face before hurrying down the stairs. Once outside the theatre she breathed in the cooler air and bright sunshine, and let her tense shoulders sag. It was harder than she thought, and Stefan obviously despised her. Perhaps she had no aptitude. But then again he'd seemed determined to dislike her.

She had to make a success of it. After all, it was the only way she could ever be able to make her way in the world. She had no money, and no way of leaving Knepp. But the new theatre was in an aristocratic part of town; surrounded by the houses of noblemen and peers. She knew from the broadsheets that the area around Brydges Street was home to the Earl of Craven, and the Marquis of Argyll. And when she had first met Killigrew he'd impressed her with the talk of how he had been 'sworn in' as a member of the Royal Household, and given ten yards of scarlet cloth for his livery. Maybe she could secure a rich patron.

She was rubbing her forehead with a hand to ease the worry there, when another large, motherly woman emerged from the door.

'Good to get out into the air, isn't it?' she said. 'I'm Mrs Corey.' She pressed her plump, scarlet-clad backside against the wall and lit a pipe. 'Want a smoke?'

'I don't, thanking you.' Tobacco reminded her of her father.

'Best thing for the voice, this baccy.' Mrs Corey inhaled and blew out a cloud of smoke. 'Stefan getting to you, is he?'

She didn't know what to say. 'He's very young, isn't he? But it's good of him to take time to train me.'

'And I'll wager he rubs that in, too.'

'I don't think he approves of me, being untrained as I am.'

'It's nothing personal. He's a moody fellow and gets jealous because he only gets servant's roles now. A few years back, he used to be as good as the legendary Kynaston. He was the best then – at playing a girl, I mean. But Stefan's not weighty enough for most mature roles, and there's still something feminine about him that doesn't make him a good male lead.'

'I've ousted him, then.'

'Not your fault, ducks. But watch out for him; he'll upstage you if he can and make you look a fool. And the other thing you need to know is that Killigrew does nothing – work-shy he is, but he's a dirty bastard. Keep out of his way if you can. Hart's all right, he's the General Manager and he cares more about the profession than most. Him and Mohun. Though they hate each other. Mohun might be short in stature but he's a powerful presence on stage. We call him the Major, because he fought for the king in the civil wars. But he's the one to settle disputes, always good for pouring oil on troubled water is Mohun.'

'What about the women?'

'Anne Marshall and Peg Hughes, they're excellent good. And Nelly Gwynne will be a fine player too, if she'd just take to it more seriously. And now there's you.'

'If I can ever learn my part.'

The door behind them swung open, and Stefan poked his head out.

'I'm waiting,' he snapped. His head disappeared again.

Mrs Corey raised her eyes heavenwards, which made Bird smile. But she hurried after Stefan, cheered by having at least one ally, and determined to glean from Stefan as much skill as she could.

In the afternoon they had the rehearsal room to themselves. The rest had gone to prepare for the late afternoon performance, and the empty room echoed with their absence. It made Bird even more ill at ease, to be alone with Stefan, who scowled and snapped at her at every gesture she made.

Finally she could bear it no longer, and threw down her script. 'I don't know what I've done to offend you, but I can manage by myself now. You have no need to stay. You have made it quite apparent you have no wish to be here, and I can read the few lines perfectly well without you.'

'How dare you? It was Killigrew's notion, not mine, to pluck someone like you from the street. And he can train you himself if he wants any more monkeys trained. As far as I can see, you're lacking in that one essential ingredient – talent.'

With that Stefan stalked from the room, slamming the door behind him so that the shutters at the windows rattled at the draught.

Bird stood in the centre of the room alone. Was he right? The hurt of it was an ache in the hollow drum of her stomach. She sagged, pulling the script this way and that in her hands. It was no use; the whole task of learning the part seemed to be moving far beyond her. She was wasting their time, and she feared Killigrew would be angry she'd rankled Stefan.

In the quiet room the rattle and clank of carriage wheels outside reminded her of Knepp and how she would be back to cleaning harness if she didn't at least try to make a success of it. If she was lacking in talent, then she'd just have to make up for it with hard work.

She smoothed out the script and began to read the lines again, playing both parts to herself, reading back and forth and acting out male and female alike.

She was just nearing the end of Act Two when a voice came from the door; 'Bravo!'

It was Killigrew. She flushed and dipped a curtsey.

'Where's Stefan? Was he not reading with you?'

'He had to leave.'

'The wretch. He gave up on you, didn't he?'

She did not reply, but felt heat rise to her cheeks. 'It was my fault. I angered him.'

'You and everyone else. What shall I do? I don't think I can keep him on. He gets worse and worse. He was bad enough with Nelly. He doesn't see that if he was just less temperamental and more reliable, I'd be more inclined to use him. No, he'll have to go.'

'Not on my account, please, sir.'

'My mind's made up. As soon as this one's played, he must go.'

Stefan would blame her, she was sure of it. An uncomfortable knot of worry formed below her ribs.

A week shot by, and she was careful to avoid Stefan, who had no major role in the play except prompter. On her first ever entrance she felt her knees shake. The crowd of faces in the pit were so close. Fortunately she didn't have to speak, only gesture, because her mouth was as dry as old feathers. The first act shot by in a blur. The smell of tallow and smoking wax, the rustle and hubbub of the crowd, all barely noticed because of the thudding of her heart, and her thoughts galloping like a horse to the next line, the next entrance, the next scene.

She barely had time to catch breath in the interval before Act Two got off to a racing start – the audience were with them; she could feel the hush as they held their breaths, then the sudden gust of laughter at the wit of the players. She delivered her final exit in her skirts, hitching them up to her knees, and pointing her toe to show off her calves just as Killigrew had told her to do. The gesture seemed to work, as piercing whistles and catcalls pursued her as she strode off and into the dark shadows of the wings.

Now all she had to do was change; a quick change, to strip off the skirt to her stays, and step into a pair of breeches. Mrs Corey was to attach her doublet sleeves to save time. She passed Stefan in the wings where he was understudying and prompting. A cold smile of satisfaction played on his lips. She shot past him and round the back of the painted backdrop to the other side of the stage where she was due to make her next entrance.

Groping her way in the half-dark past stage braces and sandbags, she could hear the other actors on stage, and the laughter of the crowd, as she passed. When she got to the chair where her breeches were laid out, it was empty. At first she thought that, being of a slippery sateen, they must have slipped off. She plunged her hands to the ground feeling for the material, for the sleeves, but there was nothing. In a panic she twisted around and about, searching the boards by feel.

Not there. But she'd laid them out herself, just before curtain up.

Frantic, she rushed to the downstage wing, thinking maybe she'd left the breeches there. Still nothing. She tore off her skirts and petticoat, until she was clad only in her stays and knee-length chemise, and then raced around the back. Maybe it was in the other wing?

'Looking for something?' Stefan asked.

'My breeches, they've been moved,' she whispered. 'Have you seen them?'

'Careless. Did you set them properly?'

'Of course I did. Have you seen them?'

He shrugged. Did not offer to help her search, but watched her with an amused expression.

The scene was nearly over. Panic made her breathless. She was supposed to appear as a man in less than a few lines. Almost weeping, she hared behind the backdrop, and to her entrance point, crashing into the side-flats on the way. On stage, Mohun shot her an irritated look.

Mrs Corey was waiting. 'Where've you been?' she mouthed. 'Where are your breeches?'

'I don't know. They were here. Someone's moved them.'

'You've only got two lines,' she said.

'Quick! Find me some!'

'But I—'

'Please!'

Mrs Corey shot off and ran back with a pair of petticoat breeches. 'It's all I could find. Quick, get in.'

There was silence on stage. Bird fumbled to hitch up the weight of material and tie it on.

The cue came again.

The breeches were too big, and wouldn't stay up. Bird shouted her line from where she was.

Mohun, who was waiting for her entrance, approached the wing and glared at her. Seeing their struggle, he went back on stage. 'It appears that like all women, my wife is taking her time to dress.'

Laughter.

Mrs Corey meanwhile had been resourceful and found some twine and was trying to attach the breeches roughly to Bird's stays. 'What about sleeves, my ducks?'

'No time,' Bird said, and she shot out from the wings into the pool of candlelight and centre stage.

A gasp from the audience, as Bird delivered her line. She suspected it was because her arms were horribly bare and she had no doublet, only her stays. The petticoat breeches were ridiculous, she knew. The audience leapt to their feet craning to see.

Bird strode forward. 'I'm a man, as you can plainly see,' she cried boldly, a line that was nowhere in the script.

Cheers.

Mohun, who was clearly used to dealing with a fractious audience paced forward and dropped his voice to a whisper for his next few lines. Anxious not to miss a word the audience quietened to listen. The scene slowly returned to the script, and Bird's terror, which she had thought might cause her to faint, subsided.

The rest of the play rattled forth, until Bird held the final bars of the song, her eyes closed to better hear her own voice as it joined the drone of the viols. A second of silence, then a tremendous noise, like a splatter of rain on wooden tiles, combined with a thousand papers rustling. Bird opened her eyes. The audience were standing, clapping and stamping. In the front row, she caught a glimpse of that man, Mr Peeps, who had taken her arm the first time she came to the theatre. His fingers were stuck in his mouth in a whistle. She threw him a smile for his presence seemed like an omen of good fortune.

'Go on, take a bow,' Wintershall and Mrs Corey pushed her forward.

Amid the tumult and the catcalls, Bird stepped forward towards the flickering row of wicks at the edge of the stage. Her heart pulsed beneath her stays, sweat sheened her face as she dipped her head and sank her knees in a curtsey. The breeches pooled around her feet, but as she stood, she stood on one of the dangling ribbons and the badly tied strings gave way.

With aplomb, she stepped out of the breeches, to reveal her cambric shift, to a huge roar from the crowd, who no doubt thought it all part of the act.

Her calves were horribly exposed in their stockings and garters. 'I did it,' she thought, triumphant but exhausted, tears filling her eyes.

She glanced into the wings, where Stefan stared sourly out at her from prompt corner. The rest of the cast ran out from behind him to join her in a long line. Mrs Corey grasped her hand as they bowed together, then thrust her out of the line again.

She bowed this time, with a flourish, like a man. From the audience, a posy, a handkerchief, some nutshells, a handful of flowers, flew through the air and landed on the boards. She bent down to step back into the breeches and held them up as she curtseyed once more.

'Show us your calves again!' shouted a wit from the audience.

She acted as if she might, by hitching the oversized breeches a little higher above her shoes, to a great roar. But then she dropped them again, to the groan of the crowd. She teased them once more, enjoying the reaction it created, before flapping her hand in the gesture of 'No.'

A glance back to the wings assured her that Stefan had gone, and instead, there was Killigrew, frantically waving her forward to take another bow. Above her, the chandelier dripped wax; she dodged the wax puddle and gazed out at the standing crowd, ready to curtsey.

Oh merciful heavens. There in the pit, her husband. She hadn't told him she was to appear.

Knepp was staring, eyes narrowed in a stony face. A fist of fear twisted beneath her ribs.

Disconcerted, she hurriedly hoisted the breeches to more applause. But just as she was about to turn and leave, she caught sight of a black arm waving, near the orange girls at the edge of the pit. It was Livvy, standing next to Rose, who had the orange basket over her arm. Livvy plucked an orange out and tossed it towards her. With her free hand, Bird caught it and held it aloft. Livvy's face was alight with excitement.

'Good catch!' shouted Mr Peeps.

Bird did not dare look at him, before rushing back behind the painted flattage towards the tiring room.

'What the hell was going on in Act Three?' Killigrew said, bustling her down the narrow wooden steps. 'But that business with the breeches, keep it in!'

In the tiring room Mother Corey enveloped her in a huge embrace. 'Well done, my dear. I thought we'd never get you on for that last act. What happened to your costume?'

'It doesn't matter, I got through it.'

'All right for you to say, but it caused me a proper panic.'

'Beg pardon, Mrs Corey, I don't know where the breeches went, they were there before the curtain.'

Mohun came past her on the way to the tiring room. 'Don't upstage me again, d'you hear? That should have been my scene, not yours.'

As he said this she caught sight of Stefan from the corner of her eye. He was staring too intently at her. In that moment she was certain. He was the only person who had the time, or the inclination, to move it.

She smiled sweetly at him. 'Well, Stefan,' she said. 'Thanks to you, I was a bigger success than I could have hoped. Enough to rattle Mr Mohun anyway.'

'Showing too much flesh is not acting,' Stefan said. He whisked his cloak from the back of the chair and went out. She winced. Her husband would probably have the same opinion.

'"Exit, pursued by a bear",' Mrs Corey said, 'as good Mr Shakespeare would say. Do you think Stefan was at fault?'

'I wouldn't like to point a finger,' Bird said. 'Anyway, leave him be. There's no harm done. At least I got to the end.'

*   *   *

When she had removed the greasepaint and got dressed, she came out of the stage door and bumped straight into Knepp.

'Get in,' he said, tersely, holding open a carriage door.

He slammed it shut after her, and levered himself into the driving seat. Through the leather-curtained window she watched his back, hunched with tension, as he steered the carriage down the crowded thoroughfares and back through the walls at Aldgate towards Smithfield. She wondered if he'd beat her, and hoped he would not mark her face or legs, or how would she be on stage the morrow?

Through the archway into the yard.

The door opened. 'Out,' he said.

She ducked and hurried into the house, as he went to hand over the horses. Lights were lit in the parlour, so his mother must still be up, awaiting their return.

Mrs Knepp was sitting in the chair near the embers of the fire, in a shawl and nightcap. She pulled herself to her feet. 'How did you fare?' she asked.

Bird gave her a tidy version that did not mention the episode with the breeches, but they were interrupted when Knepp strode in and slapped his cap down on the table.

'I will not be made into a fool,' he said. 'My wife will not be going to the theatre again. It is nothing but a whore's—'

A knocking on the door stopped his tirade.

'What?' Knepp hauled the door open to find Dobbsy on the doorstep. Bird took her chance to escape, and headed for the corridor and the stairs.

'Sir, all the carriages were taken. Every single one! I'll wager we made more than thirty pounds, in just one night! And we've repeat orders for carriages tomorrow and the next day. It's working, sir. And your missus, well, she's the talk of the town, the drivers say. Viner'll be green when he finds out.'

Knepp frowned. 'What are they saying?'

'They're asking who she is, and we're saying she's Mrs Knepp, wife of Mr Knepp of Farringdon and Knepp's horse hire,' Dobbsy said proudly. 'She's surely drawing folks' attention.'

'This could be the making of you, Christopher,' Mrs Knepp said.

Bird, who had paused to hear all this, turned. 'Told you,' she said.

'Go to bed,' he snapped at her. 'And you too, Mother. This is men's talk.' And he stepped outside with Dobbsy, shutting the door firmly behind him.

Knepp did not come to her that night, and nobody stopped her when she went out of the yard the next morning. Was it her imagination, or did the men look to her with more respect? Money talks, she thought. But probably it was Dobbsy's talk of them ousting his rival Viner that made all the difference.

Bird hurried her way into the city in the sunshine, a spring in her step.

She was going through lines with Nell when Mrs Corey came to find her. 'You've put the cat amongst the pigeons and no mistake. Mohun's been complaining that you've got no stagecraft.'

'He can never bear it if anyone else is the centre of attention,' Nell said. She mimicked him, 'You *ruined* my big scene.'

'They're all his big scenes as far as Mohun's concerned,' Mrs Corey said. 'And Stefan's been sacked.'

'What?'

'Stefan's gone. Killigrew threw him out. Killigrew asked me why you were not wearing the right costume. I told him I thought it was Stefan's fault. He went to see him, they had a blazing disagreement, and Killigrew's got rid of him.'

'Oh no. It's all my fault.'

'Don't be foolish, of course it's not. He brought it on himself. You didn't try to sabotage someone else's performance, did you?'

She shook her head. Yet she had a bad feeling about it. Her career had only just begun, and already she was making enemies.

CHAPTER 12

The next day, Elisabeth Pepys was one of Knepp's new customers.

'If we order a carriage, let's use Farringdon and Knepp's instead of Viner,' her husband said. 'Knepp's wife is the new sensation at the King's Playhouse.'

'Oh, is she?' Elisabeth's voice held an edge.

'I mean to say, I've heard Knepp's is cheaper than Viner.'

'When will we get our own carriage, *hein*?' Elisabeth demanded. 'It's inconvenient constantly sending a boy to fetch one.'

'When you spend less on rugs and curtains, my dear,' Samuel said, as he went out.

She pondered this. Yes, they had been extravagant since moving from Axe Yard to Seething Lane. Moving house had been all expense, and Viner's Carriage Hire had already had the best part of fifty pounds for moving them. Perhaps she *would* use Knepp's carriages from now on, not Viner's.

That day she told Jane to send the boy to Knepp's. She could see why Knepp's were cheaper.

The coach upholstery was grimy, and one of the window blinds didn't work. Nevertheless, it was pleasant to save some of her housekeeping money for other things, and she never did tell her husband exactly how much cheaper Knepp's was.

After they'd been using Knepp's about a month, she'd saved enough from her trips to treat herself to something. She and Jane had a very pleasant day out browsing at the Exchange. The goldsmith on the upper level was extremely persuasive, and his trays of glinting gold and pearls so tempting. How could she resist? Jane cooed over a pair of pearl drop earrings with a price tag somewhat larger than Elisabeth had bargained for. But they were so pretty, and surely she deserved them after all this scrimping and saving?

That evening she held up one of the earrings to her ear to admire its twinkle in the glass. A bargain at thirty shillings, and with real stones too; a square-cut diamond with a row of pendant sea-pearls, of a translucent cream.

Elisabeth was determined to keep up appearances. After all, the Navy office apartments were right next door to a lord. Lord Bruncker of the Royal Society, no less. Other wealthy officials of the Navy Board, and their well-dressed wives, often passed right under her window.

Not that they had made any great effort to welcome her. Madam Williams, Lord Bruncker's consort, had snubbed her as she passed. Elisabeth wished she had a friend to admire the earrings;

and now she had them on, they seemed mighty small for all that money. When they lived in Axe Yard, such fripperies would have been unthinkable. But now . . . Elisabeth let the pendants dangle and catch the light as she turned her head. Perhaps Samuel would think them too extravagant.

When Samuel came in, he went straight to Jane in the kitchen, and came back with a plate of grilled herring, which he munched his way through, making a fishy stink. He was full of his business with Lord Crew, the man who had helped restore the young king to the throne. Elisabeth listened impatiently. Lord Crew was a nuisance; he had a large rambling house near Lincoln's Inn Fields, and was always trying to persuade Samuel to buy into his estate.

'He showed a map, with a parcel of land in Cambridgeshire,' Samuel said, licking his fishy fingers. 'It's a well-drained portion. He wants a thousand pounds for it. I've a mind to offer for it.'

'What? So much? Can we afford that? This place, it is expensive, no? Now we have more servants. And if there's money to spare, I still would like a companion, someone to dress my hair properly.'

'What's wrong with your hair? It looks well enough to me.'

'It's not that; it's dull here at home with nobody to talk to except the servants.'

'Pah. You are hardly ever at home! When I handed her my hat, Jane said you went into the Exchange again today.'

Elisabeth cursed Jane and made a note to reprimand her on telling Samuel every last thing she did. 'I have to get out of this place, or it will send me *complètement folle.*'

'New earrings?'

'I've had these a while.'

'I don't remember seeing them before.'

'Then you're very unobservant.'

'Come here, let me look.' He grabbed her by the arm, and she tried to twist away.

'They're new, aren't they?'

'Are you calling me a liar?'

He sighed. 'Jane said you'd bought earrings. How much did they cost? Are those stones glass, or real?'

'If you know so much, why don't you ask Jane? You talk to her more than you talk to me, anyway.'

'That's because she has the sense to tell me the truth. Just tell me, how much did you pay?'

'They were reduced, I haggled for five minutes before I bought them. All the other Navy wives have jewels, why should I be the one who owns nothing? You never even buy me so much as a measly kerchief, you're so niggardly.'

Samuel made a grab for one of the earrings and grasped it in his fist, jerking her head towards him.

'Ow! Let go.'

'How much did you pay?'

'Let go!'

Another jerk.

The pain made Elisabeth blurt out, 'Twenty-five

shillings!' He let go, and stood with his mouth agape.

'Twenty-five shillings? On those?' His face became pinker. 'You must take them back. Now. I won't have you wasting money on such geegaws as these.'

'A trifle like this, you begrudge me, yet you think it excellent good to purchase a thousand-pound plot, is it? Land that I will never put my foot upon?'

'That's different.'

'You don't care about my feelings. Not a whit. You leave me here day after day with no company. Don't you understand? If I'm to be like the other ladies here, I must dress like them. Do you want a wife that looks like a servant? You would have me go abroad in sackcloth and you would say nothing, so long as your coffers, they are full.'

'Don't be foolish. Stop all this nonsense. Take them off right now, before I have to beat you.'

Elisabeth yanked them out one by one and threw them at him. *Espèce d'idiot!* Take them back yourself,' she said.

'You will return them wife, if it's the last thing you do. Or I'll smash them to pieces and then that will be the end of us.'

'Smash them. I don't care. *Mon Dieu,* but you're a useless husband anyway. You can't give me a babe, you're so useless. And you have to make yourself feel like a man by whoring after that Bagwell woman and any other jade who so much as throws you a smile. I should never have come back. I should have gone home to France. At least there, men are men, not beasts like you.'

'Wash out your mouth. I'm not listening to such filth from your lips.' He scooped up the earrings lying on the floorboards and cast them out of the window. 'And if those are not sold and the money on my desk by the time I get back tonight, you will be out with them, d'you hear?' He slammed the door as he went.

As soon as she could no longer hear his footsteps on the stairs, she shot out of the door to retrieve the earrings. It took her a few moments of heart-stopping searching before she found them in the dirt of the street.

That she should be reduced to this – clawing her jewels from the grit.

What should she do? She opened her palm to see them glinting there. They did not look so beautiful now. He had tainted them. She'd never be able to wear them without guilt, she knew.

'Besse?' she shouted.

The young chambermaid came running. She had a permanently frightened face under her white coif. 'Yes, Mistress?'

Elisabeth held out her hand with the earrings back in the wooden box. 'Take these back to the goldsmith at the Exchange where we bought them. Top floor, next to the glovemaker. Say you came from Mrs Pepys and tell him they don't suit. Explain that . . . say that my husband does not

195

like them, and I will be in later to . . . to try another pair.'

'Yes, Mistress.'

'Make sure to get the money back though.'

'What if he won't give me—'

'Bring me the money, or there'll be no supper.'

Besse's face looked even more scared and uncertain.

'Now go.'

Besse shot out of the door, clogs clattering. Elisabeth knew that feeling of fear. It was exactly the same fear she experienced when her husband imposed his will on her. She had merely passed it on, down to the person below her in the pecking order.

CHAPTER 13

Stefan turned at the sound of Father Bernard's voice. It was a relief that he hardly ever came up here, but Stefan kept the door locked just in case.

'Yes, Father?'

'I need you to do an errand for me,' came the voice from below.

'What, now?'

'Just come down, would you, lad?'

'Coming,' Stefan yelled, annoyed. With reluctance, he stepped out of the skirt he had been admiring only a moment earlier, and smoothed the satin under his fingers before replacing it in the trunk beneath the bed. He had sneaked it from the wardrobe of the King's Players the day Killigrew, the bastard, had sacked him. It was all the fault of that horse-dealer's wife, Mrs Knepp. She'd ratted on him for hiding her costume, the cow.

In private, up here, he could pretend he was a court lady. He had been rehearsing Olivia from *Twelfth Night*, which chimed with his favourite fantasy, which was that he was a visiting princess from Catholic Spain, and this was not an attic, but a royal apartment.

Such attachment to women's garments was unmanly, perverted, and filled him with guilt. But he loved the feel of the lush, voluminous skirts, the crush of petticoats, and the sheer abundance of fabric. It had always been the same. One of his earliest memories was of hiding behind his mother's skirts, protected by all that billowing silk from his father's ear-splitting rage. And it had imbued women's clothes with a thrilling mystery.

He thought briefly of his father. Bastard. He was a fanatic who beat the shit out of his son for his lack of interest in fighting, then hated himself afterwards for being so weak as to do it. Worse, his father resented the fact he was forced to make a confession each time before he could be cleansed of this weakness. For this humiliation with the priest his father blamed Stefan, or his mother. He beat her too.

Father Bernard had never suspected this of his father, his violence and self-loathing, and it made Stefan think him a lean-witted fool. He suspected he'd hate Stefan if he told him of his father's cruelty, if he destroyed his father's image. No Catholic was cruel, in Father Bernard's book. And Father Bernard would certainly hate him, Stefan, if he knew what he did up here.

Sometimes he wanted to shock the old man. Watch his placid, comfortable face lose its certainty. Stupid priest. He thought all women were sinners and responsible for men's fall. It seemed to him men could fall perfectly well by themselves, with no help from women whatsoever.

But the sinfulness of women only added to the illicit appeal of putting on their clothes and becoming one. Would he go to hell for doing such a thing off the stage? He was uncertain. But the pope seemed to think confessing was the answer to all. Perhaps he'd confess on his death bed in another thirty or forty years' time.

'Stefan?' Father Bernard's voice again.

He closed the lid on the peach-coloured satin and pushed the trunk under the bed with his boot, before sliding back the bolt on the door and sauntering downstairs.

'Ah, there you are. What on earth are you doing up there?'

'Learning lines. Preparing an audition for the Duke's,' Stefan said. 'Mr Davenant will see me next week.'

'That will be a shame. I've enjoyed having your company these last months. It gave us some time to get the History really underway, and I'm enjoying writing it all down. Brings back so many memories.'

'What did you want me for?'

'Ah yes. It's a parcel of poems to go to St Mary's City in the New Territories. *Hymn to St Teresa* and so forth. Do you know, they've built a church there, a wooden one? The only new Catholic church in the whole of the English-speaking world.

I won't ever see it, more's the pity. Too old for such travel. You might, one day though.'

Stefan hoped not. He'd heard stories of how the settlers in the New World had to fight off savages, and he'd never been much use with his fists.

'I've just bound and stitched them to make them last. They'll catch the trading ship *Lavinia*, if we're lucky. Drop them at Hubert's the watchmaker in the alley off Lombard Street. Sign of the Hourglass.

'Is it these?' He pointed to the wrapped packet on the table.

'Yes. And while you're out, you could call at the Spanish Ambassador on the Strand, you know, where we go for Mass, and take him this letter.' He held out a sealed missive.

Stefan took it, and scooped up the parcel. He was curious about what might be in the letter, but didn't ask. The sooner he did his errands, the sooner he could be back in his room upstairs.

Viner's stablelad, Cal, chewed at the wicks around his fingernails, and wondered if he hadn't waited long enough for his quarry in this bluster of a day. A sharp wind was blowing like the devil. Cal's stomach rumbled, and he longed for a pie or a pasty. But just as he was thinking this, the door of the bookbinder's opened and a young man with flowing yellow hair came out.

This must be him; the one he'd to watch. Goldilocks had a package in his hand, so Cal followed him, a short distance behind, making sure to keep a few other folk between him and his quarry. He was used to these sorts of duties, and it made a change from mucking out. Besides, they paid well, Viner and Bludworth and the rest of the anti-Catholic league.

He'd passed this bookbinder's many times, and thought it just a dusty old man's type of shop, not one for a fashionable young rake like Goldilocks. The man had a funny kind of walk, bouncing on the front of his feet, but it was a fast walk and hard to keep up with. Cal bounded after him, his cap jammed down on his head, the brim close to his eyes because of the wind.

Cal followed all the way to Tinker's Alley, and saw him go inside a shop with a hanging sign of an hourglass over it, before he came out again and headed westwards towards the Convent Garden and Drury Lane.

There, Goldilocks stopped right outside the King's Theatre and seemed to read the flapping playbills very intently. Cal stopped too, pretending to bend over to fix the buckle on his shoe before following again, through blowing dust and debris, down past the massive white stonework of Somerset House, a sprawling building currently undergoing renovation.

So that's where you're going, is it, Goldilocks, he thought. He'd heard a story of how Roundhead soldiers had smashed up a Catholic chapel there, but to his surprise, the young man didn't stop, but carried on, plainly in a hurry.

Fewer people were on the street here, and the tall lanky lad suddenly stopped and turned. Cal nipped into a side alley, but not before Goldilocks had seen him. Curses. He waited a little longer, kicking at the few fallen leaves with his too-big boots.

A few moments later, he dared emerge from the alley to see the young man much further ahead, and turning sharp right off the highway away from the river. Cal plunged after him. He was just in time to see him go inside a large residence on Canon Row. The building boasted a sign above it with an elaborate foreign coat of arms, but Goldilocks had no trouble gaining admittance from the liveried doorman, so perhaps he was known there.

Cal scrutinised the sign again. He was not much of a reader, and it was not a sign he recognised, but he made a note of the look of it, a central shield with an eagle and a griffin back to back, and a lot of red and yellow stripes. Some sort of official residence anyway.

He settled to wait on the corner, behind a large elm tree, just out of sight, his eyes fixed on the door. After about fifteen minutes he was getting bored, and wished the man would come out.

A hand on the shoulder made him yelp and turn. It was Goldilocks. He must have come out another way. A hand fastened around his arm.

'Were you following me?'

'What you doing? Leave go!' Cal feigned innocence.

202

'You were following me,' the youth said. 'Why? Who hired you?'

'Nobody!' Cal was wiry and tough and with a sudden twist, he jerked free. In two shakes he was off up the street, as fast as he could run. Behind him he could hear Goldilocks shouting, 'Get back here, you vermin!' and footsteps thudding after him, but his pursuer didn't know the back alleys as well as Cal.

Lost you, you bugger, Cal thought with satisfaction.

Later, as arranged, Cal tapped on the window of the Old Bull Tavern just off Cradle Alley, where he could see Viner's broad back through the smoky glass. Viner turned, and moments later lurched out, still clutching a tankard of ale.

'Yes?'

Cal told Viner about the blond lad, and where he'd been.

'Canon Street, you say? And a building with a coat of arms.'

'Yes, sir.'

'Good lad.' He produced threepence from his pocket.

Cal looked at it with disgust. 'You said sixpence.'

'You took too long, so you only get half. Now get back to the horses, and mind you change into livery first.'

Not fair. But there was no point arguing if he wanted to keep his position. He slouched away slowly, rubbing the threepence between his fingers and feeling like ramming it up Viner's fat arse.

Inside the tavern, Thomas Bludworth, the Mayor of London, and the Reverend Broadwell of St Margaret Lothbury, a balding man with a beaky nose, awaited Ted Viner's return by finishing the jug of ale before them.

'Anything?' Broadwell asked, moving his thin legs aside as Viner squeezed himself back into his seat.

'Could be. We had a tip about Bernard's the bookbinder. He rarely goes out, but there's a lad there that does his errands. A foppish out-of-work player called Stefan Woolmer. I had him followed and he delivered a letter to the Spanish Embassy in Hertford House, and then a parcel to Hubert – he's the French watchmaker in Tinkers Alley. We've tracked Hubert to the Spanish Embassy on Canon Street on several occasions, and we're fairly sure he attends Mass there two or three times a week.'

'Bloody French and Spanish again. It's a farce,' Bludworth said, his red face growing even redder. 'Everyone knows they meet in these embassies for Mass, and there's not a thing we can do about it, as according to them, the embassy's Spanish soil and London law doesn't apply.' He raised his podgy arms in disgust.

'And it's no secret that these Masses are where all the plotting against our Church goes on.'

Reverend Broadwell said. 'They flout the law, and practice idolatry, and yet we can't touch them. Do you think this bookbinder could be a part of the Popish cabal?'

'Seems likely,' Viner said. 'Someone's getting these tracts out, despite the law. We closed down the printer in St Martin's Lane, but as soon as one shuts, another pops up. They're like weevils, pull up one weed, and there's more of the creatures underneath.'

'This Bernard and his actor friend, have they a printing press?' Reverend Broadwell leaned forward on a skinny elbow. 'And have we enough evidence to convict them yet? Begging your pardon, Mayor, but nothing seems to be being done.'

'We could certainly search their premises and see,' Viner said. 'Constable Garrod's a friend of mine and I could have a word with him.' He paused, 'With your permission, Tom, of course.'

Bludworth gave a nod in response. 'If you would, Ted. Sooner we put a stop to these seditious chapbooks, the better. It looks bad if they keep multiplying during my term of office. So you'll deal with it?'

'Leave it to me. Tom. No sooner said, than done.'

Livvy gripped the heavy pail of hot water and looked right and left before crossing the yard. She didn't want to see Mr Viner. He kept appearing when she was cleaning or making the beds, and staring after her when she passed. The office was below the lodging chambers where she worked which made it awkward to avoid him, and his sneaking presence would sometimes catch her unawares.

She pulled the door open slowly so its noise wouldn't alert him, but to her annoyance she was just a bit too quick and the hinges creaked. Immediately, he appeared out of the downstairs office right in front of her. She tried to pass him, but he leant one hand on the wall next to her, like a barrier.

'What are you doing today, Livvy?'

'Windows, sir.' She put the steaming bucket down, and looked at her feet. The smell of him, his slightly sweet, soapy odour, made her hold her breath. What did he want?

But he said nothing further, made no pleasantries, no chat. He just smiled in a knowing way; a way that made her feel uncomfortable, and take a grip of her slop-apron with both hands. She had to sidle away and then walk around him, as he smiled his thin smile, like a split in his doughy face. As she passed and picked up her bucket, he put out a hand and let it trail on her breast.

The door to the yard opened again, and Tomlinson the overseer strode in, with a blast of chill air. 'Ah, there you are, sir. Lord Arlebury would like a carriage for the morning, shall I look in the book and see if one's available?'

Quick as she could Livvy rushed into the first

upstairs chamber, and put the bucket in front of the door.

So it was that way. She'd have to watch out. For all his railing against sin and the devil, Ted Viner would have her, if he thought he could get away with it. Not only that, but she knew where it would lead. He'd tire of her, then hate her, then dismiss her. She'd seen it happen to other servants and it was always the same.

CHAPTER 14

October 1664

Once a month was Livvy's full day off and she was anxious for news of Mamma and Jan, her younger brother. She cursed the cold and the rain. How come, when it was her day off, it always did this? Worse than Holland for rain, was London. Despite the wet, as soon as she'd finished the morning chores she threw on a cloak and some wooden pattens over her shoes, and set off to M'sieur Hubert's.

When she got there, there was no candle at the window. She knocked, hoping to see his familiar figure bloom through the glass, but there was no answer and the door was locked. No note pinned on the door either, but he must know she would come. She came every month now, on her day off, hoping for a letter. Last time she came, he'd given her another parcel to go to the docks, and she'd delivered it to the ship *Lavinia*'s first mate as he'd asked. M'sieur couldn't have forgotten her, could he?

She stood under the jettied overhang in her

soaking skirts as a stream of water poured in front of her into the gutter. She hadn't realised just how much she relied on his warm fire, but more than that, his welcome. Just as she was about to give up and go home, a limping figure appeared at the end of the road, pushing a handcart, with its leather cover well-strapped down. Hubert himself was so wet he looked as if he'd just been for a swim in the Thames.

'*Pardon*,' M'sieur Hubert said, his sparse hair dripping on his forehead, 'Have you wait long? I had to fetch something for a friend.'

'No, not long. Here, let me help.'

He opened up the door and hurried to unload stacks of books and pamphlets from the cart, sheltering them under his oilskin cloak.

'What is all this?' she asked, as she carried a stack of leather-bound books inside, ducking under the dripping lintel. 'Bibles?' Some of the books were embossed with a cross.

'Wait, I tell you when they are all in. Careful. Keep them dry.'

They hurried to get the things out of the rain and then to heave the handcart into the yard at the back. Books and pamphlets littered his usually tidy work space. She could see he was itching to restore order.

'Where will you put it all?'

He shrugged. '*Je ne sais pas*. But I must hide it somehow.' He went to bolt the door and close the shutters. 'We all help each other, all of us who go

209

to Mass.' He turned to look into her face. His eyes were pale and serious. 'I don't shock you, do I? You knew I was a Catholic when you delivered my parcels?'

'Yes. I knew it.'

'I'm sorry. I should have trusted you. But I didn't want to risk that you know too much. It makes danger for you.'

'What I don't understand is the difference between one Christian and another. What is Catholic and Protestant? Same God, isn't it? Except that they fight like dogs over who is right.'

'It's complicated. I'm not sure I understand it all myself, but a lot of it is to do with honouring our parents. We honour their faith. And I think we fight for the right to pray how we please.'

'And if they won't let you, you do it in secret anyway.'

He laughed. *'C'est vrai!* True. But it's dangerous being a Catholic. We'd hoped the king's marriage to a Catholic might give us . . . how you say? Some breathing space. But it is the English people who hate us. They send spies to search us out, and we hear rumour they have warrant to search Father Bernard's house. If they find these books, they could put him in the Tower, and then he'd hang.'

'So Father Bernard is safe, and now *you* have these dangerous pieces of paper.' She held up a thin chapbook and flapped it so the pages fluttered. 'They are just paper. It is wrong a man can be killed for this.'

'Not just paper. Ideas.'

'I keep my ideas safe in my head where no-one sees.'

'Very wise.' He tapped one of the books with a forefinger. 'Though I'm more afraid of what's hidden in men's heads, than anything written in here.'

She thought of Mr Viner and his silent stalking, and suppressed a shudder.

M'sieur Hubert shivered and pulled off his wet boots. Livvy saw him glance at the fireplace and went to the tinderbox to strike a light. Within a few moments the fire crackled in the grate, and they stood side by side to enjoy its heat. He was the same height as her, she realised, but that was probably because one leg was withered, and his back a little stooped. As she thought this, she caught his eye. Both instantly turned away. Had he been thinking the same? Thinking she was as tall as he? She moved away, feeling too tall and ungainly.

'That's better,' he said. 'Now. Let's see.' He opened up one of his longcase clocks and withdrew the pendulum, before stacking a pile of books inside. 'Folk might notice they show the wrong time, but that is not so strange in a repair shop, *n'est-ce pas*?'

'Very neat, M'sieur,' she said. She helped him fill two more clocks until the small room was clear of Catholic books.

'So you know now, when I send you with my parcels, it is a risk you take.'

'I knew before. But I do it because you help me read what Mamma writes.'

'And I have another from your Mama,' he said, pulling open the desk drawer and brandishing a sealed letter with a grin. 'That's the advantage of reading,' he said. 'Sometimes it is good, to see inside someone else's head.'

She spent another hour in his company enjoying small talk from her mother and brother, before a customer's insistent knock made M'sieur Hubert return to business. By the time she left him the rain had stopped, but she still needed to be careful of the swimming channel of refuse flowing down the street.

She dawdled on the way back, because she didn't want to go back to Viner's until the last possible moment. As she passed the corner of the road she saw a poster for a horse-hire company with a woodcut of a prancing pair of horses before a speeding carriage. She stopped because the word at the top was not Viner's. She knew the 'V' letter because it was in her own name. She tilted her head to try to make it out.

Then she recognised it, the straight line and sideways V was the same as on Knepp's sign. The sideways V that meant Knepp's. She smiled. Good. Knepp's were obviously taking on Viner's. A moment of regret, as she remembered Bird's shining face on their outing to the theatre. And now she'd wrangled it so she was actually on the stage. Mrs Knepp, the actress. Who would have believed it? Livvy chuckled to herself, lost in thought.

It was then she noticed a wiry lad lounging against the vintner's wall, observing her from under his sodden cap. It was Cal, one of the stable-lads from Viner's, a sack over his shoulders to keep dry, and wearing a pair of boots much too big for his feet.

'What are you doing here?' she asked, annoyed that he'd caught her daydreaming.

'Nothin'. Just on my way back to the yard, that's all.'

'Where've you been?'

He looked momentarily confused. Then a reply came, 'The bridle repair shop.' He wasn't carrying a bridle, and her sharp look made him babble on, 'They kept it in, stitching was broke, and the leather all worn through, they couldn't fix it straight away.'

A tight feeling in her stomach made her sure he was lying. But why? Had he been following her? Was Viner that smitten that he'd set a boy to find out where she went? She stared at him, until he stuck out his tongue at her and ran on ahead. She watched his skinny legs weave through the pedestrians and the cluster of coaches and sedans. As he went, the wind blew off his cap to reveal a shock of bright red hair. Hastily he grabbed the cap back up, and was soon out of sight.

★　　★　　★

Bird stared out at the audience as she took her bow, smiling and curtseying. Like always, she snatched glances along the rows, scanning the audience, searching for her father's face. He was never there, of course, yet still she could not stop herself looking for him. One day he'd see her there, and see her speak up, and be amazed at her eloquence and skill. Of course she had no proper speaking part yet, but one day she would, she told herself. One day she would be famous and he'd have to beg for an audience with her.

Her eye skimmed the benches one last time, as Hart tried to drag her off-stage. Her gaze alighted on Mr Peeps. He was always there somewhere, that man, his eager eyes full of heat and enthusiasm. She blushed. Every time she looked for her father, he would catch her eye. Did he think she was searching for him?

She hurried off into the wings, and the hustle of the tiring room. The winter weather was cold and her arms were rough with goose-pimples as she changed, in a rush to get into warm flannel petticoats and her warm bodice and shawl.

'Good performance, Mrs Knepp,' Killigrew called as he passed on his way to the men's chamber. 'We'll make an actress of you yet.'

Pleased, she stuck her hat on with a hat-pin and covered it with a shawl, before heading for the street outside. She let Nell go first because Nell loved the crowd, like it was the air she breathed. The stage door was thronged with young rakehells and the rougher sort of lad, all anxious for a feel at a pair of legs or a backside.

Nell burst out of the door and was immediately submerged under a crowd. Behind her, with her shawl pulled over her face, Bird managed to skirt past the crowd and around the corner to Catherine Street. It was almost empty; her husband's carriages had gone with their wealthy occupants, there was just one couple climbing aboard one of Knepp's carriages with its brand new livery emblazoned on the side, and its lamps lit. It looked well. The green-and-burgundy livery had been Mrs Knepp's idea, and it had made Farringdon and Knepp's carriages distinctive.

Bird preferred to walk; the carriages were for hirers, not her, and it wasn't late, though at this time of the year it was dark, and the torches were already lit on the outside of houses. She summoned her usual link boy to light her way home, and he walked slowly so she could enjoy the frosty night air. London was beautiful at night; the ancient huddled streets nestled beneath the starry sky. She walked slowly because she dreaded arriving home.

The horses whickered as she arrived, and she heard the clank of a bucket as the shadowy figures of the stable lads watered the horses. In the parlour, Widow Knepp was already abed, and snoring.

The fire was almost out but she roused it, and boiled up milk to make a hot drink of milk and honey. Buoyant because of Killigrew's praise, she decided to be kind and take a cup to Knepp.

She knew where he'd be – playing cards in the tack-room with the grooms. She took the steaming cup across the yard and pushed open the door. To her surprise, he was there alone, sitting morosely in the dark.

'Where is everyone? I brought you a drink,' she said.

'What for?' His tone was annoyed.

'I thought you might like it, as it's such a cold night. It's what wives do, for their husbands.'

'No need. I'm going to the coffee-house.'

He stood, and walked past her.

'That's right, ignore me! I try to please you, and I get it thrown back in my face. Damn you to hell!' she shouted, and threw the cup down onto the cobbles. The white liquid steamed among the broken pieces.

He slapped her, a stinging blow across the cheek. 'You'll pay for that from your housekeeping,' he said in a tight voice, before striding out of the gate.

No use to pursue him to the coffee-house where women couldn't go. She stared at the broken cup in frustration. She had never yet managed to penetrate the wall that seemed to be around him, the invisible spiked barricade that would let no-one in. At first she'd been afraid of him, but recently she'd begun to suspect he was afraid of her. Whichever way, no matter how she tried to be pleasant or placate him, he'd lash out at her, as if the very sight of her made him angry.

★　　★　　★

216

Elisabeth reached for Samuel's shoulder again, to make him roll over towards her.

'Give over, wife,' he said, pushing her away with a jab of his elbow.

'Sam dear,' she said breathily, persisting, reaching under the sheets to the soft plumpness of his belly.

He brushed her away like a fly. 'Tickles.'

She kissed his cold ear, gently, above the blankets, and stroked the hollow of his neck; a move that when they first met, used to have him shuddering with excitement.

'I'm tired,' he said, plucking off her hand and shuffling further away.

She sat up and pulled her nightgown down a little to expose her breasts, and leaned over him. 'It's still early,' she said, 'hasn't my Sammikins got a kiss for his Lizzie?'

One eye opened. 'For God's sake, woman. Have you no shame?'

'Shame I have. That I am childless still. How can we . . . if we never . . .?'

He turned over, and pushed her away. 'Tush woman! Why must you hound me so? If you left me in peace some nights, instead of your peck-peck-pecking, I might get enough rest to feel like it.'

'You never feel like it.'

'Don't be ridiculous. You just always choose the wrong—'

A crash. Actually there, in the bedchamber.

Elisabeth shot upright in bed at exactly the same time as her husband.

Samuel fumbled for the flint and taper. 'What the devil—?'

Jane's querulous voice. 'I didn't mean to break it, sir. T'was an accident.'

'What the blazes is going on? What on earth are you doing creeping round in the dark?'

'Looking for the key, Master,' Jane said.

'What on earth for? Don't you have your own?'

'Mistress has it, sir. She lost hers.'

Oh, the shame of it. How much had Jane heard? Elisabeth scrambled out of bed in a fluster, and struck a flint to light the candles.

Samuel heaved himself up with a huff of annoyance, and grabbed the candelabra, waving it round the room. 'What was that crash?'

'Careful sir,' Jane said. 'There's glass.'

The hearth glittered with pieces of the vase that had until recently stood on the edge of the mantel. Its matching pair was still intact on the opposite side.

'Not my Venetian glass!' Samuel cried. 'I'll never replace it. What were you doing, stupid girl? Go and get a brush and pan.'

'Sorry, sir, but the key—'

'Never mind the damned key! My wife will bring you it.'

The key was in the closet. She'd forgotten. She stormed downstairs on bare feet, in search of Jane.

She accosted her in the parlour, 'Don't you ever, ever disturb us again, d'you hear?'

'I had to.' Jane did not drop her gaze. 'It's breaking the law to have no lantern lit on a winter morning.'

From her slight smile, Elisabeth guessed she'd heard everything. 'Don't talk back. You should have thought of it before we retired.'

'You've got my key, Mistress. You borrowed it when you lost yours.'

Impertinent madam. Elisabeth thrust the key at Jane. 'Well *you* have it now. And the price of that vase, it will come straight out of your wages.'

Jane slouched away, a venomous look in her dark eyes.

Elisabeth hitched up her nightgown and with as much dignity as she could, went back up the stairs. Their night was ruined. Ruined. She'd never get him to do it now.

'My best vase. It won't do,' Samuel said. 'You need to control your servants better. And fancy losing your key!'

'It's not my fault.'

'It never is!' He was shouting now. 'All you have to do all day is keep an eye on the servants, and you can't even do that. It's not much to ask is it?'

'Jane's a lazy girl, she never—'

'It's you. You're the lazy one. You do nothing all day except spend my money and mope about the house complaining about the servants. I've better things to worry about than your petty domestic squabbles. Like the Dutch breathing down our necks threatening invasion. I've got to sort out the entire Navy and you want to wake me at all hours

219

with your lewd tomfoolery. I'll be up to my ears in it tomorrow.'

'Oho,' she sniped. 'A busy day with Mrs Bagwell, is it?'

'Not that again. I told you before; she is petitioning for her husband.'

'Every other day, from what the clerk Hewer says,' she said. 'Does her petitioning involve lifting her skirts? You can do it with her, can you, but not with your wife?'

A fist shot out and a sudden bloom of pain and shock, like an explosion. Elisabeth reeled back, her hand to her face. She ducked away, hands covering her throbbing cheek. When she looked up he had hidden his hand behind his back.

'You hit me.' Her voice came out tiny, like a child.

'Damn fool woman. You drove me to it with your nonsense. Waking me up in the middle of the night, like a harlot. And then accusing me of all sorts of lewdness!'

'But you hit me in the face.'

'A lot of fuss over nothing. It was only a tap.'

'But you've broken my nose! Look! I can hardly see.'

'Don't exaggerate, woman.'

'By my troth, I shall leave again! I shall go home to France where men are more civilised!'

'Then go. My life would be far easier without you.'

Elisabeth picked up her clothes from the chair

and dragged them from the room. When she got onto the landing it was to see Jane's door above in the attic suddenly close. She'd been listening all the while. She twisted the fabric in her hands and pulled. She had never wanted to throttle someone so much in her entire life.

Elisabeth calmed her ragged breathing, took her clothes to the parlour and then stood a moment, looking in the glass that hung over the mantel.

Her eye was already beginning to close. She would be unable to go abroad, and Christmas was almost upon them, with a mass of engagements. She would be stuck here, in the house, unable to show her face.

He would expect her to hide away, to preserve his good name. Well, she would not. Let them see it. She didn't care who knew. Let them see the sort of Christmas gift you give your wife, she thought.

CHAPTER 15

December 1664

Bird pressed one hand on the walls of the houses as she tottered and slid down the icy pavement towards Cradle Alley and Viner's yard. Over one arm she held a basket of greenery and a wrapped parcel of soulcakes she'd made herself. It was weeks since she'd had time to call on Livvy, and last time she went, Livvy had looked peaky; thinner and with a guarded look around the eyes. Time to take her some Christmas cheer. By now she knew to be careful, and go around the back to the tradesman's entrance, then sneak in and try to spot Livvy in the brewhouse or the lodging rooms and beckon her out.

Today, Viner's yard was busy with a bustle of shoppers, ladies carrying parcels and gentlemen dressed for the winter in fur-lined cloaks and beaver hats. She was lucky and saw the familiar figure of Livvy just crossing the yard with an armful of laundry.

She rushed up behind her and tapped her on the shoulder. 'Livvy!'

Livvy turned so quick she nearly knocked Bird over. And the look of fear in her eyes made Bird instantly contrite.

'It's only me,' she said.

Livvy pulled her by the arm, 'Quick, Viner's out with his wife and children. We can go up to my chamber.'

She followed Livvy into the building where the office was, and up the stairs. Livvy dumped the washing into the nearest door, an empty chamber with the horsehair mattress stripped back to its ticking cover, before unlocking the door of the very end room.

It was barely bigger than a cupboard, with a single pallet bed, neatly made. There was no fireplace, just her servant's box at the end of the bed. The windowsill housed a collection of horseshoes beneath its single oiled linen curtain.

Livvy saw her looking. 'I collect them if one of them casts. Can't have too much luck, can you?' She sat herself down. 'Good to get the weight off my feet, though I can't talk long. Tomlinson the overseer, he reports me if I've not got all the beds done by noon.'

'I brought you this.' Bird passed over the basket. 'It's not much, but I thought you could put the holly round your room to give a bit of cheer. Lots of berries, this year. And I made the cakes myself.'

'You made them for me?'

'Old Mrs Knepp loves them. It's all I can do to

223

keep her thieving fingers out of the tray when they're done.'

'But I haven't anything for you. I didn't think. I've had a lot on my mind.'

'What is it, Livvy? You nearly jumped out of your skin, when I called you.'

'The constable came. He wanted to know how I knew M'sieur Hubert. I tell him the truth; how we met in St Paul's Church when I was looking for work. M'sieur, he help me read the notices on the *Si Quis* door.'

'*Si Quis*? What's that?'

'M'sieur Hubert say it means 'If anyone'. It's Latin. It's a door where masters pin up posts asking for serving girls. That's how I got to Knepp's in the first place; Knepp put up a note for a brewing girl and laundress. I tell him I could do both. Always he want to save money, Knepp.'

'But what's this about the constable?'

'He came to Viner and ask for me. It make a cartload of trouble. Constable ask me how long I'd known M'sieur Hubert, and where he go to church. I told him I didn't know. He ask me if Hubert ever got me to take messages.' She twisted her fingers in her apron.

'What sort of messages? Is this Frenchman some sort of crook? He's not hurting you, is he?'

'No.' She squirmed and began to pluck the feather ends from the mattress. 'But I do take messages and parcels for him.'

'Why? Do you know what's in them?'

224

'If I tell you, do you promise not to tell anyone else?'

'I'm not sure—'

'You have to promise, or I can't tell you.'

Curiosity got the better of her. 'Cross my heart.'

'He's a Catholic. He sends books and papers to the colonies, and to the Catholic embassies. It is a network. There are many Catholics, all over London.'

'But it's illegal. You know that, don't you?'

'I know it. But I must do it for M'sieur. M'sieur Hubert is my friend. He helps me read my letters from Mamma, because I can't read. He is a good man, I swear. But now I'm worried that they will find out he is Catholic and take him away.'

'Did you tell the constable anything?'

'No. But I know they watch me. I feel their eyes everywhere. And Viner, he is a friend of this Constable Garrod. He drinks with him and that hog-faced Bludworth, the mayor. It makes me uneasy.'

'Be careful, Livvy. If you get mixed up in any Catholic plot, it will mean arrest. Especially if the mayor and the constable are involved. And they're never kind to women, especially—'

'Don't say it, black people. I know. So how is life on stage?'

She was changing the subject, but there was little Bird could do. She sat down next to Livvy. 'It's good news. It's taken months, but Killigrew's finally raised enough money to produce his play of all women, and I will have a part where I get to speak as well as sing.'

'You were a treat in *The Silent Woman*,' Livvy said. 'So proud. So upright. It surprise me. You were right, it suits you being a player. But I don't know how you persuaded Knepp.'

'By tying my profession to his business. He's not enamoured of it, though. He tolerates my playing just as long as I bring in the custom for the horse-hires. I have to mention Knepp's at every turn. But it's a small price to pay.'

'What about old Widow Knepp?'

'Just the same. Feigning weakness when I know she's tough as old leather. She thinks I'm out ordering the Christmas goose. Lord knows where she puts all the food; she's still thin as a stick. But it would be a miserable Yuletide without some festive fare. Knepp is so unbending, and we never entertain. I tell you, Livvy, without the theatre, I swear I'd just wither away from lack of a happy face.'

'But you prosper more than before?'

'Knepp buys more horses. We have twenty-five now. But somehow, it never pleases him; the more successful he gets, the more miserable he gets. And the house itself looks just the way it always has. Mrs Knepp begged him for new drapes and he gave her a shilling. A shilling! I ask you. I bought a cushion instead, and he wasn't amused. But now I can get away from him, at least some of the day. Lord, how I wish I was rich, and could buy myself a billet somewhere else. I think of my father, and how he lives, and it makes me want to spit.'

A noise from below made Livvy leap up. She hurried to the window. 'Quick. It's the Viners' carriage. He mustn't find you here, or I don't know what he'll do.'

'I wish you a merry Christmas,' Bird said. She reached out to give her a quick embrace.

'Season's wishes to you too.' Livvy gave her a rueful smile and a brief hug then hurried out and locked the door. Her expression had changed to one of desperation. 'Please, go now.'

Bird hurried downstairs, and out into the frosty yard.

Livvy followed behind with the armful of sheets and turned sharply round the corner to the wash-house.

It made Bird ache inside to see her run like that. Livvy looked so alone, and the thought of all those powerful men, like the mayor and the constable, persecuting her, made her long to smash something. But it was dangerous to dabble with anyone involved with the Romish church, and she hoped M'sieur Hubert was really as kind as Livvy believed.

She was just thinking that when she saw Viner striding towards her. Hastily she pulled up her hood and hurried out of the entrance, but not before she saw him go in the office building. Moments later, Viner's white, pudgy face appeared at Livvy's window. It must be hers – the end window. What was he doing in Livvy's room? He yanked the curtain shut, and the window became a black hole. She supposed he had a key. But why did he need to draw the curtain in the daytime? Did Livvy know he was there? Something about it didn't seem right.

She hurried back and round to the wash-house. Livvy was just thrusting the sheets into the steaming copper.

'Livvy, I just saw Mr Viner in your chamber.'

She stood back to upright, eyes scared. 'You're mistaken. He hasn't got a key.'

'I swear it. I saw his face at your window.'

'Can't have.'

'Well, I just thought you should know, that's all.'

An awkwardness arose between them that hadn't been there before. 'Thank you,' Livvy said stiffly. 'Now get yourself away, I've my work to do.'

But as she walked away, Bird couldn't help feeling uneasy.

CHAPTER 16

Seething Lane, February 1665

Elisabeth examined herself in the looking glass. In the last few weeks the yellowish bruising around her eye had completely gone. She was able to go abroad now, without everyone staring. Over Christmas she'd become tired of the neighbours' knowing looks, tired of pretending she had fallen into a door. Samuel's shifting gaze alone was enough to tell everyone that his fists were the cause of it.

Now she put down the glass and wondered if she dared go out unaccompanied for dinner. She had had words with Jane, the cook-maid, only the night before, because Jane'd been prattling about Samuel and Mrs Bagwell, implying some sort of dalliance between them. Incensed, she'd dismissed her. Good riddance. She'd never liked the woman anyway. Didn't like the way Jane looked down on her. Of course Jane was taller, but did she need to keep that scornful look on her face? Maids shouldn't be allowed to be tall and look down on their mistresses.

But it still left a problem with her dinner. Samuel was out today which was a blessing, dining with his Uncle Wight, so he wouldn't care, though he'd been annoyed when she told him Jane had gone. He'd always liked her. But then Samuel liked any woman who smiled at him, Elisabeth thought grimly, tying on a woollen cap over her coif, and teasing the ringlets out to hang becomingly over her ears.

There, she was ready. She damped the fire and covered it with the *garde-feu*, bracing herself for the February chill. She would be daring and go out to dine alone, to the bakery on Pudding Lane to treat herself to a calf's foot pie. Samuel hated them, but they reminded her of her childhood in France. And then another thought occurred to her – she could visit Edlyn, the astrologer. Mrs Pierce had recommended him; 'I decide nothing without Edlyn, my dear,' she'd said.

In the hallway Elisabeth put on her warm cloak, and hung her velvet muff around her neck on its cord. She looked for the house-boy to tell him she was going out for dinner, but then remembered; he'd gone with Samuel today. With Jane gone, and little Besse's day off, she was alone in the house.

It felt odd to lock the door herself, as if she was suddenly untethered, drifting. She wondered what would happen if she never came back. Not much, probably. Samuel would replace her with another woman easily enough. He'd find another

Jane to cook his food, and a willing maid to warm his bed.

Elisabeth wrapped her cloak tighter around her as she made her way down Seething Lane towards Thames Street. She was convenient, that was all. And the child-bearing years were passing. She felt the possibility of each child, like a ghost passing away, every year. At first she had not worried, but now it was nine years, and she veered between desperation and hope.

Each time her monthly bleed arrived, and no child, it made her feel more like a failure. Their friends were all dandling their children in front of her. Every woman she met seemed to be in confinement, big with child, or waiting for her churching, when she'd be 'clean' enough to come forth after childbirth. Mrs Pierce, not content with being the most beautiful woman in their circle, and with setting Samuel's eyes on stalks, seemed to be in a continual round of fertile production these last five years, with barely room to breathe – like a constant reminder to the whole assembly of Elisabeth's increasingly obvious inadequacy.

As she walked down the frost-rimed street, she wondered if it was her, or Samuel. The desire to know consumed her. She wouldn't blame him, but she would just like to know. If she could wager on such a thing, she'd wager it was when he had had his operation. Such a lot of chopping about *down there* to get the stone out.

Last night in bed she had asked him, 'Do you

think it could be because of your stone, when they cut for it, perhaps—'

'Nonsense. I'm as fit as ever I was. You must try to be calm. Worry only makes it less likely.'

She felt as if it was her fault then, and turned away from him, banging the bolster with her fists.

'Why can't you be patient?' Samuel asked, irritably. 'Children will come in God's own time, and besides, they are a mortal trouble when they do.'

But they hadn't come. God was certainly taking his time. And without a child, she felt as if she was disappearing. What was a woman *for*, with no child? But maybe Edlyn would have an answer for her in the stars, and know who was at fault, and tell her which days were auspicious for . . . that business. Elisabeth headed for the city walls with a new sense of purpose.

She turned down Little Eastcheap, past the butchers with their flitches of bacon, to emerge behind the Star Inn and Farriner's bakery on Pudding Lane. It was busy as usual with red-cheeked apprentices buying their dinners. Samuel used Farriner's to supply the Navy with bread and the dried stuff they called hard-tack, but it was best known to locals for its hot pies. She queued against the wall with the rest, where she could feel the heat of the ovens through the brick, and smell the savoury salty smell of pastry baking. When she got to the front, Hanna, the daughter, served her as usual. She watched as she pulled the pie out of the oven, dislodging a coal. Hanna kicked at the glowing ember with her boot until it turned grey, then trod the sparks to dust in the sawdust.

Seeing she was alone, with no maid to carry for her, Hanna wrapped the calf's foot pie in paper and put it in a paper bag with a string for a handle. Elisabeth could hardly wait to tear it open, but forced herself to find a spot in an alley near the Thames where she could eat it un-noticed.

She bit into it and let the salty juices run into her mouth. Samuel would reprimand her if he saw her eating like a peasant in the street, but the pleasure was all the sweeter because it was forbidden. Oh, the bliss of that hot trickle of savoury gravy on a freezing day! After she'd licked her fingers, and wiped her chin, she felt more cheerful and made her way to Edlyn's, above the Four Swans in Bishopgate Street. On a swinging sign above the tavern, a blue, painted hand with an outstretched finger pointed upwards, to shutters helpfully emblazoned with a moon and stars.

Elisabeth hitched her skirts and made her way down the side alley to find the stairs. At the top of the staircase she paused in front of a low dark door, to read the ragged notice pasted there.

Richard Edlyn Esq.
Available each day between nine and five for the astrological judgement of diseases, nativities, and horary questions. All enquiries strictly confidential. Enquire within.

She didn't knock, but just walked in. The man she presumed to be Mr Edlyn had his feet on the desk and a plate of eels in his hand. The nest of papers on his desk seemed to already be suffering from the remains of other dinners. Behind the desk, a coal fire glowed with an orange heat, and the fishy smell of eels pervaded the room.

Edlyn, a bug-eyed man with receding hair, leapt up, swallowing hastily, and dumped the plate on top of his hat which lay on the chair beside him. A quick wipe over his drooping moustache with his sleeve, and then he ushered her into the seat opposite.

'Pardon me for interrupting, Mr Edlyn. Your sign led me to think—'

'Yes, yes. Always open. The stars never cease moving, and we must move with them. What can I do for you, Mrs . . .?'

'Brown.' She dare not use her real name. If word were to get back to Samuel, he would be most displeased. He didn't hold with what he called 'fortune-telling'. He prided himself on his scientific knowledge. Scientific knowledge which didn't extend as far as where to find his clean shirt.

She leant forward. 'I hear you can cast a horoscope. I need to know if I will . . . if I will bear children.'

'You have no children now?'

'No.'

'Then you are indeed fortunate. This is a year

234

of trial and tribulation. Have you not read any of my pamphlets?'

'No, I don't think I—'

He jumped up and searched the bookcase behind him, which was stuffed with piles of chapbooks and pamphlets. On the wall next to it was a painted glyph of the planets, each with a symbol next to it; the scales, the virgin, a horned goat. On top of the bookcase was a lop-sided broken stand with a dusty brass telescope, and a brass calendar showing last week's date. Not good signs, she thought.

But by now, Edlyn was talking at her very slowly as if explaining to a simpleton. 'The last time there was a conjunction like this, plague appeared in London. I warned people, but nobody would listen. And now, word of it is in every tavern.'

'Are you sure? I mean . . . I have heard nothing and—'

'Already St Giles is rife with plague, so I hear. They try to suppress the news, but the stars are quite clear on the matter. Not only that, but there are signs of a great conflagration. My advice to you would be to forget about the idea of children, and to sequester yourself in the country. The city is in grave danger, but will they listen? Pah. I can't even get an audience at court.' He leant over the desk towards her. 'Our lordly monarch saw fit to disband the Society of Astrologers and now he relies on the Royal Society for the Advancement of Science. Doesn't he know that science and astrology are one and the same?'

During this impassioned speech, Elisabeth watched the greyish juice from the tilted plate seep into Mr Edlyn's hat. That, and the thought of the plague, made her nauseous.

He would calculate her chart; she was determined. 'But won't you look at my chart, Mr Edlyn? Perhaps that might tell me whether to leave for the country, or no.' Or perhaps her future was in France?

He sighed. 'Place of birth?'

'Bideford, Devonshire.'

'Date?'

'23rd day of October, 1640.'

'Ah. Sign of the Scorpion. Just over the cusp. Unusual.' His face became more animated, and he drew out a sheet of paper and cleared a space on his desk. 'You may come back later this afternoon; it will take a few hours for me to draw up the chart, and then . . . well we shall see what we shall see.'

Elizabeth settled back in the chair and folded her arms. 'I'll wait.'

'Wait? But Mrs Brown, it will take me until at least four o'clock. These things can't be rushed; accuracy is everything.'

'Don't mind me, Mr Edlyn. I have nothing pressing to do. I'll wait, as I'm paying you for your time.'

'Oh.' Mr Edlyn's face fell, but he could hardly disagree. She watched him pick up his plate again and grimace as he saw what it had done to his hat. He reddened as he wiped the brim on his sleeve. 'You could do some errands; as I said, it will take a few hours.'

'I'll wait,' she insisted.

She watched him sigh and consign his plate to the wicker basket by his desk which was almost overflowing with papers. She was aware of his discomfort, but had no desire to move on. She watched his scribbling, his frantic drawing with a metal compass, and his listing of calculations with interest.

After a mere half-hour, he announced, 'It's finished.'

'Already?' Elisabeth blinked. 'And?'

'Well, it really is most interesting. You are married to someone whose fame—'

'Never mind about him. Will I have children?'

Edlyn cleared his throat and looked at the floor. 'No. No children. Your husband . . .'

Disappointment swamped her like a cold wave. She knew it was coming, but somehow, no amount of armour could protect her heart from those words.

'A relief, I'd say,' Edlyn continued in a placatory voice, 'because as I said—'

'I know, I know,' she said huffily, 'plague and hellfire are coming.' She stood and brushed down her skirts.

'Wait! Mrs Brown! I haven't finished.'

'Your office smells of fish,' she said, choked.

'Mrs Brown, perhaps my interpretation is wrong, perhaps there are children after all . . .'

She looked back at him with a look that could freeze. 'Do not take me for a fool, Mr Edlyn. There will be no children. That's what you said.'

He held out his scribbled maps and pieces of parchment towards her, 'But, Mrs Brown, if you'd only look—'

She snatched them from his hands. '*This* is what I think of your chart!' she tore the papers in half. 'And *this*! And *this*!' The rasp of the tearing filled the silent room. She threw the remnants towards him. His face sagged into a white mask of disbelief.

Elisabeth didn't wait. She heard Edlyn protesting and his footsteps pounded down the stairs after her, but she ran up the road clutching her skirts as if hounds were baying for her blood. She had never run so fast, her breath spurting in gasps.

'I hate you,' she wheezed, when she finally came to a stop. 'I hate you!' Who, she did not know. Edlyn, Samuel, the whole world.

No children. He'd said the words. The world had become empty and pointless in an instant. She turned. Edlyn was nowhere in sight. He would have to whistle for his money; she'd never go back there, not for all the tea in the Orient.

Instead, she set off clutching the stitch in her side, to the offices at Seething Lane. The great collection of brick buildings that was home to all the business of the Navy. The buildings that dwarfed their house, which was a small apartment within the vast number of offices and official residences. The Navy was drowning them, she thought. Their marriage was squashed by all this business, and she, Elisabeth, was the least important part of this lumbering ship of which her husband was supposedly the captain.

CHAPTER 17

March 1665

The inside of St Paul's Church buzzed like a hive of black bees. Every spare seat was occupied by knots of gesticulating men, and the aisle thronged with dark-cloaked merchants and worried traders, all clutching the latest broadsheets.

Livvy, who was merely passing through on her way to the tannery with a broken bridle, spoke to one of the servants hanging around the font. 'What's to do?' She put the sack holding the bridle on the floor to rest her arms. 'Is it the plague? Has it spread?'

'We're at war.' He smacked his lips, satisfied.

'With the French?'

'No. The Dutch. The bleeding Hogen Mogens.' His tone spoke his disgust. 'About time too. My master says they've been opening fire on our ships in the Channel for no reason. Bastards.'

Livvy grabbed her sack, clutched it to her chest, and backed away, her thoughts reeling. It couldn't be true. They couldn't be at war with the Dutch

240

again. It was what she'd been dreading. *For no reason*, the boy said. Yet everyone knew more than two hundred Dutch ships had already been captured from the colonies and brought into English ports. She'd seen them herself, and witnessed the celebrations on the Thames, whilst mourning each one of her poor nameless drowned countrymen. But nobody mentioned them.

Beside her, a be-wigged merchant let out a throaty laugh, at the news that the English had insulted the Dutch again. Livvy bristled. If ships met in neutral waters, the Dutch were supposed to raise their flag to salute the English first. A treaty of law had been passed to say so. But recently, English sailors had deliberately provoked the Dutch, by thumbing their noses and not saluting in return.

'The beggars! It knew it would lead to trouble,' the merchant said, eyes full of glee.

Such a small, petty thing could start a war? She pinned back her ears to try to learn more. It was so frustrating not to be able to read. From another man, she heard that the Dutch government had tried to calm the hot tempers by ordering its men to continue saluting first, but many Dutch commanders could not bear to, and refused. And who could blame them?

Every way she turned there were men talking of the Dutch as if they were savages. 'Butterboxes', they called them, because of them keeping dairy herds, but it made her people sound fat and greasy, and lacking in brains.

If they were at war, her life would be harder from now on; without doubt. It would be even more dangerous to be Dutch. What would she do if she was to be found out? Around her the men were discussing what this would all mean for trade; how much money would be lost, whether it was worth speculating on spices, and whether they would be able to ply their usual routes.

They were like vultures pecking at a corpse. She shot out of there into the squally rain, and hurried to M'sieur Hubert's shop on Tinker's Alley.

'Soon as I heard, I knew you'd come.' He looked up from his scatter of glinting watch parts as Livvy appeared.

'What shall I do?'

'Nothing.' He sighed and put his tweezers down. 'There's nothing you can do.' He stood up with difficulty and limped over to put a hand on her shoulder.

It brought water to her eyes and a lump to her throat. She shrugged away, unwilling to show emotion. Servants were expected to have faces that revealed nothing, and it was a hard habit to break. 'No letters, I suppose.'

'No. And you can't send them either.' He caught hold of her hand. 'But she'll understand why.' His eyes were warm with sympathy. He was not an attractive man, everything about him was nondescript, except his limp. But he had a kind face, she realised. It was something she hadn't really noticed before. She looked down at her dark hand, the way it sat in his soft white one. He squeezed.

'I wish I could go home,' Livvy said.

'*Non, ma chérie. Pas possible.* Not until this war, she is over. It was the same for me, when they were at war with my country. And last year it was the Spaniards. The English, they love being at war. It will end soon, and they will find another country to fight.'

She turned to face him. 'My mother will worry if my letters stop.' She took a sharp breath as she felt her eyes prick. 'And me so useless with no lettering.'

Hubert passed her the small cloth he used to polish his watch dials. 'Don't cry.'

'I'm not crying.' She pulled away from him and turned her back to sniff and wipe her face with her sleeve.

'I can't scribe for you now, though. All letters going to the Dutch will be intercepted.'

'Oh.' There was a silence as they both considered this. Livvy realised there would be no more excuses to come here to M'sieur Hubert's shop. He had been part of her life, a regular occurrence, for six years. The thought of it stopping gave her a tight feeling in her throat.

She reached out to his desk and picked up a delicate flywheel from a watch, laid it on the palm of her hand, where it was light as a moth. He was so clever. He fitted all these tiny intricate parts together to make a machine that went all by itself, and had its own little heartbeat. She loved to see him pick up the tiny cogwheels that were jewels in themselves, or see his long fingers turn the miniature screws that held together the case.

If she stayed long enough she'd hear all his little bells ping the hour, and that was her favourite part of her visits; that and his smiling welcome. She would miss him. He was the only person who spoke to her as if her opinion was important.

She put the flywheel back down, aware she had not spoken for a while. 'Then I suppose there is no need that I bother you again, M'sieur Hubert.'

'Robert. Call me Robert.' He pronounced the word, 'Rob-air'. He paused, and then his voice came again, softer. 'How will this suit? You keep coming like you always do, and I can read you the news-sheets instead of the letters. Tell you how the war goes.'

'Would you?' She looked back at him to see his face had turned blotchy and pink.

'Assuredly, I would.'

'Then I thank you most kindly, M'sieur . . . Robert.'

He smiled, and the smile lit up his eyes, turned them blue as cornflowers. It gave Livvy a feeling, deep in her chest that she had never known before. As they stood smiling in the dingy shop, the watches began to chime the hour like bells.

CHAPTER 18

'Here's your part in Dryden's new one,' Mrs Corey said, leaning forward from her chair to pass Bird the master script. 'You've to copy your part ready for Monday. It's the beginning and end, and then the dancing spirit in the middle.'

Bird took it and thumbed through the pages, searching for her name beside the lines. '*The Indian Emperour*,' she read. Only a few lines top and bottom by her name, and none at all through the text. 'Am I only to have the sung Prologue and Epilogue?' she asked, disappointed.

'You have a fine voice, it will suit you well. And you've good legs for dancing. There's a dancing tableau, with you and Nell as ghostly spirits.'

Ghostly spirits? Was she destined never to speak as a character on stage? Bird stood up and paced up and down the chamber, which was still chill as no fire had been lit. 'I'd hoped to have a speaking part,' she blurted out. 'I should have been Lucetta in *Thomaso*, and Nell was to be the courtesan, but then Killigrew cancelled it. I couldn't believe it, not after all our work.'

'Blame Hart and Mohun. And Sedley, too. I've found out what happened. It appeared the men created a stink because there were no parts for them, and they threatened they'd go over to the Duke's Company, unless Killigrew reconsidered. His idea of putting on an all-woman play really riled them all. If you ask me, they were cowards – afeared it would be too much of a success.'

'But it's not fair! We women get hardly any lines as it is.'

'Tush, girl. You don't know you're born. When I was your age, Cromwell was in charge. There were no plays allowed at all, and certainly no acting parts for women. So think yourself fortunate. Anyway, London needs something cheerful, now the Dutch are after our throats, and there's to be a grotto scene, with spirits making incantations, and fountains spouting real water.' She pointed to the corner. 'If you want cheering, go take a look over there at what Killigrew's friend, Mrs Behn, has brought back from her travels.'

Bird walked over to the wicker travelling basket and creaked it open to reveal a gaudy mass of feathers, with colours bold enough to make her eyes hurt. She lifted out the shimmering cloak, and realised how it would impress an audience. But the dazzle of it made her uncomfortable. She wanted to speak truth, to be a real person on stage, like the first play she ever saw, not more of this show and pretence.

'Who else is to play in it?' Bird asked, stroking the iridescent feathers of the cloak.

'Mohun will be the Emperor, Hart will play Cortez, and Kynaston's coming in to play Guyomar. Stefan tried for it, but Killigrew still won't have him back.'

'Huh. I should have guessed. All men, then.'

'No. Mrs Marshall will be Almeria. And of course you will start and end the play.'

'But what about you? What role have you?'

Mrs Corey pressed her lips together a moment. 'Nothing this time. I'm too old for dancing, and there's no role for an older woman. Tom Killigrew told me this morning.' She sighed. 'The audience want young, beautiful women, not old broilers like me, and the time had to come, I suppose. They'd rather make a young woman look old, than use a genuine mature woman. So I've been given my marching orders.'

'What? For good?'

'Fraid so, ducks.'

'But that's unfair. You've been here for years. Here am I complaining, when you haven't even got a part at all. What will you do?'

'Oh, something will come along. I could try the Duke's.'

They looked at each other. Both knew she wouldn't. It would be like admitting failure to their arch rivals.

'See, I had my chance, and I never made much of it, to be honest. I kept thinking that the big

247

part would come, that I'd be famous, that I'd have the audience right there.' She pointed to the palm of her hand. 'But it never quite happened. I never got to be the lead, never made much money neither, and now I wonder what all those wasted years were for.'

'Don't talk like that! Every person in a play is valuable. Even the courtiers and the servants give the thing life. And it can't happen at all unless everyone pulls together.'

Mrs Corey shook her head sadly. 'My time's up. But you'll sing your Prologue and Epilogue like it's the only thing that matters, won't you, ducks? Whilst you've still got the chance.'

'Oh, Mrs Corey.' Bird sat down next to her and wrapped her arms around her large back. 'I'll miss you in rehearsal,' Bird said.

'And I'll miss you, ducks. But I'll find something. You know they can't keep me away from those boards. You just get on that stage, miss, and make us all proud.'

Later, as she learned her two songs, she couldn't help thinking about Mrs Corey, and wondering how she would feel if she spent her life playing prologues and epilogues, and never had the chance to show what she could really do. The fear of it wormed deep inside. What if she was never the talk of the town? What if her father never heard of her again?

She made a detour on the way home and went into Hardman's the booksellers by St Paul's. After browsing the shelves, she bought a book for orators and actors called *The Natural Language of the Hand*. It showed how to convey reason and feeling by the use of gesture, all illustrated by woodcut pictures. She took a sixpence from her purse, and passed it over. Knepp always checked her wages, so she'd say Mrs Knepp's laundry bills had gone up. He'd never know.

She bounded from the shop clutching the precious parcel to her chest. She'd have to study it hard. She didn't intend to be one of those posterity had forgotten. No, she would not be full of regrets like Mrs Corey.

June 1665

The Indian Emperour was a great success, and ran for weeks. Many remarked on how sweetly Bird sang, and the gracefulness of her gestures, though she wished for a more substantial role. Again, she had seen the Peeps gentleman staring up at her from the pit. She asked Killigrew about him, and he said his name was spelled 'Pepys' and he was a friend of the king, and had always been an ardent theatre-goer. She felt vaguely let down that it was the plays, and not her own person, that held the attraction.

Still, the King's Company had managed to hold their own against their arch-rivals, the Duke's, who were staging the popular *Mustapha* as part of their summer repertoire. Knepp's hire business continued to flourish, and with his new clientele, began to even rival Viner's.

Bird hurried down Drury Lane towards the theatre, avoiding the centre of the thoroughfare where flies gathered around the rotting ordure, putrid in the heat. She could tolerate her situation at home, as long as she could escape to the glow of the candles, the soaring viols, and the glisten of sweat on paint.

She was glad to get away from old Mrs Knepp, who was a permanent fixture now. Knepp's brother's legs had not set well, and the poor man had been confined to a wheeled chair, so Knepp had no alternative but to keep his mother at Smithfield. Her distress, and the fact she was to stay, had at last managed to persuade Knepp to install a few home comforts, like a rocking chair, and thicker curtains for the windows.

Bird glanced up. A storm was coming. The sky was the colour of old pewter and the clouds hung thick as curds above the skyline of steeples and chimneys. Even in her summer linen Bird was already perspiring just from the walk from Knepp's. Her stays pinched and rubbed, and in the distance she heard rumbling, and a crack that could have been thunder or could have been Dutch cannon fire.

Grinstead had told her that morning that the English fleet had sailed out from Solebay and were chasing the Dutch out to sea. On his way to work he'd passed crowds gathered along the

250

Thames waiting for news of their menfolk, but so far there was no news of a victory, and all the city was on tenterhooks, in case London should be invaded.

As Bird turned into Drury Lane she recited her lines under her breath. *The Indian Emperour* was to finish, and Bird was anxious to rehearse her new role, an actual speaking part in which she was to play a merry wife. A crowd gathered on the opposite pavement made her hesitate. Were they staring at her?

She glanced behind her, momentarily confused. Then she saw it.

The door behind her was daubed with a ragged red cross. She flinched and stepped away. The paint was still congealing and glistened too brightly on this muggy day. Someone had scrawled 'Lord Have Mercy upon Us' in black coal on the window shutters which were tight shut.

Plague. Oh Lord, not here.

It was too close. Too close to the theatre.

She moved to the opposite side of the street, but the knot of people had moved off. She saw them look across again and followed their gaze.

Three more houses with the red daub dripping. She started to run.

The heavens opened and raindrops the size of bees began to fall. Ducking her head, she arrived breathless and bedraggled at the stage door, and shaking off the wet, made her way down the corridor. She glanced into the theatre, but it was empty and there were no scene-shifters getting ready for the performance, and the Italian designer was nowhere to be seen. Where was everyone? She clattered up the stairs to the rehearsal room. As soon as she pushed open the door, she knew it was not good news by the fact that the whole company was there, mired in gloomy silence.

Killigrew was staring morosely out of the window. He didn't turn as she came in.

'You've seen it then,' she said to Mohun. 'The doors on Drury Lane.'

'It's worse than that,' Mohun said. 'We're to be closed down.'

'What?'

'All public gatherings are forbidden. By order of the king.' Mohun shrugged, but there were lines of tension between his eyebrows.

'That includes us,' Nell said cheerfully.

'But we have the King's Livery, and he promised us his support, he can't just leave us with no livelihood,' Anne Marshall said.

'Oh, yes he can, if it's a case of saving his own skin,' Hart said. 'The king's going to Salisbury, and then on to Oxforde.'

'But what will we do?' Bird was seized by cold panic. 'What about our play?'

'I'll try to persuade him he'll need entertainment in Oxforde of course,' Hart said. 'Isn't that right, Killigrew?'

Killigrew turned. He looked old and haggard, his Indian robes suddenly appearing tawdry and limp. 'All that work. And for what? All wiped out in a day.'

'Not if I can help it.' Hart stood up and threw open his arms. 'We must petition the king. Get ourselves lodgings near the court in Oxforde. What say you all?'

Bird's heart froze. Knepp would never give his permission for her to go to Oxforde. And he would never leave his horses.

'But what about today?' Peg Hughes asked. 'Will we still play this afternoon?'

Killigrew held up the paper dangling with its royal seal and shook it. '*From henceforth*, it says. There'll be no more plays until this curse is lifted from us. You can all go home. First the Dutch, now this.'

'No,' Bird said, unable to take it all in. 'Can't we petition the king to reconsider?'

Several people laughed and Bird lowered her gaze, feeling small and foolish.

'It's not just that,' Mohun said. 'Now there's plague in Drury Lane we'll get no audience neither. Didn't you hear? The mayor's forbidden gatherings.'

There was a hubbub then, of everyone speaking at once. Hart trying to persuade people to sign a letter to the king, Nell saying she'd always wanted to go to Oxforde, and Anne Marshall warning everyone not to tarry but to leave London before they were struck down themselves.

'Go!' Killigrew shouted. 'Get out of here. I can't

253

bear to listen to you all. Bunch of chattering monkeys. I'll send a message if you are required.'

Still gesticulating and arguing, they went from the room. Anne Marshall, purveyor of ever-sensible advice, took Bird by the arm and led her downstairs. 'Keep out of company,' she said. 'It will pass, as it always does, but make sure you're not one of those it settles on. Wash in vinegar and breathe only sweet smells.'

But Bird barely heard her. 'You go on ahead,' she said. 'I just need a few moments to take it in.'

Anne Marshall squeezed her arm, 'Go safe,' she said as she headed out into the rain.

The theatre was cool and dark as Bird pushed past the curtain to the pit, and made her way towards the cone of daylight which poured through the roof. Nobody had closed the roof shutter, and rain was pouring in. It reminded her of the illustration in her mother's Bible where God sends his shaft of light down to earth. She climbed the stairs from the auditorium and stood in the pool of light, rain falling over her shoulders, gazing out at the empty rows. The silence was heartbreaking.

What would she do, with no work? With no theatre open, how would Knepp's fare? The whole yard relied on the custom from the theatre. All the stable-boys and grooms. The idea of going back to cleaning saddlery in Knepp's dark tack room, and worse, to spend time with only Knepp and his mother for company made her despair. Already she felt stifled; as if she couldn't breathe.

How long would the theatre have to be closed? If Knepp's found some other trade she might never be allowed to come back. She might never be able to sing on this stage again. A lump came to her throat. Just when she was starting to feel like she *was* someone, the plague had turned her back to nobody.

She would have to make sure she went to Oxforde, with the company. Not to, would be like putting a nail in her own coffin. At the edge of the stage she wound the handle that worked the pulley for the roof shutter. Above her, it closed like an eye, blocking off the light.

CHAPTER 19

News of the plague had come to Ted Viner's yard, and two smiths were fitting a set of large iron gates to the entrance, with the aim of making his premises secure. The Bills of Mortality had confirmed plague in St Giles, and already, now the rain had stopped, people desperate to flee the city crowded the yard, wanting to hire a horse and not bring it back. He feared someone might try to steal a horse. Ted watched the queues with satisfaction. As horseflesh grew scarcer, and every other carrier left London, he could profit handsomely. He hoped the plague had got to Knepp's. If it had, he could buy up his stock. That man was a thorn in his side, a bloody nuisance, always copying everything he did.

He shouted instructions to the ironmongers installing two troughs just inside the gates. These were to hold vinegar for washing. There would be no more paying guests, he knew. He gave orders to take down the lodgings sign and put it in the lumber room. No-one would pay to come and stay in London, and he'd best get someone to clear the rooms and distemper them. Livvy could clean them when she got back from the morning errands. The thought of her face made him angry; she was so closed and still, with her eyes always shifting away from him. There'd be no work for her with no paying guests, so he'd have to think of another excuse to keep her on.

He'd best lock up the rooms on both floors whilst he was about it. On the upper floor at the end of the corridor, he paused outside Livvy's door, the temptation strong in his loins. He pushed against the door. Locked as usual. He slid his bunch of keys from his belt and finding the correct key, turned it in the door. When he went in, he inhaled deeply. There was a sweet smell in the room as usual. Was that what black women smelt like? He was curious.

The room was tidy, the bed neatly made, with a pair of worn felted slippers standing by it, as if she had just slipped them off her feet. He picked one up, rubbed his thumb along the worn spot at the heel, brought it to his nose. It smelt of dust and the wool it was woven from; he wanted it to smell of her. He longed for the musky smell of sweat, for the feeling she had stood there inside them in her night things, her body black as a devil inside the white of the shift.

He prowled to the end of the bed where her trunk rested, solid and wooden like all servants' boxes. It had no lock; they never did. Servants were expected to leave their trunks open, to deter thieving. He lifted it open as he had done the other times he'd been here, and a small maggot of guilt squirmed in his chest. He ignored it. She was a servant, and a Negress, with no right to complain. Not a slave, though the thought of that excited him. He imagined her manacled, begging at his feet.

The trunk held her few underclothes, but that was all. They were always meticulously folded. He let his fingers trail down the length of a stocking, surprised at how illicit it felt as he imagined it was her leg. He strolled to the window and pulled the curtain across.

What did she need with all these horse-shoes? Some superstitious hoodoo, perhaps. He went back to lock the door, leaving the keys dangling in the lock. Holding the stocking to his cheek, he began to rub himself. He lay down on her bed, imagining slipping himself inside her black nakedness. A rustle of paper. Curious, he threw back the covers but could see nothing, just an expanse of flat sheet. He felt along the sheet with a palm.

A crackle of papers under the sheets, and the bulge of something. He untucked the sheet and reached his arm under it, up to the elbow. What he drew out was a bundle of letters.

He saw that they were addressed to Livvy at a different address.

Care of Robert Hubert
Sign of the Hourglass
Tinker's Alley,
off Lombard Street
London

He unfolded one of the letters and spread it flat on the sheet. It was foreign. He stared at the loops of the letters, but couldn't make out the words. The writing style was unlike anything he was familiar with, and there were strange marks above the letters. It wasn't French, he knew that. Was it German? A different tongue; that much was certain. He squinted at the letters again, and it came to him suddenly. Why would she hide them, unless . . . unless this was Dutch.

England was at war with the Dutch. Why was Livvy receiving letters in Dutch? He opened another. They were all in the same hand, with the date written at the top and the same closing greeting. 'Mamma'. That word had to mean 'mother'.

Just then there was the rattle of a key and his keys jiggled in the lock. She was back. He heard her trying to turn her key, and a sigh of frustration that it would not work. He didn't bother to hide the letters, but walked over to the door and unlocked it. When the door opened her eyes dilated in shock, but then she took a step backwards onto the landing.

'Come in,' he said.

She shook her head, but he grabbed her arm and yanked her over the threshold. He saw her gaze go to her open trunk, and then to where the letters were spread out on the bed.

Her mouth began to quiver. 'What you do in my room, sir?' she asked.

'I am checking that there are no Dutch spies on my premises; what do you think?'

A moment in which she looked desperately around the walls before she made a sudden move as if to bolt from the room, but he was too quick for her. He kept his grip, and dragged her back. Then he turned the key in the lock. He dangled the bunch of keys from his fingers. 'The letters are from your mother,' he said. 'So don't tell me they are not.'

'You can read Dutch?'

'Enough to tell me that. So the question is, what do you write to her in return?'

'I can't write. You know that.'

'But I presume that Robert Hubert, whoever he is, can. Is he a spy?'

'No. Not a spy, sir. I didn't know the English would want to fight my country.'

'Would the constable believe that, I wonder?'

'Please sir, I meant no harm. Only to be good daughter.'

'They hang spies, you know that. They would be interested to know about you and your friend Hubert.'

She ran her pink tongue around her lips. 'What do you want, sir?'

So she had seen it already, that there was a bargain to be had. He moved closer, traced a line around the base of her throat, down to the dark cleavage between her breasts. 'You know what I want.'

She backed away from him towards the door. He could see a slight sheen of sweat around her hairline, where the black furze of hair met the white coif. She was afraid.

'I do extra work,' she said. 'Shine your shoes, make cool drink. Will be nice on this hot afternoon. Lemon water, yes?'

'Extra work,' he agreed, pocketing the keys. 'Yes. But not those tasks. Unlace your stays.'

CHAPTER 20

'We can't pay the feed merchant, Mr Knepp,' Grinstead said. 'It looks bad. We've more horses than before, and no hires coming in.'

'It's not my fault the theatres are closed,' Knepp snapped. He blamed Mary Elizabeth for getting him in this mess, though he knew in his bones that was unfair. He'd bought too many horses, and if the theatre was shut there'd be not enough money coming in to feed them. The feckless king was leaving London, too. He wished he'd give some sort of useful guidance instead of taking his rakish rabble with him. Oh, how he loathed taking those fops in his carriages. He hated Viner's toadying to the aristocracy, yet here was he, unwittingly doing the same.

Over the next week more people begged him to sell his beasts so they could leave for the country. One by one, Knepp let the horses go, to people who were leaving London. The profit paid off the feed merchant, but now he was back where he'd started a year ago; mired in debt.

His mother was panicked by then, 'Can't we go too, son?' she asked.

'And leave our house to looters? No. That's just what Viner wants.'

'But what if we take sick?'

'We won't. I've never been ill in all my life.'

'Aye. You've a strong constitution,' she said. 'But age weakens a person. Won't you think of your poor old mother?'

'You'll be well enough here indoors. You never go abroad in the summer heat anyway.'

Mary Elizabeth came in from the brewhouse. She'd obviously overheard. 'We should go to Oxforde,' she said, 'to where the king is. There would surely be haulage work there, with all those fine dandies.' So she was determined to follow the players, was she? It made him even more reluctant.

'If Viner stays, we stay,' he said. 'Or I'll have no business to come back to.'

Part of him wondered why he couldn't stop being so awkward, but in truth, he'd forgotten how to be any other way. To concede to these women might seem weak.

One morning as he was passing through the yard on the way to the tack room, Dobbsy arrived looking grey and gaunt. 'It's Purler,' he said. 'He's gone.'

'What do you mean?' Knepp asked.

'The plague. His house is shut up and there's a cross on the door.'

'He's left London?'

'No sir . . . he's dead.'

Knepp stared at him in disbelief. 'Not Purler? But he was fit as a flea the day before yesterday.' He couldn't take it in. He heard himself say, 'It'll make more work for the rest of you.'

Dobbsy shrugged. 'And I think it only fair to tell you, me and my missus, well, we're going to my sister's.'

'Are you, indeed?' Knepp said, feeling panic flood through his veins. How would he keep afloat with no staff? 'If you leave now, there'll be no month's pay and no work for you when you come back,' he said.

'Don't be hasty, husband—' Mary Elizabeth was passing and had obviously heard the exchange.

Why was she always trying to interfere? 'Who runs this yard?' he asked. 'Keep out of it.'

'I should've known,' Dobbsy said. 'I've been a good worker all these years, yet you won't throw me a line when I need one.'

That was unfair. Knepp felt his temper rise. 'You've been a lazy worker, and you know it. Always taking the extra five minutes when you thought no-one could see. You're no loss to me.' He turned as if to walk away.

'And you're a tyrant and skinflint,' Dobbsy replied. 'No wonder Viner's does so much better than you.'

The barb hurt. He swivelled and his voice was low and hoarse. 'Get out. I don't want to clap eyes on your face again. And don't come grovelling to me for a horse or carriage to get you out of town;

if you love that bloated bullfrog Viner so much, you can go to him.'

Mary Elizabeth shook her head at him, as if he filled her with disgust, then walked away quickly to get out of his view. How had he got to be so despised? It had just happened, somehow, and he didn't know how to remedy it. Didn't know if he even *wanted* to remedy it.

Before the end of the day, Grinstead stuck his head around his office door to tell him two more of the grooms had also resigned their positions. Grinstead scuttled away as if he, too, was afraid of him. Knepp put his head in his hands over the desk and rubbed his forehead. What was he to do?

Two weeks later

'It seems the world's leaving London,' Mrs Knepp complained as Bird and Anis prepared the carrots and turnips. 'We're the only ones left here.'

'He won't give in,' Bird said, 'not unless Viner goes. You know what he's like. He's as stubborn as an old donkey. There'll be no jockey work here, though, if everyone flees the city.'

'Can't you find out if Viner has plans to leave?' Mrs Knepp asked. 'I'm afraid to stay here. I heard the passing bell tolling from St David's. It hasn't stopped all morning and it's only two streets away.'

'I don't know. I could ask Livvy. You know? The maidservant that used to work here? She works at

Viner's. I'll go in the morning and find out if Viner's following the court. I need a reason for Knepp to go to Oxforde.'

'His name's Christopher.'

'I'll see what I can find out.'

So the next day Bird went to find Livvy at Viner's. 'I wondered if you'd still be here,' she said, watching Livvy polishing the boot scraper by the office door. 'It seems like the last few weeks everyone's leaving.'

'Those that can afford it,' Livvy said, spitting into the rag again.

'Has Viner no plans to leave?'

'He's closing these rooms. No more paying travellers, so I've to clean them and shut them up.'

'He's staying?'

'He knows that as horses get scarcer, he can charge a bigger hire fee. He'll wait until the last minute. I can tell you something, though.'

'What?'

'He's after hiring stables in Oxforde, where the king's men will lodge.'

'The devil he is. How do you know?'

'He tell me. He likes to boast. He sent a letter this week, I had to post it.'

'Where? When will he leave? This week?'

'Soon as he has the stabling, I think.'

'Then we'll have to be ahead of him. And it suits my purpose. The playhouse is shut and I want to follow the king to Oxforde, but Knepp won't hear of it.'

Livvy glanced nervously over her shoulder, 'Let's get out of view.'

'Will you get in trouble if they see us talking?'

'Trouble, yes.' Livvy pulled her by the sleeve around the corner out of view of the yard.

'Is it M'sieur Hubert? Has the constable been again?'

A stubborn shake of the head.

'And Oxforde – will you tell me the name of where Viner'll stable his horses?'

Livvy twisted the rag in her hands. 'I can't. If I do, then he might not go after all, and I want him to go.'

'Why? What is it? Are you well, Livvy? You look thinner.'

'I'm well enough.' She dropped the rag back in the bucket.

'You'd tell me, wouldn't you, if there was something ailing you?'

Again, a shake of the head. 'There's nothing.'

But Bird could see that Livvy's face had lost its roundness, and that her hands now plucked nervously at her apron, as if she would have the conversation over quickly. She wondered if it was trouble at home.

'Have you heard from your mother recently?'

'No. But my elder brother has. He's in France. He write me and say Mamma worry about the war, that the English might come ashore. She say my little brother Jan is going to learn his letters so he will be able to write for her, instead of the white servant. He must be getting big now he's seven summers old.'

'You should learn your letters too, Livvy.'

'Me? Why would I? Then I would have no reason to go to see M'sieur Hubert.'

'Is it him? The problem, I mean?'

'No, no. M'sieur Hubert, he is . . .' She paused, thought a moment. 'He is good man. Kind. We have understanding.'

Bird gave her a knowing smile.

Livvy frowned. 'Not that kind of understanding.'

Bird laughed, but it wasn't reciprocated. The carefree Livvy was gone. 'I miss your company, Livvy.'

'And I yours.'

'I must go.' She moved back into the open space and Livvy followed.

As she turned to take her leave, she saw the anxious look had returned to Livvy's face.

'Farewell,' Bird said. 'I may not be able to visit for a while. As I say, I hope to go to Oxforde. Perhaps we'll be able to meet there, if Mr Viner goes there. Try to persuade him to take you with him.'

'No. If he goes, I'd rather stay here.'

'But—'

'I can't go.' Livvy's expression took on a sudden urgency.

'Why? It will just be until the plague lifts and then—'

But Livvy's eyes were fixed over her shoulder.

She swivelled, to see Ted Viner approaching from the offices behind them.

'Finished your duties?' he said to Livvy, with a raised eyebrow.

'Sorry sir, I was just doing the chambers and—'

'Mrs Knepp is not welcome here. I thought I'd made that clear. She will leave now, or I'll find a man to escort her. And Livvy, if you've spare time for gossip, I'll give you something worthwhile to keep you occupied.'

Bird did not like the way Viner took hold of Livvy's arm. But what made her most angry was Livvy's whole demeanour, which had become that of a slinking, cowering mouse. There was something here that was not right, and Bird suspected she knew what it was. A creeping rot festered behind Viner's clean and tidy façade, she'd swear it.

If only Knepp's could buy out Viner's.

July 1665

Bird walked to her father's house, just for a look, she told herself. She was anxious to know if he was all right, and whether he had been affected by the plague. In this area of London whole streets were deserted. Most of the street was shuttered. Even the top windows of her father's house had boards up, but there were no red crosses on the street. The rich men had obviously fled. She stood in the middle of the thoroughfare, staring at the blank façade, unable to believe he had actually gone without telling her.

Where had he gone? What if he never came back? Had he forgotten her to the extent that he couldn't even send a message? A panic assailed her. Perhaps he was on his way to see her right now. Yes, that was it. Their paths must have crossed.

She hurried home, but there was no sign of her father.

'Has my father been here? Mr Carpenter the lawyer?' she asked a stable-boy.

'No, Mistress. Nobody's been.'

The pit in the centre of her chest grew deeper. It was always with her now, this feeling of not belonging to anyone.

She went to search out Knepp, but he was in the office with Nipper and Grinstead. Again, she stood outside the door, invisible, listening to the men's voices within. Knepp had obviously had a swift change of heart. Nipper had already found out that Viner was trying to negotiate stabling in Oxforde, so Knepp was ordering them to take a coach and four to see what could be done.

Viner. Viner. Always that man. And nothing about him that was admirable, so far as she could see. Why must Knepp be always be snapping at his heels?

It wasn't until a few days later that she found out what the plans were for the theatre. She had just come back from the brewhouse with a jug of ale and had set it on the table where Mrs Knepp was feeding her canaries, her twisted, bumpy fingers somehow managing to hold a single seed.

'A man came knocking at our door, earlier,' Mrs Knepp said, turning. 'Strange-looking individual dressed like an Arab. I got Anis to deal with him.'

'Killigrew.'

'Yes. How can you take orders from such a peacock? He brought you a note. I told him to leave it there on the table. With the pestilence so rife, I didn't want to touch it, in case it was tainted. Can't be too careful, can you?'

'No other letters?' Was it foolish to hope she'd hear from Father?

She opened it and read:

'The company leave for Oxforde on Friday by Royal Warrant. Men will lodge at the Black Boar on Corne Market, ladies with a Mrs Tennent on Eastgate. Mrs Marshall is already gone and will join us there. Rehearsal will be in the rooms above, in Convocation House. I urge you to reply with all haste whether or no you will be in our company. If so, coach will leave Drury Lane at 7 matins. We are to play nightly and will need our full repertoire. God save the King.

Killigrew'.

'What says he?' Mrs Knepp asked.

'It's about the players going to Oxforde. I'll have to persuade Knepp.'

'You won't leave me here alone, will you? James

was always leaving me on my own. Everyone's always so busy. Nobody has any time for me any more.'

'I'm sure he won't leave you, Mrs Knepp, don't worry.'

Bird was crossing the yard with a bucket of corn when Grinstead returned from Oxforde. She slowed on purpose so as to discover the outcome. Knepp, too, who was curry-combing a horse, had heard the carriage, and he leaned over the stable door to see who had arrived.

'Did you find us stabling in Oxforde?' Knepp asked, flapping away wisps of gingery horsehair.

'An old farm, right near the river close to the castle. On the edge of the open ground they call Paradise Fields,' Grinstead replied. 'Good for watering the horses, and close to the bridge for passing trade.'

Knepp came out of the stable. 'Did you find out where Viner lodges?'

'I did as you asked, and we've snaffled his preferred billet. The farmer was happy to take our higher offer. Viner will have to look elsewhere.'

A nod of satisfaction. 'Tell the men to prepare to move us all out.'

'I'll tell your mother, shall I?' Bird asked.

'No. The womenfolk will stay. There are no suitable billets for women, and my mother is too frail.'

Too frail? She was tough as bootleather.

★   ★   ★

'Christopher's going to Oxforde?' Mrs Knepp shut the cage door and gave Bird her full attention. 'Why didn't he tell me?'

'I've only just found out. Ask him. You and I are to stay here, whilst all the menfolk go. He makes excuses to leave us behind. He says you are too frail to travel.'

'Poppycock. Apart from my legs, I'm perfectly fit.'

When it suits you, Bird thought. 'The travelling blacksmith that came last week said there are more than a thousand dead in Whitechapel already. That's less than a half-mile from here. If we wait, the plague will come upon us for certain.'

Mrs Knepp looked genuinely shocked. 'A thousand! I will speak with him. Oh mercy, I have so few years left.'

She didn't have to wait long, for Knepp appeared in the doorway, and came straight over to embrace his mother. She wasted no time. 'What's this I hear about you going to Oxforde?'

Knepp cast Bird a cold look. 'I was going to tell you, Mother. I am moving the business temporarily to Oxforde, where we will still be able to do business with the court.'

'I am coming with you. No, don't protest. If you do not take me, I shall follow behind you in one of Viner's coaches, and tell everyone that you cared so little for your ailing mother that you left her behind to die.'

'Don't be foolish. If you stay indoors as usual,

there is no need to disturb yourself. Mary Elizabeth will look to your needs.'

'Mary Elizabeth should be with her husband, or people will talk. Besides you could be away for months, and you need to be . . .' she paused, flapped a wrinkled hand, 'you just need to be together, that's all. Maybe the country air will do the trick.'

'No, Mother. It will not be suitable,' Knepp said. 'There is no appropriate accommodation for women.'

'Then find some. I meant what I said.'

Knepp turned on Bird. 'What did you say to her? This is your fault, stirring up trouble.'

'I told her the truth. That there are a thousand dead in Whitechapel, and Smithfield could be next. Would you have me say this foul disease is a mere cold?'

'Obedience is the first rule in a marriage. You will bide here as I say. You think I don't realise you want to follow that scurvy troupe of whores with their damnable plays. Well, I don't need you to play now, for Killigrew signed an agreement with me that he will use my coaches and none other.'

'Then he can be persuaded to unsign it, is that not so, Mary Elizabeth?' his mother said, rising from her seat, eyes dark with anger. 'I am not staying here to die before my time. We come with you, both of us, or I will do everything in my power to make sure Viner gets that work instead of you. I shall tell folk your coaches are infected.'

Knepp's lips tightened, but he said nothing. He turned on his heel and strode out in an atmosphere taut as a bowstring.

'He'll do as we ask,' Mrs Knepp said. 'I know my son. And I also know the power of women is that folk listen to their gossip, whether it is true or false, and he knows it. Fetch my travelling trunk, I need to pack.'

CHAPTER 21

Elisabeth squinted her eyes against the sun, watching the other craft sail by. She hadn't wanted to leave. She'd tried the excuse that a carriage couldn't be found as both Knepp's and Viner's had left London. But Samuel had an answer to that, and called a wherryman to take her by boat to temporary lodgings with a Mr Sheldon at Woolwich, further down river. Where it would be safe, he said.

She sniffed. Of course Samuel would not be joining her; according to him, Navy business was far too important to be set aside for something as trivial as the plague. So she and her new paid companion, Mary Mercer, were to be banished beyond the city walls where there would be little to do, and she would have to bear the odious Mrs Sheldon, who was a fusty bore with no interest in anything but housewifery and knitting.

Sacré bleu, but that sun was fierce. It would surely burn her nose, out here on the water. She glanced behind to where Mary sat amongst their bags and trunks, picking at her nails with a sour expression. Elisabeth reached into her bag and

276

offered Mary a forbidden sweetmeat, and it brought a wan smile.

A comfit always made everything sweeter. As Elisabeth licked powdered sugar from her fingers, the wherryman rowed them steadily downstream with the tide, the back of his neck red as a plum. At Woolwich the Sheldon's carriage awaited them on the quay, and his men soon had everything lugged on board.

'It's a pretty place,' Mary said, casting her eye over the empty street.

'But quiet,' Elisabeth said. 'What do people *do* here?' There was only the sound of a cow lowing in a back yard, and not a single carriage to be seen.

The Sheldon's lodgings were solid and comfortable, but pitifully old-fashioned. No wall tapestries, no Turkey carpets on the tables, and the bedchamber with a hard straw mattress. Elisabeth unpacked her trunks feeling exiled. She had a feeling Samuel had sent her here not to keep her safe, but to keep her out of the way.

She laid her nightdress under the pillow and sighed. What would he do all day? The war had moved over to New Netherland across the Atlantic, so London was at least temporarily safe from invasion, if not the plague. He'd be up to his usual tricks, and there was not a blessed thing she could do to stop him. The only women left in London would be common women of no breeding, Betty Martin and Doll Lane, and that new actress he was always talking of, Mrs Knepp. Still, he couldn't go there – the theatres were all shut. But perhaps that would leave the women on the loose? Well, if he caught the plague from one of them, she thought, it would serve him right.

In less than a week the Knepps were also on the road, bumping down the long trail to Oxforde. Mrs Knepp, Bird and Anis were to share a poky chamber on the first floor of the farmhouse, but Mrs Knepp's gout was bad again and in the end Bird set out a cushioned chair and footstool in the downstairs parlour, and with Anis at her side with her 'Yes, Madam's', Mrs Knepp rarely moved from there.

This meant Bird had the luxury of a room to herself, and Knepp took the adjacent one, and thank heaven, all this upheaval had diverted him from the idea of begetting an heir. The first few weeks of being in Oxforde the players played in two of the taverns to earn some money, and to make their presence in the town felt, and until Killigrew could persuade the king to fix a date for their performance.

The players were to perform for the king in a room off the Geometry School close to Convocation House, so the next morning Bird set off to walk there for rehearsal. As Bird headed down the path towards the honey-coloured walls of Oxforde, the sweet-smelling river slid by, filled with the glitter of light, so different from the dark, brackish Thames.

It was harvest-time; the musky scent of the hayfields filled her nostrils, and the mowing men raised their heads briefly from their scythes to nod as she passed.

When she got to the rehearsal room she was early, but she pushed the door open to find a panelled chamber which seemed poky after the bright outdoors. A slim figure, with a quill in hand, was bending over the scripts with his back to her. At the creak of the door, he turned and hastily thrust some papers out of sight.

'Ah, Mrs Knepp, the warbler,' Stefan said, his tone mocking.

What was he doing here? She felt a tinge of annoyance that he was to be one of the players. She ignored his comment and went to sit alone on one of the leather seats pushed against the walls, watching as he set out the players' scripts, and the list of rehearsal times.

Shortly afterwards Mr Mohun and the rest of the company arrived in a great gaggle, full of good humour and banter.

Anne Marshall whipped off her sun bonnet and sat down next to Bird. 'Warm today, isn't it?' she said.

Mohun clapped his hands for the assembled company to be silent.

'Clap for yourself, would you now?' Anne said, winking at the others.

'Oh, ha ha. Very droll. You'll stop your jests when you realise you've just three days to learn your parts. And what's worse – we can only have this room for rehearsal on two afternoons.'

A general outcry which Mohun had to hush with a flapping hand.

'Given that this is a unique opportunity to please his sacred Majesty and his Royal Court, and thus increase our coffers, please make sure you are word-perfect when we next meet, Wednesday this week.'

'It's too short,' Anne said. 'Killigrew's lost his mind.'

'Where *is* Mr Killigrew?' Nell asked.

'He has an appointment with the king to finalise details of our play, and cannot be with us today, or for the rehearsals.'

'You mean he's bowing and scraping,' Nell said.

'He has duties as the King's Groom of the Bedchamber.'

'Exactly. Fawning on the king, the lazy bag of toads.'

'Who'll run the rehearsal then?' Anne asked.

Mohun raised a hand. 'Killigrew's put me in charge. Stefan here's been persuaded to join us, and he will act as my right-hand man, and prompter for our performance, and will also stand in, in the event one of us is ill, or cannot play on the night.'

Stefan gave a thin, obsequious smile. Anne dug an elbow in Bird's ribs and gestured to Stefan. 'Trust Mohun to bring in his scurvy friends by the back door.'

Mohun glared at her and she shut her mouth. 'Now, Stefan, hand out the scripts. It's *The Committee*, a new play by Sir Robert Howard. You'll see your name next to the part you are to play. There'll be no changes, so it's no use arguing that you want another part. The casting's been set by Killigrew and the king, and I'm just delivering orders.'

There was silence as everyone received a copied manuscript and turned to the list of characters.

'What's it about?' Nell asked.

'It's about a scheming Puritan who wants to take some Royalist lands,' Mohun said. 'The committee in the title is the Sequestration Committee from just after the civil uprisings.'

'And don't tell me . . . the Puritan is beheaded by the end,' Nell scoffed, miming slitting her throat.

'Wrong. It's a happy ending,' Mohun said, 'with feasting and a double marriage.' He gave a mock-yawn.

Bird heard little of this. She was staring at the list in front of her. It made no sense. She'd been given the biggest female part in the play; Mrs Day, the role she'd expected Anne Marshall to have.

'Excuse me, Mr Mohun, is this right?'

He raised his eyebrows skywards 'There always has to be one. What did I just say, Mrs Knepp? No arguments.'

'But am I to sing the prologue and epilogue as well? It's a lot of—'

'Afraid of hard work are we now?'

'No, it's just that—'

'Oh, save your breath for acting. You'll need it.'

Bird stared down at the script, and flipped through the pages, feeling her face redden. She certainly would need it, for she was to be in nearly every scene! It was what she'd always dreamed of. A proper part with a substantial number of lines. She glanced at Anne who must have been expecting this role herself, and Anne, who never blushed, had two splashes of hot colour in her cheeks. Seeing Bird's glance, she deliberately turned her back and looked away. So she was offended. The set of her shoulders was too rigid and fixed. Bird bent over the script feeling like she had stabbed her friend in the chest.

But what a chance! Bless Killigrew. He at least must have faith in her. She'd work hard and make sure she knew every word. And before the king! Already her stomach fluttered with nerves.

'We will meet here again on Wednesday,' Mohun said, 'by which time we should have procured the relevant properties and garments.'

Nell came over as Bird stood and tucked the script into her basket. 'Shall we take a stroll around Oxforde, Mrs Knepp? It looks a mighty fine town. So many young blades here for their learning. How's about I teach them a thing or two?'

'Sorry, Nell, I can't. I've got a lot to remember this time.'

'Go on. You can spare an hour or two for carousing.'

'Not if I'm to play Mrs Day.'

Nell stepped back and raised her eyebrows. 'The wife? Really? Oh you are favoured.' She whispered into Bird's ear, 'I say, you didn't let Killigrew give you one, did you?'

She gave Nell a playful slap. 'Wash your mouth! And anyway, I wouldn't. Not if he were the last man on earth.'

'Then what did you do?'

Bird shrugged. 'Nothing. But I want to get it right if I'm to play before the king.'

Nell pouted. 'I've got Arbella, the Irish orphan. She don't have many lines, but I hope she flashes her titties. The king's partial to a bit of flesh, so I've heard. And if I can't catch meself a nice young blade, I'm going to catch me a king.'

Back at the farmhouse, Bird set to work on the script, repeating the lines over and over to set them in her mind. The play was better than she hoped. The character of Mrs Day was ambitious, selfish, and unscrupulous, but also possessed of a powerful will. Bird looked forward to conveying her with vigour.

'In the first place – observe how I lay a design in politics—'

Over and over she said the words until a cry came from below, 'For pity's sake, desist! Mary Elizabeth! My head is bursting.'

Bird put her head over the banister.

'Must we have all this declaiming?' Mrs Knepp

complained. 'I can't get any rest. And you're upsetting my birds.'

'I'm sorry, Mrs Knepp, but I'm to play before the king, and I must have it perfect.'

'That young pup. I remember when I was received at court. It was his late father then, of course. I've lived through three kings.'

Bird came down the stairs. 'You were received at court?'

'Don't look so surprised. I was quite a catch then.'

'Tell me.' Amazed by this confession, Bird sat in the chair beside her and put down the script. In the bird-cage on the table, the two canaries cheeped and fluttered.

'Oh yes. I met Christopher's father at the opening of the Banqueting House in Whitehall. Sixteen twenty two, I think it was.' Mrs Knepp's eyes lit up with sudden animation. 'What a night! There was a masque by Mr Johnson, which was quite spectacular. Elegantly costumed, and silent except for the sound of the tambours and viols. Not like these modern plays, that seem to be designed to show the very worst side of people; everyone arguing like cats. No, in my day the theatre was uplifting.'

'So how did you meet your husband?'

'Roland wasn't a courtier; he was one of those in the Horse Guard. I saw him dismount from his horse as I passed through the courtyard, and I thought him so handsome. I suppose I was staring, and it caught his eye. He raised his eyebrows at me, and in that moment I thought, "that's the man I will marry." Foolish, hey? Of course, my parents would have been horrified, and indeed they were, and now I see it was just a young girl's fancy. But he came to dance with me at the masked ball, and I was so breathless I almost fainted. Now fetch me my small trunk, the marquetry one under the side table.'

Bird had bumped into the thing several times and wondered why Mrs Knepp had to bring it with her everywhere she went. That, and her caged birds. Now she did as Mrs Knepp asked and dragged out the box, even more curious about the contents.

'On the table, Mary Elizabeth, where I can reach it.'

Bird hoisted it up, and Mrs Knepp unlocked it and pushed up the lid. The first thing to come out was a pair of yellowing gloves, 'See these? I wore those then, and I've kept them because he kissed my hand, and it was the first time Roland ever kissed me.'

She laid them over Bird's knee as she reached in to pull out something else. Bird looked down at the thin fingers of pale kidskin that had stiffened with age, and couldn't see how Mrs Knepp's knobbly fingers could ever have slid into these.

'Now, look.' A wired garland of paper flowers embellished with tiny seed pearls was waved before her. 'I wore this in my hair when we were wed, but of course it had real flowers twined into it then, lily of the valley, but those have disintegrated since.'

Bird tried to imagine Mrs Knepp as a young woman, and when the circlet was passed to her, she experienced a stab of regret that her own wedding had been nothing like the one Mrs Knepp must have had.

'It's beautiful,' Bird said tightly, and put it back on the table in a hurry.

'Yes, so delicate,' Mrs Knepp said, her gaze diffusing into the distance.

'It sounds as though you loved him very much.'

'Then, yes. But humours change. I was dazzled by him; by the uniform, by his long legs, his dark curling hair, his wild enthusiasm for everything, his wickedly intimate smile.' She shook her head and sighed, pushed the circlet back inside the box. 'He, of course, was dazzled only by my wealth and position. I was Lettice Hawtrey then, daughter of one of the noblest families in the land, and he was a mere horse guard.'

'Does Christopher take after him?'

A mirthless laugh. 'I hope not. No, not at all. Though he worshipped him. To a child, he must have seemed entirely admirable.' She paused, her mouth working.

Bird waited, the gloves still on her lap. It looked as if the old lady had swallowed something hard that was stuck in her throat.

Eventually she got the words out. 'Roland was

cursed with melancholia. Something of the devil's darkness. He would soar like a kite one moment and sink into a pit of despair the next. He would rouse all the servants at four in the morning, full of mad excitement, and announce a hunting party, and then ride like a man possessed, leaping hedges and ditches with no thought for anyone's safety. Everyone would love him.'

'He sounds like quite a character.'

'Yes, he'd be leaping with joy like a March hare one day, then the next he would hardly stir from his bed, snapping at anyone who came near, convinced all the neighbours were housing a conspiracy to kill him. We soon lost friends, and servants never stayed long. Once, Jennings, the gamekeeper, found him with a noose about his neck, hanging from the barn roof. If Jennings hadn't arrived in time, Roland would have been dead. In some ways, looking back, I almost wish . . . almost wish Jennings *had* been too late.'

There was nothing Bird could say, so she kept quiet. How terrible for his sons.

As if reading her mind, Mrs Knepp spoke again. 'Of course James and Christopher found out, and it made their lives hell. Servants will gossip, and what better, what more scandalous gossip than that?'

'How dreadful. I had no idea. He never talks about his childhood.' Or indeed to me about anything at all, she thought.

'It terrified both the boys. They were afraid of

losing their vivid jovial father. I made sure they were schooled; got them away from the house, but their questioning faces when they came home nearly broke my heart.'

'He . . . he must have been hard to live with.'

'But he was charming, that was the trouble. So handsome too. At first I only saw his exuberant side. The first time he showed me what he called his "black bear", I couldn't think what I'd done. He accused me of plotting against him, and I just couldn't fathom it. In the end I both loved and hated him.' She swallowed, her eyes blinking too fast. 'The boys must have felt the same; they were so afraid to displease him, it made him a tyrant. They feared setting him in a black mood and making him want to end it all. We all walked around him like creeping on ice, afraid it would crack without warning and drown us. You must be thankful; at least Christopher has never had that weakness.'

'No,' Bird turned the gloves on her lap. 'But he—'

'You do not love him. I can see that. I had hoped you would, for his sake. But for yours, I am glad you do not. Everything hurts so much more, when love enters in,' she said. A moment's pause. 'I should never have loved his father.'

'Did your husband try again? To end his life, I mean?'

'Did he?' A dry laugh. 'It was his obsession. But he could not. We all watched him like owls. Watched for signs his mood was changing, hid the

288

key to the gun cupboard, locked up the poisons, made sure one of us was always there. You see, we feared the shame of it. We knew it would reflect badly on us, that if he were to succeed we would be blamed, that we would have failed him in the worst way, and we would be proved unsatisfactory as a family. He would escape, you see, but we — we would be left to bear the indignity.'

The door opened and Knepp appeared. Mrs Knepp shut her mouth and gave Bird a warning look.

'I need another bag of change from the strongbox,' Knepp said. His gaze lighted on the open trunk. 'Reminiscing again, are we, Mother? I don't know why you must drag that heavy thing everywhere we go.'

'It's my past, Christopher, that's why. It reminds me of who I've been. When you're old, people only see the bent and wizened person. They don't see that the younger woman is still there inside, hidden away, just like the things hidden in this trunk.'

'I would have thought you'd want to forget, not remember,' he said, unlocking the strongbox. 'No good comes of dwelling on ancient history. Why don't you do something useful? There are girths that need mending if you've time to spare.' He plucked out a clinking moneybag and re-locked the box. 'Sitting gossiping is no use to anyone.' With that he strode out again banging the pouch of coins against his thigh.

'He doesn't understand. How would he like to

be sitting here day after day with no-one to talk to except that maidservant? Nobody ever talks to me. It's the first time you've ever listened to me.'

'I'm sure that's not true,' Bird said.

'It is. You're always too busy with the plays and all your make-believe people. You've no time for real people at all.'

Was it true? She hadn't paid Mrs Knepp much attention, except as a nuisance to be endured. She'd never really thought of her as having a life before she came to London. 'You should ask your son to take you out sometimes for a drive.'

Mrs Knepp sighed. 'Christopher's looking older. His hair is greying already. He needs a child to keep him young.' She turned and fixed Bird with a questioning eye.

'Then he should have married earlier,' Bird said. She picked up her script again and pretended to pay it close attention.

'You're ignoring me again, Mary Elizabeth.'

Still Bird did not answer.

'Mary Elizabeth?'

Bird stood up, frustrated. 'I'm not ignoring you, but what am I supposed to say to that? I'll have you know I do my duty, Mrs Knepp, as a good wife should. I can do no more. It is in the hands of God, as you well know.'

She left Mrs Knepp and went upstairs, guilty because she knew exactly why no child would be forthcoming. She sat in the window where the light was best, looking over the long rows of harvesters sweating in the fields, her script open before her, determined she'd have Act One word-perfect by the morning. But she couldn't seem to concentrate, and soon put it down on the window-sill. She felt sorry for her mother-in-law for she saw now that her life was a lonely one. Living with Knepp's father must have been a kind of hell, and she understood at last why Christopher liked to have such rigid control over everything that went on in the yard. Christopher. It was the first time she had thought of him by name, or with any sympathy at all.

She bent her head to the text again. She'd show them all; even the king. Everyone, all over the land, would hear of Mrs Knepp. If it weren't for summer and these light hours, she would never have managed. Her head was so stuffed full of words, she thought they might leak out of her ears. But still, she found it hard to settle to her learning. Mrs Knepp's talk of her marriage and her children had unsettled her.

She imagined her character, the strident Mrs Day, telling Mr Hart, who was playing Mr Day, what to do. In the play, it was easy to say the lines and give orders. Not so easy to do it with your real husband.

After three solid days of learning Bird was anxious to show them at Convocation House what she could do in rehearsal. She had discarded the script, which lay in her basket and, after her first sung prologue at the opening of the play, she let the note die away before asking Mohun, 'Am I to stay on stage, or shall I go off?'

'No, no!' Mohun said, impatient. 'Get into the wings, then come on for your cue.' She almost protested, for it seemed stupid to go off, then come straight back on again. But Mohun seemed harassed, and she didn't want to cause a fuss, so she did as he asked.

'Scene one, please,' Mohun called.

The company entered – Bird as Mrs Day, followed by Anne Marshall, Nell Gwynne, Mr Wintershall, who was to play Colonel Blunt, and Stefan, slouching behind as the stagecoach man. Bird launched into her opening speech:

'Now out upon't, how dusty it is! All things considered, it is better travelling in the winter; especially for us of the better sort, that ride in coaches. And yet, to say truth, warm weather is both pleasant and comfortable—'

'What are you doing?' Mohun leapt out before her.

Bird stopped, confused. 'I've another four lines,' she said.

'No. Stop fooling.' Mohun raked a hand through his curly hair. 'Where's Mrs Marshall?'

'Here,' Anne said.

'Anne, you're wasting time,' Mohun said. 'Start again, please.'

'*Now out upon't, how dusty it is! All things*—' Bird began.

'Stop! Let Mrs Marshall say her lines.'

'But I speak first,' Bird said.

'You try my patience! Anne, give us Mrs Day.'

'But why?' Anne said. 'I'm to play Mrs Ruth, aren't I?'

'What?' Mohun's mouth opened like a fish.

Anne talked to him slowly as if talking to a simpleton. 'Killigrew, in his infinite wisdom, cast me as Mrs Ruth, and *her* as Mrs Day. I thought you knew. Though I have to say, I thought it mighty strange, as I already know Mrs Day's part from the readings in town.'

Mohun threw up his arms. 'Nonsense. Tom told me you were to play Mrs Day, since you know the part already, and Mrs Knepp was to take on Mrs Ruth. I'm quite certain of it.'

Anne glared at Bird. 'It's her. She must have got inside Killigrew's breeches somehow.'

'I did not.' Bird said. 'How dare you! If Killigrew wanted me to play the part, it was because he believed in me and wanted to give me a chance to show what I can do.' But even as she spoke the words, a seed of doubt made her last few words less certain.

Mohun shook his head. 'This is most queer. I only spoke to Killigrew yesterday and he never mentioned any cast change, and he gave me the scripts himself.'

'Well mine clearly has my name written next to

Mrs Day,' Bird said, feeling suddenly vulnerable. There had been some mistake, and somehow she was at the heart of it.

'And mine had Mrs Ruth,' Anne said. 'But the top page was in a different hand from the rest.'

'Ah. Now we are getting somewhere. Let me see,' Mohun said.

Anne hurried off to fetch her script, and Bird followed suit. They lay them side by side on the table.

Mohun took out an eyeglass and peered down at them.

'See?' Anne said stabbing her finger on her name. 'Mrs Ruth.'

'But on mine, it says you are to play Mrs Day.' William Wintershall placed his script next to the other two.

'And mine,' Mohun brandished his copy.

'Egad. Some mischief at work,' Stefan said. 'These two have been altered, and the names copied out again.'

'But why would anyone want to do that?' Bird asked.

'Why indeed?' Anne said, with a pointed gaze.

Bird was stung. 'You can't think that . . .? You can't seriously think . . .?'

'You can write, we all know that. And Mrs Day is certainly the bigger part,' Anne said. 'Mrs Ruth has little to do. But I had never thought you quite so ambitious.'

'I'd never do anything like that!' She glanced

round the company, but not a one leapt to her defence. They all stared at her with disbelief, as if seeing her for the first time.

'Oh pish and pizzle!' Nell piped up. 'I don't care which one of you plays Mrs Day. And neither will the king, so long as you're bare chested. We just need to get on with it. Go on Mohun, choose.'

'But what will Killigrew say?' Wintershall asked.

'He's not here,' Nell said. 'So nothing.'

Mohun stared at his copy of the play a moment, ruminating. 'Very well. Who has Anne Marshall as Mrs Day on their script?' Everyone raised a hand, except Bird and Anne. 'Seven. Then Anne has it. Mrs Knepp, you will play Mrs Ruth.'

Bird wanted to protest, to say she hadn't learnt it, but her throat was so tight she couldn't speak. All those hours learning, all that time thinking that Killigrew actually thought her good enough. And it was all for nothing. A mean trick played by someone out to avenge himself.

The worst of it was, she could guess who was responsible. Hadn't she seen that vile youth Stefan with a quill and ink just before the scripts were handed out? But she'd fallen for it, as he knew she would. She'd been so puffed up with her own importance that she hadn't seen how unlikely it was. She should have questioned it more. Her face burned with humiliation and shame.

For the rest of the day she was forced to witness Anne playing the part she, Bird, had worked on for so long. Nobody cast her a smile or a friendly word as she struggled through Mrs Ruth's few bland lines with a script in her hand. She knew she was mangling the part, for she had no understanding of Mrs Ruth's person, and it was as if she was speaking with a weight pressing on her chest. Perhaps she should give up.

At the end of the rehearsal she waited before the door. Stefan was the last person to leave, as he was responsible for putting away the properties and storing the theatre swords safely in a locked case. She stood aside to let the others go by. None would meet her eye, except Mohun.

'Be sure I will tell Tom about this little fiasco,' he said. 'He can deal with it himself. I told him women acting would cause us all mighty grief.'

'It's not of my doing,' she said.

'Who else would benefit?' Anne said as she marched past.

Mohun took her by the arm. 'You've let the thought of the king turn your head. So let me give you this advice; if you wish to stay in this company, you had best keep out of Anne's way, keep your trapdoor shut, and con the part of Mrs Ruth with all good haste. Good day.'

Stefan, who had been listening, whilst surreptitiously putting things away, picked up his cloak, about to follow Mohun out.

'A word, Stefan.' She shut the door and turned. The brass door handle pressed into her back.

'Get out of the way.' He too would not meet her gaze, but frowned in a surly way at the floor as he stepped towards her. She noticed his face was red, and greasy in the way of young men's complexions. When she did not move, he made an attempt to push her aside, but she held firm, spreading her legs wide, blocking the closed doorway.

He paused, inches from her.

She looked up at him. 'Why do you hate me?' she asked quietly. 'I know it was you; you changed those scripts. But why?'

'Let me go by.' He wiped his nose, and shuffled on the spot, red-faced.

'No. You heard Mr Mohun. You made a fool of me, and worse, of Mrs Marshall. I saw you tamper with the scripts, and I will tell that to Mr Killigrew. How did you think you could get away with it?'

'Oh, you think you know everything, don't you?' His eyes met hers with sudden venom. 'You can just walk in off the street and expect everything to fall into your lap. Even an audience in front of the king.'

'That's not true. You have no idea of how I had to wrangle to get taken on by the players, nor what I will go back to, if I fail.'

'You're a wife, aren't you? Isn't that enough? Let your husband keep you. I worked to the bone for five years to learn how to play those roles, and unlike you, I can't take a husband. There'll be no man earning for me. You women are all the same; you're just playing at it. You should go back to your cookery and sewing. You are not fit to grace the London stage; all that posturing and pouting.

297

If you cared enough to look, you'd see that real women don't behave like that. All that mannered gesturing. It just looks fake. Killigrew should have given Mrs Day or Mrs Ruth to me; I'm old enough by now.'

'You're telling me what's real? That's rich. Can't you see? Times have changed. The old theatre has gone and the audience wants reality, not men dressed as women. They want to see themselves on stage, the women too, so why shouldn't we women have a voice, one that's not stolen by men?'

'Stolen? It's against the natural way of things.'

'And I suppose you know all about what's natural, do you? You, who have to dress up as a woman to feel like a man?' The instant the words were out she regretted them. Stefan looked stricken. His silence told her she'd hit a raw place inside him.

'Get out of my way!' His voice finally broke. Now there was no stopping him, he pushed her roughly aside and fled out through the lobby and into the street.

'Wait! Stefan!' But he was loping away, cloak flapping above his spidery legs.

'Curses.' She took a deep breath. He was just a young man, with barely a beard, and she'd only made things worse. And a part of her felt sorry for him. He was an unpre-possessing youth, and would never make a good leading man. What would he do, if he had no profession? But at the same time, the thought of how much trouble he'd caused rankled. The other actors no longer felt able to trust her, and she'd a whole new part to learn.

To make things worse, when she got back from rehearsal, Knepp was waiting.

'You spend too much time with those vagabonds, and you neglect your wifely duties.'

'Why so? Food is on the table, the linen is clean, the house swept. Anis sees your mother wants for nothing. What more do you expect?'

'Those are not the wifely duties I mean. My mother is right. I saw Viner's eldest son Georgie in Oxforde. He was driving a carriage already. Time passes, and still there is no son in my household. Soon you will be past your prime.'

She stiffened, but kept her tone light. 'It is not something that can be ordered. It is under God's jurisdiction, not ours.'

'There will be no more sleeping in separate chambers. Not until you are quickening with my son.'

'And if I refuse?'

'Then I will keep you from your precious theatre until you agree.'

CHAPTER 22

The plague was still rife in London, but the King's Players were finally to get twenty pounds to perform before the king. Not that she'd see more than a few shillings. But it was a relief, because there had already been a month's delay whilst the king was occupied with political trouble with the French. What an honour, to be part of a private performance for the king! She was determined it should go well, after such an inauspicious start to rehearsals. She'd go early to the rehearsal room to check her costume. She couldn't afford any mishaps, and she wanted to make sure that weasel Stefan hadn't been anywhere near it.

Knepp drove her to the centre of Oxforde in their convoy of carriages, in the hope his men would pick up extra fares for the day. He dropped her by the spire of All Hallowes, on Highe Street.

'Do you know how many you will play to?' he asked her after she got out.

'No,' she said. 'But just the thought of it makes me shaky.'

'He's just a man,' Knepp said. 'In a fancy suit

of clothes. And a worse man than the last king. But he'll want to be entertained like all the rest.'

'I suppose so.' She wasn't convinced.

'I wish you luck,' he said. She was surprised; he rarely showed her any kind of care. 'And don't forget to mention Knepp's Horse Hire if you can.'

She lifted her hand in a wave to show she'd understood that she was to capitalise on the opportunity if she could. She was too frayed with tension not to be on the move, and she still had to walk to the rehearsal room. The morning sun lit up the spires of Oxforde as she hurried along. The town was filled with beautiful stone buildings, quadrangles of green grass and knot gardens laid out in the French style. Though smaller, it was certainly as prosperous as London.

The rehearsal room was open and she went in, glad to find she was alone. There was a smell of beeswax polish, and new rushes had been laid, so the sound of her feet was like a whisper, not her usual clatter.

The adjoining room was to serve as their tiring room, and at the last rehearsal they had set up temporary rails hung from the rafters so they could hang their costumes. Bird was about to enter when she caught sight of movement through the door. A glimpse of a woman, as she walked by.

It was Anne, rehearsing Mrs Day. She paused to listen, reluctant to disturb her. She knew all the words, for she'd learnt them herself. But Anne was giving the words depth and substance. Her voice was deeper and more melodious. The lone rehearsal was obviously paying off. Bird was fascinated. She pushed open the door and Anne whipped round.

But it wasn't Anne. This was a woman she'd never seen before. Tall and slim, with blonde hair under the blue hat. It was Mrs Day's costume, but that wasn't Anne wearing it.

'What are you doing?' The words were out before she could stop them.

The woman's eyes were enormous in her pale face, but there was something familiar about her.

'Stefan. I should have guessed.'

His eyes shifted away from her, and his pale hand plucked at the skirts. 'I was just . . .' He swallowed, struggling for words.

'What? Are you planning some other trickery?'

'I just wanted to try it on, that's all.' He began to unlace the front of the bodice. 'I meant no harm.'

'What would Anne say if she caught you here, dressed in her costume?'

'I just wanted to try it. Mrs Day should have been my part. I know all the lines. I could do it better than she would. Better than either of you.' He let go of the laces and began to untie the sleeves.

'Stefan, Killigrew will never give you a woman's part again. Those days have gone. You just have to come to terms with it.'

The sleeves wouldn't come loose. 'Curse it,' he

said. His face crumpled. 'I suppose I'm to play a servant all my life?'

'I'm sure not. Come, you're getting in a tangle. I'll help you.' She went to unthread the laces from the sleeves. 'I never wanted to make an enemy of you,' she said quietly. 'I admire your talent. When I heard you just then, I thought you better than Anne.'

His head turned. 'Do you mean it?' His eyes were alive with yearning.

'I believed in you. When Anne acts, it is as if it is still an act. She speaks well, and her voice carries, but they don't feel true. You spoke the words as if they were real.'

He reddened. 'To me they are real. When I'm in costume, *I'm* more real.' He paused. 'Sometimes I think it's a sin to feel this way.'

'We all feel something for the art of it.'

'No. I meant . . .' He took off the hat and threw it down. 'Have you ever felt that the outside of you doesn't match the inside? Like you've no place to feel comfortable?'

Bird felt a bolt of recognition and it silenced her. She waited as he wriggled out of the sleeve.

'This might be the last time I can dress like this.' His voice held a choke in it as he smoothed the folds of the blue silk skirt. 'Without it, I think I'll disappear, become nobody at all.'

She looked up at this strange young man then, and saw a sort of torment in his pale eyes.

'There'll be other roles,' she said, 'for a fine actor like you.'

'But not where I can be a woman.' Sadly, he stepped out of the skirts to reveal his breeches beneath. 'I had the best of it, and now it's over.'

She took the skirts from him. 'Don't give up on the theatre, Stefan. We need good actors like you.'

'There's nowhere else I could go. My parents are dead, and I know of no other life. I live with a friend of my father who will never understand me, and will think me a monster if he knew what I really am. The theatre is a place of more possibilities for a person like me, a place where the boundaries between things can blur.'

She knew what he meant. The theatre was the only profession in which a man could both hide and be seen.

Stefan shrugged. 'Maybe Killigrew's right. He says we are all looking for the lost bits of ourselves in the parts we play.'

'Well he should know,' she said. 'If you ask me, most of his bits are missing!'

Stefan laughed, a giggle that was like a trill of running water. It was infectious, and soon the pair of them had to sit to wipe their eyes.

'Share the jest?' Mohun said, arriving through the door.

Stefan caught her eye and again they burst into peals of laughter.

The performance of *The Committee* was over, and Bird was slumped in a chair, her head hanging.

She'd forgotten her words and had had to be prompted by Stefan.

Worse, out of the corner of her eye, she'd caught the king's lowered eyebrow as she waited for the line. She didn't want to speak to anyone and Killigrew ignored her as he rushed by in the wake of the exiting king and courtiers.

'Why so glum?' Stefan said. 'It was a great success. The king just told me so. He loved it.'

'I forgot my words. I could curse myself.'

'It happens to us all. It's part of the territory, and you have to bear it. That and bad reviews. If it's any consolation, we've all been given extra coin for playing. Here.' He fished in the money belt to draw out some coins. As he pulled out his hand, something fell rattling to the floor. They both pounced to pick it up together, but Bird was quicker.

She handed it over, but not before she'd felt it in her hand and seen what it was. It was a rosary, rows of ivory beads with a heavy gilt crucifix on one end.

Stefan reddened and shoved it back in his pouch. 'So what?' he said defiantly. 'Will you report me?'

'Of course not,' she said. 'It's a stage property, isn't it?'

'Of course it is.' His face opened in relief. 'Yes. A stage property.'

She gave him a smile. 'Though I'd be careful to keep it at home in future, if I were you.'

He handed her the extra payment and she

watched him as he went out of the chamber. Such a complicated young man, and a Catholic too. It made her think of Livvy and her French friend. She hoped they were safe. She had written to tell her where they lodged, and a reply had come that morning, scribed in an elaborate curly hand – by M'sieur Hubert, presumably – to say Viner had decided to leave Livvy in London after all. The plague was less, though London was still reeling from the number of dead. Livvy warned Bird to keep well away.

But now the king's play was over, she hankered to get back. She sang at various evening concerts, but that was not the same as becoming another person on stage. And she had the feeling the more she clung to it, the more the theatre was slipping out of her grasp.

Time passed, and the nights lengthened and days shortened until the day Killigrew stopped her on her way to the tiring room, and said, 'We return next week, God willing. The Bills of Mortality show the plague is passing.'

He watched the shifting emotions on her face. 'It's been long enough. Aren't you glad?'

Bird twisted her neckerchief in her fingers. 'I can't wait to get back on the boards. It's just . . . I don't want to go back to the life I had before.'

Killigrew put a hand on her arm. 'You won't. I will see to it. I know your husband is not the easiest of men. But good singers are hard to find.'

'It's not just the singing. It's the acting. I'd hoped . . . I'd hoped to . . .' What? She wasn't sure what. She just knew she came to life on stage inhabiting someone else's lines. She felt heat rise to her neck. She put her hand there to cool it.

'Don't be embarrassed. I can see you care about it, as I do. Why do you think I do this? For the money? No. There is some magic that happens when the audience see themselves reflected on the stage.'

'The first time I saw a play, I wanted to get up there with the players. And now I've tried it, I've found it feels like nothing else. When I cast myself aside I can breathe deeper, and then I'm bigger than I thought, two people instead of only one. It's . . . exhilarating.'

He laughed. 'You have caught the theatre, and no mistake. You'll soon be unable to live without your daily dose of greasepaint and candlewax!'

She looked at the ground, abashed. 'When do you plan to leave, sir?'

'A few days hence. There'll be alterations at the theatre that I want to oversee. New machinery, and a bigger apron to the stage. A bigger, better theatre for all my lovely ladies.'

He reached his hand behind to pinch her buttock, but instead of slapping it away, she took hold of his shoulders and gave him a smacking kiss on the lips. 'That's for taking a chance on me, and for letting me play before the king.'

'Egad! Then I should do it more often!'

That night as she lay tossing and turning in the shaft of moonlight filtering in through the casement, she was wary of her good fortune. It seemed every time her fortunes turned a corner, Lady Luck would change her mind.

As if to echo her thoughts, the door swung open, and Knepp was there in his nightshirt.

CHAPTER 23

Knepp prowled the lodgings, snapping at his mother, unable to be still. Despite doing better business than Viner here in Oxforde, the restless feeling persisted. He'd seen Arabella today, and her children, passing by in Viner's monogrammed carriage, noses in the air as if they owned the street. They were a proper upstanding family, whilst Mary Elizabeth had grown ever-more distant, and seemed unable, even after all this time, to give him a child.

He went up to their rooms and paced. It was his fault, he knew. A voice inside him said he was brutish and ugly and he hated the way Mary Elizabeth turned away from him when he came to her room at night for their conjugal duties. She confused him. On stage she was all softness, all open eyes and fluttering fan; a pretty Mary Elizabeth, full of smiles he had never seen at home.

With him, she was as hard as a plank of wood. He picked up her nightdress from the chair and put it down again, wondering how it had become so difficult to cross the divide with his wife. He had no idea who she was at all. How did other men talk to their wives?

He wandered through to the closet and saw her things laid out there: the cream for her face, a bottle of rosewater, a box of powder with a swans-down puff. He opened the box and smelt the scent of her which was so subtle as to be hardly there. She was young; surely she didn't need all this paraphernalia? In the table was a small drawer, and within it, a leather box. He flapped it open and saw two limes, and another cut in half, hollowed out. He picked out the hollow one, and wondered what it was for.

A voice behind him said, 'There you are. I lack company.'

His mother. 'Is your gout easing, Mother?'

'No. It's like red hot knives in my big toe, but I wanted to talk to you about getting Mary Elizabeth to buy me some new material to sew nightdresses, and I can never catch you. Isn't she back yet?'

'She's still at rehearsal. Look at all this stuff. Beats me why you women need to do all that messing with your skin. What do women use these for? Whitening?' He held out the lime-skin on his palm.

His mother's eyes narrowed. 'The vixen. So that's it.'

'What? What's the matter?'

'Don't you know?' Her tone was scathing.

'Know what?'

310

'Women use these . . . these things to stop themselves getting with child.'

He stared blankly at it.

'Down there.'

He stared down at his hand and then threw
the thing down onto the bed. 'How do you . . .?'
But the thought was too much for him. That his
mother should know this, and his wife, and yet he
was ignorant of it. What a fool he'd been.

He made for the stairs. His mother's voice
followed him. 'You'll have words with her, won't
you?'

He hurried out to the yard, the feeling of shame
and anger knotting his chest, so he had to get
away. Run, somewhere, anywhere. But then, how
did you run away from yourself?

Bird knew something was wrong; an instinct
curled her gut. When Knepp collected her from
the rehearsal that day he was even more tight-
lipped and silent than usual.

'Upstairs,' he said, when they got back to their
lodgings.

She looked to Mrs Knepp, but her eyes shifted
away, back to the bobbins and the lace she was
making to edge a cap.

'Now?' Bird tried to think of an excuse, but
there was no excuse she could give. 'Why? What's
the matter?'

She followed him to the bedchamber and saw
his gaze move to her leather box open on the bed.

311

How had he found this? He must have been prying into—

'Don't try to lie to me.' His voice interrupted her thoughts. A lime-skin lay next to the open box and he pointed at the offending object.

There was no possible answer.

He swept it off the bed with his arm and kicked it away across the floor. 'I knew you were up to some trickery. Did you think I didn't know? This has gone on long enough. People are saying I have no firepower. But it's you. You whore-faced vixen. You've been cheating me.'

'You shouldn't be looking at my things—'

He took her arm in a tight grip and manoeuvred her back to the bed. 'You will give me a son. That's what wives are for. Yet you deny me. All these years of trying and it was never going to happen, was it?'

'I deny you nothing. I do as a wife should. T'is God's will no babe comes.'

'We'll see about God's will. You'd fool Him as well as me, would you?' His eyes were hard and dark, and a vein stood out on his temple.

He took her by the shoulders and threw her flat on the bed. His hands were like iron on her shoulders. She lay still, like a corpse, her eyes tight shut, making no move. She could have been stone. She felt him lift her skirts, but stayed rigid, put all her energy into the idea that his seed should not stick. She imagined a castle wall around her womb. For how would she play if she was with child?

Suddenly, the weight lifted. 'Damn you,' he croaked.

She opened her eyes to see him buttoning himself again and storming from the room.

He had not forced himself on her. Why not? It was his right.

She got rid of the lime-skins and did not dare buy more. One week later he approached her again, in the dark of the night. She endured it the way a wife should, praying this was her least fertile time.

When it was over, she tried to get up, but he put a hand on her shoulder. 'Lie still. You must lie flat.' She tried to stand again, but he pressed his big hand down, almost with regret. It was this that made her despise herself, and shrink from him more, this confusion between his force and his apology. She prayed to God no child would come, for if it did, it would be black with hate.

CHAPTER 24

London, November 1665

K nepp rubbed his hands together to get the feeling back. The journey back to London from Oxforde had been cold, the carriage draughty, and his hands were like lumps of ice. Returning to London after Oxforde had shocked him beyond words. It was like visiting a house where someone had been bereaved. Folk still spoke in whispers. Many shops remained shuttered, many houses were still locked; weeds grew between the cobbles on the thoroughfares.

He stood a moment in the Smithfield yard, taken aback. Why, the place looked completely down-at-heel. How had he not noticed the stable doors were peeling, and the tiles were off the roof of the hayloft? To put it right would cost money, and for a moment just the thought of all he must do overwhelmed him.

His mother stopped him as he passed through the house carrying his luggage from the carriage. 'Are there no servants here, son, who will do that for you?'

'It's quicker to do it myself.'

'What about my luggage and Mary Elizabeth's?'

'I suppose I could ask one of the men. But I want them to get the horses settled. They need to be earning. All this disruption does them no good.'

'Nor us.' She cast her eyes around the chamber. He followed her gaze and took in the pockmarked walls, the soot-stained ceiling and the worn-out upholstery. 'This place does look shabby after Oxforde,' she said.

'We are alive, Mother, so we should be thankful for small mercies. Most of the good folk of London moulder in the plague pits. I have lost most of my best clients. London's like a graveyard.' He sighed and dumped his valise on the flagstone floor. 'Why is it good men have to die, and cheating rogues like Viner still survive?'

'Never fear, son; when the theatre opens again, business will soon rally. Mary Elizabeth will tell the theatregoers about Knepp's, I'm sure. I'll say this for her; she didn't disgrace herself before the king. She's doing her best to mix with the king's musicians – that lutenist, and the musicians of the court. And you have to admit, they are using your coaches more than they did. Maybe it's a godsend she's not yet with child after all.'

He curbed his temper by taking a deep breath. 'What she brings, it's nothing but piecemeal. Not the good solid trade I need. I should never have married her.' Even as he said it, he knew it sounded churlish. Mary Elizabeth's contacts were all that

315

kept the business afloat; not that he'd admit that to his mother.

'She's not still using that—'

'No, Mother, she's not. And I'd thank you to keep your nose out of my affairs.'

Christmas was coming, and to Bird's frustration, the King's Playhouse was still closed for refurbishment. The actors cursed Killigrew, but there was little they could do. He had ceased to pay his labourers, and they had downed tools, and the whole building charade proceeded in fits and starts with much ill-temper on both sides. With business slow, Knepp had agreed Bird should accept invitations to sing from anyone with contacts at court. Bird was elated, for tonight she was to sing for Mr and Mrs Pierce, a well-esteemed merchant and his wife. They had friends who were musicians at court. She had a good feeling about it, and the music was sure to be the best.

'Treat it as business,' Knepp said, and he had given her leather tokens with *Knepp's Horse-Hire* stamped into them. These she was supposed to give out to the gentry. She dreaded the embarrassment this would give her, but she agreed to try to keep the peace, and because otherwise he'd forbid her the chance to sing. Since the lime-skin incident, she felt like a leper in her own home. Knepp barely spoke to her, and Mrs Knepp, too, had been shorter with her than usual.

As soon as she was out of Smithfield, she exhaled.

Determined to make an impression on the Pierces, she went to the theatre and borrowed a pink silk dress. It still needed more colour. A vivid cerise-coloured wrap from the wardrobe rail took her eye, and she swathed it around her neck. That's better, she thought. Now she was dressed for Yuletide merriment. Extra feathers in her hat, borrowed from the theatre's Henry VII cap, gave her a jaunty air.

The stars twinkled above her, and the air tingled with new possibilities. When she arrived at the Pierces' new house in Covent Garden, the sound of trilling voices drifted down, though the shutters were closed. She paused on the doorstep a moment, watching smoke plume from the chimney, her head cocked, separating out the voices in her head to hear the individual harmonies. She knew it was unusual to travel alone, but she had deliberately not persuaded Knepp to accompany her. She knocked loudly and confidently, and a maidservant appeared.

Inside, Mrs Pierce, a pale-skinned beauty of aristocratic bearing, welcomed her with a kiss that didn't touch her face, and indicated with an expansive gesture the way to the upstairs parlour. Bird picked her way past cloaks dangling from the banister, and weapons cluttering the stairs.

Lanier, the serious-faced court lutenist, his pointed beard more grey than ginger, was already plucking away at a madrigal and acknowledged her arrival with a dip of the head. She smiled at him, for despite all that was wrong in her life, she was itching to sing to his accompaniment. Also in

317

the party, and bellowing the tune with enthusiasm, was Captain Edward Rolt, a tenor, who it was rumoured was a cousin of Oliver Cromwell. She could well-believe it as, despite only being in his thirties, he favoured dark clothing and wore his hair unfashionably short.

Standing around him, music sheets in hand, were Mr Coleman, a dapper little man who was a celebrated music master, next to him, his wife Catherine, exquisitely dressed, and the short, square figure of Mrs Worshipp and her equally square daughter. The tune finished and Mrs Pierce urged her to join the group for a rousing version of *The Sweet Trinity*, so Bird took on the high part and as she sang, she poured her feeling into the song.

> '*Sir Walter Rawleigh has built a ship,*
> *In the Neather-lands*
> *And it is called The Sweet Trinity,*
> *And was taken by the false gallalee,*
> *Sailing in the Low-lands, low.*'

During the last verse she whipped off the cerise scarf and eyes closed, wafted it like a sail before her. When she opened her eyes, it was to see two other people had come into the room.

'Samuel! Elisabeth!' Mrs Pierce hurried over to the newcomers.

Bird startled at the names. Elisabeth was a pale-skinned brunette, fussily dressed in a blue gown which had rows of ruffles and ribbons on the stomacher, and more ribbons dangling from lace-edged sleeves. Everything about her was flyaway, from the ribbons on her sleeves, to the way her hair fluffed around her face, to the way her eyes darted around the room. But it was her husband who held Bird's gaze.

It was him; the man from the theatre. Her eyes locked on his.

'How fine you could join us,' Mrs Pierce said. 'Elisabeth, you must tell me all about Woolwich, we missed you this last six months.'

Bird swung her gaze away in time to see Elisabeth kiss Mrs Pierce on both cheeks, and bundle her cloak and hat into her maidservant's arms. 'I simply had to come. I couldn't bear Woolwich a moment longer,' Elisabeth said. 'There's nothing to do. I must come back to town soon. I'd rather die of the plague, than stay, my dear, I really would!'

Samuel smiled at Bird, eyes alight, as if greeting an old friend, and waved his hand at her in a regal kind of way. It made heat rise to her face. He was holding a flageolet, and she wondered if he was a musician. But he seemed too well turned out for that; he sported a periwig and the latest tied silk cravat, and his shoes were adorned with expensive red shoe-roses. She smiled back at this man who had escorted her the first time she had ever been inside a theatre. He had taken her arm and led her through the crush. The memory of that day was seared into her mind as if branded with a fire-iron. It seemed as if it was the first day of her life.

As the musicians got ready to play, Samuel passed the flageolet to Elisabeth, who was deep in giggling conversation and promptly put it aside without looking at him.

He came to stand next to Bird and looked down on her with a grin. 'I met you before at the theatre,' he said, 'before you trod the boards. I'm right, aren't I? I never forget a face.'

'I remember you. Can you believe, that was my first visit to the theatre?' she said. 'But now I am part of the King's Company.'

'I know,' he said. 'The theatre is my chief pleasure. I've seen you in many a play. I first saw you in *The Silent Woman*, last year, the first time I ever saw a woman in the title role, and you played it to perfection. I went to see it again the next week. It was a pity though,' he said, 'the performance was interrupted by that dreadful hailstorm.'

'Oh! Were you there that night? I was so nervous, it being such a big role and so much to remember in the way of business, if not talk. But what a disaster! We lost half our audience!'

'I must admit, I was one of them. I had so much hail down my neck I almost rattled.'

'Oh, let me introduce you,' Mrs Pierce glided over. 'Mr Pepys, this is Mrs Knepp.'

'We've already met,' she said, 'in a hailstorm, *inside* the theatre.'

Mrs Pierce looked bemused.

Mr Pepys and Bird exchanged a conspiratorial

look. 'Enchanted,' he said. His warm smile lifted her spirits.

As Mrs Pierce drifted away, Bird glanced to Pepys's wife. Elisabeth Pepys was the centre of attention, talking animatedly to the Worshipps about the re-opening of the shops in the Exchange. She did not seem to notice her husband.

'Shall we?' To her surprise, Mr Pepys picked up a viol that was propped against the wall, hitched up his breeches and sat down to play.

Lanier nodded to him, '*Fain Would I Wed*, Mr Pepys?'

'Fine choice.' Pepys picked up his bow and drew it across the strings with confidence.

How he could play! His rhythmic bowing was more accomplished than she had imagined; his fingers pressed the strings with precision. He signalled to begin with a smile and a nod of his head, and Bird launched into song. Captain Rolt, the brazen devil, tried to outdo her. As she increased in volume, so did he, until everyone stared and the two of them were rattling the rafters.

Mr Lanier and Mr Pepys plucked and fiddled for all they were worth until the very last line when Bird and Mr Rolt drew out the long note in 'forth' until Bird thought her lungs would burst.

'Bravo!' Mr Pierce applauded from the door, just arrived, and still in his travelling cloak and muffler. 'I could hear you from Oxforde!' His wife hurried to welcome him into the party.

In the fuss around the return of Mr Pierce, Mr Pepys caught her eye. 'That was marvellous. What next? Have you a favourite Mrs Knepp?'

She sensed her blood fizz under his gaze. 'I love Johnson's poem – 'The Bright Lily'. Can you play that, Mr Pepys?'

'It's one of my favourites. Come, let's play.'

She regretted choosing it almost immediately. It spoke of a lost innocence, something close to her heart. It gave too much away, but now she'd begun she didn't know how to back out. The men were already playing.

'Have you seen but a bright lily grow
Before rude hands have touched it?
Have you marked but the fall of snow
Before the soil hath smutched it?'

But as she sang, she forgot everything except the song. The last few notes she sang low and soft, and the viol resonated in a silence after Mr Pepys had lifted his bow from the strings.

When she opened her eyes, Mr Pepys was gazing at her with the sort of scrutiny you might give a never-before-seen creature from a far-off shore. She felt awkward, her borrowed dress too loose around the waist, her hands too big and red, clutching her scarf. Immediately she asked for another more rousing song, 'This Merry Pleasant Spring,' she called.

'But it's December!' Mr Pepys protested, laughing, raising his palms.

'Even more reason to sing it. It's bitter out. Perhaps we will bring spring early. And I'll dance a jig to make it come quicker too.'

'Now that I *would* like to see,' Mr Pepys said, striking up the note.

Bird picked up her cerise scarf and hopped from foot to foot in a mad caper, to dispel the feeling that he'd seen something of her she did not want to show. Only half-way through she realised she must look a bedlam fool, but by then it was too late to stop. Elisabeth Pepys was watching her, mouth open, from the corner, then whispering something to the other ladies that amused them.

It's me, Bird thought. I'm the cause of their amusement. But she kept the smile pinned to her face, kicked her feet and acted merry, all the time willing the song to end.

Mr Pepys seemed to have noticed nothing amiss as she sank gratefully onto a stool, and wiped her curls away from her forehead with a shaking hand. How foolish. She was hoping to impress these people, after all Mr Lanier was often at court; she'd seen him in the king's company in Oxforde. What a fool she was! All she'd done was convey the impression she was touched in the wits. It made her feel queasy. Too much dancing on an empty stomach.

Mr Pepys lay down the viol and hurried to the side table where a tray was set with cakes and ale. She watched his neat legs in their tidy blue silk stockings as he went, but was surprised when he returned to her.

He held out a small cup of ale like a gift. 'Here, my dear Mrs Knepp, you deserve that after your exertions,' he said.

She took it and sipped, determined not to make a show of herself again.

'That scarf has made a red mark on your neck,' he said. 'The dye must not be properly fixed.'

'Oh.' She felt heat rise to her face. 'Yes, I borrowed it from the theatre.' She put a hand to her throat.

'You have a fine voice,' he said, leaning in towards her. 'Do not be ashamed of—'

'Samuel!' Mrs Pepys was upon them, all flap and flutter, and he had to break off.

He looked at his knees as if caught doing something improper.

Mrs Pepys frowned, 'Come and sit by me, Samuel. I refuse to lose you to that infernal din, *all* night.'

'Certainly, my dear,' he said, rising to follow her.

She watched them go. Elisabeth had ignored him most of the time, and then at a whim expected him to be at her beck and call. She wondered what it would be like to be Mrs Pepys instead of Mrs Knepp. This was the type of man her father should have found for her. Someone who loved music as she did, a man who brought her a drink without any bidding, instead of demanding one, a man who could appreciate poetry and not just horseflesh.

CHAPTER 25

'Another letter came for Mary Elizabeth. It appears she has yet another engagement tomorrow.'

At his mother's voice, Knepp looked up from the table where he was wrestling with the morning mail. Bills, demands, final reckonings. The plague months had taken their toll. His fortunes were plummeting again.

'Third one this week,' his mother said, interrupting his thoughts. 'And leaving me on my own again with only that scrap of a servant for company. My, Mary Elizabeth must be popular.'

'Well it hasn't resulted in much more trade.' Her popularity pricked like a thorn. He threw down the bill he was holding. 'I want to see what my wife does at these "entertainments". Trade is just the same. I think they're a waste of time. She earns a pittance and could be doing something more useful in the yard, until the theatres re-open.'

'Getting the name Knepp into court circles can't be bad. She's not a bad wife. You could do worse, you know, Christopher.'

'How? She disobeys me at every turn.'

'It's how you ask. Try to be a little soft.'

'She's my wife, for God's sake. She took a holy vow to obey me, and by God I'll make her if I have to.'

Mrs Knepp sighed. 'Then I see I will have no grandchildren to comfort me.'

'Don't be foolish, Mother.'

'Just try a little softness.'

The door from outside swung open and Mary Elizabeth came in, muffled in her winter cloak and dragging a basket of laundry. She looked dishevelled and her nose was pink from the cold.

'I'll come with you tomorrow night, to Mrs Pierce's,' Knepp said. 'I have a mind to hear this singing you spend so long over.'

Mary Elizabeth dropped the basket to the ground. 'What? It's not at Mrs Pierce's, it's at Mr Pepys's temporary lodgings. It's all the way out of town.'

'Then I'll accompany you to the Pepyses' lodgings.'

Mary Elizabeth frowned. 'It won't be very merry. There's no good players, and the company will be very dull.'

'I daresay I'll survive it. I want to see what you do.'

She was silent; her expression mutinous. He was about to take her to task again when his mother interrupted. 'He just wants to meet these fine friends you've made.'

Mary Elizabeth picked up the basket again. 'But Mr Pepys didn't invite him,' she said coolly.

Now he felt the anger rise in a tide. 'Damn you. I'm coming with you, or you don't go. Your choice.' And with that, he stormed from the chamber.

First thing in the morning Bird arose and had to vomit into the chamber pot. She was shaking, her legs like feathers. Pray God it was not the plague. Probably something she had eaten at Mrs Pierce's, a reaction to the night before last. She'd been feeling unwell yesterday. But the thought of plague had taken root, and she trembled so much that she had to strip off her clothes and examine herself all over for blemishes. But she could see nothing amiss, though she twisted and stretched to see her back in the hand-held looking glass.

By the evening the sickness had abated, and it stemmed her fears about the plague, though another worry had lodged in its place. Knepp still insisted on joining her, and she worried he would humiliate her and make her talk of money before the guests. She had given him a clean shirt but he had chosen not to wear it. Instead he was wearing stained breeches, an old-fashioned doublet over his work shirt, and his jaw showed two days' worth of stubble. His cloak stank of horse and tobacco. She knew she would be ashamed, and fall in the estimation of the company. It was point-less to argue, the more she tried to keep him away, the more he was determined to come.

They travelled by boat to Greenwich in frosty silence. He'd ruined it all. She had looked forward to singing with Mr Pepys, and now she would be afraid to enjoy herself.

After they'd travelled about half-way, Knepp suddenly said, 'Why is Mrs Pepys lodging at Woolwich, when Mr Pepys is at Greenwich?'

'Mrs Pierce says it's because Greenwich is near the dockyard where he does his important business. He said Woolwich was too inconvenient. Though it's safer. It's four miles further down the Thames, away from the plague.'

'Still seems a strange thing to do to cast your wife off like that. Why didn't he stay at home?'

'I expect there were no servants there to look to him.'

Knepp fell back to silence.

Winter was coming and the sky held the threat of snow. Bird shivered as the sky darkened and the lights along the banks began to glimmer through the rising mist, but she was grateful for the gloom which meant she did not have to look at her husband.

As the boat bumped against the landing stage, her stomach churned with agitation, and she slipped on the wooden jetty and had to clasp the rail, her heart thudding as she felt herself almost topple into the icy water.

'Boy!' Knepp summoned one of the link boys with a crooked finger. 'Light us to Remmer's Row. Mr Pepys' lodgings.'

'I know it, sir. This way.' The boy set off eagerly into the twisting alleys leading from the water.

Knepp strode after him, hands stuck into his breeches' pockets, his breath wreathing around his head. Bird stumbled after, clutching her borrowed cloak to her chest, determined to be at his side when they arrived.

The house was a large three-storey building of brick with half-timbered upper storeys and lights showing in every window. She could imagine what Knepp was thinking: wasteful.

He threw the boy a token and rapped on the door as if he would wake the dead. Mary Mercer, the Pepys' new maidservant, neat as a bodkin in starched cap, opened the door and divested them of hats and cloaks.

The company were already assembled. Elisabeth Pepys, come up from Woolwich, in another over-wrought gown, greeted Bird with an airy false kiss to each cheek, before joining the others in staring at Knepp. He scowled and looked defiantly at them all, rubbing his whiskers.

'My husband, Christopher,' Bird said. His name seemed completely foreign; nothing to do with the man standing next to her with his hunched shoulders and belligerent glare.

There was a mumble of acknowledgement. Mr Pierce approached hurriedly and tried to engage Knepp in a conversation about horses, but his answers were terse, and Pierce soon drifted away. Knepp scowled at his back and found himself a hard-backed chair in the corner of the room.

Mr Pepys appeared in a great fluster, having

come from the Navy office. Bird tried not to stare, though her attention drifted to him, and she got the impression from his side-long glances that he had spotted her too. He was soon the centre of attention with rip-roaring tales of the Duke of Albermarle and Prince Rupert who was to go to sea in the New Year against the Dutch.

'Mrs Knepp!' he finally exclaimed, hurrying over to her and taking her by both hands. His eyes twinkled at her with lively interest. 'Such a pleasure to see you again. I'm so glad you could come.' He held onto her fingers as if he did not wish to let them go, and the sensation raised a flutter in her chest, along with a twinge of guilt.

She reluctantly withdrew, and pulled him over to meet Knepp. 'Mr Pepys, this is . . . my husband.' This time his Christian name stuck in her throat.

Knepp did not stand, but sniffed and nodded insultingly from his chair.

'Good to meet you, my man,' Mr Pepys said.

Knepp slowly looked Mr Pepys up and down. Bird was acutely aware of Samuel's lace-edged cravat, and his general air of genial but patronising good humour.

'We are so glad you invited us, aren't we?' she prompted Knepp desperately.

'Your wife is a fine singer,' Mr Pepys said.

'Then let's hear her,' Knepp said. 'She doesn't sing at home.'

Mr Pepys gave a nervous laugh, as if to make a jest of it, and took her by the arm over to the music stand. As he played, and Bird sang, the conversation flowed around them, all seemingly without penetrating Knepp's surly exterior. Bird could feel the storm brewing, but was powerless to do anything about it.

The musicians struck up a dance and she was obliged to dance with Mr Pierce, Mr Coleman, and finally Samuel Pepys.

'Doesn't your husband dance?' Samuel asked her, glancing at the stony figure in the corner.

'No. I don't believe he ever learnt.'

'A shame. He's missing a great pleasure.' Mr Pepys said. 'Especially with a partner such as your good self.' The music whirled faster and Mr Pepys held her tighter and spun her around the floor. She felt as if her feet were flying, but the sick feeling in her stomach rose again.

'Please, put me down Mr Pepys.'

'Do you not like this tune?'

'I do, but my husband . . .'

'He cannot mind. I meant nothing by it, just a dance. It can't harm.'

'I know, but he . . .' She shook her head, unwilling to explain. She could not tell him that he could not even imagine what her life was like at Knepp's yard. And from the corner of her eye she could see Knepp leaning forward in his chair staring at her through narrowed eyes. It made any light conversation impossible. And Mr Pepys was so charming, so much the gentleman. He could have no idea.

'Samuel.' Elisabeth ran over to claim him at the sound of the tinkling bell that summoned them to their places for supper. She was seated opposite, whereas Bird was seated with Knepp on her left, and Mr Pepys on her right.

They were to begin with oysters, steeped in lemon juice, he told her. Lemons in December! They were at least six pennies a piece. But as soon as the plate was set before her, she began to feel queasy again. She picked up her knife, but dizziness made her set it down again.

Pepys placed a hand over hers. 'Are you all right? You're grey as a goose.'

'I've had too much wine, is all.'

Elisabeth Pepys put down her napkin with a flounce and glared at her.

In Bird's ear on her left came the clipped words, 'Get that filthy dog's paws off you.'

She pulled away from Pepys as if burnt, and turned to face Knepp.

In an undertone he said, 'If you make me look a fool, you'll be sorry.'

Bile rose in her throat. She stumbled to her feet and out of the chamber, blundering to the closet where she was just in time to vomit into the porcelain washbowl. She really couldn't sit and look at those slimy oysters. Her mouth was full of a strange metallic taste. It could be fear, or it could be . . .

Oh, please God, not that. Not a baby.

She leant up against the wooden shutters. The image of Knepp's dour face shot into her vision.

The thought of having something of his inside her made her quake with revulsion. Could she get rid of it? She would be unable to be a player if she was having a baby. The thought had no time to lodge before the other thought was upon it, that even to think such a thing was a mortal sin.

When she got back to the company, her husband had already left to check Nipper had arrived with his carriage to take them to the boat.

'Mrs Knepp, are you recovered?' Mr Pepys put a soft hand on her shoulder. 'What did your husband say to you, to upset you so?'

'He is always angry if I am merry,' she said. 'It's as if others' enjoyment reminds him how melancholy he is.'

'How sad that he—' Pepys stepped away as Knepp glowered from the door.

'Mary Elizabeth.' Knepp beckoned her with a sharp incline of his head. 'Have you been paid?'

'Oh, of course.' Mr Pepys reached into his pocket and drew out a sovereign.

It was far too much. It made her feel cheap, as if she'd been bought. Knepp glowered at it with a black expression. With a dip of a curtsey, she took her leave of Mr Pepys. Her last sight of him was as he stood uncertainly on the doorstep, rubbing his chin.

On the wherry home, Knepp ignored her, and it was just as well, for her thoughts tangled in webs that she could not unravel. Maybe the sickness really was the plague, and she would die. Or she would die in childbirth. It would mean the end of her career in the theatre; that much she knew. Men had no such worries, they could sow their seed wherever they would, and never have to worry.

How would she survive it? She would be confined at Knepp's. It would be like a prison sentence. When the theatres reopened, she would be at home nursing Knepp's baby. Her life in the theatre was over.

CHAPTER 26

Livvy tucked in the corners of the sheets with knife-like pleats, and smoothed them over the mattress. Viner and the men would be back soon, and the thought made her stomach tumble and her mouth parched as dust. The war with the Dutch was going well for her countrymen, but it made her nervous about her own fate.

Was it bad to wish the plague would stay longer? She hoped that Viner's fancy would have moved on, since he'd been away. Or that he'd pay more mind to his wife. Arabella Viner never came near the yard or the horses, though she'd seen her ride, once, and been impressed with how natural she looked on horseback. Rumour was, she hated the whole dirty business of horses and muck, and saw herself as a cut above everyone else, but whenever Livvy had seen her she looked lost. A sadness around the eyes like a dog to slaughter, her hands unable to be still, always twiddling with something: her hair pins, or her collar, or the edges of her sleeves. Poor woman, she thought. Though by rights, she, Livvy, should be the poorer.

Livvy inspected the bed she was making for wrinkles and stood up to stretch her back. She was just unlocking the next room when a voice called out to her, 'Livvy!'

She turned, and there was Bird Knepp, her old mistress, nose red with cold, and lacking her usual smile.

'So you're back,' Livvy said. 'How was Oxforde?' Straight away she felt something amiss. 'What's the matter?'

'I'm with child.' It came out defiant.

'You certain?'

A miserable nod. 'Sure as I ever can be.'

Livvy pursed her lips. 'Guess by the look of you, that's not good.'

'Livvy, can we go inside?' Once in the chamber, Bird said, 'I can't keep it. It would sentence me to a life behind Knepp's closed doors. Do you know someone? Someone who . . .'

'You sure 'bout this?'

'I just want rid of it.'

'Mrs Megg's girls say that too, but there's many as change their minds.'

'I won't.'

'It's dangerous and it don't always work, you know that?'

She nodded, but Livvy knew Bird didn't really understand the whole mess of it.

'It'll make you grieve,' Livvy said.

'It'll make me grieve more to birth it.'

'And the guilt. It makes girls waste away like

336

ghosts. It ain't easy to live with yourself if you make something die.'

'What would you do, in my place?'

'I'm not you, am I? If you be looking for me to say it don't matter, you'd be a fool.' Livvy sighed. 'There's an apothecary next to the whorehouse on Seddon Street. It's where Nell's mother's girls go if they need to . . . well, lose something quick.'

'Will you write it down?'

'Can't write. It's the sign of the Pestle and Mortar. You can't miss it.'

'Oh.'

Livvy saw she was waiting for something more. Perhaps she hoped Livvy would go with her, but this was something a woman had to do on her own, no-one holding her hand. She didn't want no-one saying it was her fault after. Servants were too easy to blame. Livvy's heart ached for Bird, but she kept her mouth shut.

When Bird was gone Livvy paced the room, back and forth in her old felt slippers. Had she done right? All these deaths these last months, why would anyone need another?

By the time she'd finished cleaning the last room, the yard had erupted into a frenzy of activity and the hire-horses and carriages clattered back into the yard. From the window Livvy watched the entourage arrive; Viner's weak-chinned son, Georgie, was driving, but didn't help his mother get out of the carriage, and neither did Viner. She watched their heads in their fur-lined hats as they strode off towards the offices below. Mrs Viner struggled out of the carriage alone and lost-looking, and had to holler to get the men to fetch the trunks into the house.

As Viner passed, he glanced up to the window. Livvy shot back, out of sight. The look filled her heart with foreboding. She understood instantly. Nothing had changed.

Killigrew had called Bird to rehearsal. Any other time she would have leapt to it. But now? Oh, why couldn't the theatre alterations have taken longer? Determined, she pretended all was well, quipped and jested with the rest, and played with passion, though inside she felt bitter. First the plague, then this. She'd been cheated. The cheerful company only grated, and all day she struggled to concentrate, what with the sickness, and the weight of the worry.

After rehearsal Bird speeded her step towards the apothecary's. Now or never. A week, she'd waited. If she was going to do something about her predicament, it would have to be tonight, because Knepp was away. Mrs Knepp, the fool, had sold her last remaining gold necklace and with the proceeds Knepp had taken a coach to Northampton horse sale, to buy more horses. He'd heard Viner was back in town and was anxious, as usual, to be one step ahead of him.

Bird approached Coal Yard Alley warily. Nell's mother ran a bawdy house here, and it was where

Livvy used to live, though it was not an area Bird had ever been to before. She was aware of stares from upper-floor windows. The further she went, the more the uncomfortable feeling prickled; as if she was being watched from the depths of the ancient, cramped alleyways. The way grew darker and dingier; the houses perched in ramshackle rookeries. Smokestacks perched higgledy-piggledy on top of roofs peppered with pigeon shit. Every house seemed to have broken tiles and shutters and an air of seedy neglect.

She paused under the sign, willing herself to go inside. The apothecary's had no windows, only a shutter to the street, which was battened down. She took a deep breath, and burst inside. The shop stank of something sharp and vinegary, though the counter was ringed with grease and dust, and bottles of leeches squirmed on the shelf behind.

She gagged and almost ran out, but forced herself to stay rooted.

The apothecary sidled to the counter. A man who looked as though he had died and not quite come back to life. A head like a skeleton, with a few wisps of hair on his bald skull, and bony hands with long, yellowing fingernails.

She quelled the quaver in her voice. 'I want something strong,' she said, 'something that will get rid of something I don't want.'

'Who sent you?' he croaked. 'Mrs Gwynne from next door?'

'No,' she said rather too sharply, offended he

should think her a whore. 'And it doesn't matter who sent me, can you help?'

'Maybe. Babe is it? How many weeks've you been sickening?'

'Four weeks, maybe? Could be five.'

He sucked on his teeth. 'It's late. Late accidents cost more to loosen.'

'I'll pay.' She took her house-keeping purse from her hanging pocket and let the weight of it clink down on the counter under her hand. She prayed the cost of what she needed would leave her enough left to feed the men tomorrow in Knepp's absence.

He licked his lips. 'Aye, well in that case . . . you must follow my instructions exactly, or the remedy might not work. And I'll have you know, in these late cases there's no guarantee.'

'Make it double strong then.'

He reached for the jars marked with *pennyroyal*, *rue* and *rosemary*, and tipped a little into the mortar for grinding. A slosh of amber spirit on top, and a nub of wizened root. She tilted her head to read the label. *Stinking gladdon*. An odour of rotting meat. She pressed her kerchief to her mouth as he scraped the pestle round the bowl.

'Excuse me,' she said, hurrying out of the door. She spit bile into the street, watched by several amused whores from next door's window.

By the time she came back he had emptied the mess into a wide-topped jar and corked it. 'Half just before you retire for bed, half as you rise,' he said. 'Hold your nose, and straight down. Best have plenty of chamber pots ready and clean sheets. Don't be tempted to drink any ale or other fluid, no matter how thirsty it makes you. After the bleeding ends, you must take this.' He tapped out a small scatter of brownish green powder into a paper.

'What's that?'

'Blood stopper,' he said as he twisted the paper closed. 'Dried stag's urine and violet leaf to tighten the womb afterwards. Mix it with milk.'

Would she be able to swallow any of that stuff down? It had the taint of a magic spell about it, and it made her conscience rise in protest. She must force herself. After she paid, she hid the jars in her basket to keep it out of the sight of Knepp. So far she'd managed not to alert him to her sickness, but since the lime-skin argument, he or his mother would be bound to ask questions if he found anything from the apothecary in her possession.

She took the remedy straight home and as she crossed the yard, Knepp and the stable lads were saddling the horses and a pack-mule for his ride out to Newbury. He barely looked in her direction. By the time she set off to rehearsal, having hidden it under her nightclothes in the small chamber, he'd left with not even a goodbye.

Tonight, she would have to do it, and she hoped the affair would be quiet and painless.

★   ★   ★

341

'I'll not stay up for supper, my head's banging,' Bird said.

'What is it?' Her mother-in-law's eyes became alert. She heaved herself up from her day-bed. 'Have you examined yourself?'

'No need. It's not the plague. I just have a bad head. A hard day of rehearsal, and too much of Killigrew's pernickety criticism. Or maybe I've eaten something.'

'Are you sure? It starts that way, I've heard, with an ache in the head or gripes of the stomach.'

'It's not the plague.' She tried to keep the annoyance from her voice.

'It could be. You—'

'It's not. It's just a bad head. I'm going to bed. I'll sleep in the small chamber tonight, as Mr Knepp's away.'

'But that's why I gave Anis the day off. Who'll help me undress?'

'You'll have to manage. I need to lie down.'

'You do look pale, you should try to—'

But Bird didn't hear the rest, she was already hitching her skirts and with a determined step, heading upstairs. In the dark cold of the chamber, Bird lit the candles on a branched candlestick, drew the jar from her pocket and uncorked it. Even the smell made her want to gag. She held her stomach for a moment, a shiver of regret in her chest. What she was about to do was a mortal sin, and it wasn't easy to imagine forgiveness for taking a life, especially one so blameless. Her stomach was still taut and flat; the babe must be tiny, a pearl inside an oyster, and now here she was, ending its little life before it had begun. At the thought, her eyes blurred. She swallowed hard.

Hands in a clasp over her belly, she closed her eyes. 'I'm sorry,' she whispered. 'God forgive me.'

She reached for the remedy. Her hand hovered a moment, and then with a wordless prayer she upended the jar into her throat. One gulp and she was left with a pungent sour aftertaste, like vomit itself, that threatened to surge back into her mouth. She willed herself to hold it down, though her throat convulsed to bring it back up. She was still swallowing frantically as she tore rags from an old pillowslip, and dragged the chamber pot from under the bed.

At first she felt nothing, just the bitterness in her throat. Sitting on the bed, she rocked back and forth with a sudden swell of love for her own body and the babe nestled within. Too late now. Tears came but she would not allow herself the luxury of sentiment, and eventually, exhausted, as nothing seemed to be happening, she slept – a sleep of the dead; numb and dreamless.

In the middle of the night she woke, arms thrashing. Her stomach possessed a life of its own, inhabited by a thousand squirming eels. Immediately she had to vomit, and then use the chamber pot. After that, the pain, unbearable, a dagger in her stomach, twisting and writhing.

Groaning, she grabbed the sheets and bit down

onto them, but the pain had stronger teeth. She clenched her fists into her guts, and still the agony did not cease. She cursed Knepp, and she cursed the apothecary. An hour later she was drenched in cold sweat, but still the babe hadn't come.

Another griping pain seized her and she let out another groan and grabbed the bedpost. She vaguely registered a noise outside on the stairs, but she couldn't leave go.

The door creaked open. Mrs Knepp clutched the door frame for support, her sparse grey hair unpinned, her nightdress flapping under a heavy knitted shawl. 'Is it the plague?' she asked.

Bird couldn't answer, except with a painful and empty heave towards the chamber pot.

In a blur, she realised Mrs Knepp was limping past her towards the window ledge, clinging to the furniture as she went. Her gaze was locked on the bottle still uncorked on the sill. With a cry, Bird lurched from the bed and tried to grab hold of it before Mrs Knepp could reach it, but her legs were like straw, and buckled beneath her.

'What's this?' Mrs Knepp swiped it off the sill. 'Is it a plague potion? It has no label.'

'A tisane for my bad head,' Bird said weakly. She was cold now and shivering so hard her teeth chattered.

Mrs Knepp wafted the bottle under her nose and recoiled. 'That smell. I recognise it. It's iris root – stinking gladdon. Why do you need a purge like this for a headache?'

The cramps came again, as if they would wring her out. Bird let out another moan. The room was churning, Mrs Knepp's face swam before her as if underwater.

She saw Mrs Knepp hold the bottle out at arm's length, scrutinising the contents. 'I've only ever smelt this stuff once before,' Mrs Knepp said, 'and it was thirty years ago when I wanted to dispose of . . . an unwanted bundle. I'll never forget it; it was a horrible business. The pain, the blood, and . . .' She paused, staring hard at Bird. Silently she re-corked the bottle and placed it back on the sill. 'Tell me it's not true.'

Bird shook her head for an answer, but doubled over, overtaken by another twist in her guts.

Mrs Knepp's face loomed close to hers. 'Are you with child?'

When she didn't reply, Mrs Knepp took hold of both her shoulders with her claw-like hands. 'Answer me!' Her nails dug into Bird's collarbone, but Bird evaded her eyes. She was too exhausted to argue, and besides the babe was still clinging on inside her.

'You dare to do this to Christopher?' Mrs Knepp thrust her roughly away, then seized the bottle again.

Bird knew what she would do. 'No! Don't! I need the rest—'

But she was too late; Mrs Knepp pulled open the casement and emptied it into the yard with a splatter.

345

Bird fell back onto the bed, her stomach still cramping as she ground her teeth together and prayed for the pain to stop. Had it all been for nothing? She turned her back on Mrs Knepp, curled herself into a ball and put her hands on her belly.

All night dark waves of pain surged and withdrew. The child did not come.

'All right,' she whispered to her belly. 'You win.'

The next time she became aware, dawn had lit up the window with a rosy glow. Bird peeled up her nightdress and peered under her skirts. Nothing – no blood, no courses.

'So you're awake.'

Bird started. Mrs Knepp was still there, a wraith-like figure at the foot of the bed, sitting very upright on her hard bedroom chair.

'I feel shivery.'

'You deserve it.' Then quietly, 'It's a sin.'

Dim memories of the night before re-surfaced. 'Then you should know. I presume the remedy actually worked for you.'

'It's been a stain on my life all these years, and I've always regretted it. All this time, and I still can't forgive myself.'

Bird pulled herself up in bed against the pillows. 'God forgives. Did you pray?'

Her face took on a hollow expression. 'Every blessed day. When I birthed Christopher, it was like the torments of hell. They say you forget. Not true. It lasted three days, and the midwife who helped me . . . well, she was no use. I could see the terror in her eyes, and in the end I was so weak I could not push enough. She panicked and got some men to try to pull the babe out by the heels with a crook, and it nearly tore me apart. They cut me to do it, and I lost so much blood I nearly died. So, you see, I just couldn't face the terror of that, or the knife again. I had my two boys to carry on the line. What good was another? But my husband would go into one of his wild enthusiasms and insist . . .'

'So you took remedy and Christopher was your last.'

'Thank God. Or I swear I would not be living today.'

Bird drew her knees up to her chest. On the mantel the last candle guttered, leaving them in the pale dawn light. She gazed at her stomach. 'This child will take away everything that makes my life worth living.'

'But you have no children. At least I had two boys. What is worth more than a child if you have none? The playhouse? What's that next to the love of a mother for her son? Sometimes I love Christopher and James so much it makes me double over. I ache for them. So much aching, sons bring. Even though they are grown men.'

'Your son never really sees me. On the stage I am visible . . . to someone. When I sing, I become myself again. Without that to sustain me, there would only be misery and drudgery. In the theatre, though it is only a pretence, it's my window to the world I used to know. I can be who I used to be. I can pretend I never married; that I am someone else.' She paused, examined her pale hands where they trembled on the coverlet. 'Your son; he is a tyrant, just like his father.'

The old woman shrugged, and passed her a glass of water. She sipped at it gratefully. 'You should feel sorry for Christopher. All women are his enemy.'

'Then why did he marry me? For spite? He acts as if he hates me. Yet with the horses he is so gentle. If he gave me half the care he gives them—'

'He cannot. He cannot love you. He cannot love anyone. He had his heart broken, and it has never mended.'

'He has no heart.'

Mrs Knepp stood. 'That's not true. You should have seen him when he was a boy, romping in the fields with his dog; he was good-natured, full of warmth, and he worshipped his father. Christopher took his father's death hard, but worse was the fact that he could have prevented it.'

'Why? I don't understand.'

'Christopher was betrothed to Arabella St John. Of course they knew each other as children, but she was sent away to an aunt, and when she returned at age eighteen, he became besotted with her. I have never seen a boy so smitten. She was handsome, with a mass of curly hair and that long aristocratic nose. Add to that she was a fearless rider to hounds. She'd hunt anything; buck, fox, deer, otter. But able to hold her own in any company, too. Christopher doted on that girl, and she led him to understand they'd be married – that our two good families would be bound together by blood.'

'Would he had married *her*, then.'

'He would have, but for Cromwell's war. We were unlucky. Our home was sacked, and the contents sold or plundered. There were debts. My husband had pledged his land to buy arms for the king. Of course he had no doubt the king would win. Foolish man! We lost everything. Christopher and James found themselves heir to a patch of nettles and a pigsty.'

'The pigsty is still here.'

A tap on the hand. 'Do you want to know, or not?'

'Go on.'

'Well, James was lucky; he was already wed, and possessor of a fine house, the property of his lady-wife. But Christopher was unfortunate. When we lost our estate Arabella believed she could do better for herself, and she married another man.'

'Don't tell me.'

Mrs Knepp nodded. 'Ted Viner. When nothing could be done, and Arabella's wealth could not save him from debt, my husband finally threw himself under the mill wheel. It took two days to find him, and four men to drag him free.'

Bird was beginning to see.

'Christopher blamed Ted Viner, but worse, he blamed himself. He vowed to oust Ted Viner from the horse hire business and win back the hand of Arabella. He cursed himself for losing her, and because he couldn't keep her, for his father's self-murder. It's become an obsession with him to get her back. He's been trying for eighteen years.'

Eighteen years. The idea was both poignant and horrifying.

'But that's madness! I always thought him unnaturally obsessed by Viner, but I never understood why. Does this woman Arabella know he's still pursuing her?'

'I expect she must. And it hurts me to see my son made a laughing stock. I think he married you to cock a snook at the Viners, but of course they don't care. They haven't seen his pain. To them he is just this pathetic little man, following them around like a tail. But to me, he's my son, and I just can't bear to see it.'

'That's no reason for him to hate me so.'

'No, no, no! It's not you he hates! Can't you see it? He hates himself. If you'd seen him, when she first threw him over, he could not even drag himself out of bed. He'd lost his father and never properly grieved; but now, here were two griefs together. Anyone would be crushed by them. And the more people told him to get over it, the less he could. I tried everything, priests, cunning women, astrologers. No-one could do anything. In the end he got over it by passing on his pain

350

to everyone else.' She edged her chair nearer, and leaned in. 'So you see, you must give him this child. It might bring him back to love again.'

'You ask too much! I have no feeling for your son. I could never love him. He has abused and humiliated me at every turn. Do you think I want to risk it, that a child might be treated as he treats me?' She hit a fist down on the counterpane. 'And what would my life become, tied here to a life with no music in it, no singing or company?'

'You could carry on, once the babe is born.' Mrs Knepp leaned forward, an eager light in her eyes. 'I will mind the child, love him as I loved Christopher.'

'He would never permit it. And you are old; too old to run after a child.'

'Where there's a will . . . after all, I made it up these stairs, didn't I? And the child seems to be sticking, whether you will it or no.'

The silence hung in the room. Mrs Knepp took hold of her hand. 'Please, Mary Elizabeth. I will love it. This house needs some love.'

Bird was warmed by the gesture, and by the soft use of her name. She lay back on the pillows, exhausted.

'We won't tell him yet,' Mrs Knepp said. 'It can be our little secret.'

CHAPTER 27

January 1666

London was stiff and creaking with frost, and still half-empty from the populace that had fled the plague. But the bells had stopped tolling, and for once the citizens could take an unfettered breath in the knowledge that for now, at least, the great beast of the plague had slunk away.

On the Strand the shops had opened again, though many of the windows bore black-edged notices, or writs affixed to the door, saying that the hours would be shorter until they found new staff.

In the dark chamber at Hubert's watchmaker's, Livvy and Robert sat side by side, their breath steaming in the cold air. Livvy was darning a pair of woollen stockings as he read to her from the broadsheet. She was desperate to know whether the war was going to end soon, for whilst the Dutch were the enemy, she could not leave Viner's without the risk he would betray them both as traitors. And whilst she stayed, she must suffer Viner's foulness whenever he demanded.

She shivered just thinking of him.

'I'm sorry,' Robert said, 'but since I've been away these last months, I didn't buy coal, so I have no fire.'

'It doesn't matter,' Livvy said.

'But I know you feel the cold.'

Livvy gave her knee a slap. 'Under here I have a good thick flannel petticoat.' She paused and looked down. The mention of her underclothes hung between them.

Robert coughed, and rustled the paper.

'Did Petersen's ship get to France? Did he tell you how it goes with your father?' she asked hurriedly. She knew Robert had just returned from Sweden aboard a ship captained by a friend of his father's – a Swede called Petersen, who often travelled to France bringing iron from Sweden for the clockmaking business. In return the Swede took timepieces back to Stockholm.

Robert's eyes glowed with warmth. 'Papa is well. He never changes. He is very strict, very precise. Petersen is great admirer of my father's skill. He say last time he visit the shop in Rouen it is filled with the smell of my mother's *madeleines*. Can you believe, people stand outside just to smell it.' He shook his head. 'I miss them both. But most the *madeleines*.'

His grin confused her. 'Good cooking,' she said gravely. 'Stomach first, my mother say.'

'And your father, Livvy . . . is he . . .?'

The question came too quickly, like a dart in

353

the flesh. She hadn't prepared an answer. To her surprise, the truth slipped out, defiant.

'Dead. He was a slave on an English plantation in the Indies. He spoke against the foreman. So they whipped him until he died.' She stuck the darning needle in her apron and busied herself winding wool onto the ball.

When she looked up, Robert blinked and blinked again. His expression looked like he would speak, but then he thought better of it. The silence lengthened; bloomed.

'The Dutch war goes ill for the English,' he said, finally, pointing to the paper.

'I'm glad,' Livvy said, recovering herself. 'My mother and brother will be relieved. They live in Terschelling, by the Dutch coast. Tell me what else it says. Does it say who will win, and when?'

'It's complicated.' He scanned the page. 'Ah, but you will like this. The Dutch have rebuilt their ships with heavier guns, and the paper says they plot to join the French to come against England. Huzzah!'

'Then we will be allies against the English.'

He smiled and rested his hand on hers. 'We are already allies.'

She looked down at the way his white hand covered her black one, and was surprised that it should be so warm. He took it away immediately, but she still felt its heat.

'I wish the war would be over.' She spoke with venom. 'I hate the English.'

Robert put the paper down. 'They are stupid and stiff, I agree. But they are the same as any other people. Some are good, some bad.'

'You wouldn't say that if . . .'

'If what?'

'Nothing. It doesn't matter. Forget I spoke.'

Robert looked into her face as if he would read her thoughts; rested a hand on her knee. 'You can talk to me. Whatever is hurting you, I would keep it to myself.' His face was creased in concern.

Livvy swallowed the lump in her throat. 'Mr Viner, he—'

The door opened and banged against the wall, and a bitter blast of cold air whistled in. Livvy leapt up, pulling away from him.

'Sorry, Hubert,' the man said, grabbing the door to force it shut, 'the wind caught it. Cold as the devil out there.'

'Ah, Mr Browning. Your watch is ready.'

'Good, good. Girl, take my hat.' Browning held out his beaver fur hat to Livvy, who took it without a word and hung it on the stand near the door. Robert threw her an apologetic look, just before she hurried from the shop.

After his customer had gone, Robert stared down at the broadsheet. Now Livvy was gone, it had lost its appeal. What use was news with no-one to share it with? He put it to one side, his mind haunted by the thoughts of the man falling beneath the whip.

★   ★   ★

Bird still had said nothing to Knepp of her condition, though her breasts had begun to swell and she was bone-tired. Mrs Knepp had rather pointedly begun embroidering a baby blanket, but as usual Knepp never took much interest in what his mother was making. Over the last weeks the morning sickness had abated; everywhere she went, though, she seemed to see babies. How had she never noticed them before? She pondered about Dorcas, and her father's child, but pushed thoughts of it away. Their new babe might be born by now, and Father hadn't even sent her a message. Was he returned to London? If so, he never brought Henry to visit. In fact, she hadn't seen any of them for nearly two years, and it gave her a tight, breathless feeling of rage.

Today she had been invited to sing at Lord Bruncker's house with her other theatrical friends. Knepp had satisfied his curiosity about the company she kept, dismissing them all as 'good for nothing dandies', so she was to go with Mrs Pierce.

She had yet to sit down in the carriage when Mrs Pierce grabbed her by the arm, her eyes a-glitter. 'Can I tell you something?'

Bird slammed the door shut, and squashed herself in.

'I'm to have another child! I thought I may never have another, as it's been so long coming. Mr Pierce is marvellously pleased.'

'My felicitations, Mrs Pierce, that's splendid news.' Her words felt empty. Would Knepp be 'marvellously pleased' when she told him? She doubted it. She dreaded the thought of it all. The fuss, the sudden feeling that your body belonged to someone else, that everyone would have opinions about what she ought to do.

As soon as she arrived at Lord Bruncker's, a fine big set of chambers within the impressive brick-built Navy Buildings, she was aware of feeling someone's eyes on her, by the prickling sensation on the back of her neck. Startled, she whipped round to see Samuel Pepys watching her. Even as she handed her cloak to the maid, his eyes sought hers, and she was flattered, though she placed her hands over her stomach as if he might see the bulge. She ignored him at first, so as not to show how pleased she was to see him.

He was talking with Lord Bruncker's consort, Abigail Williams, a part player at the Duke's, a coarsely handsome woman with a predatory manner, and hair as black as jet. Vixen. She'd hemmed Samuel into a corner, talking animatedly, with one hand resting languorously on his arm. Samuel saw Bird looking and raised his eyebrows in a helpless shrug.

Finally Mrs Williams sauntered away from him, with the air of a cat dropping a mouse. Bird's irritation subsided as the music began, and a barrel of Malaga sack appeared. Glasses were filled and re-filled until the rest of the company – Mr Minnes and the Turners – were quite drunk. Bird only sipped at her drink; she didn't want to be made a fool, and besides, the gleam in Samuel's eye made her heart feel fluttery.

He caught her eye, spluttering with laughter as Mr Minnes and Mrs Williams mimicked the king and Mrs Castlemaine.

'Stop, stop,' he wheezed, 'Let's have more music before I die of mirth!'

'What would you sing?' Bird asked, walking over.

'Your choice, Mrs Knepp.'

'There's a ballad I'm fond of; one I used to sing as a child.' Bird took a piece of music from her bag. She had written it out especially, hoping he would ask.

'We will need to share the music as I have only one copy.' She turned to the lutenist. 'Do you know it, Mr Lanier? It goes like this.' She hummed the tune.

'Ah yes, I know the tune, Scottish, I think.'

'That's the one.'

He struck a few chords and Bird began, singing the tale of two lovers who died for love. Samuel held the music for her, and began to join in the chorus.

'Again!' he said. 'I know it now. Let's sing it again.'

This time his arm crept around her waist and they sang together, acting it out with large gestures.

Barbara Allen was buried in the old
* churchyard*
Sweet William was buried beside her,
Out of sweet William's heart, there grew a rose
Out of Barbara Allen's a briar.
They grew and grew in the old churchyard
Till they could grow no higher
At the end they formed, a true lover's knot
And the rose grew round the briar.

On the last line he squeezed her waist and his lips came close to her ear. 'Oh that was sublime,' he whispered.

'Once more then?' Bird asked.

'I wish I could, but I cannot stay. I must to the office now, for it is post night, and I need to get the Navy dispatches sent.'

'So soon?' The thought was out before she could hold it back. She flushed.

'I'm loath to leave my Barbary Allen, but duty calls. Fortunately, I don't have far to go.' He took her hand in his and made a little bow, his eyes locked to hers. It was a romantic gesture, such as a lover might make, and it made a sweet pain in her chest. As he let go, his fingers brushed hers, soft and feathery, like the wings of a sparrow. 'I have written a song. Nothing much; quite short, but I'd love to hear it sung. I wonder, Mrs Knepp, if you might do me the honour of learning my song?'

'I'd love to,' she said, heat blooming on her cheeks.

'A moment then.' He hurried out to the hall. Lord, he was a fine figure; so dapper and neat, and his face so open and enquiring. She wondered in that instant about his wife, whether she was waiting for him at home, but it was a thought she did not want to acknowledge.

A few moments later he was back, pink and beaming, and holding out a paper with the notes to a song pricked out on it. '"Beauty Retire". It's my only copy,' he said.

'Oh, are you sure?'

'It will give me great pleasure to hear it in your sweet voice.'

'Then I shall take care of it with my life,' she said.

His hand reached out to her shoulder and his touch sent another shudder of pleasure through her spine. It was his farewell, and as he detached himself, she felt a pang of loss.

She watched him stride purposefully over to say his farewells to Lord Bruncker, and call for his boy who was with the other servants below. The boy brought his hat and a heavy cloak, which he swung over his shoulders. As he went out of the door he turned and raised the hat to her, a big smile lighting his face, before blowing her a dramatic farewell kiss. She made an extravagant curtsey. It was as if they were the only two in the chamber.

When the door closed behind him, the room became drab and colourless. What would it be like to live with a man such as him, instead of with Knepp? A man who made an impression every-where he went, a man of culture and education, a man who loved music as she did? She was taken with him, no denying it. And was it sinful to think that way with a bellyful of another man's child?

She must put him from her mind.

'Will you sing again, Mrs Knepp?' Lanier inter-rupted her thoughts.

'Oh yes. Yes.' But not Samuel's song. And she no longer had the heart for any other. Her thoughts were with Samuel, heading through the frosty night, with his serving boy skipping at his heels.

She put Samuel's music in her bag and at the end of the evening two of Knepp's coaches arrived and she crammed herself in, next to Mr Boreman and Mrs Turner, already dreading the thought of going back to Smithfield. Next to her, Mrs Turner fell against her, tipsy from drink, but Bird pushed her off; she had barely touched a drop. She placed her hands over her stomach. Once it thickened, there would be no more gambolling abroad, or singing with Samuel Pepys.

She was mulling on these thoughts when Mr Boreman, who had his head out of the window shouted, 'Stop!'

The coach had hardly gone a few yards when it drew to a halt making them all fall forwards.

'What is it?' Mrs Turner asked in a panic. 'Is it highway thieves?'

'Well, would you believe it, it's Mr Pepys again! He's flagged us down.'

Bird's stomach lurched.

The door of the carriage flew open, and Samuel climbed in and tried to squash between her and Mrs Turner, but there was no room. Elbows jabbed, knees poked, hats were knocked askew.

'Samuel, you oaf,' Mrs Turner said, 'you're treading on my foot!'

'Barbary Allen, you must sit on my lap,' he said, pulling her to him in the confusion. After much juggling, he got his backside on the seat and dragged her back sideways onto his lap.

'I thought you had to go to the office?' she said, to cover her embarrassment.

'I needed more of your company.' He gave her thigh a firm squeeze. 'I finished my work, sent the boy with the despatches, and came back to Bruncker's hoping to catch you for another song.'

She put the baby firmly from her mind. 'Then let's sing,' she said.

Through her skirt she felt the heat of Mr Pepys' legs as he stamped his foot to beat time. He pulled her to him, holding her solidly around the waist.

'Are you cold?' His voice was breathy in her ear. He smelt faintly of madeira wine.

She shook her head and leant back, enjoying the warmth of the contact. His hand brushed her hair away from her collarbone in a tender way, before he squeezed her waist again. The feeling made her want to cry. She glanced down at his square fingers with their neatly pared nails. When his hand crept upwards to her breast she did not stop him. She wanted him to like her, and didn't dare reject him for fear of giving him offence. And his hands were playful, not rough and wrenching like Knepp's. The sensation of his touch made her giddy and breathless, but she did not want to break the spell by turning to look at him. His hands explored her, and the sensation was so exquisite she almost wept.

Too soon they arrived at Smithfield. Bird struggled to her feet as Mrs Turner opened the door of the coach, with an expression of disapproval that was as cold as the night air. From outside, the meaty smell of the boiling vats of the tannery caught in Bird's nose.

'Must you go, my sweet Barbary Allen!' Samuel sang, tugging on her sleeve, to stop her leaving.

'Not Barbary Allen,' she said. 'My mother used to call me "Bird", on account of my liking to sing. But leave go, you know I must away.'

'You'll always be Barbary Allen to me.' He kissed her neck, then looked up with a wistful expression, which was replaced immediately by a smile.

'Then you must be Sweet William.'

'Or Dapper Dicky!' He laughed at his own ribald jest, but his eyes were searching her face for approval. She could not hold his gaze; she feared he would see her fancy for him too clearly.

She bundled herself out and banged on the door to send them on their way.

The carriage rattled away over the frosted cobbles and around the corner. Bird stood in the archway to the yard where a sole lantern hung. Her shoulders sagged. She was not Barbary Allen. That was a dream that could never became substantial. No, she was still Mary Elizabeth Knepp, failed actress, wife of a horse-trader and horse hirer, and a woman bearing a child of a man who despised her.

Through the arch was the real world, the one of a threadbare existence, as lacking in affection as it was in any other comfort. The world where sorrows past had made them all into beings who could never quite trust life to give them anything good.

A whicker told her one of the horses had noticed her arrival. No indoor lights showed so her husband would already be asleep, and she was glad. He hated her to have these friends, even though it was these very people that lined his pocket by hiring his horses.

She paused under the arch, on the shadowy threshold between their world and hers. Once she told her husband about the child, she would be trapped in his world, and there'd be no more plays, no more music. No more flirtations with Samuel Pepys.

Perhaps she could wait until the babe showed. She pressed her hands to her belly, 'Oh what's to be done, little one? You're a fighter, that's certain.' A sigh. 'Not much of a mother, am I, bringing you to this?'

★　　★　　★

A few days later, Knepp leant over the table, reading the catalogue of the forthcoming horse sale at Norwich by candlelight. His mother was stitching, in the corner by the fire, swathed in a moth-eaten knitted shawl.

'You were right. Mary Elizabeth spends too much time with those people from the theatre,' Mrs Knepp said.

'I know,' Knepp said, not looking up. 'But it brings in business.'

'Don't you worry that she is making a fool of you?'

'How so?' He paused, his finger still resting on the list.

'Well, a note came for her the other day from Samuel Pepys.'

'And?'

'Your wife turned a pretty shade of pink when she read it, and she took pen and replied straight away. Like she couldn't wait. When I asked her what Pepys said, she couldn't tell me.'

'What are you saying, Mother?'

'I'm not saying anything.'

'Will you stop speaking in riddles! If you've something to say, just speak plain.'

'She shouldn't be gallivanting in her condition.'

He stopped what he was doing.

His mother fidgeted, twining and untwining her fingers. 'I think she's with child.'

'How do you know? She looks the same to me.'

'There've been signs – sickness in the morning, and she just looks different.'

'Has she said anything?'

Mrs Knepp contemplated the needle and thread a moment, held it up to the lamp. 'Not exactly. But I think you should ask her. And she should be resting quietly at home.'

'Where is she now?'

'Gone out with Mrs Pierce.'

CHAPTER 28

Bird was quick to sense the change in atmosphere the next day over breakfast. Usually Knepp ignored her, intent on his bills, his auction catalogues and his inventory for fodder stock. Today he watched her as she got up to fetch the curds and the steaming pan of oatmeal, and again as she sliced the bread. Intensely conscious of her thickening waist, she held in her stomach. Could he know? She threw a glance at Mrs Knepp, who merely smiled benignly and carried on chewing through a crust with her few remaining teeth.

She still felt his assessing gaze on her back as he spooned his gruel. He was interrupted when a stable lad came, saying a client was asking for him. He hurried past, grabbing his muffler and hat from the hook with his free hand, but not without a backward glance at her as he went.

'Have you said anything?' Bird turned to Mrs Knepp accusingly.

'No. But you need to tell him. Maybe he's noticed the change in you.'

'He wouldn't notice if I turned blue and spouted

Dutch. No, if you've said nothing, then he's got something on his mind.' And she wouldn't be comfortable until she'd found out what. Today was an afternoon rehearsal, and she fretted about how she would tell Killigrew. She knew she wouldn't be able to play once she began to show.

By ten of the clock, she and Anis had got Mrs Knepp washed and bundled up in a fur cloak, no mean feat in this freeze, so she could take her to the scullery to scrub her few remaining teeth.

They'd only just gone out when there was a knock at the door. Bird went to answer it to find Samuel Pepys's boy-servant on the doorstep with a letter.

Behind him Knepp was approaching with a long stride. Bird's shoulders rose.

'What is it, boy?' Knepp said, holding out his hand, his breath standing in a cloud.

'Letter to Mrs Knepp from Mr Pepys, sir. I'm to wait for a reply.'

Bird held out her hand for the letter, and the boy passed it towards her.

In that same instant Knepp intercepted it. 'Go and wait over by the mounting block,' he instructed. 'It will take us a few moments to write a reply.'

'Very good, sir.' The boy went, his hands tucked tight under his armpits against the cold.

By now Knepp was unsealing the letter.

'It's addressed to me,' Bird said, her mouth dry.

He ignored her and read in silence. His mouth

tightened. He pulled the door behind him shut with an almighty bang, sealing the room from the ears in the yard. Bird's body prickled, alert like a deer ready to run.

'*Barbary Allen*.' A sneer. 'Is that what he calls you?' He tore the paper in two and cast it down on the table.

'He doesn't mean anything by it; it's just the name of a song, that's all.' She tried to be casual, but of course he saw through it and was advancing. She could feel his anger, pulsing through his calm. She stepped back.

'And tell me, why does he name himself *Dapper Dicky*?' He held up a hand, 'No, don't answer. Because he gets up your skirts, doesn't he? That's why you are always sniffing round him. *Dapper Dicky*.' He laughed, as if it might choke him.

'We're just friends, we make music together, ask Mrs Pierce. Ask anyone.' She was protesting, though part of her knew she was being false to herself. She had done nothing, yet there was no question they were more than friends.

Knepp took hold of her arm and raised a threatening hand. 'Don't!' she shouted, doubling over, surprising herself. Why had she done that? The child. A coiling fear inside that he might hurt the baby. She dropped to her knees.

'You whore.' He raised a boot and kicked out, but she rolled sideways. His foot connected with the wainscot with a bang.

'Christopher.' Mrs Knepp appeared from the

scullery at the back. 'Take care,' she said. 'Remember the child.'

So she'd told him, just as she thought.

Anis stopped in the middle of the room, eyes wide.

'The child,' Knepp said bitterly. 'Ah yes. Then the only question is, whose child is it?'

Bird scraped up her skirts and gathered them around her to protect herself. 'It's yours, I swear it.'

'And why should I believe you?'

'I have been a faithful wife. The child is yours.'

'And yet you didn't think to tell me?' His eyes went to Anis. 'Get out!'

Anis hurried back into the brewhouse and shut the door.

'I was going to tell you, but I didn't want to get your hopes up. Because so much can go awry—'

'I told her she should tell you.' Mrs Knepp folded her arms.

'I'll not be palmed off with another man's bastard. I don't want this child.'

'Samuel Pepys is just a friend. I haven't—' she said, but he raised his voice over her.

'A friend who sends you smutty little messages. Pack your bags. You can go home to your father.'

'Christopher—' Mrs Knepp tried to block his way, but he shook his head at her and made for the door.

At the last moment he turned his head. 'That messenger boy is still waiting. You can ask if

'*Dapper Dicky*' will take you in, always supposing there's room in his bed next to his wife.'

The door slammed behind him.

In the ensuing silence, Mrs Knepp walked awkwardly to the table where she picked up the pieces of the letter. She jig-sawed them together with her gnarled hands, but Bird was at her side in an instant.

'Don't.' She snatched them up.

Mrs Knepp stood away from the table fixing Bird with her shrewd eyes. 'I want to know one thing,' she said. 'Can you swear on the Bible it is Christopher's child?'

'Yes. And I wish to God it was not.' Then in a smaller voice, 'Do you think he'll send me away?'

'If it's his child, I'll see he does not.'

'My father does not want me.' The words in themselves were like a knife. As she said them, she realised it was true. 'I can't go there. And there's nowhere else.' She gulped for air. 'What will I do?'

'Knepps always look to their own.' Mrs Knepp held out her arms and without thinking, Bird stepped into them. Mrs Knepp smelt of camphor and dust, but her grip was firm and the firmness of it loosened something, and hot tears began to flow.

A rap at the door. Both women jerked apart, startled.

'I'll go,' Bird said, wiping her eyes with her sleeve, her hand still wrapped around the wad of paper.

On the doorstep was the boy. 'You forgot. You forgot the reply.' His tone was accusing.

'No. Just wait a moment.' She blinked again; her eyes wouldn't stop streaming, damn them. She went to the side table and smoothed out the pieces of the letter.

Sweet Barbary Allen,

I was mighty disappointed not to see you at Lord Bruncker's again last night. I so enjoyed our singing; it was quite the finest musique I have heard in my life! This evening we are to sing at my house in town. Will you join us? I have an urge for your company.

Dapper Dickey

The very joviality of his words made her shoulders heave with renewed sobs. What could she say? That she was having a baby? That their whole delicate liaison, so tender and fresh, like a young shoot, was crushed before it had even begun? A tear fell onto the table, but she smeared it away, angry that her body would make such a fool of her. She braced herself and wrote a quick note.

We have guests, and I must look to them. Perhaps another time. Barbary A—

But there couldn't be another time. She could tell him nothing. She scratched out the words in vicious, black strokes of the quill.

The boy stared at her curiously as she returned to the door wet-cheeked and empty-handed.

'No message,' she said, raising her chin. 'I changed my mind.'

The boy gave a squawk of indignation and

marched away, certain of his righteous anger and his place in the world.

Bird turned back to Mrs Knepp. 'I want the babe to be loved, that's all.'

Mrs Knepp rubbed her aching knees, and wished she was twenty years younger. Young folk didn't have any common sense. No child should have to bear the stigma of being born illegitimate, and especially not if the babe was really Christopher's. She was still ruminating by the embers of the fire by the time her son appeared from the stables.

'Where is she?' he asked, moving to stand before the heat.

'Sleeping.'

'She should be gone. Getting wed to her was a mistake; that greasy-faced Carpenter fooled me – he said she was well-mannered and gentle.'

''Tis done now,' Mrs Knepp said in a placatory tone. 'You're man and wife. And she says it's your child.'

'She says whatever suits her.'

'But what if it's true? How will you feel in a few years hence, if your child is lost to you, in the city somewhere, knowing nothing of you at all?'

'I shan't care.' He slumped into the chair; stretched out his boots. 'But you will. That's what you're saying, isn't it?'

He'd seen it; the longing for a grandchild she'd thought to hide. She picked her words carefully. 'I think she speaks the truth.'

'Why? She's paid to pretend every day on that damned stage. I tell you, I won't support it, this lewdness with Pepys.'

'Hold fast. She's brought you prosperity with her playacting – a better class of customer and—'

'God's breath!' He thumped the arm of her chair, making dust fly. 'You talk as if it's all her doing. I'm the one who has to fulfil the contracts.' He prodded a finger to his own chest. 'It's my horses and carriages that do the work.'

'But if she goes, you'd lose all that. All the theatre carriages, all the well-paid business.' She made her voice soothing and reasonable. 'And you can't send her home to her father. He has shown no interest in us since you wed. Thinks he's a cut above us. Like him or not, he has prospered mightily since she came here. Lord knows why, but I read the news sheets and he's one of the best-known lawyers in London. He'll speak ill of you abroad if you throw her out, and then your reputation will be mud.'

'*My* reputation? It's not me dallying with Pepys, is it?'

'No, but a man's only as good as his reputation; your father should have taught you that.' She paused to let the truth of it sink in, as she picked at the fringe of her shawl. 'And unfortunately, your wife has a good one. She has become well-known in certain circles. Court circles. It may not please you, but you are known as Mr Knepp, husband of the actress.' She saw his horrified expression

374

and wondered if she'd pushed him too far. She added a hasty postscript, 'Of course only in theatre circles, with the playgoers. And I daresay Pepys writes these little notes to all the women. It's the sort of thing these loose men do. And he's married, that Pepys, to a French aristocrat. I can't imagine him risking his good standing for anything other than petty dalliance.'

'But I'll never be able to be sure whose child—'

'Why not talk to Pepys? Ask him if . . . well, if he's had *relations* with Mary Elizabeth.'

'Don't be so witless, Mother. I can't lower myself to that. You want me to be laughed at from here to Wapping?'

'Then there is no way to know.' She'd pushed him into a corner. 'You have a choice. Throw away all you've built up, and lose the business to Viner, or accept the child as yours.' Viner. She watched him wince. The name was like the last arrow into a dying man.

The next day Bird heard Knepp moving around as he usually did in the morning, the click of him closing the closet door, the tread of his stockinged feet creaking down the stairs, and murmured voices, followed by the front door and the bark of Fetch, the collie, in the kennel outside. He'd not been in to tell her to leave, but that didn't mean he would not. There was no predicting with Knepp. She pressed her palms down on her belly, circling them over its smooth mound, as if to soothe the child within.

When she got downstairs, Mrs Knepp was already awake, ready to be washed and dressed. Anis helped her into her stays, and as Bird took a comb from a basket so she could dress her hair, Mrs Knepp whispered, 'He won't make you go.'

'What did you say to him?'

'I told him I believed you about the child.'

Anis's face grew taut, listening.

'Anis, fetch me a handkerchief from upstairs, would you?' Mrs Knepp asked.

Bird paused with the comb in her hand, moved she should suddenly have an ally.

'I made him see it would be bad for business if you were to part,' Mrs Knepp said.

'Oh. I see.' So it was not sympathy for her or the child, but hard-nosed greed. She passed her the comb and moved away. 'So he did not believe me.'

'He can't trust any woman, I told you that. Or indeed any man.'

Bird knew she must return Samuel's song. If Knepp found it in the house, Lord knows what he'd do. It would only lead to more strife. The next day, she wrapped it in oilcloth, for the January rain was horizontal, and she was scared his precious manuscript would get wet. It was his only copy. She tucked it under the leather flap in her basket, and as she caught the wherry down to Pepys's lodgings in Greenwich, she kept checking it was not flying open in the wind. She strained past her cowled hood to see where the jetty was.

Carefully, she stepped out on the slippery, greasy wood, and then hurried up the road, head down in the wind, clutching her cloak across her chest and stomach. She hoped she'd find Samuel at his lodgings, given that she knew he was moving back to town soon. When she got there, it was to find him all in disarray with papers everywhere, and books stacked on the floor.

He was clearly surprised to see her. 'Good Lord above! My dear Barbary Allen! But you're soaked through.'

'I needed to return your music and—'

'Be careful!' he said, steering her dripping figure away from his books. 'I don't know,' he said, picking up a stack of books and depositing them in a large wooden crate. 'It's a mystery how I've accumulated so many books in so short a space of time!'

'I'm sorry I could not send a message about your musical evening. You must think me very rude.'

'I would never think that of one so charming.' He cleared a chair of ledgers and urged her to sit down. 'I'll call for refreshment.'

'No need, I can't stay.'

'Of course you will.' He flashed her a smile and disappeared downstairs. His resonant voice echoed up the stairs as he ordered refreshments from the landlady.

Whilst he was gone, she put down her basket and peered onto his desk, moving aside a letter to reveal accounts signed from William Howe, who she knew to be clerk to Mountagu, the Earl of Sandwich. A man of standing.

Then there were all the books. He must be in the middle of packing. She ranged round the room to look at the wooden cases which littered the turkey rug, most of them half-filled. The sight of so many volumes gave her a pang. She bent down to read the titles. Science, religion, even lost ancient monuments. It was all here. There were no books in Knepp's house, except the few she'd found by his bed. She remembered asking her father if Knepp had books, and him telling her it was not important. It *is* important, she thought. It shows you are interested in the wider world, and that you are willing to learn something from others. It shows you are curious, and that what others think and believe is important to you. Knepp had thrust books out of his life, yet she knew him to be educated and intelligent.

Samuel returned bearing a tray of hot posset and some wafers. Finding nowhere to put it, he rested it on the floor until he could clear a space on the table.

Bird stayed standing, watching the steam rise from the cups. 'I really can't stay,' she said. 'I just brought you this.' She offered him the oilskin parcel.

'What is it?'

'Your music. "Beauty Retire". I had to wrap it against the rain.'

'Have you learnt it?' His eyes lit up.

'Yes. I mean, not entirely. But I can't keep it. My husband won't allow it.'

'Oh, I see. That's a blow. I did rather get the impression he didn't approve of me.'

'He intercepted the note you sent me, and he tore it up.'

'Ah.'

'He thought it . . .'

'Too intimate.' He finished the sentence for her, immediately understanding. They held each other's gaze a moment. 'I see.'

She felt the need to apologise. 'I know the names were only meant in jest but—'

'He hasn't hurt you, has he? My boy said when he left you, you were crying.'

She felt herself blush. 'I was angry, that's all. Because of his harsh words and . . . and because soon I will be unable to sing or play on stage, for I will shortly be confined.' Seeing his blank expression, she said gently, 'I'm with child.'

'With child?' His eyebrows shot up. He rubbed his chin, back and forth, back and forth, seemingly lost for words. 'An actual baby?'

He didn't meet her eyes again but began to bustle about, moving piles of books from place to place in a kind of panic. 'My dear Barbary Allen, please sit down. What am I thinking? But this is a disaster! How will Killigrew go on without you?'

He took her by the arm and forced her to sit, by which time he'd reconsidered his words. 'But that's marvellous! My felicitations, if you will accept them. Your husband, is he pleased?'

'Hardly. He calls me whore and suspects me of liaisons with another man, so it's better for me if he doesn't know I have your music.'

'The devil he does.' But then he backed away, his face suddenly wary. 'He doesn't think . . .?'

'Indeed. He accuses you of being the father of my child.'

'But that's absurd. It could ruin me! Besides, I would never . . .'

'Wouldn't you?' A sadness welled up in her throat.

'My dear Barbary Allen,' he put a hand on her shoulder, 'of course I would . . . I mean . . . oh dear. A child.' He grabbed a cup of the steaming posset, and a translucent china plate with a wafer and passed it to her. Bird sipped the pale, milky drink and bit into the crunchy wafer, the plate on her lap. Everything was sweet and delicate and refined. It was a hundred miles away from Knepp's house. She could not bear it. She set it aside on a pile of books. 'I'm sorry. I've no appetite.'

Samuel hurriedly removed it back to the tray. 'Of course not. No matter. I suppose this changes everything. What will you do?'

She swallowed. 'There is nothing to be done. The babe will come, that's all.'

'But we can still be friends, can't we? As long as . . . as long as we are discreet.'

What did he think? That she would still be able to flirt with him, whilst it could never come to anything? She shook her head. 'I must be careful who I befriend, if I don't want to incur my husband's wrath. He'll use his fists if he thinks I transgress.'

'Men shouldn't use their fists on their wives. A switch or rod is the decent thing. Oh, Barbary Allen! I shall miss our singing together.' He paced up and down before the window. 'But wait! If we're to be friends, it will look better to your husband if you spend time with my wife.' For him. It would look better for him, he meant.

'I would be pleased to meet with her, should she wish it,' Bird said. There was nothing she'd like less. But Samuel was already drifting away from her, the child had seen to that. Perhaps it would keep her in their minds, in the swim of society; prevent her being forgotten completely.

'Then that's settled,' he said, wiping down the front of his waistcoat with satisfaction, as if that had solved the whole problem. 'I'll arrange it.'

She wanted to scream at him then, 'It's you I want, not your stupid wife!' But instead she stood. 'I must go.'

'Will I see you again? In mixed company, I mean.'

'Perhaps. I had a message from Mrs Pierce this morning inviting me to sing in town next week.'

'Oh, yes. Mrs Pierce is to have a baby, too.

Perhaps it's something in the air . . . yes, the Pierces'. I shall try to be there.' He took her cold hand and pressed it to his cheek. His skin was warm and soft as a peach, and she saw the flare in his pupils that gave her a corresponding lurch in the heart. 'Your husband should appreciate what he has.'

There was no reply she could give. He reached to take her shoulder and gave her a deliberate dry kiss each side of her face. The sparkle between them had evaporated into politeness. She stumbled away down the stairs, but not before she heard him whistle, and the scrape of packing cases being dragged across the floor.

CHAPTER 29

Valentine's Day, Mrs Mercer's House,
Crutched Friars, London

The dancing had finished and Bird was resting, sandwiched on a chair in between Elisabeth Pepys and Mary Mercer, Elisabeth's paid companion, and daughter of the hostess. Samuel had done as he suggested and pushed his wife, Elisabeth, and Bird together. Bird found Elisabeth to be more entertaining than she had hoped, although she was unfortunately tone deaf as far as singing was concerned. Pepys himself was apparently 'too busy' to attend the soirée. Valentine's Day was a disappointment. But then what did she expect? Bird pretended not to care, though she still felt sore to think of him.

'I'm done for, Mistress,' Mary Mercer said to Elisabeth. 'My feet are so blistered I can't dance another step.'

In the corner, behind the rolled-up rugs, William Howe was still fiddling away on the viol, and Lanier the lutenist plucked gamely for the remaining dancers, who were dancing a quadrille, feet tapping on the bare boards.

'I'll have to go soon, too,' Bird said. 'My husband's sending a gig for me.'

'Spoilsports,' Elisabeth said. 'It's not yet midnight.'

'It's all right for you, you're staying the night here.'

'You could stay too,' Elisabeth said. 'Mrs Pierce won't mind. We could have another song.'

'No, I think my babe's had enough of my caterwauling,' Bird said patting her stomach. 'Besides, I must be up early to see to old Widow Knepp.'

'Thank the Lord my mother is still hale and hearty,' Mary said, looking over to the fireside where old Mrs Mercer was presiding from a high-backed chair.

Bird fetched her outdoor clothes, bid them good night and thanked the dame for the evening's entertainment. The babe made her weary, and she longed for bed. Downstairs, she pulled on her gloves to wait for the carriage. Yellowish fog wreathed the street, and she could barely see a few yards across the road. The lights of several carriages rattled past, dispelling the fog into wisps for an instant before it closed in again, but none of the carriages stopped. After a quarter hour, the door behind her opened and the gentlemen musicians burst forth.

'Oh. Mrs Knepp? Are you still here?' Mr Howe asked.

'My carriage hasn't come. I expect it'll be here soon. It must have got held up.'

'Do you want to walk with us?' Lanier asked.

'No, it's kind, but I'm going all the way to Smithfield.'

So they left her, their cloaked backs melting into the fog.

Another quarter hour and still no sign of it. What was she to do? She couldn't walk home alone. But if she didn't go home, Knepp would be angry. But then again it was his carriage that was supposed to fetch her.

She looked up at the house. There was still a light showing through the cracks of the shutters. She knocked timidly on the door. When no-one came, she knocked again louder.

Mary came to the door. 'I thought you'd gone home.'

She explained.

'Best come in then, though I don't know where we'll put you. You'll have to go on the truckle bed. Elisabeth and I have got the big bed.'

Elisabeth was already in the four-poster bed in her nightdress and cap, the covers pulled up to her chin. 'Men,' she said. 'You can never rely on them, can you? They say one thing and do another.'

'I hope I find a good one,' Mary said, throwing Bird a blanket. 'And handsome. If your carriage comes we'll ignore it. I'm not getting up again, and you'll have to sleep in your shift, I suppose. There's still hot water in the ewer.'

'You wouldn't want a husband like Samuel,' Elisabeth said. 'He never listens to a word I say.'

'I thought he was a good listener,' Bird said.

A bitter laugh. 'To you, yes. Always he listens to other women, but never to me.'

Bird went to the ewer and washed her hands and face, during which time Mary had got into bed with Elisabeth, and Elisabeth was complaining about her cold feet.

'Keep them off me! Snuff the lights before you get in, Mrs Knepp,' Elisabeth called.

Bird did so and crept gingerly to the truckle bed. The room was pitch black with no lights, but Bird was glad the other women could no longer stare at her, and at the slight swell of her stomach.

'Mrs Knepp, your husband's a lot older than you, isn't he?' Mary said. 'Just think; when he dies you'll be a rich widow.' She giggled.

'Mary! Have you no tact at all? Mrs Knepp doesn't want to think of her husband dying.'

'On the contrary, I've often thought of it.'

Silence, followed by an explosion of giggles.

'I could murder mine, sometimes,' Elisabeth said. 'His eye roves over every woman we meet. He thinks I don't notice, fool that he is. But I can always tell when he takes on that eager expression.'

Bird leapt to his defence. 'Oh, Mrs Pepys, I'm sure he doesn't—'

'There's that draper's woman, Betty Martin, and her sister Doll Lane for a start. And then Mrs Bagwell, the carpenter's wife; he makes far too many unnecessary appointments with her. I tell you plain, he'll stare at anyone in a skirt. I even thought he had his eye on you, Mrs Knepp.'

Bird stared through the dark towards the ceiling, uncomfortable. 'I'm sure not,' she said. 'We share a love of music, that's all.'

'Mary knows what he's like, don't you, Mary?'

A moment's pause. 'Well, Mistress, I don't know what he's like with other women,' Mary replied, 'but at least he doesn't beat you.'

'But he does! Do you not remember my black eye last Christmas? Oh, of course you don't. I went nowhere. I couldn't face the shame of it.'

Bird stared into the darkness, gripping the edge of the blanket. So she was not the only woman he flirted with. How could she have been so foolish as to think Samuel really cared for her?

'I never understood why he hit you, though,' Mary said.

In the dark, Elisabeth was still talking. 'We had an argument over my servant, Jane. She's another he's tried it on with. But it's not the first time. I tell you, a woman has to be a saint to put up with him.'

'He keeps you well though,' Mary said. 'Your house wants for nothing. The plasterers and joiners have only just left.'

'The house. Yes, the house is fine. But what use is that, when so little affection is within?'

Bird was silent. She heard the wistful tone in Elisabeth's voice, felt the echoing emptiness in herself.

'Mrs Knepp?' Mary whispered.

Bird did not answer. She pretended to be asleep. She still smarted from the idea that she was just one in a long line of Samuel's 'ladies'. She lay rigid, wondering why Knepp had not sent a carriage and what sort of welcome would await her at home. Nor could she shift from her mind the thought that Samuel Pepys was a wife-beater just as bad as Knepp, and none of his fine clothes and sweet words could hide the fact he was an inveterate rake. The thought of his sudden coolness when she told him about the child made her grip the blanket tighter. Samuel Pepys was not the gentleman she thought he was, and his betrayal made her wince. But not as much as her own foolishness for believing the whole fantasy of it.

CHAPTER 30

The next day, one of the stables was empty. Knepp had been forced to put down Hector, his favourite riding horse, who had got colic late into the night, which was why he hadn't sent her a carriage. He'd been so concerned with his horse, he'd forgotten all about her, until the next morning, when the knackers arrived, and he remembered to send Nipper with a carriage to fetch her. Knepp offered no apology, but she had been surprised to see his eyes wet when he told her of the loss of his horse. She wanted to reach out to hug him, but reined in the desire. She feared showing him any comradely affection lest it be hurled back in her face.

Months passed, and Bird grew heavier. She had told Killigrew and he had taken it well, casting Mrs Marshall in her upcoming role instead. So she was replaceable, was she? It hurt. And she missed the familiar bustle and banter of being in the company. Life was going on without her. Nell had braved Knepp's bad temper to call in and tell her that Samuel Pepys had been on a tour of the theatre and admired the new machinery and the painted backdrops. The thought of him still made a pinch in her heart, a yearning for his company that gripped like a fist.

Knepp, though ignoring her as always, accepted the well-wishes of his workers and began to talk of the coming babe with a certain pride. Bird continued to sing for pin-money whenever she could.

She couldn't quite believe that these might be her last days of freedom. Mrs Pierce insisted on giving her well-meaning instructions about midwifery and swaddling, and Lord knows what else. The mysteries of childbed still seemed distant and unlikely, as if it might be something that would never happen to her.

This particular morning, she woke as dawn was breaking and a pale light crept through the shutter to stripe the floor. She was restless, unable to sleep for an ache in her back; she peered out of the window across the rooftops and spires, towards the market. A fog drifted up in the chill air; the breath of all the beasts to be slaughtered that day was rising from the pens and stalls in a great cloud.

It was then she felt it. A sensation in the pit of her stomach. A tautening. Then a flutter.

She placed her hand there and held her breath.

Again, the tiny movement, like a quiver.

She gasped. The child. It was alive.

Bird pressed her hand to her belly, listening with her spread fingers. Another faint push.

A spurt of joy. 'My little one,' she said, encircling

the bump with both hands. 'You will have a good life, I promise.'

Again the movement within that filled her with a swirl of emotion. She had the urge to tell Knepp, his baby was moving!

A faint clatter of cutlery as she went gingerly downstairs to where Anis was putting out the bread and meats for breakfast. In the gloom of the parlour guttural snores could be heard emanating from the curtained alcove in the corner.

'Not awake yet?' Bird asked.

'She sleeps like the dead,' Anis said.

Bird sank into a chair and leant her hands on the table. For the first time the fact of the baby became real. Inside her, a boy or girl was waiting to be born. The thought was amazing. She remembered Mrs Knepp's description of birthing Christopher and shuddered. Times had changed since then, surely? Less women died in childbed than they used to. Still, a mixture of fear and anticipation made her unable to be still, and she set about pouring ale into the jugs.

Knepp arrived from the yard a few moments after and went to scrub his hands in the basin in the scullery, before sitting at the table and helping himself to bread. She stood to pass him a napkin, which he ignored.

'No singing engagement today?' he asked.

'Tonight. At Lord Bruncker's. Abigail Williams has invited me to sing.'

'Will Pepys be there?'

'I expect so.' She didn't mention the fact that Elisabeth was out of town this week.

'Make sure you get the money first, hear me? No more singing for nothing. Mr Pierce still hasn't paid you for the last time.'

Unable to keep it in, she bust out, 'I felt our baby move today.' She twisted the napkin in her hands.

He looked up briefly, then returned his attention to his food. She hoped he might want to feel the baby move, but of course he would not. The mysteries of a woman's body did not seem to interest him.

'Good. That's good it's healthy. Though it will be more expense when it comes,' he said.

Disappointment swamped her. 'But the plague has left us. Maybe the theatres will have been re-opened by then, and your carriages might return to their rank on Catherine Street,' she said.

'Perhaps. But you needn't think you're going back to the theatre. Not with a child to mind. And more will probably come, too.'

'More?'

'More children.' He waved the butter knife vaguely in the air.

She hadn't even considered that. That he might want more, with this one not even birthed yet. A pall of weariness descended on her. How quick her feelings came and went; one minute elated, the next dark as thunder. She made herself go over to Mrs Knepp's bed alcove and draw back the curtains. No point in moping. Life had to go on.

'Mrs Knepp?' She helped the old lady to sit up, and then brought her a cup of ale.

'The baby moved,' she said.

Mrs Knepp took hold of her by both arms, eyes alight with excitement. 'My grandson! God be praised!'

Tinker's Alley, June 1666

Livvy picked up one of the 'diurnalls' that Robert had laid out before him on the table, and fanned her face. Saints alive, but it was hot. Barely a breath of air anywhere in London. It made her sweat. That morning Viner had visited her room again. Months she'd endured it. He was too big, too rough. He ate up all the air. She could still smell him. He smelled of pig and too much heat. She dragged her attention back to Robert's voice, and blinked hard to lock the memory of Viner away.

Robert was still reading from the other paper in his precise monotone, and she wafted the paper towards him to give him some breeze. He looked up over it and smiled.

'Is the English fleet sunk yet?' she asked.

He put down the paper. 'Haven't you been listening?'

★   ★   ★

'Of course I have. The English fleet is in trouble, yes?' She had only half-heard the news that English ships had been fired and no money was left in the English coffers to rebuild.

He sighed. 'Livvy, you have to tell me what is wrong. You have been staring into the corner all afternoon.'

'Nothing,' she said. How to tell him she felt dirty all over? She shouldn't even be here. What if Cal had followed her? Viner could use it against Robert. Yet Robert drew her like a bee to honey. All sweetness.

She raised her eyes to his face, his forehead creased with worry, his hair sticking up in tufts. He was such good man. Crazy, but good. Who else would care about a blackamoor maid?

'Livvy?'

'I can't tell you. I'm just not the person you think.'

He stood and hobbled around the desk, put his thin wiry arms around her shoulders. 'None of us are. We are all holding secrets; trust me, I have my own. But I care about you. You can tell me. Whatever it is, it won't make any difference.'

She leant into him, rested her forehead against his chest; the bone buttons of his waistcoat pressed against her cheek. She said nothing. Of course it would make a difference, whatever he said to the contrary.

'I just wish the war was over,' she said eventually.

He rubbed her back, up and down, like you would

an infant. 'Would it be . . . I mean would you mind if . . .?' She looked up; his eyes were shining with a strange light.

'What?'

He swallowed. 'Can I kiss you?'

She gave a long slow nod and closed her eyes, her face tilted up to his. She closed her mind to the tumble of thoughts and made herself like a statue. She could give her friend this one little thing.

The chair creaked as he leant his weight on it, then a soft, barely perceptible, touch of his lips on hers. The sensation was brief and hesitant before he pulled away. She snapped open her eyes to see his face, serious as if he had made a great decision, and felt the slight damp coolness on her lips. She wanted to pull him closer, bury herself in his goodness, but the moment had gone. Tears sprang to her eyes.

'Don't cry,' he said, touching her tenderly on the temple with his long, white watchmaker's fingers.

She wanted to shout, *Why you want me? Why you want a woman like me?* But instead she stood up, brushed herself down, wiped her eyes with the backs of her hands. 'Thank you for reading to me. I must go. They'll be looking for me at work.'

Out of the door, hurrying as if it were the devil himself she was running from. She heard his shout from the doorway; 'Livvy!' but she didn't stop. Not until she was right at the bottom of Lombard Street.

Damn fool woman, she chided herself. *Why you running from a kiss?*

Because it felt more dangerous than a beating. Because a beating could only hurt the outside of you, whereas love could pierce your soul.

CHAPTER 31

Smithfield, 4th July

W hen the first pain came, Bird ignored it. She was too afraid to admit that something might be happening, and she didn't want to call Mrs Grinstead, wife of the clerk, and the pinch-faced woman who Knepp wanted to act as midwife. Nor did she know enough women for the usual custom of childbed lying-in and gossiping. She had no female relatives standing by, no lace-edged childbed linen inherited from her mother, as other women did. She had written to her father, to tell him her time was near, but no reply had come. Not a single word. Devil take him.

The yard was quiet; it was fast day for the plague, and few called for coaches. The men usually spent fast day cleaning out the stalls, mending harness and sweeping the yard. Before she was confined, Bird would have been working with them, but now she was too heavy. Women in such a large state were not permitted abroad, as if the act of a woman producing children were something faintly disgusting.

She stayed upstairs, by the open window, making a mess of the stitches on a small nightgown for the child to come, and fanning her face to try to get some air. The second pain made her clutch her stomach.

'Settle down, now,' she said to her belly.

The talk in the yard below was all rumours of the war with the Dutch. Word had come that it was a great victory, and the tang of the smoke of the celebratory bonfires drifted through her open window. The smell made her nauseous, and the pains began to pull her regularly, like sirens dragging her onto rocks.

Sweat beaded her brow. Still, she pretended it was not happening. Later in the day, a customer told the stable hands the English victory was a lie; he'd seen our ships limping back to port, broken, battered and full of blood-soaked casualties. The men cursed and swore, and beneath the window, they argued about what the English should have done to save themselves; that they should have formed a line, that they shouldn't have run aground on the Galloper sandbank, that it was all Prince Rupert's fault.

By now the cramps were so bad she was gasping. 'For God's sake hold your peace,' she cried.

She couldn't pretend any longer.

'Anis!' she shouted.

After what seemed like hours of shouting, Anis burst in. 'Is it coming?'

'What does it look like? Fetch Livvy. Livvy Black from Viner's.'

'Master won't—'

'Just do it. I trust her. Hurry!'

She heard Anis's voice shouting as she went through the house, 'Mrs Knepp, wake up. It's the mistress. It's her groaning time!'

The room grew fuzzy with pain, her back felt like it would break in two.

The door creaked open. Mrs Knepp had struggled her way up the stairs, one arm full of white sheets. 'They're clean,' she said. 'How long have you been like this?'

Bird couldn't answer, her teeth were gritted too hard against the iron grip that cleaved to her belly.

'I'll call Mrs Grinstead.'

'No!' But it was too late. Mrs Knepp had gone below, her feet clomping unevenly on the stairs.

Hours passed in a blur. At one point Bird opened her eyes to find Livvy's face staring down at her, and the sweet smell of almond oil, as Livvy massaged her belly, feeling for the position of the child. 'All right now,' she said. 'Everything's fine. The babe's head is down. Just hang on to my hand when the pain comes again.' She moved away and then held a cup to Bird's dry lips. 'It's betony. It will ease the pain.'

Bird gripped her slippery hand tight. 'I can't do this,' she said.

'Any woman can. Just takes time, is all.'

The light gradually faded from the outside window, and still the child had not come. Instead Mrs Grinstead had arrived, full of disapproval. She glared at Livvy. 'What's that darkie doing here?'

'My daughter-in-law asked for her,' Mrs Knepp said, 'and I see no harm in an extra pair of hands.'

'How can you see with no candles lit?' Mrs Grinstead lit every candle in the place then, banishing the comforting dark and making Bird feel like an exhibit to be stared at. 'When did she start?'

'Yester afternoon,' Mrs Knepp said, her voice full of fear.

'She should be delivered by now,' Mrs Grinstead said. 'We might have to help her.'

'No!' Mrs Knepp said. 'Not that.'

'You can't hurry nature,' Livvy said. 'The babe might not be ready.'

Mrs Grinstead insisted, 'The babe might die if we don't—'

All the women were silenced as Bird let out another moan and grabbed the head of the bed. She'd get the babe out. She bore down and began to push. She was breaking in two, but she still couldn't do it.

Mrs Grinstead took a fearsome-looking metal implement from her basket.

'Get away from me,' Bird screamed.

Mrs Knepp took hold of Mrs Grinstead trying to pinion her arms. 'Push. You can do it, girl,' she shouted to Bird.

'Leave go!' Mrs Grinstead cursed and struggled until Livvy stepped in to thrust her away. She crashed against the wall, gasping with outrage.

'Come on, Mary Elizabeth, one big push,' Mrs Knepp cried.

Bird took a deep breath and strained for all she was worth, and suddenly she felt something slide out of her.

Livvy was there to catch it. 'Oh, my goodness, Bird, it's a boy! A beautiful boy.'

The sound of a baby's cries tugged at something deep inside her. Had she done this? Had she made this new human being? She let out a whimper and held out her arms.

Mrs Grinstead hastened away to fetch Knepp and convey the good news. Livvy stayed beside Bird and cut the cord and wrapped the baby, whilst Mrs Knepp, overcome, wept and prayed in the chair in the corner.

Livvy passed the bundle back to Bird, and there he was again, a tiny perfect human being. Perfect little nose. Eyelashes all there. Fingers moving, clenching and unclenching.

Her son. She could hardly believe it. How was it possible? That she and Knepp could have made such a thing was a miracle.

A knock. Knepp pushed the door open quietly. How odd that he should knock. But he seemed uncertain as he crept towards her. She turned the babe slightly so Knepp could see his face.

His eyes widened. He paused, hat held to his

chest, then reached out a gentle finger to touch his cheek. 'Little fella,' he said.

'He's got your nose,' Mrs Knepp said.

'He's beautiful, isn't he?' Bird said.

Knepp could only nod and turn aside. His eyes were wet with tears.

'Here,' Bird said, with sudden generosity, 'you hold him.'

Knepp's mouth worked, but he let his hat fall and reached out and took the babe gently to his chest. 'Who's a big strong lad, eh?' he said.

Knepp passed the babe back to Bird and wiped his eyes with his sleeve. He didn't seem able to speak. He just stood staring at his son. 'He'll need baptising,' he said suddenly.

'What will you call him?' Mrs Knepp said.

'Christopher, of course,' Bird said. 'Christopher Roland.'

A muffled sob from Knepp, who tried to hide it with a cough.

'Decent godparents,' Mrs Knepp said. 'Someone of standing, someone that can help him up in the world. How about the king's Navy man, Mr Pepys?'

Bird looked to her husband, unsure. He gave a nod. He seemed to take a moment to unglue his mouth. 'We need two men, so Grinstead of course. And a woman. Someone from the theatre,' he said gruffly, 'that my wife chooses.'

It was his way to make amends, she knew. 'Mrs Williams then, consort to Lord Bruncker.'

'A Lord.' Mrs Knepp was impressed. 'My, then

my grandson will be even better-connected.' Bird did not enlighten her as to Abigail Williams' reputation, but she did want her son to have the best possible start.

'Very good,' Knepp said, recovering his composure. 'I will send paper and a quill for you to write and forewarn them. Then I must go and register the birth, and see when the church can hold the ceremony.' He meant, go to the tavern and celebrate, but Bird was too euphoric to care. 'Shall I write to your father?'

'No.' The one word was all she could manage.

Knepp leant forward and wonderingly, he touched the babe again on the forehead. 'He does have my nose, Mother,' he said.

A moment later, Bird felt a dry kiss on her cheek, and then he was gone.

Bird slept, and the next few days passed in a blur. She woke to the baby's cries, to feed and change his nightdresses or his swaddling bands. Many of Knepp's acquaintances visited to stare at the new arrival, who she called Roly, a name much disapproved of by Mrs Knepp, who thought it disrespectful. But how could she call someone so tiny Christopher? Besides, his official name would be confused with his father. 'Kit' was unthinkable – not if the boy was to grow up with the surname Knepp.

Mrs Knepp wanted to hire a wet nurse, but Bird refused all offers of help. She drowsed contentedly with Roly in her lap as the early morning sun streamed through the windows. In the evenings she often awoke to find Knepp sitting on the end of the bed, staring down at them both.

'He's a fine-looking boy,' Knepp said. 'As soon as he's old enough I'll teach him to ride. My brother and I had such fun on our ponies when we were small.'

She eased herself to upright on the pillow. 'It will be harder in London, with no fields to gallop in.'

'I'll have to take him out of town. I'll keep my eyes open for the right pony.'

'He's not even a week old! And I don't believe all your mother's nonsense that you could ride before you could walk.'

He smiled, and it made him look suddenly younger. 'But I could take him to look at the horses, couldn't I? Just a look can't hurt him. He'll be inheriting the yard, won't you, my little man?'

'In a few weeks maybe, you can take him. But he's just so little. Look at those tiny fingers.'

Knepp put his forefinger into Roly's hand and the babe clung on tight. 'He's going to be a great little rider, I just know it. Feel the strength of that grip.'

Bird was now lying in state in the big bedchamber. Mrs Knepp had furnished the room with fresh linen and Anis had thoroughly cleaned it. Last night Knepp had crept into bed next to her, unwilling to be too far from his son. He had not tried to touch her, but merely taken hold of her hand and squeezed it before falling asleep.

Anis delivered a note to Livvy and she came to admire the new arrival again, and see how Bird was doing.

'Well, aren't you the mistress?' Livvy said, admiring the new surroundings. 'Here, I've brought you a tonic,' she said. 'I used it on all the babes at Mrs Gwynne's. Those that wanted to keep them, anyway.'

She peeped into the crib at the end of the bed, where Roly was sleeping, swaddled tight in his bands.

'He's asleep now,' Bird said. Earlier, he had grizzled a little, but now he appeared to have settled.

'Are they letting you rest?' Livvy asked Bird, plumping down on the edge of the bed.

'They are. Mrs Knepp has got a new lease of life. She's got quite sprightly. She even made me a chicken soup yesterday, and she simply can't do enough for Roly.'

'And Master? What about him?'

'He seems different. The boy seems to make him soft. I never thought he'd ever look with affection on anyone, but he looks at Roly like he's an angel just dropped from the sky.'

'Does it not crack his face?'

Bird giggled. 'It's a relief. I feel safe, which I never did before.'

'Well, watch out. That usually means something bad's coming.'

'Tush. What's the news from town? Have you seen Nell? I miss my theatre friends, and I'll be lying in for another week.'

'Nell's just the same, playing the jade with everyone in town, pushing herself at all the king's courtiers. She's got the luck though, that one. There's something golden about her, like life is just meant to be merry.' A bitterness made Bird stare at her. Livvy sounded jealous. She used to be so cheerful; now she seemed intent on spreading gloom.

'How is it at Viner's?'

Livvy got up from the edge of the bed and turned away. 'Don't ask. He takes advantage. It's a common enough tale for a servant and master.'

'Oh, Livvy.' She knew straight away what that meant. 'Is there nothing you can do?'

'Not unless the war with the Dutch is over, then he wouldn't be able to threaten me.'

'Why? What difference does it make?'

'My family are in Holland.'

'In Holland?' Things began to make sense.

'I was born there, so I am Dutch. My mother's still a slave, sold and transported from Suriname to Holland because she wept so for my father.'

Bird watched Livvy turn her face away and take a deep breath.

When Livvy turned back, she held up a hand. 'You don't want to know. Anyway, the English didn't want Mamma on account she was sickly and weak, and sold her to the Dutch who were trading in those parts. But she was sickening with child, see? And in Holland a person is born free. When I was born she begged him to enslave me too, but the new master didn't want to own me. Didn't want to pay bed and board for a useless girl. He already had enough house slaves. So Mamma had to earn my keep by sewing nights, until I was old enough to stitch. It was mortal hard.'

Bird was silent, her mind spinning. She'd seen slaves, but they were mostly small boys, used by aristocrats to denote their power. The idea of Livvy's mother, a grown woman with no freedom, made her pause for thought. It made her realise how much of her own freedom she took for granted.

'So I can't leave Viner's, not with no reference,' Livvy said, 'and I need money to feed my brother back home.'

'How old is your brother?'

'Must be eight summers by now. He was sold on with Mamma on account he was only a bitty babe and too small to fend for himself. She earns no pay in coin still, and him too young to earn aught but a pittance.'

'I'll speak to Knepp, see if I can get you your old position back. He might be better about it if I explain how skilled you were when you delivered Roly.'

'Viner won't let me leave,' she said dully. 'He'll have me slung in gaol as traitor first.'

'Is there nobody you can trust?'

'Only you. And M'sieur Hubert. He reads me news of home from the paper. He's a good man.

I hoped . . . it sound foolish, but I hoped he might wed me. Mad-fool pipe dream prob'ly, for a Frenchman to take a darkie. But even if he did, Viner would never allow it.'

A wail from the crib stopped their conversation.

'He needs his feed,' Bird said.

Livvy hurried over to pick up a red-faced Roly and pass him over.

A noise on the stairs. These days, Mrs Knepp's gout had miraculously improved, and she seemed anxious that her grandson should not be usurped by a stranger. 'Let me change his swaddling bands before you feed him,' she said.

'You'll spoil him,' Bird said, smiling.

Mrs Knepp picked him up and began to unwrap him, but his crying would not stop. 'Hush now! What a pair of lungs!' She paused with the bandages looped over her arm. 'What's this?'

Her expression had changed to one of concern. Bird held out her arms. Roly's chest was peppered with red spots. 'Maybe he's too hot,' she said. 'Open the window.'

'Let me look,' Livvy said. She put a hand to his forehead. 'A rash. And he's burning hot. It could be scarlatina. Nelly had that when she was a child. I don't like the look of it; not when he's only a few days old. Best send for a physician.'

'Here, little one,' Bird said pulling him to her breast, but he would not feed. She got up out of the bed on wobbly legs and walked him back and forth, as he whimpered.

408

'I'm sorry, but I must bid you farewell,' Livvy said. 'Or I'll be courting trouble. I hope Roly gets better soon. Shall I fetch the master on the way out?'

'No,' Bird replied, 'he said he'd be out all day. He's driving one of Mr Pepys's friends to the country, and I can't reach him.'

'Then find someone to ride after him, girl,' Mrs Knepp said. 'I'll send for Hopkins at the staff and snakes on Harley Street.'

'Not Hopkins!' Bird cried, remembering the leeches.

But it was too late; Bird heard her dot-and-carry footsteps clunk down the stairs.

'I'll do as she asks,' Livvy said. 'Don't get into a fret.' She stroked Roly's chest but it set him crying again, a cracked, desperate wail.

Livvy left as Bird bundled Roly against her, for now he was shivering. She was seized with a terrible sense of foreboding. Was it her fault? Had she brought this on him with that vile liquid she'd drank? She had wanted him never to be born. How could she? How could she ever think about harming this beautiful boy? Thank heavens the potion had failed. But the sin still stared her in the face. Was this God's punishment?

'Please, let him get well,' she prayed.

By the evening both Bird and Mrs Knepp were distraught. The doctor had been and insisted on bleeding the babe, and now the infant was oddly motionless in the cradle, his body pale and flaccid, the spots scarlet like pinpricks of blood. Bird stood over him, watching for any sign of a change. Mrs Knepp kept the big black Bible beside her, and muttered constant prayers. At the least sound from outside, both women started. Night fell, and in the big bedroom with the round window, the two women barely spoke. They lit the candles slowly, each moving silently around the other, afraid to waken Roly, intent on listening to the slightest sound from his lips.

At the clatter and ring of hoofbeats on the cobbles outside, Mrs Knepp pressed her face to the window. 'Carriage lamps!' she said. 'It could be Christopher. I'll go down.'

Bird knelt by the crib to press a kiss on Roly's hot forehead, and look under his covering. In only a few hours the rash had turned into one big red blur, all over his tiny body. Fear made Bird unable to be still. She walked up and down, eyes constantly on the cradle until she heard the crash of Knepp's footsteps running up, and the door flew open.

'Where is he?'

Bird pointed wordlessly to the cradle.

'What did the doctor say?'

Bird explained, but her explanation was cut short by Roly's sharp cries of pain.

'You woke him,' she said.

Knepp turned to Bird, as she picked him out of the cradle. 'Can't you do anything?'

Bird's legs shook. She was faint from the travails

of labour, lack of sleep, and the fact that none of them had had time to eat. She swayed on her feet. Carefully, she unswaddled him a little. The babe's face was contorted and his fists, escaped from their wrappings, waved angrily in the air

Mrs Knepp took her by the arm. 'Get back into bed, Mary Elizabeth, you shouldn't be up. We'll look to the child for an hour or so whilst you get some rest.'

'Put him by me,' she said, passing Roly to Mrs Knepp. She was so weary she could hardly lift her legs into bed, but finally she was up and under the covers, and lay back, so Mrs Knepp could rest Roly in the crook of her arm.

'I'll watch him,' Knepp said, sitting in the chair. 'You and Mary Elizabeth can get some rest, Mother.'

'Men shouldn't be here, in the lying-in,' Mrs Knepp said. 'Not for a few weeks.'

'Don't be foolish, Mother. He's my son.'

'He's my grandson.'

'Stop it, both of you.' Bird said. 'You can both stay, but stop your arguing. Just wake me the moment anything changes.'

Roly seemed to have worn himself out with crying, and finally Bird let herself doze in the flickering shadows of the candles.

CHAPTER 32

When Bird woke, she couldn't understand what was happening. The room was full of people. Mr and Mrs Grinstead, and the vicar, Anis the maidservant, and Hopkins the doctor. Knepp was clutching Roly in his arms.

'You have to let him go,' Mrs Grinstead said to him.

'No, give him to me,' Bird said.

Nobody moved.

'He'll need feeding. Pass him over.'

Again, nobody moved, but their eyes slid to one another.

'What is it?' The room was too quiet, it was as if a blanket had descended, suffocating all noise.

'He passed away,' Hopkins said. 'Just before dawn. I'm sorry, we did what we could.'

'No.' It couldn't be true. They were making it up. She turned to Knepp. 'Give him to me.'

Knepp's eyes burned into hers. 'I couldn't do anything. He just went stiff, twitching all over, and the next he was gone.'

'I want my baby.' Her voice sounded oddly high-pitched. 'Give him to me.'

Knepp lowered Roly gently into her arms. He was heavy in a way he had not been before. She put a finger to his cheek. Cold.

'What did you do to him?' She fired the question at Knepp.

'Nothing. I swear. There was nothing we could do.'

'Why didn't you wake me?'

'We went to find the doctor first. Then he tried to make him breathe. We did what we thought was best.'

'You let him die. Without me. And I made him a new nightdress.' What was she saying? Of course the nightdress wasn't important. It was as if her mouth had disconnected from her head.

She looked down into Roly's face, unbelieving. His eyelids were still faintly blue, the soft feathers of lashes so motionless and doll-like. His head was covered in a fine dusting of dark hair. She wanted to shake him, yet something hard and solid inside her prevented it. And then she wanted to crush him to her, but was afraid to, in case she hurt him, in case he . . .

Something inside her began to move, pushing, like something trying to be born, and she heard her voice fill the room with a surging wail of grief.

Of course Roly hadn't been baptised and so he couldn't lie in holy ground, but must needs be buried close to the churchyard wall of St Sepulchre's. The followers were few. There had been so many

plague deaths of late, and Knepp had never bothered to win himself many friends. Mrs Knepp had
elected to stay behind, suddenly an invalid again.
And indeed, she looked gaunt, her skin papery
white as they left the house. Knepp carried the
tiny coffin by himself, a broken man. On the other
side of the wall was a plague pit, with the sour
stench of decaying bodies and quicklime.

Bird followed behind him, in a kind of daze, her
black dress too warm and scratchy for the summer
heat. It was all so quick. She could not believe she
had become a mother, and then it had been ripped
away from her, all in the space of a week. It was
as if she was confused about who or what she was.
Every action seemed mechanical, every speech like
a pretence. She could be quite calm one moment,
and wracked with sobs the next.

Knepp's eyes were red with crying, and when
he had to lower the little wooden coffin into the
ground his shoulders heaved, but he stood up
straight and rigid, as the vicar spoke the blessing.
Bird could not take in the words, just the sound
of the spatter of earth on the coffin lid.

On the way home from the church, Knepp held
out his arm to her. She took it, grateful for the
support. She was dry-eyed now and numb. It
seemed impossible they were going home without
him; that Roly would always be lying there, in the
hard ground, when only yesterday he had been so
loving and trusting in her arms. 'We failed him,'
she said.

'I'm sorry,' he said. 'I would I could bring him back.' His voice cracked and broke, and he paused to gather himself.

'Why?' she asked. 'Why our son, and not another's?'

'Only God knows, wife. Let's pray that he is safe in heaven.'

'I don't know how I can go on,' she said. 'It is shaming, that I was not enough of a mother.'

'No. It was a sickness, and nothing to do with your care. I've heard it is common in new-borns that they succumb to such things. 'Tis the same with horses, and all beasts.' He pressed his hand on her arm. He was reassuring her. It was clumsy, but she felt his good intention behind it. For the first time, perhaps ever, she felt that they were man and wife.

But the son that should have united them was gone, and nothing in this world could ever replace him. *Flesh of my flesh, blood of my blood.*

Together they walked back to the yard. When they arrived, all the stable-boys and grooms were lined up in the yard, hats pressed to their hearts. Bird felt the tears come again, as her husband steered her in through the front door to the darkness of the hall.

CHAPTER 33

Seething Lane, London

When she heard the knock, Elisabeth sighed and put the book to one side, annoyed at being interrupted whilst reading her latest French romance.

'It's Mrs Knepp,' said Janey Gentleman, the new maid, apologetically.

'Oh, no. Well, I suppose it's too late to say I'm not at home.'

Janey swayed side to side on her feet and said nothing.

A sigh. 'Better fetch her up, then. And tuck your hair in your cap, before you go.'

A few moments later, Janey ushered the visitor in.

'Oh, Mrs Knepp, how very nice of you to call. How are you?' Elisabeth said.

'Well enough, considering,' Mrs Knepp replied.

Oh saints alive. She shouldn't have asked after her health. *Quel faux pas*. She should have offered condolences. Now she would think her heartless. Elisabeth ushered her towards a chair, only now noticing she was in a sober navy gown with no rouge or patches to be seen.

'Wait a moment, Janey,' Elisabeth said, as the maid was just disappearing out of the door. She took a quill and ink and scribbled a hurried note asking her husband to come home. 'Nip around to the office and take this to Mr Pepys. Quick as you can.'

Then she turned back to Mrs Knepp. 'Make yourself comfortable, I'll fetch us some cordial.'

'If the maid has gone out, there's no need to trouble yourself on my account,' Mrs Knepp said.

'No trouble,' Elisabeth said. She didn't know what to say to her. What on earth do you say to someone who has just lost a child?

When she returned with the tray, Mrs Knepp took the cordial and sipped it, but did not offer any small talk the way she usually did. She looked as if all the life had been drained out of her, and immediately Elisabeth felt a pang of compassion.

'I came to thank Samuel,' Mrs Knepp said. 'For agreeing to be a godparent—'

'It was nothing. I mean, he would have been glad to . . . such a terrible thing, your loss. Samuel told me.'

'It was unexpected. Roly was right as rain one moment and . . . the physician said scarlatina. We don't know how he caught it. We had a few visitors, but none confesses to being in contact with the disease.'

'Still, I suppose you can take comfort in the fact

you are not the only one grieving,' Elisabeth said. 'Mrs Pierce lost hers, you know. Still born. And so many must have lost children in this pestilence.'

Mrs Knepp's lips tightened and she gave a slight inclination of her head, but did not reply. Oh, *mon Dieu*, it looked like she might cry. Elisabeth picked up her drink and put it down again, filled with a sense of uselessness. She was failing, she realised. She didn't know how to help, but couldn't admit it. She cast about to change the subject.

'Do you know if the theatres might re-open soon? Mr Pepys does miss it so.'

Mrs Knepp swallowed. 'Soon, I hope. I need something to distract me. Killigrew has been an age finishing all his alterations, I hear, though I haven't ventured down there recently, being . . . confined.'

'I hear it's taking so long because of all the new machines – moving scenery, like at the Duke's,' Elisabeth said.

'If so, I wager they'll be cheaper. He's a skinflint, as far as spectacle goes, but he does care about the words. And actor managers like Hart don't like their money to be put at risk. Whenever there's talk of improvements, there's always mighty arguments over profits.'

'Really? It doesn't show in the plays.'

'Tom's not good at managing people,' Mrs Knepp said. 'So many actors have left the King's with bad feeling. Of course, now there's talk of the theatre re-opening he wants to woo them back, but he's competing with the Duke's, who seem to treat their actors with more respect.'

'Would you ever go over to the Duke's?'

'There are less roles for women with Betterton's troupe. I'll be lucky to find a part again with the King's Men. I'd barely got started when the theatres closed, and now . . . well, I feel—'

The noise in the hall alerted Elisabeth to Samuel's arrival. She rushed into the hall. 'Mrs Knepp's here,' she whispered. 'I don't know what to say to her. I think she might cry.'

She followed him back inside, where Mrs Knepp stood to greet him.

'Oh my dear Barbary Allen,' Samuel said, and enveloped her in a hug.

Mrs Knepp sobbed discreetly into Samuel's shoulder, at which point he produced a kerchief. Trust Samuel, he always knew how to butter the women. Elisabeth told herself not to be uncharitable. The poor woman had just lost her child. But did Samuel have to hug her quite so tight, and for quite that long? Samuel caught her disapproving expression and moved reluctantly away.

'Why not sing?' Elisabeth asked huffily. 'That's why you came, is it not?'

Samuel cast her an aggrieved look, and asked Mrs Knepp about the child, telling her how he regretted losing the chance to be a godparent.

Mrs Knepp wiped her eyes, took out the sheet music from her bag, and Samuel put it out on the stand. Mrs Knepp began singing, and Samuel sawed away at his viol. A maudlin song about a lost ship at sea. Elisabeth pretended to enjoy the resulting noise. True, Mrs Knepp did have a deep resonant voice, but she disliked the way they gazed at each other, as if she, Elisabeth, didn't exist. And besides, wasn't it a little unseemly to sing so, when one was in mourning?

To make matters worse, Mr and Mrs Pierce arrived shortly afterwards, all clad in black with black weepers on their hats. Mrs Knepp and Mrs Pierce embraced and tried not to weep, while the men looked on with piteous looks. Elisabeth began to feel she was the only one who wasn't grieving for a dead child. Samuel was all concern, to the point where she was quite nauseated and wanted to slap his face to wipe off his mournful expression.

Mr Pierce paid her little attention; his eyes were firmly on his wife and the singing duo of Samuel and Mrs Knepp. Eventually they joined in to make a cosy little quartet. Elisabeth suffered it in silence, except for the occasional sigh which everyone ignored.

Finally she stood up. 'Excuse me,' she said. 'I have a headache.' And then to Samuel, 'Call me when they've departed.'

She caught his sideways look to the company, which plainly said, my wife is a fool, and it hurt. She slammed the door as she went.

A few moments later Samuel came after her.

'Why must you be so rude?' he said.

'Me, rude? Why they paid me no courtesy even in my own house! Nobody invited *me* to sing.'

'We didn't know you wanted to.'

'You're right. I don't want to caterwaul with those whores, who fall with child like rabbits.'

He put a hand out to her arm. 'What is it?' he asked earnestly, looking into her eyes with a worried expression. 'Why must you be so . . . so ill-mannered? What is it that irks you so?'

'Nothing,' she said, brushing him off. Nothing she wanted him to see.

He stood a moment, holding out his arms in a sort of mute appeal. Finally he sighed and said, 'I'll send the boy for a carriage. Will you come with me to see them away?'

'No. I told you, you've given me a headache.'

He bowed out then, and she heard the doors close as everyone left.

Why hadn't she gone with them? It reminded her of the first time she'd come to England, and needed a hat against the rain. When she was on the way out of the milliners, proud of her purchase, all wrapped in straw in its hat box, she overheard the two serving girls mocking her choice of hat, and her English. She had gone back in and shouted at them, but it only made it worse. She came out the second time humiliated and amid peals of laughter. She felt like a foreigner, then, and she still did.

Except now she was a foreigner to motherhood. To the whole business of childbed.

CHAPTER 34

The Netherlands, 20th August 1666

At the town of Terschelling, Livvy's mother, Bo, watched the sea with growing unease. The rain was slanting down; grey needles into a pewter sea. At first, she thought it was the storm. But now she was not so sure. She stared at the flares in the sky from the window whilst she was closing the shutters against the night. She feared that the flashes were fire-powder, not lightning, and that the dull thud that echoed under her ribs was not thunder, but cannon.

'How far away are they?' her mistress asked, reading her thoughts.

'Closer,' Bo said. 'I can see masts and sail. Many ships. They are gathering in the Vlie.'

'I hate this war,' her mistress said, putting aside the linen coif she was sewing. 'Why must men fight so?'

Bo did not answer. It was not her place to do so, and she had heard this many times from her mistress. She and her husband were Mennonites and followers of Simons, who preached peace to all. Except to their slaves and servants, of course.

'Are there lights at the warehouses?'

'Yes, Mistress.'

'Then my husband must still be there, and there's no need to worry.'

Bo did not tell her mistress that last night she had seen plumes of smoke billowing into the night sky from Vlieland, the island opposite them across the mud flats, and that the sight had given her an oppressive feeling of dread.

'The supper is ready for when he comes?'

'It is laid out in the kitchen.'

'Go and fill the ewers then, and turn down the beds.'

Bo went, and as she smoothed the coverlet on the four-poster bed, she glanced again out of the window, and stopped dead. In the water close by, there were warships burning. They looked different from the usual sloops and whalers; heavier, squatter, like fighting dogs. Were they Dutch or English? She couldn't tell. English boats made her think of Livvy. Whatever they were, they were close; she could see small dots of men flailing in the water. Another boom that shook the window panes with a metallic rattle. She squashed the sudden panic that rose in her throat. Should she tell Mistress? Master always said the seafarer St Brandarius would protect the town. His lighthouse on the hill was kept lit day and night, to keep the whalers off the sandbanks and mud. Her next thought was for her son, Jan, who was down in the kitchen as usual, cleaning out the grate for tomorrow's cooking. He'd be scared.

She hurried downstairs but breathed a sigh of relief. He was squatting down on his heels, scraping at the remains of the peat with his shovel.

'Their fighting is bad tonight,' she said.

He turned and looked to her, a dark shadow against the darker grate. 'Will it come here, Mamma?'

'No, don't worry, chick.' She reached out to rub his wiry hair.

'If it does, can I fight?'

'It won't come here.'

A crash of the door against the wall, and the noise of men running into the house. Bo looked up to the ceiling.

She hitched up her heavy skirts and ran up the stairs. When she got to the top she saw the master and three of his men dragging their arms from the case in the hall. She had never seen him hold a gun in his life, and the sight of him ramming it with powder and shot made her put a hand to her mouth to stifle a cry.

'No, husband,' her mistress shouted. 'We must not! We took a vow.' She tried to wrestle the gun from him, but he would not let go.

'Do you want to die where you stand?' he cried. 'The English are coming. They're right behind us. I saw them cut Lieke down.'

She let go. 'Old Lieke?'

'She's dead. Hacked to pieces. Now get out of

my way.' The mistress stepped back, uncertain, her eyes dark with shock.

Bo ran down the stairs and almost hoisted Jan off his feet. 'Hide,' she said urgently. She threw open the big cupboard where they kept the fishing tackle and the pails and brooms.

'No!' Jan fought her off as she tried to bundle him inside. 'Why, Mamma? What is it?'

'Because I say so.' The harshness of her voice silenced him. 'Stay there until I see what's afoot. Stay, do you understand? And whatever you hear outside, you don't make a sound, until you hear my voice. I'll come for you when it's over. Do you understand?'

He nodded, dumb at the urgency in her voice. She shut the door on his wide-eyed face, locked it with the key from the chatelaine at her waist.

Up the stairs again, and the men were at the windows now, muskets poked through the shutters.

The mistress grabbed her by the arm. 'The key! Quick, lock the door.'

Bo grabbed the key from her belt and ran to the door, but just as she was closing it, it crashed into her from the other side. It hit her squarely on the shoulder and she tumbled backwards into the room. After that it was all confusion. A shot, and the dark man in the doorway fell, but immediately more pairs of boots stepped over him. They passed by her face amid the sour smell of shot, muskets to their shoulders. They fired at point-blank range.

The men jerked and fell where they stood, with no time to turn and defend themselves.

Bo put her hands over her ears, cowering to the wainscot.

Jan. He must stay where he was, they mustn't find him.

'Wait!' she heard her mistress cry, but it was too late, the master turned, there was a crack and a billow of smoke, and his chest exploded before her. The mistress was pressed back against the wall, her gown spattered from hem to neck with her husband's blood, her mouth in an 'o' of terror.

She would not have had time to speak because one of the men grabbed her roughly by the shoulder and swiped a blade across her throat. Bo crawled slowly towards the stairs, but one of them caught her movement, and turned, pistol in hand. She saw his look of triumph as he levelled it, saw its nose point to her forehead and his quick recoil before everything bled to black.

Jan heard the foreign voice giving orders, though he didn't understand the words.

'Search everywhere. Then fire the place.'

Hunkered in the cupboard, Jan squeezed both arms tight over his head. Shots made him shoot further back, and the clomp of running feet echoed above his head, but he did what Mamma had told him. He was quiet as a mouse.

Now they were so close he didn't dare breathe. Shadows passed the crack under the door; men laughed and jested to each other in their foreign tongue. Beside him, the noise of drawers hurled to the floor, the cutlery rattling down. A knife sped under his door. Still he didn't move.

A shout. More orders. Something dropping and smashing close to his shoulder on the other side of the door. The footsteps ran away.

He waited. Mamma always did what she said. She'd come back for him when it was all over.

Finally it was silent. There were no more shots, no more crashes. Instead there was another noise, a crackling noise. The space inside the cupboard got warmer. Flakes of dust fell from the ceiling and when he rubbed them between his fingers they were hot. Then he smelt it. Smoke. It crept under the crack of the door like a white snake.

Should he call out? Mamma had told him not to. Still he kept quiet. Then he began to cough, his throat on fire. He smothered the noise with his sleeve but couldn't catch his breath. He slumped to the ground amongst the brooms, but cowered away as the one nearest the door suddenly burst into orange flames. He dared not scream. She'd be here any minute he thought. He was a good boy.

CHAPTER 35

Robert Hubert hurried along the road towards Viner's Horse Hire in his usual uneven gait. He must get to Livvy. He'd hoped to tell her gently he was going away for a few days, sailing with Petersen again back to France, but now he felt guilty already about leaving her, but knew only he could be the bearer of such terrible news. The summer sun made him go hatless, and he flapped it at his face to try to get some air. He had the latest broadsheet in his hand, and a letter. His stomach was hollow and his mouth dry. She would not like him interrupting her at work, but it had to be done.

When he got to the place it was swarming with customers. Two carriages were just going out of the gate and a group of three well-dressed men on horseback. He asked one of the stable lads where he might find Livvy.

'In the bed-chambers. We had six in last night, so she'll be putting the chambers to rights. I'll fetch her if you like.'

'No, if it is not trouble, I'll go up.'

'Master don't like strangers in his house.' The boy stood in his way to deter him.

'I'll be only two shakes,' Robert said, holding up two fingers. He drew an old rose farthing from his pocket and held it out. 'I just need a private word.'

'All right.' The boy took the coin and reluctantly led the way. At the bottom of a flight of wooden stairs he pointed above. 'Up there.'

Robert grasped the rope banister and climbed up. At the top all the doors were open, and he glanced in each one. They were spartan but clean, the mattresses plumped, bolsters standing upright to air.

The last door was closed. He was about to knock when he heard a man's voice behind the door. He paused; his hand in mid-movement. The voice had stopped but now there was a sharp cry of distress, or was it pleasure? A woman.

He stood, unsure whether to go back down, but compelled to listen. Was Livvy in there? He heard the noise of the man again, grunting, and the noise of something banging. He knew the sound, and feared it. He looked out of the landing window but saw nothing. His attention was all on the sounds behind him. The sounds were unmistakeable. The man sounded like a bellows; puffs and grunts. Robert bit his lip. Then he slowly walked back down the corridor and downstairs, on tiptoe, lest anyone should hear him. He squeezed the letter in his hand. Should he still deliver it?

She'd betrayed him. The tearing sensation in his chest increased as he felt both the vengeful pleasure and the awful pain of giving her such a letter. Undecided whether to go or stay, his tangled thoughts were interrupted when the door flew open, and a man came striding down the stairs, still buttoning the fly-flap on his breeches. Red in the face, he straightened his periwig, which was askew, then glanced at Robert, who was off to the side of the door.

'Can I help you?'

'I'm booked in room four,' Robert said.

'That way,' the man said. Evidently deeming Robert to be of no special notice, he ignored him, only pausing to smooth down his suit and breeches, and put on an air of superiority, like a cloak.

Robert tensed, watching him go. The stableboys bowed low to him, and the men waiting doffed their hats. This must be Viner, the man in charge. It made Robert hate him the more.

From up the stairs came the noise of water splashing in a pail. A little while later, the scratch of the besom sweeping on the floor. Both sounds made him wince.

Robert called up, 'Livvy? Are you there?' He was surprised when his voice sounded just the same.

He heard her intake of breath. A moment later she appeared, tucking her muslin kerchief into her bodice. 'Robert. What are you doing here?'

'I came to see you. You'd better come down.'

He watched her descend the stairs, the swing

of her skirts swaying over her bare ankles, and as she did so, he hardened his heart. She was just a black serving woman. She wasn't anything to him.

When she got to the bottom, he saw one eye was swollen and bruised. 'What did you do to your eye?'

'Nothing. I hit it . . . on a shelf.' She looked away over his shoulder. Her lower lip quivered, before she pressed her lips together.

'Who was that man? The one who just came down?'

Her eyes flared in surprise, but she masked it. 'Mr Viner.' Seeing him waiting, she folded her arms across her chest. 'He likes to check the rooms.'

Robert said nothing. He knew how it was between master and servant. But it didn't make it hurt the less.

'What is it? What was so urgent?' she asked.

'I'm going away,' he said, his voice strangled with emotion. 'To France. I sail on this afternoon's tide. I have a collection to make. Some watch parts. I'll be a week, maybe ten days.'

'Oh.'

'So there'll be nobody at the repair shop if you call. But a letter, it came for you, so I had to bring it. I'm sorry, I read it . . . well, I didn't know the hand, so I open it. I'm sorry, it's bad news. Your town, it was burnt down in a raid by the English. There's braziers and feasting all up and down the quays.' He heard the words come out, and was

431

glad to hurt her. But then immediately, he felt sorry. He saw her brown eyes shift in confusion.

'Feasting? Where? What do you mean?'

She hadn't understood. Now the words wouldn't come. He stammered, 'Terschelling, where your family are. I remember the name, so I come to say. It was burnt down, fired by English troops, by a man called Mr Holmes. The English, they call it "Holmes' Bonfire".'

'Why?' She still hadn't grasped what he was telling her.

'There's a letter. Not in your mother's hand. It just arrive this morning. From France. Livvy, you should sit down while I read it.'

Her face registered shock then, and pain. She hadn't heard the words, but read the bad news in his eyes. His heart didn't know whether to be glad or sorry.

'I don't need to sit down,' she said. 'Just read it.'

He unfolded the letter. 'It's in French. Bad French.'

'Just read it for mercy's sake!'

He kept his voice flat; neutral, translating as he read.

'*My dear sister. Our mother and brother Jan are dead in the English raid on Terschelling.*

Five hundred are dead, burned to death. God rest all their souls. The news came to me from a friend who fled here. He saw their house, but it was a . . . I think it say *. . . a ruin, and no-one survives.*'

He looked up to see if she was taking it in. Her

face had turned still as stone, but she clutched her skirts with pale-knuckled fingers.

'Should I carry on?' he asked.

'Read it all,' she said, flatly.

He lifted the paper again. '*I asked my friend if there was hope. He said, none. Friends dragged the bodies out afterwards for burial. Heaven rest them. I have no place to offer you here, sister. I am indentured. My friend helped me set down these words. Stay safe, and may all the powers curse the English.*'

He stopped reading and looked up.

'Mamma.' She gulped the word. 'Jan? What both?' She turned from him, pressed her head into her hands, rocking back and forth on her heels. After a few moments, she swivelled and stabbed a finger towards his news-sheet. 'What does your broadsheet say?'

His belly tightened. 'They rejoice in the city at the number of Dutch dead. Talk of it is everywhere.'

She snatched it from his hand and tore it in pieces before casting it down. Her whole body was shaking. 'Filthy English. They are not human beings. They steal, and burn and treat us like . . .' Here her words ran out.

'Livvy, I—' He reached to comfort her but she slapped him away.

'Viner found our letters. He threatens to tell the constable about you. That you are Catholic spy. So I let him do what he wants. Now I am a woman worth nothing.'

'No. You shouldn't have done that!' He tried to take her by the arm.

Mason, one of the uniformed grooms, was staring at them, bucket in hand.

'Don't touch me! They have burned down everything I love! I will burn them. I will make inferno of hell. Let them see what the Dutch can do. I will burn down this city until they scream for mercy.'

'Wait! Livvy!'

He ran after her, stumbling, catching at her sleeve, but his lame leg meant he could not catch her. His last sight of her was her flying skirts and the ties of her apron streaming behind like tails.

CHAPTER 36

Livvy did not stop running until she reached the church of St Paul's right in the middle of the city. She dived inside out of the bright sunlight. Gaggles of men had congregated around the news stands, staring at the headlines, but Livvy didn't stop, for she could not read. The only word she could recognise was '*Dutch*' – the word Robert had taught her, with its curving belt-buckle of a capital and its cross in the middle.

She ignored the crowds of bustling shoppers and the scantily clad streetwalkers, and marched straight down the aisle towards the altar. Years of being forced to worship on Sundays had made her familiar with the English church. The altar – that was the holiest place. She took a front-row pew, daring anybody to stop her. Here she'd bargain with their God. She always thought of him as 'their' God, something separate from her, for her mother had told her that she had been forced to Christianity in Surinam, under the whip. When she was a child there had still been hidden whispers to the ancestors, rites for the blessing of trees, and castings of sacred water in her mother's prayers, in the curious mixture of Christianity and what her mother called the Old Faith.

Livvy knelt on a hard, embroidered cushion and closed her eyes tight to block out the hubbub, and the light which rippled from the leaded glass in the windows. Over years, she had learnt that in any catastrophe, and she had seen many, it was better to be calm. She remembered her mother's voice, 'Nothing good comes from tears, nor from raging.'

She offered her questions up towards the rafters. 'Why did you let the English kill a child like Jan? Why does Mr Viner feel he can still sit in his pew on a Sunday, like he done nothing?'

She knuckled her brow with her hands, waiting for an answer. Surely, if He could hear her, Christ would answer. Losing a mother and a brother gave her the right to be heard.

The silence about her grew. The echoing English voices became just a hum.

No answer came. Maybe the Christ-God was a master who thought he didn't need to answer someone like her? After a half-hour, her anger grew hot again. Unable to stay still a moment longer, she turned her back on the altar and with long decisive steps made her way out into the air. She could not go back to Viner's yard. She headed down Fish Street Hill towards St Botolph's Wharf.

As she approached the edge of the Thames, she could already see a column of smoke rising into the sky. A bonfire of pallets and rags blazed on the thin shore. Surrounding it, a crowd of men were carousing, ale cups and flagons in hand. Further down the shore towards the customs house, more pinpricks of flame and smoke could be seen.

'Death to the Dutch!' one of them cried.

'Fry them alive!' shouted another.

Livvy shut her ears and hurried down towards the stone steps where the water lapped by the wharf.

'By all that's holy,' she let the thoughts intensify, 'I'll not let them win.' She scraped up a spar of driftwood and spat on it. An idea came to her. A wicked, sinful idea, but one that eased the storm in her heart.

'This is Viner.' She held up the spar of wood and spoke the words aloud. It felt good, to be mistress of her own fate. Closing her eyes, she unpinned the darning needle from her apron hem, held out her palm and stabbed down hard. A gasp. The sharp pain felt like nothing in comparison with the pain inside. A bead of blood appeared, red and shiny like a berry. She used her index finger to smear it over the driftwood 'man'.

'By my blood,' she said aloud, 'I call on my ancestors, make vengeance on this man. Bring death to him and his warmongering city.' Two sharp stabs with the needle gave him eyes, and the satisfaction of hurting him.

I'm a witch, she thought wonderingly. A black witch. She laughed. They had driven her to reclaim the thing they feared most.

She picked up the puppet. She'd have vengeance on Viner, cast him into the Thames, let him drown.

But then another voice seemed to whisper to her. No. Let him burn, and his city with him.

She turned and, gripping the effigy in her hand, walked towards the bonfire.

~ ACT THREE ~

'It made me weep to see it. The churches, houses, and all on fire, and flaming at once; and a horrid noise the flames made, and the cracking of houses at their ruin.'

Samuel Pepys, *Diary*,
2nd September 1666

ACT THIRD.

CHAPTER 37

Bird had been sent a script by Killigrew for *The Silent Woman*, and was sitting in the parlour turning the pages, but with her thoughts drifting. She knew the part already, and these days she couldn't seem to nail herself to anything. She let her eyes fall on the vase of flowers on the table. Yellow flag irises in a blue-and-white jug. Knepp had taken to riding out of town at first light alone, and yesterday he had brought the flowers back and put them before her on the table.

'Thought you could do something with these,' he'd said.

He'd turned and gone into the yard before she could reply, and she was left staring at the damp bundle. The slim, green leaves and the sunshine yellow petals were shockingly bright.

'Aren't you going to put them in water?' Mrs Knepp had asked, from her bed. 'There's a jug I brought in my trunk – in the plate cupboard.'

So she had found the jug, and somehow her hands had arranged the irises to stand tall and upright, something she thought she might never persuade her own body to do again. She gave an involuntary shiver as if to shift a weight from her shoulders, and let her gaze rest on the petals, which were already curling at the edges because of the dry summer heat.

From the corner, she could hear old Mrs Knepp's breath subside into snores, and huff in and out as she slept, one hand dangling over the edge of the bed.

A knock at the door.

Anis went to answer it and came back saying, 'There's that blackamoor at the door, Mistress.'

'Livvy?' Bird roused herself and went to see.

'I need a place to stay.' She was rubbing sooty hands down her skirts, and her hem and shoes were filthy. 'And work if you've got it.' She looked over her shoulder as if expecting to see someone after her.

'Come in; shut the door.'

Livvy's eyes shifted around the room. 'I've left Viner's. I thought . . . maybe you need a servant.'

'I'll have to speak to Knepp. And I don't like to bother him now, not since . . .'

'I know it's a bad time. I'll be no trouble. I can sleep anywhere; a stable, or a stall, if need be.'

'You know Knepp, he doesn't like anyone going near the horses.' She gestured to Livvy to sit, but she did not, just stared back at the blackness of the window.

'There's plenty of empty rooms upstairs,' Bird said. 'And you're welcome. No-one lives in now.

We lost some stablelads in the plague, and we thought to decorate the rooms for paying guests, but then with Roly . . .'

'Grief's like that. It saps you, once the anger's gone,' she said. 'Your babe had a burial and folk to mourn him. That's more'n some children get.' Something in her tight manner forbade further questions.

'Livvy? Is it something I can help with?'

'No. Nothing gonna help. 'Cept you take me in.'

'All right. When will you come?' Bird asked, too weary and heartsore to gainsay it.

'Now,' Livvy said. 'I'm not going back.'

Livvy had no luggage with her, not even a night-gown. 'Is it Viner? What about references? Does he know you've gone?'

'I don't want him to know where I am. I don't want nobody to know. I'd go for my box, but I daren't go back. I'll manage without.'

'Are you in some kind of trouble?'

Livvy tilted her head on one side, eyes lowered and her mouth pressed hard shut.

'Knepp might not let you stay, if you're in trouble. And we can't afford another servant. Business has been slack enough with no playing in the theatre these last months. Not that I feel like it. I can't seem to rouse myself to anything, these days.'

'I don't need no pay. Just a place to stay.'

'There's no home comforts here, you know that.'

'I don't need none. A bed's comfort enough.'

443

A piercing scream. Mrs Knepp was by the open birdcage, one of the birds lifeless in her hand. 'It's Thimble,' she cried. 'He's gone.'

A week later, Seething Lane

'Wake up, sir!'

Elisabeth disentangled herself from the dead weight of Samuel's naked leg, and squinted through the dark to see Janey Gentleman's face peering around the edge of the door.

What was she doing? Kitchen staff were not allowed up here. And she and the other servants were supposed to be abed.

'A fire, Mistress! Quite close by. Thought I'd better come tell you.'

'Samuel!' Elisabeth prodded her husband in the back.

'Don't try your antics again, woman,' he mumbled.

'A fire! I can see it from my window. Looks like Fenchurch Street, but I can't rightly say. Close though.'

She pushed Samuel out and he stumbled to the window.

A sharp cry of realisation. Hastily, he covered his nether parts with his hands and leapt back into bed. 'Pass me my nightgown,' he snapped.

Elisabeth found it under the pillow and threw it at him, but when she turned back, Janey's face had disappeared.

'It'll be nothing,' Elisabeth said. 'She makes a fuss over nothing, that girl. What is it with servants called Jane? She's as bad as the last one. No common sense.'

Nevertheless, she sat up in bed and pulled a shawl over her shoulders.

Samuel, now dressed in his nightgown, was at the window. 'Can't see a thing from here. I'll go up to the maid's room and look out from the flat roof.'

Elisabeth hurried to slip her feet into her mules and clop after him. She told herself it was to see the fire for herself, and not to check if he was up to anything with Janey.

Samuel was out on the flat roof. 'Careful, sir,' Janey said.

Elisabeth peered over Janey's shoulder. There was an orange glow a little way off, on Marke Lane.

'Fancy you waking us for that,' Elisabeth said. 'It's just someone's bonfire. Someone could piss it out.'

'It's not far away,' insisted Janey.

'Stuff!' Elisabeth said. 'It's celebrations for our victory against the Dutch, I expect.'

Samuel climbed back in. 'I'm going back to bed,' he said. 'It's something and nothing.'

Janey looked mighty disgruntled. When they woke in the morning, a cursory glance out of the window showed smoke billowing further away. 'See,' Samuel said, 'it's almost out.'

As they were eating breakfast, Janey poked her head around the door again. 'Thought you should know, sir. That fire you were going to piss on, well it's burned more'n three hundred houses right down Fish Street, and it's heading for London Bridge.'

Robert Hubert saw the smoke from the dock even before he disembarked from Captain Petersen's ship, the *Skipper*, that early Monday morning. He held his hat on with one hand against the wind, and squinted through watering eyes at the streaks of flame on the horizon. *Mon Dieu.*

Livvy's words came back to him; her threat to burn the city. She couldn't have done it, could she? *Non. Pas possible.* It was just a house fire gone astray, that was all.

But the nearer they rowed, the worse the scene became. The whole east side of the city was alight. He always thought fire to be orange, but here as well as orange, the flames were green, blue; unearthly. The air swarmed with sooty particles of dust, and ahead lay a clear view of St Paul's church which had never before been visible from the river. The sight of the tower, stark and tall, un-nerved him; it was an accusation from God, a sign pointing at something, or someone.

As the boat forced its way up the Thames the stench of burning caught in his throat. A man with a large moustache coughed and took out a scarlet kerchief to cover his nose. Robert's heart thudded uncomfortably in his chest as the wherry ploughed through the debris-strewn river. People's possessions bumped about, half-submerged in the oily water. A barrel of wine floated by, and a woman's hat. A portrait of a gentleman in a gilded frame sailed past like a raft.

Where had all these boats come from? He'd never seen so many boats on a river at once, not even on the Seine. They had to veer side to side to avoid these small craft; scullers and rowboats, all jammed to bursting with people and goods, and all fleeing in the other direction.

Further up, shouts, as families flung their goods into the river. From this distance, the wharf teemed with running silhouettes against the brilliant light of the flames. Anxious lest the fire should engulf his shop and his lodgings, Robert stood up with several others to get off at Old Swan Stairs, but the warehouses and offices, the gantries and loading tackle, even the wooden stairs and jetty, were gone. Half-burned joists, patterned like snakeskin, floated by. He had to shield his eyes, as burned bits of sacking and ash whipped into his face. On the wherry the men were too awed by the sight of the charred devastation to speak.

'We'll have to go further up,' the wherryman said. Then as an afterthought, 'You'll need to pay double.'

Uproar on the boat, such that Robert thought it might capsize.

Everyone protested at once. Robert was last off.

Others were steadier on their feet. So there was nobody left to trolley his luggage – the heavy boxes of enamelled clock faces, watch-springs and chains. No small boys hung around the stairs hoping for work. Their absence was disturbing.

What should he do? Should he abandon his stock on the side of the river to be seized by thieves? But he couldn't carry it all, and there was nobody to help. At the same time, the fear of what might have happened to his shop and his livelihood made him want to drop it all and run.

He emptied what he could into his travelling case, and bowed down with the weight, staggered towards Thames Street. He wasn't the only one with a burden; everyone he passed was the same. The landscape of London was like a mouth with missing teeth, full of blackened stumps and gaps. The view was alien; unrecognisable. Half-burned joists and rafters stuck out from church steeples, in the distance something exploded.

He grew hot as he walked, the smell of burning moving with him as he picked his way through the embers of what had been a warren of streets, and was now, unaccountably, open to the air. Burning debris blew into his hair and his beard. He had to claw it away as the heat bit into his skin.

Out of the burnt-out streets and into more familiar territory, where the buildings were still intact. He paused to wipe his eyes, and saw in the distance a large, unruly crowd. The uniforms told him it was one of the trained bands, the King's Militia that was supposed to protect the city. At the centre, a group of them hammered on the front door of one of the tall, jettied houses.

Moments later they dragged out a ginger-headed woman by the hair and pummelled her down the street. The crowd surged towards him, with cudgels and flails, filling the narrow space, surrounding a knot of men and women being driven like geese down the street.

Robert retreated, fearing to be mown down.

'French pigs!' shouted a man in a knitted cap, on the fringes of the crowd. He picked up a loose cobble and flung it hard towards the cowering woman. It struck a young freckled man on the side of the cheek and he fell. Robert rushed forwards before he could think.

A booted guard, face black with smuts, stopped him with a pistol to the chest. 'Out of the way,' he said. 'Move along.'

'What's happening?' Robert shouted, over the mêlée.

'The plot by the French and Dutch to fire the city. We're taking suspects to the Tower.'

Robert abruptly shut his mouth. The crowd surged past him. Immediately he was ashamed. He should have done something. But what? He was a small lame man, he'd be no match for them. But still. He had not stood up for his countrymen. It shamed him as he pushed his way through the straggle of people up the alley. Every window broken; every door staved in. And yet the fire hadn't touched these houses. A mangled loom had been upended on the cobbles, its luminous white silk trampled and sooted, and he realised this was the weavers' street, all of them houses of French silk weavers.

Where was Livvy? If they were dragging the Dutch and the French away, would they have Livvy? The tightness in his chest made him breathless. It was no use. He couldn't carry his load any further. He let it drop to the ground, and loped with his uneven gait towards Goldsmiths Row and the yard behind; his lodgings and shop.

A sign used to hang above the door, *Le Sablier*, the sign of the hourglass, which he had put there last year because French goods were fashionable. He searched for it, but it was gone. Two loose chains dangled, the broken links evidence it had been torn down. He stared up at them where they swayed in the wind, a cavern growing in his chest. In the fierce wind, his door flapped with a rhythmic bang.

He knew what he would find when he went inside, but still, he had to look.

Not a drawer left closed, not a single watch or clock. The prayer-books and missals ripped from the long-case clocks, torn and scattered. Every cabinet broken into. The breath whooshed from him, and he sank onto his backside on the stairs. He remembered the long years of patient study; his father's trembling hands trying to show him how to fix the tiny springs, and his own youthful voice, '*Ne te dérange pas, papa. Je peux le faire moi-même.*' It's all right Father, I can do it myself.

He didn't know if he had the courage or the will to re-build it all. 'I'm so sorry, Papa,' he said.

Shakily, he stood and turned his back on it. He had the feeling of being caught in something too big for him to understand. There was a heat and tension in the air that was not just from the flames. He wanted answers. But most of all, he needed to see Livvy. Was she the cause of all this? He couldn't believe she'd do anything so wicked. And what would Viner do to her, if he thought she was responsible?

From the street he could see the lowering cloud of smoke. Like an omen, it seemed to be hanging right over Viner's Yard. He set off towards it.

CHAPTER 38

In the yard at Farringdon and Knepp's, the queue for horses and carriages was six deep. Bird and Mrs Knepp peered from the parlour window as the queue grew ever deeper. Anis had told them about the fire in the east of the city, and how it had spread in the teeth of the wind. The clatter of hooves coming and going, the shouts of the men, the bedraggled appearance of the women begging for someone to save their belongings, all led Bird to see that something urgent and calamitous was happening. Yet inside the parlour, nothing had changed. The clock ticked. The ache in her heart split her open just the same.

'Look at all these people queueing. He'll make his fortune!' Mrs Knepp said.

Even if he did, what difference would it make? It couldn't bring Roly back.

The door flew open. Knepp's face was pinched, his forehead rimed with sweat. 'It's much worse than we thought,' Knepp said. 'Nobody can get in or out of the Cinque Ports. Lord Arlington has banned it. There's an embargo, to stop anyone who might have fired London from leaving.'

Livvy, who sat in the corner darning a pair of socks looked up, suddenly still.

'But worse,' Knepp went on, 'there will be no imports either, and they're saying the hay ware-houses near the Ropery are in danger. The waterwheel under London Bridge is in flames. If the warehouses go up, we won't be able to feed our horses. Our business will be finished. We'll have to get as much hay out of there as we can. I can't spare a driver, look at the queue – but one of the stable-lads will help me load it. I need someone to hold the horses while we do it. Will you help?'

'Me?' Bird asked.

'You and Livvy. It wouldn't involve any lifting, just holding the reins and keeping them steady.'

'I can't. I . . .' She didn't know why not. Just everything felt too much.

'Mary Elizabeth, the horses will starve if we don't, and they won't be able to work, and . . . it would be the end of Knepp's.'

'I'll do it,' Mrs Knepp said, rising from her seat. 'I can hold a horse.'

'Don't be foolish,' Bird said. 'Sit down. You haven't the strength. I'll go.' She heaved herself out of the chair. 'I'll just fetch a cloak.'

'Are you mad? You won't need one,' Knepp said. 'It's hot as hell out there.'

'Livvy?' Bird went to where she was still sitting, unmoving.

She was fixed in place like a stone, her eyes fearful. 'I don't want to go out.'

453

'Why? Knepp took you in, didn't he? Now he needs you to help.'

'I'm not moving. I stay here, look after Mrs Knepp. The fire only small. It will be out soon.' The mutinous look in her eyes held something more, but Bird was at a loss to understand what.

Frustrated, she raised her voice. 'If you don't come, I'll . . .' What? Would she be prepared to throw Livvy out? Beat her? No. She sighed. 'Make sure there's food ready when we come in then.'

Ted Viner pushed his eldest son, Georgie, into the carriage with the other four children. He was twelve-years old, and big enough to be responsible.

Georgie looked sulky. 'I want to stay here, Father.'

Arabella Viner put her head in through the coach window. 'Don't fuss, Georgie. Someone needs to look after your brother and sisters. The fire's too close for comfort.'

'You always treat me like a baby.'

Viner pushed Arabella aside. 'On the contrary, I'm giving you a great deal of responsibility,' Viner said. 'Tell Uncle Benedict we'll be following directly. We just need to collect one or two things.' He turned to Arabella. 'You've spoilt that boy, turned him into a molly-boy.'

'You were the one who gave him everything, not me,' she said. 'You should've given him more guidance.'

Stupid woman. She always had something to say.

Around the front of the carriage he spoke to Tomlinson, his overseer and whispered, 'Make sure they get to Storey House, Whitehall, won't you?'

He looked up. The sky was a strange purple colour as the sun tried to penetrate the thick pall of smoke. Arabella had turned her back on him and was walking away, her skirts blowing in the breeze, her hand to her hair which was whipping across her face. She disappeared through the front door.

To his relief, the carriage clattered away. It was good to get the children out from under his feet. One less thing to worry over. Servants pulled another carriage out of the bay, and readied it in place, whilst Cal and another of the stable-boys went to fetch the horses.

Viner issued orders: 'The cellars first, the trunks of coin there. Then the plate in the dining hall, and the silverware in the cupboards. By then we'll have packed the rest.' He strode away and followed his wife into the house.

As he went a gust of wind brought sparks and debris raining into the yard. A flaming piece of straw landed in front of him. He extinguished its red glow with his boot, grinding it into the dust. Bludworth had better be getting that fire under control. Damned inconvenient, having to move everything, like this. Still, better be cautious.

Inside the house he puffed his way up the stairs to find Arabella staring out of the window.

He joined her there and looked out.

'Christ almighty.' The whole of the adjoining street was on fire. How had it grown so fast?

'Quick,' he said. 'Get a basket! Your jewellery, the silver candlesticks.'

Outside, the shouts of his grooms, 'The well! Fetch water!'

He ran out of the room and into his adjoining chamber where he threw open a leather case and swiped his gold snuff-boxes into it, off the night-stand. Pouches of gold coins followed. What else was small and valuable? His eye fell on the family Bible, but he dismissed it. Too heavy and bulky. But he'd be vulnerable with all this gold. He buckled on his sword belt and armed himself with his best steel sword.

What else? He couldn't leave the full barrel of brandy in the cellar. He'd best fetch it out.

'Don't forget the miniature of my mother!' he yelled through the open door as he passed. The other room was oddly silent. He paused and peered in.

Arabella was still at the window.

'For God's sake, woman, get a move on.'

'It's too late,' she said.

He was over in two strides to look.

The back of the carriage store was already burning. He shook her by the arm, 'Call the servants! We've got to get everything out.'

'No,' she said, pulling sharply away, a wild spark in her eyes. 'I hope it all burns to the ground. Your whole empire.'

He couldn't take it in. 'Hurry! Do you want to burn to death?'

She seemed suddenly bigger. He took a step back.

'I am walking out of here,' she said, 'and I'm walking out on you. No. Don't try to stop me. For years you have made me serve your ambition. You have gambled and whored, and treated me like dirt, and all the time pretending to be a good upright Christian. Well now God is giving you retribution. And it shall be my greatest pleasure to watch it happen. I hope there is not a stick left, not even a toothpick.'

She was away down the stairs before he could stop her. 'Arabella! What about the children?'

She turned back, pausing on the stairs. 'If you know so much about raising them, then do it yourself. I'm sick of being your brood mare. Five children and four more dead at birth. Well, no more.'

'You need me. You'll be nothing without me.'

'I shall be everything without you. I shall be free.'

At Knepp's the heavy horses were already in the traces with Purler, the stable-lad, lounging in the back of the cart like a king. He grinned at the idea of this great adventure. Bird couldn't help but smile back, though she knew lugging trusses of hay would be heavy work. She hoped the watchmen and the beadle would have got the fire defences properly organised by now.

As soon as they were outside, she realised they were going in the wrong direction. The street was jammed with mules and people hastening westwards, bundles of possessions clasped in their arms. They were pushing against the tide. The horses wouldn't go forward, and Bird and the boy had to get out and lead them on, shouting 'make way,' as they went.

They headed for Thames Street, jostling through the crowds, until suddenly they came out of a narrow thoroughfare into open space. Such was the shock, it was like falling off a cliff. Knepp hauled on the reins and the cart creaked to a standstill.

Where was London? This place was unrecognisable. What should have been Thames Street was a smouldering, blackened field, the roads only visible because they were criss-crossed by trudging queues of people.

Even the boy was speechless, retreating back to stroke the horse's nose, as if to gain some comfort. The glint of the Thames was just visible past the ruined scaffold of a church tower. Bird hadn't ever seen the river from the city. She stopped a woman hurrying past with a basket hitched on her hip. 'The warehouses by Three Cranes . . .?'

'You'll be lucky. Nothing left standing in the East End. I saw one of them warehouses just go up. Boom! A fireball. Spice warehouse I think it was. Stank to high heaven. The whole city's ablaze. Can't stop it. We had it coming, didn't we? Killing the king.'

'Is it still going?' the boy asked eagerly.

'Aye. It's headed for King's Head Court now, and they say there's no saving it.'

'The warehouses have gone. And the fire's got to the King's Head,' she shouted to Knepp.

She had barely time to take in the information before she had to leap sideways to avoid a cart lurching crazily towards her, piled high with furniture and draperies.

In the opposite direction one of the new fire engines clanged a bell as it was pushed down the crowded thoroughfare, and turned left towards the streets that were still standing. A group of men hurried beside it dragging buckets and a rolled-up leather hose.

Knepp was yelling over the noise. 'Did you say The King's Head?'

'Yes, she says it's right in its path.'

'I'm going to take a look. Viner's is right by there, on Cradle Alley.'

'No. It's not right to gloat.'

'I'm not going to gloat.'

'Then why? To watch it burn?'

No answer.

'Stay here, Mary Elizabeth,' Knepp said. 'It's no place for a woman. Boy! Get back up.'

The boy leapt onto the tail-gate, just as Knepp plied his whip to the rump of the matched pair of horses. They shied and tossed their heads, reluctant to trample into the surging mass of people.

'Stop; wait for me!' Bird shouted, running after him.

Then it came to her. He was going to find Arabella Viner. And leave her behind. How dare he? The thought of it stung. With amazement, she realised she was jealous. She'd be damned if he'd go without her.

Fortunately, the cart's progress was slow, hampered by the mass of people swarming by. A man shook his fist at them, and a woman came past dragging a scrawny brown-and-white cow by a lead, her husband following with a bogey with the butter churn strapped to it. As they grew closer to the seat of the fire, the air swirled with microscopic black, like a cloud of midges.

The heat and smoke were choking. They were heading right for the heart of the conflagration. She shouted to Knepp, 'Go back! It's madness!'

But Knepp had his kerchief pulled up over his nose and ears and didn't hear her. The road ahead cleared and the horses shied and quivered, refusing to go on. Knepp used the switch, but they side-stepped and neighed their fear in high-pitched whinnies.

Had he lost his senses? Bird leapt to control the horses and try to reason with him. Surely everyone in Cradle Alley would have evacuated by now; they must turn back. The air was thick as soup in the back of her throat. But it was what she saw that made her retreat backwards.

A solid wall of heat shimmered before her, the

460

half-timbered houses wavering as if underwater. Bird put up an arm to shield her face. About a hundred yards away, orange flames dragged sideways by the wind, like fiery hair, licked up the sides of the King's Head tavern, from where rats scurried forth like ants.

She ran to the back of the cart. 'Go home,' she said to the boy.

His eyes were glued to the flames ahead.

She tugged him off as he struggled against her. 'Now! Go home!' she said. 'Back to the yard. It's too dangerous. Just get out of here.'

The boy came to his senses and ran. Knepp was already turning the cart left, to wind past King's Head Court towards Cradle Alley, with Bird haring after him, panting, her sleeve pressed to her nose. Beneath her shoes the pavement was hot through the leather. At the end of the row she passed the mayor's men pulling down a tavern with billhooks and shovels. A smith with bulging muscles was destroying the lath walls by hurling his weight behind a spade.

Knepp forced his horses past, but then the whole of a side of the building came down, dragging rafters and thatch, and the horses bolted forwards.

At Viner's Yard all was disorder. The wind had changed direction and now thick clouds of smoke enveloped the yard in a choking pall. It didn't take much to see that the back part of the stable block was already alight, sparks flaring upwards from the wooden-tiled roof. As they approached,

461

a wild-haired woman was shouting, 'Burn damn you! Burn!'

A red-haired lad grabbed the woman by the arm to pull her away, but she almost bodily lifted him off the ground and threw him aside. With a terrified look, he scrambled back to his feet, and ran.

'Arabella?' Knepp leapt off the cart. 'Are you all right?'

'Best I've ever been in my life.' The woman was perspiring, her hair fallen from its pins at the back, the underarms of her dress, dark.

'Where's your husband?'

'In there, trying to get his gold out. I hope he burns.'

'Wait here,' Knepp said, running through the gates. Above the carriage house door, the roof and the fancy sign below it were already burning.

Viner was trying to put a horse in the traces of a coach, but the horses' eyes were white and rolling with fright. As they approached, he yelled at Knepp to get out of the way.

The horse snorted and stepped on the spot.

'This is the fault of your damned maid, Knepp,' Viner said.

'What?'

'Your black maid that you sent here. She's part of this devilish plot by the Dutch. One of my grooms heard her boasting she would burn down the city.'

'Which groom?'

'Mason. But he's gone. They all have. They saw

the fire coming and fled. Bloody cowards. Now get out of my way.'

'What about the horses?' From the stables came the frantic whinnies and the thuds of thrashing hooves.

'I'll have to leave the livestock to take their chances. The fire's at our backs; there's no time.'

'You'd leave the poor beasts to fry?' Knepp said. 'Where's your harness room?'

'None of your business.'

'You're not leaving until every horse is out of here,' Knepp said, standing in front of the coach.

'Damn you,' Viner said, climbing up onto the driver's seat. 'Get out of my way. Do you want us all to die?'

'There's not enough time,' Bird shouted, 'Look!' The roof of the stables was silhouetted against a flicker of flame and a haze of heat.

As Knepp was distracted Viner cracked the whip and the carriage careered out of the yard.

'Watch out!' Bird grabbed Knepp and pulled him to the side.

Knepp shouted after him, 'Wait!'

'Madman! He nearly mowed us both down.'

'Help me,' Knepp said, rushing to drag the gates closed. 'Unbolt all the stable doors.'

The bolts were hot and swollen with the heat. Bird pulled one set free and a panicked horse shot out, neighing wildly. The next stable was open at the top, smoke already billowing from the top door, but Knepp dived in and came out bearing

463

an armful of ropes, halters and leading reins. He thrust those and a pile of sacks at Bird's feet and went back in for more.

She grabbed the ropes and headed for the nearest loose box.

As soon as she opened the door, the big iron-grey hunter barged past and shot out into the yard, nostrils flaring, but finding its way blocked by the gates, let out a piercing whinny, causing more uproar in the boxes. It galloped around the perimeter looking for a way out and away from the heat and smoke.

Lord, she'd be knocked flat. She pressed herself back against the wall, to keep out of the way of the flying hooves, as Knepp came past dragging a heavy dray horse by the halter. He'd thrown a sack over its head, and with practised efficiency he lashed it to a ring by the mounting block. Bird dodged the loose horses and tugged back the bolt on the next box, relieved to see a smaller horse churning its straw as it turned round and round. This one, she managed to get a head-collar and a sack on, though it bucked and neighed as she fastened on a leading rein. She led it out behind her to tie it up, and it half-dragged her across the yard.

Four more she fetched in this way, until she thought her lungs would burst from heat and smoke. 'No more,' Bird shouted, eyes pouring, 'We've got to get out.'

'Back up the cart then, whilst I let the last ones

out,' Knepp said as he ran past. 'Wait for me outside.' But she couldn't cross the yard – by now it was full of terrified horses. A crack like thunder, and the roof of the house next door fell in, throwing out sparks and debris like rain.

Immediately a series of small fires started in the tinder-dry grass in the gutters, which were soon burning fiercely. Bird ran for the cart. It was gone.

'Clear the gates,' she shouted, 'I'll have to let the rest go free.'

She squeezed through the small turnstile near the big gate and yelled at everyone to clear out of the way.

Arabella Viner was still standing there, her hands black, her cuffs filthy. She looked old; worn-out.

Knepp corralled the loose horses up to the gate.

'Arabella, you need to move, the horses are coming out,' she shouted.

Arabella ignored her. She was standing right in their path. With horror, she saw her pick up a still burning lath and throw it into the yard. It narrowly missed Knepp's horse.

'Burn!' she cried.

'Arabella. Get out of the way!'

'You can't make me.'

Had she lost her senses? Behind Knepp the horses were crowding into a crush of heaving flanks and shoulders, the heat was pushing them forwards. She couldn't wait any longer. She opened the gate and a mêlée of thrashing hooves shot out. Horses galloped in all directions. Knepp hung onto the reins and leant back in the saddle to haul his mount under control. Tight against the wall, Bird covered her head with her arms.

A peek, and she saw Arabella, her arms waving like a crazy statue. They'd mow her down! Somehow with their innate wisdom, the horses pounded past, leaving her still standing in a swirl of dust. Knepp had pulled up, jouncing on a saddled horse, with four others, two on either side, and three more trailing on ropes behind.

He dragged his horse to a standstill next to Bird. 'Where's the cart?'

'Stolen.'

'Hell's breath. Can you ride astride?'

She nodded.

A huge crash and flames shot up into the air. All at once, Viner's yard was invisible under a crown of flame. Arabella leapt up and down and whooped. The horses bucked and pulled, and two more got loose and fled, trailing their ropes. Bird grabbed hold of the bridle of the nearest, put a foot in the stirrup and heaved herself up.

'Arabella!' Knepp called. Obviously, he couldn't leave her there. What would she do, with her home in flames?

Knepp dismounted and went to her. 'Come with us,' he said softly

'No,' she said. 'Keep away from me! I'm no-one and nobody now. I've had years of buckling to the needs of this yard, and now it's gone, and nobody can tell me what to do.'

'But you'll have no roof over your head. No money.'

'You think that's important? Money? Ha. It just binds you, that's all, like chains.'

'But how will you live?'

'Like the rest.' She pointed to the bedraggled crowds making their way in long lines through the rubble.

So many with no place to go, Bird thought.

'It's a purification,' Arabella said. 'London needed it. What we need is a new London now. A kinder, more tolerant place.'

Arabella took one last look at Viner's, threw one last loose cobble, and turned to go. She had no luggage, nothing but the clothes she stood up in. Soon she was swallowed into the crowds of refugees picking their way across the wreckage. Bird couldn't help but feel the tug to join her.

'She has nothing,' Bird said in a choked voice.

'We are lucky,' Knepp said, mounting again. 'We have each other.'

Why was it that at the very time she longed for freedom most, she was offered some kind of affection? She looked at Knepp's face. He looked weary. The father of her son. Though Roly was no longer with them, she felt his presence now, and it moved her.

'Let's go home,' she said.

Stefan's arms ached from passing buckets up and down the line. Should have kept up his archery practice. He'd never had much muscle, and his shirt was wringing with sweat and clung to his back. He winced as another bucket came along; his hands were raw and sore. He glanced up. The fire was at the end of the street, blazing like a malevolent devil, and he was desperate it should not get to Father Bernard's. After all these years of hating him, now he wanted to save him. How witless was that?

He prayed under his breath, 'Holy Mary, Mother of God,' but not loud enough for anyone else to hear.

Father Bernard was an old man, and he'd have nowhere else to go. And he couldn't carry all those Catholic tracts. If he was stopped, he'd be lynched. Folk were already blaming Catholics. Since the Gunpowder Plot, any fire was always blamed on them.

The bucket arrived again and he passed it on, but they were coming less frequently now, and the man next to him, their neighbour, the elderly red-nosed wine merchant, suddenly dumped the bucket.

'It's useless,' he said. 'I need to get my ledgers out.'

Stefan picked up the bucket and ran with it to the next man, but he too just raised his arms and shrugged. Stefan ran towards the blaze but he couldn't get near enough to do anything. The heat drove him back. With horror he realised the fire was half-way up the street.

He set off at a run. Up past the wine merchant's,

through the door and in to where Father Bernard was loading panniers with books and tracts. The inside of the house was hot as an oven.

'The History. Upstairs, you'll have to fetch it, my legs won't carry me up there. We need to get it to France.'

Stefan leapt up the stairs two at a time. At the top of the stairs, smoke was already seeping through the rafters. Suddenly there was a massive bang, and the windows flew in. Stefan threw himself on the ground as a series of smaller explosions shook the house. The wine merchant's, he realised, as a smell of brandy and burnt cork hit the back of his nose.

He grabbed the handwritten pages, crammed them into a leather binder and stuffed it down the front of his jerkin. He must get Father Bernard out. They would only have a few minutes if the wine merchant's was burning.

Father Bernard was trying to drag the panniers out of the door. The walls were already buckling from the heat.

'Leave them,' Stefan said, dragging him by the sleeve. 'Have you seen the size of the fire? They'll lynch you soon as look at you, if they catch you with these.'

Without warning, the roof beams, where they joined next door, crackled and burst into flame. Father Bernard grabbed frantically for a Bible from the top of the pannier as Stefan physically hauled him into the street.

'This way,' he said, pushing him forward away from the fire.

Not a moment too soon. In the space of a heartbeat the downstairs of Father Bernard's house was an orange inferno.

From a hundred yards away, they watched the building burn. Ashes floated towards them on the breeze and settled on the cobbles before them. Stefan picked a piece of burning paper from Father Bernard's shoulder. It was a piece of a Latin Bible. All those religious tracts reduced to ash and dust.

'They will blame us,' Father Bernard said.

'I know. That's what I've been trying to tell you.' Why was the old man so slow?

'You must get the History out of England. To France. Or Spain. It won't be safe to stay.'

'What about you?'

'I'll trust in God. Follow the rest.' He indicated the people fleeing behind him. 'Now go, or two years of work will never see the light of day.'

Knepp was riding astride with another five horses on reins around him. All he could safely take, Bird guessed. No horses were left at Viner's; they were all out.

Just in time, for the whole building was roaring like an angry beast. She never knew a fire could make that much noise; it filled her ears with a rushing so she couldn't even think. The next time she turned, the fire had moved further up the street and the building was empty space and smoke.

'Stop!' A man jumped in front of them waving his arms.

Knepp was forced to rein his horse in, or mow the man down.

'Have you seen Livvy Black?' he shouted. 'Negro maidservant that lodged with Viner?'

'She's not there,' Bird said. 'She'd left before it went up. Who are you?'

'A friend. Robert Hubert.'

'The Frenchman?' He wasn't what she was expecting, this wizened, little, fair-haired man.

'Do you know her? Where is she?'

'You'd better take a horse,' Knepp said, 'She's at my house. I'm Knepp, the carrier she used to work for.'

By the time Bird rode under the archway into Knepp's yard, she was exhausted. Her eyes stung, and her hands were blistered from untying rope from hot metal rings, and from gripping the reins. She looked back to see Hubert, white in the face and clinging to the horse's mane. The stable-boys ran out when they saw the sooty cavalcade with its extra mounts, and hurried to stable them and take them water.

Hubert almost toppled off his horse, and sat down on the mounting block, his head slumped over his knees. A stable-boy hurried over with a cup of ale. One or two of the horses were limping or had burns and Knepp gave instructions for them to be treated with liniment and bandaged.

471

'Six more,' Knepp said to the boy. 'The rest loose about the city. From Viner's. Poor beasts would have perished, else.' His coat sleeve was scorched through to the lining and the lines in his forehead black with soot. He turned to Bird, his eyes soft. 'Let's get everyone inside.'

Bird dismounted and her knees buckled. She was still weak from lack of exercise, and the sheer effort of pulling the horses free of the fire.

Mrs Knepp regarded the dishevelled group with astonishment. 'It's bad then?'

'The worst; like a scene from hell,' Bird said.

'Nobody can stop it. Half of London's gone,' Knepp said. 'There's no hay; the warehouses, the whole of Eastcheap and Cannon Street have been blotted out like they never existed. Viner's is a ruin; nothing left. He'll never recover. I can't bear to think of it. Imagine, if it happened to us? A whole life's work, gone.'

Livvy came forward out of the shadows. Her face was drawn with shock. 'Viner – is he dead?'

'No,' Bird said. 'Fled. The family all survived.'

Livvy sat down heavily on a chair, taking deep breaths, her shoulders convulsed with sobs.

Hubert appeared at the door.

'Come in, Mr Hubert,' Bird said.

Hubert limped forward. 'Livvy,' he croaked, eyes full of tears. He held out his arms towards her. 'It's a disaster, my house is a—'

'What you do here?' she said, angrily, rubbing her face dry.

He stopped short, a confused expression flitting across his features. 'I look for you. I thought you might be . . .'

'I don't want to talk to you.'

Bird hurried to interrupt. 'Where do you live, Mr Hubert?'

'I was in lodgings, but they've been . . . I mean, I can't go back. They smashed everything. They blame us, the French and the Dutch.' He sagged, and put a hand to his forehead. 'I feel most unwell.'

Bird fixed Livvy with a disapproving glare, then turned to Hubert. 'If Knepp can stable extra horses, he can certainly find room for you,' Bird said. 'Livvy, go and see what you can find to make a bed for Mr Hubert. Use straw, and horse blankets if necessary.'

Livvy seemed to be in a world of her own.

'Livvy?'

'Yes, Mistress.' She hurried away upstairs.

Mrs Knepp limped in with a basin of water and cloths. 'A wash, that's what you all need.'

Bird turned to Hubert. 'Viner said something to me . . . that Livvy was responsible for the fire. Is it true?'

Hubert shifted his eyes away from her. 'Viner, he's a bully and a liar.'

'He said she deliberately started it. He was adamant. His groom overheard her talking to someone.'

Hubert flushed, but he still looked at the floor. 'It was me she talk to. He's a bad man.' Then he

473

looked up, defiant. 'The English slaughtered her family. In Holland.'

Bird took this in without saying a word. No wonder Livvy was so strange. She must blame them all. She sighed. 'You go upstairs. I don't need Livvy for a while. Perhaps it will give you time to talk.'

Livvy was banging a pillow to soften it when Robert appeared at the door.

'Why you hounding me?' she asked.

'Did you do it, Livvy, *ma petite*? Did you set fire to London?' His voice was soft.

She hugged the pillow to her chest. 'I don't know.'

'You must know. Did you do something to start the fire?'

'I pray, that's all. I pray as hard as I could and then I . . . I call on the ancestors to burn this place. Now they do it.' Her lower lip trembled and she bit down on it. 'I never expected it to do anything . . . but I was angry. Now I think maybe they hear me. My mother maybe. That's all I do – pray.'

'Oh, Livvy. I know one thing – the ancestors did not make the fire. Some human did, with a forgotten candle probably.'

'But they say the fire's so big. It's burning down whole streets. A candle don't do that.'

He rested his hands on her shoulders. '*Le vent*. The wind. The wind blew the fire half-way across

474

the city. If you did not light anything, then it's not you. *Pas toi, ma chérie.*'

'But what if it is?' she pleaded with him. 'Some magic I don't understand? I make a spell. A wicked spell of revenge, and I pray and pray again, but it don't stop.'

He pulled the pillow away and let it drop. Then he closed his arms around her. 'I would have done the same in your place. I thank God you're safe, that I find you. I ran everywhere, then I see Viner's place burning, and my heart, she breaks, thinking of you inside.'

'You came to find me?' She let her arms wind around his back. He smelled of bonfires and sweat.

'Of course. I look for nobody else.'

Livvy pulled away. She picked up the pillow and threw it down onto the bed she had just made up. 'Why? Why d'you want me?'

'Because I like the look of you. I like the way you listen when I read, with your head on one side, like this.' He demonstrated. He looked comical.

She grimaced. 'Do I look so stupid?'

'No. I like it. And you are quiet. And you don't touch my things on my desk without asking. I like that.'

It wasn't what she was expecting, but it was honest. He hadn't tried to touch her, or force her into anything. Her shoulders released.

'There's one thing though,' he said.

She caught the regret in his eyes.

475

'The fire's still blazing, and they think you started it. I know this is false. You didn't, hear me? Words don't start fires. But the soldiers, they take all foreigners, especially the French and Dutch. They round them up and beat them and take them to the Tower. I don't want them to find you. They need someone to blame, and we are the easy targets. Especially you. The stable man, Mason, he's telling everyone he heard you say it, that you will burn the city.'

'What will I do?' She put a hand to the wall to steady herself.

'Hush. We'll go to France,' Robert said, '*Demain*. Tomorrow. Once the word is out for you it will be *difficile*. A black woman is so easy to see. We must go to Chatham and try for a boat to France.'

'My brother's in France. My only family, just two of us now.'

'I know, I know.' He took hold of her hand and pressed it. 'We will have good life there. We will be nice companions, yes?'

She placed her other hand on top of his. 'I will come with you.'

CHAPTER 39

Bird slept with Knepp that night. She no longer cared about the state of the bed, or that despite his wash, he still was grimed around the neck. She moved up close to him for comfort and fell into an exhausted sleep, the first for weeks.

The hammering on the door had them both out of bed in an instant.

Bird peered over the banister. There were two soldiers and a constable in the parlour. Mrs Knepp was sitting up in bed, white-faced.

'Is it the fire?' Knepp asked, hurrying down and tucking his shirt in his breeches. 'Has it spread?'

'I answered the door—' Anis said, clutching her lantern.

'And they just barged in,' Mrs Knepp said. 'Without invitation.'

'We're looking for a negro woman called Livvy Black.' The constable braced his back. 'She's Dutch. Ted Viner told the mayor she threatened to fire the city.'

'Dutch? Are you sure?' Knepp said. 'I thought she came from Africa?'

'Ah, so you know her. Has she come here? Did she ever mention a Frenchman, a Catholic called Hubert?'

Knepp glanced Mrs Knepp's way, and she threw him a frantic look.

Mrs Knepp saw the look and was about to speak, but seeing her son silent, shut her mouth.

Bird took herself out of sight just as she heard the words, 'We'll need to search your premises, sir.'

By the time Bird entered the spare chamber, Livvy and Hubert were already up.

'The constable. Go quietly,' Bird said urgently, 'through the corridor past the grooms' lodgings and down the back stairs. Your best chance is to go the back way to the theatre. Go to Nell, and I'll meet you there later with a horse and carriage.'

Hubert's brief nod showed he understood and, carrying his shoes, he pushed open the door into the dark corridor. Livvy whisked through after him.

Downstairs, Knepp's voice drifted up. 'I really think this is unacceptable. Fancy waking a man at this hour for some fugitive, when London's still burning!' he protested.

'Bludworth's orders. And we shall do it, with or without your permission.'

'Who's upstairs?' A soldier's voice.

'What is it, husband?' Bird came down, feigning sleep.

'Some trouble with one of our servants.'

'At this hour? I'll need to dress.'

'No, Madam, you can dress later. This way, men.'

They clattered past her up the main stairs, lanterns bobbing and weaving.

Bird held her breath. Above them the noise of them searching in the chambers above, the scraping of boots on floorboards.

Disgruntled voices. Soon they reappeared on the stairs. There was no sign of Livvy or Mr Hubert. Bird felt tension drain from her.

'Very well, Mr Knepp. But if she should come here, you must send someone for the constable straight away.'

'Sir!' Nipper was at the door, come from his night-watch at the stables.

'Not now, Nipper. Wait until I've seen these gentlemen out.'

'But sir—'

'I said, not now.'

Nipper glowered but closed his mouth.

Knepp saw the constable and his men out into the yard and watched them head down the street to Whitehall.

'You should've let me speak. I saw two people run out of your back door. Hiding their faces, they were. Looked mighty suspicious. If he'd let me speak I could have told the constable.'

Thank God he didn't, was all she could think.

God speed, Livvy, she thought.

Elisabeth Pepys looked out of the window to the back lawn where Samuel was digging, in his shirt sleeves and no coat. Fool, he looked like a peasant.

Earlier in the day he'd buried papers from the office, now he was burying his wine and Parmesan cheese by moonlight. *Quel insensé*! Of course he had not offered to bury anything of hers. Typical of him, to think only of his stomach at a time like this.

Two days on, and the fire was still raging. Why had nobody put it out? Gross incompetence; that was what it was. Even Samuel agreed, he'd written to Sir William Coventry asking the Duke of Yorke's permission to pull down more houses. Told him plain that losing the Navy office would cause the king a mighty inconvenience. As of yet, he'd received no answer.

Samuel turned towards the window, pointed to the hole, grinned broadly, and made a gesture of victory with his fist. She smiled. His cheerfulness won her over. She watched him lower the wheel of cheese in its protective sacking, into the ground. When she was small, she'd thought the moon made of cheese. Today the moon was almost obscured by smoke. He didn't really think their house would burn down, did he? Perhaps he wasn't so stupid after all.

After supper she begged Samuel to take her to see the fire. They walked in the dark down to Tower Street. But further down there was no need for link-man or bellman – the darkness was lit by an unearthly glow. Smoke rasped raw in the back of her throat.

A huge bang, and Elisabeth grabbed Samuel by

the arm. The street seemed to shudder and a house rose as if on air and then collapsed amid a pall of dust, white against the black smoke.

'It's all right, wife, they're blowing up houses to make a fire break.' He pulled her close to reassure her.

The crowd stood around to watch with ghoulish apprehension. Elisabeth found it both thrilling and frightening. Would they do that to the Navy offices?

Sacrebleu! But Trinity House on one side was on fire, and the Dolphin Tavern on the other side, far too close to Seething Lane for comfort.

A couple staggered past, weeping, the man carrying a basket of goods on his hip, and supporting the woman with his other arm. She was well-dressed in a silk dress with embroidered stomacher, and a fine velvet bonnet. He had silver buckles to his shoes, and a fine long periwig.

Elisabeth stared at them as they passed. The basket looked pitifully small.

They're people like us, she thought.

Up until this point she had thought of the fire as only affecting the nameless poor. That it could destroy lives like theirs made her stomach plummet. All at once she felt her good fortune. Her lovely house, her fine possessions, this dear man who was good and solid by her side.

'Samuel!' She tugged urgently on his coat. 'I can't bear it. I want to go home.'

'No need to fluster, wife.' He hugged her tight, and she felt his dry kiss on her forehead.

But when they got home, Samuel's clerk William Hewer, his fair hair grey with soot, arrived with worse news.

'It's nearly at the city walls to the west. Cheapside's in ruins, not a shop left standing. And I had to move my mother to lodgings in Islington. I paid fifteen shillings for a handcart. A handcart! She's lost everything. Her house at Pye Corner is completely destroyed. There'll be nothing left of London. Now it rages towards the fleshmarket at Smithfield.'

Elisabeth thought of her father. News would have reached St Martin-in-the-Fields by now, and he would no doubt have fears for her.

'I must write to my father,' she said.

'You can't,' Hewer said. 'The post-office has burnt down.'

Tuesday 4th September 1666

Stefan hurried westward through the streets, the Jesuit History stuffed down his jerkin. It was all very well for Father Bernard to tell him to get to France, but he'd nothing now except what he was wearing, and no money to pay for a passage. Last night he'd kipped down on the stony earth of Moorfields, huddled with the rest of the bewildered refugees, most of whom, like him, had been stripped of everything but the clothes they stood up in. He winced as he felt for the History again. One of his hands had somehow got burned, and was now stinging and raw.

There was only one hope; the theatre. The fire might not have reached there and he could try to screw some wages from that dog, Killigrew. And borrow a suit of decent clothes, too, or at least a cloak that wasn't black with soot. And a bag, to put his precious papers in.

Watling Street was not so much a street as a path through a forest. Fallen timbers littered the ground, and scorched chimney stacks were the only thing remaining upright. At one point he passed a house still standing, but when he drew closer, one side was completely gone, its innards of wall-panelling, carpet and furniture still intact. There was even a portrait on the wall, and platters on the table. But the staircase was gone and the house open to the air. Why had God spared half a house?

His feet suddenly slid and he floundered to stay upright. He looked down to see the pavement slick with molten lead, smooth and grey, and now set solid in place. Ahead of him the churchyard of St Paul's, usually a circular enclave, was filled with rubble. St Paul's itself lay, collapsed like a dead beast within.

He stopped dead. He couldn't help himself.

God be damned. This must be the devil's work. No matter what he thought of the rest of Christendom, he would not wish any church brought so low. He took a step away. The lead he was standing on was the remains of the molten roof.

Around the walls of the churchyard, people thronged four deep, staring silently at the wisps of smoke that rose from the rubble of the collapsed corpse.

He must get out of here. Carrying this cursed Jesuit History in his jerkin was akin to carrying a barrel of gunpowder in this fiery city. He crossed himself and headed towards Ludgate Gatehouse. Parts of the gatehouse still stood, the buckled bars of the jail beneath open to the air. The statue of Lud, founder of the city, lay cracked in pieces blocking his way.

Perhaps London deserved it for killing the king. First plague, then this. The enormity of the destruction numbed him. Was it of God? He didn't know. He crossed the Fleet Bridge and hurried onwards, leaving the stench of burning and blame behind.

In the distance, the fire raged northwards towards Smithfield.

CHAPTER 40

In Smithfield the smell of burning could no longer be ignored. With the help of Nipper, who was stronger than his small frame suggested, Bird dragged the cart from the carriage bay and Knepp helped her put a horse in traces. The cart was heaped with Mrs Knepp's possessions, because she wouldn't leave without them. In the wicker cage the lone bird tweeted on its perch. Mrs Knepp herself lay in the back of the cart propped up on blankets and pillows. Her face looked bone-white in the light, and creased with wrinkles.

'Thank you, son,' she said. He smiled a cracked smile.

'Closing for business was a good idea,' Bird said, touching his arm.

'If we don't want the fire to reach us, then all fit men must fight it,' Knepp said. 'My stable hands will be paid the same for carrying buckets against the fire, as for watering the horses. But I want you to take Mother somewhere safe, so she's out of the way if the worst happens.' He passed her a rolled-up document.

She pulled it open to see a parchment map of London and Essex. She baulked at the winding road she must take.

'You must go to Romford straight away. Grinstead's sure the burning of the city's a Dutch plot and fears the Dutch will invade whilst we are dealing with the fire. Take Anis, and return Mother straight to James's in Essex. My brother won't be expecting you, there's been no way to send a letter, but I'm sure he will welcome her.'

'What if you need to move the horses again?'

'I don't know. But I'll stop the fire if it's the last thing I do. Not enough people are fighting back, all too intent on saving themselves. But I haven't spent a lifetime building this business to see it go up in flames. I'll be calling on everyone I know. All the beef traders from the fleshmarket, all the fodder merchants, all the milkmen. I owe them all money, and I can't pay, but now's a chance to give them something back.'

She nodded. 'Take care,' she said. A shiver of apprehension for his safety.

'I've ordered Grinstead to go with you. He was reluctant, but I told him his job depended on it. He said he was too ill to fight fires, so I set him this task instead. He hasn't a choice, as his house is a ruin and his wife's had to prevail on her sister for a bed.'

Bird did not relish the thought of Grinstead's company, but knew Knepp would not let her travel alone. When they were ready, Grinstead took the reins, with Bird in front next to him. Knepp clanged the gates shut and locked them behind them. As they drove away, she heard the crump of more explosions in the city. More houses blasted into rubble. She quashed the fear in her gullet. That was the least of her worries; first she must persuade Grinstead to take a diversion, and see if she could help Livvy and her strange Frenchman.

Grinstead was already complaining about the smoke and his lungs, even though the fire was still at a distance. 'I shouldn't be on such a long journey, not with my weak chest,' he said.

'I don't suppose many of us wish to be travelling,' Bird said sharply. 'But we have no choice, and the whole city is on the move after this calamity.'

Then she had a thought. This could work to her advantage. 'You know, you're right. You don't sound so good, Mr Grinstead. Perhaps you shouldn't be driving after all.'

'Essex's too far for me to be driving at my age,' he said. 'All that jolting on bumpy tracks. Knepp should have sent Nipper.'

'Maybe you're right,' she said. 'My husband has little sympathy for those who are ill, as you well know. But I can see you are ailing. I don't like to think of dragging you so far when you're unwell. Perhaps I should drive there myself. I could drop you at a coffee-house, and you can wait there until I return. Knepp need never know.'

'I can't do that,' he said. 'If Knepp was to find

487

out, I would lose my position.' Something in his tone was undecided.

'What are you talking about? I can't hear you.' Mrs Knepp called from behind.

'Nothing, Mrs Knepp, just the difficulties of the road, that's all.' She turned to Grinstead, determined. 'Really, Mr Grinstead, I insist. You look most unwell.'

'Do I really?' The reins dropped loose in his hands, and Bird gathered them up.

'You rest, Mr Grinstead,' she said. 'There's the Three Crows Coffee House close to the theatre on Catherine Street. It has rooms too, if you've the money. We'll go there.'

'But it's miles out of our way.'

'Not at all. It'll be quicker to skirt the city walls than to drive through the town with all the blockages, and people on the move. No, we'll go around it all.'

Mr Grinstead took out his kerchief and blew into it. Bird clicked the horses on, and no more protests came from Grinstead's lips. She left Mr Grinstead in the coffee-house and immediately turned the horses to head for the theatre.

When she drew up in Catherine Street, Mrs Knepp called, 'Why have we stopped? Where are we?'

'Wait here with Anis, Mrs Knepp. I won't be long.'

'Don't leave me!' Mrs Knepp stared around her, hands shaking, suddenly looking old and vulnerable.

'It's all right. I'll be back in two whiskers,' she said.

As she expected, the theatre was thronged with people. The whole building stank of smoke from the gathered refugees, and an assortment of over-flowing bags, furniture and bedding littered the floor. On the stage itself the scene shifters and property men were packing up armfuls of costumes, masks and wooden swords into wicker trunks. Charles Hart was there, handsome as ever, but looking harassed as he barked out instructions.

In the auditorium every seat was full. There was even a milk ass tethered under one of the boxes. Bird took one look and decided to try the tiring room. Bird spotted Livvy and Mr Hubert in the corner, squatting on a bench talking to Nell.

Livvy stood up when she saw Bird, but her expression was worried. She bent to talk to her in a low voice. 'Armed soldiers are guarding the city gates, but we dodged them by going through Newgate Street and cutting across the Fleet. Nell says the trained bands are everywhere because the Dutch will invade, now they've weak-ened the city. Is it true? I don't know what to do. Whether to go or stay. What if my countrymen are coming?'

'I don't know, Livvy. It's chaos. But Viner's roused the constables, and they're locking up all foreigners, and we know they've got orders to look especially for you. They'll flay you alive if they find you. You need to get away from the city as soon as you can. Outside, I've horses and a cart ready, but you'd better find something to hide your face.' She turned to M'sieur Hubert. 'Robert, the cart is just outside with old Mrs Knepp and Anis. Best you wait with them until I come for you; they're vulnerable to thieves without a man there. But don't talk to anyone; I fear your accent will draw attention.'

Robert went, and Bird and Livvy made their way to the costume store in the room next to the tiring room. The room was a dark musty closet with no windows. A tall, skinny figure was already there before them, rifling through a costume basket and shoving clothes into a bag.

'Stefan!'

He almost shot out of his boots, and turned, white-faced.

'Are you burned out?' she asked.

'Completely. I've only what I stand up in. I came for a bag and some sort of weapon, and to try to get Killigrew to pay me my dues. But there's no sign of him, the dog. He's left Hart and Mohun to fight it out as to who's in charge. I'll get no pay from them and I've not even a penny for ale.'

'Will you stay here? It's not safe out there. The streets are full of angry men looking for someone to blame.'

'I'm for leaving London, as soon as I've got myself a decent suit of clothes, but I'm unarmed, and I'll have to beg my way. There are no real weapons here, only wood; some men came earlier, screaming about the Dutch invasion and took everything.'

'It's bedlam out there. This is my friend Livvy; they're after her blood. Orders are out for her arrest. 'We're looking for a hat, something to hide the face, such as a woman might wear against the sun. Have you seen one?'

'No, nothing like that, sorry. Try the top shelf.'

They pushed over the wicker trunk, so Livvy could stand on it. She reached up to the shelf to pull down some hats.

Robert arrived, breathless at the door. *Mon Dieu*, I found you. The king's soldiers they check the theatre. They clear it out; they arrest anyone foreign. Livvy, I'm afraid for you. You stand out too much, they'll stop you, for certain.'

Livvy climbed down.

A moment where they all looked to each other before Livvy suddenly said, 'The trunk.' She threw open the lid. 'Can you carry me?'

'We'll have to try,' Robert said.

'Quick, then,' Bird said. 'Get in. And don't come out until we're well away.'

They dragged out all the garments within, Livvy hoisted her skirts and got into the basket, and Bird threw a cloak and some extra garments on top.

'Which way?' Robert grasped one of the rope handles.

'The stage door,' Stefan said, grabbing his bag.

Bird tried to lift the other end of the trunk but

although Livvy was slight and thin, it was too heavy.

'Let me.' Stefan grabbed the other handle and he and Robert struggled down the corridor with Bird following behind.

Thank God the cart was still there with Anis and Mrs Knepp's anxious faces peering out from amongst the luggage.

Robert and Stefan heaved the trunk aboard, with Bird putting her shoulder beneath to help it up.

The doors of the theatre opened and a crowd of people poured out onto the street, dragging their belongings with them. Behind them the King's Guard harried them forwards, shooing them like livestock.

Bird leapt up to the driver's bench, and Stefan sprang up after her. 'Can I come with you?' he asked.

'Where are you going?' she asked.

'France.'

'Why?' Bird asked. 'What are you running from?

'You know. They think it's another Gunpowder Plot.' He gave her a look, and she understood. He was Catholic, that's why.

She cracked the reins and shouted to move the horses forward.

Too late. A guard stood before them to block their path. 'Names?'

'I'm Mrs Knepp, of the theatre. These are all actors; we're moving everything out of town in case of a Dutch invasion.'

'Mrs Knepp! I remember you. You sang beautifully in *The Indian Emperour*.'

'Thank you.'

'Move along then,' and he cleared the way for them to trot by. She breathed a sigh of relief.

Once they'd covered about half a mile, she turned to Stefan. 'Can you drive?'

'No. Never had the need to handle horses.'

Bird sighed. 'What's in your bag?' It was bulky, that was certain, and he was clinging onto it like it contained something of value.

He reddened. 'Nothing; just clothes and shoes.'

'For an actor, you're a useless liar. We were lucky that time. What if they stop and search us?'

He had no answer. He was a risk. The bag was probably stuffed with Jesuit Bibles. Bird gave him a long slow look. His face was pinched and his eyes bloodshot with smoke. He deserved a chance. 'Very well. But you'll find a pistol and shot in that leather case,' she pointed to it, 'and I expect you to use it if we meet highway thieves on the road. Rumour is, footpads and highwaymen are having a field day with all of London fleeing the fire.'

'What's going on?' Mrs Knepp asked, coming around from her doze. 'Why have we stopped? Who's this?'

'Just Stefan, a theatre friend, Mrs Knepp, going the same way as us, and M'sieur Hubert. We're giving them a ride, that's all.'

The journey around the edge of the city was heartbreaking. They could still see flames and a thick pall of smoke, and Bird imagined Knepp in the thick of it. She mustn't look back. She must concentrate on driving.

They were not the only people on the road, but there seemed to be no armed militia this far out, only poor folk such as themselves, their carts and carriages loaded up with their goods. Gradually, the travellers thinned out. As soon as the road cleared, she hauled the horses to a stop; they took a moment to stretch their legs and she opened the lid of the wicker trunk. Livvy climbed out of her hiding place. 'Is it safe now?'

Anis's eyes opened wide in amazement. Mrs Knepp shot backwards away from her. 'What's going on?'

'Didn't mean to scare you, Mrs Knepp,' Livvy said. 'I'm grateful to travel with you.'

Livvy pressed Mrs Knepp's arm, but Mrs Knepp withdrew it hurriedly as if she didn't want to be touched, and looked at Bird with fearful eyes.

'Calm down. It's only Livvy,' Bird said, walking round to lean over the edge of the cart. 'We're taking her out of town.'

'You should've told me! It's confusing, all these strangers. Why's she hiding? Why did the constable come for her?'

'She's done nothing. Is a misunderstanding, that's all,' Robert said.

'It's all right, Mrs Knepp,' Livvy said. 'We'll be getting out of your way soon.'

It took a while to settle everyone again before

494

they could move on. Stefan was responsible for keeping a wary eye out for thieves on the road, but they saw no-one, only harvesters in the fields. The spires of Romford rose from the horizon long before they reached it.

Bird reined in the horse. 'I can't take you any further,' she said. 'Here's coin for your passage, and there's spare bags behind with some bread and a few pears. I took them from Knepp's before we left.'

Livvy climbed down. 'I'm sorry. I didn't mean to bring you no trouble.'

The look of sadness in her eyes made Bird reach out to embrace her in a tight squeeze. She took out the lucky hare's foot and pressed it into Livvy's hand. 'You'd better have this back. And stay safe, hear me? Write from France; Robert will help you, won't you?'

'Soon as we are safe on French soil. Thank you,' Robert said. 'From now on, we take our chances, but sincerely we thank you. Your kindness.'

She embraced Robert in turn, and finally Stefan.

'You are a fine actor. Don't forget it.'

He held out the pistol, but she pushed it back towards him. 'Keep it. You won't need it, but better to be prepared.'

He nodded gravely. A shiver of apprehension riddled her stomach. She had an urge to tell them to forget the whole enterprise; to come home with her again, but it was too late. She watched them as they walked away from her into the light; the tall, thin silhouette of Stefan, the bulky holdall bumping his thigh, the skinny black woman holding the arm of the limping Frenchman. Something about them walking away to an unknown future made her unutterably sad.

Knepp scooped up water with gritted teeth, for the fire was already at the bottom of Duck Lane, less than a hundred yards from Knepp's Yard. The heat seemed to skin his eyes.

'Heave,' Knepp shouted in a rhythmic chant as he sent the buckets along the line, 'heave, heave.'

He'd collected every bucket and container from the stables and organised a relay from the Fleet River at Holborn Bridge. The Fleet was a filthy dung-encrusted channel and Knepp's arms were the colour of shit. The summer heat had dried the river to a mere slick of mud and shallow water, but it was the only water they had.

Bastards. He cursed the private carriages that kept passing by them on the bridge; shiny monsters come from the big houses on the Strand, the rich merchants who were only now beginning to fear the fire. He cursed the men gliding by, who never deigned to get out and help. Oh God, he was losing. They'd have to work quicker.

Frantically he grabbed and filled any container that came his way: barrels, cauldrons, buckets, even a chamber pot. Further up the line the water sizzled onto the flaming buildings, but the fire had taken hold in so many places that as soon as one spot was extinguished, more flames burst forth from somewhere else.

A sob rose in his chest. He was going to lose everything. He'd have to give up soon, and get the horses out, just like at Viner's. Bird was right, he'd have to salvage what he could. He hoped she had got to his brother's and they were all safe there.

A noise of trooping feet behind him and he turned. 'What?' he asked the next man.

'It's the Earl of Craven's men, come to help at the bridge.'

'Thank God. We can go to Cowe Lane, further up, see if we can knock houses down, stop it there.'

He rallied his workers and they ran to Cowe Lane where they found a group of well-dressed men staring hopelessly at the burning buildings.

'Have you fire hooks?' he cried to the man in the white cravat, who was obviously in charge.

'No,' the man said glumly. 'Not a one.' By the unsullied state of his clothing Knepp could tell he'd been nowhere near a bucket or the fire.

He grabbed the man's sleeve. 'Sir, it's reached Pye Corner, we must demolish the houses in the neighbouring streets and make a fire break, or the whole of Smithfield will go up.'

'We haven't any equipment,' the man said, withdrawing his arm and brushing off his sleeve.

'Who's in charge here?' Knepp turned desperately to one of the other men.

'Sir Richard Browne.'

'Well, where is he?'

'You were just talking to him.'

Knepp sighed in frustration. His arms ached, his back ached and his feet ached. His palms were blistered from bucket handles and smeared with soot. He couldn't give up. A sudden anger filled him that the rich men of the city idled by, whilst his livelihood was about to be incinerated.

'Men!' He shouted out to those tradesmen in aprons who had gathered with him. 'We need fire-hooks. Anything that'll serve – pitchforks, spades, picks and hoes. Anything at all. We need to smash down some buildings if we're to save Smithfield.'

The call went out and five minutes later they were on Giltspur Street hacking away at the smallest of the houses. He had a momentary pang, as he saw candlesticks on the mantel and realised it wasn't just a house, but a home.

The next moment he'd steeled himself and the spade someone had thrust into his hand smashed through the window. Fortunately the house was wood and lath and only bricks for the chimneys, so with fifteen men they began to make an impression.

Standing in a pile of dust and render, he hacked at the wall like a madman, as the heat grew, and pieces of burning debris began to rain onto his shoulders. Everything was hot. He tore at hot timbers and nails with his bare hands. He glanced up the road. The locked gates of Knepp's Yard floated eerily in the swirl of yellow smoke. He began to cough, but still could not stop hacking at the walls.

'Watch out!'

The shout behind him was too late. The ceiling crashed in, and a beam hit him hard on the collar-bone. He fell to his knees amid the falling plaster, pain shooting down his arm. Immediately sickness overtook him. He crawled out of there and vomited into the dust.

Fingers of fire tickled at the roof of the house next door. The heat singed his hair, his throat felt like it was on fire.

'Clear the space,' he yelled, dragging his spade free of fallen rafters.

His left arm was like lead but he couldn't stop. 'Help me!' he said, dragging timbers away across the road. The building was down now, and miraculously the wind had turned. It was blowing away from them now, down towards the Thames.

They cleared the space where the house had stood, crunching over broken stools and crockery, over bedding and the spilled contents of a pantry. One room seemed to be full of rolls of cloth, now grey as the smoke pouring from the house next door.

'I think we've done it!' Nipper said. 'It's blowing away from us now.'

From the street came a huge cheer.

'Here.' Someone passed Knepp a bucket and he heaved it onto the ruin of rubble. Pain shot up his arm. Other men around him did the same, dousing the whole place with water. He had another bucket in his good hand when a slight man in a woollen cap came running up, shouting.

From a distance his words were unintelligible, but he kept on coming. By the time he arrived he could hardly speak.

'What have you done?' A barely intelligible croak. His face was grey, his clothes patched with smuts. He grabbed Knepp by his bad shoulder, and Knepp grimaced with pain. 'What have you done to my house?'

'I'm sorry, we had to stop it. We had to create a gap.'

'But I was fighting the fire by Temple Bar! You should've come for me.'

'There was no time.'

The man ran into the house and scrabbled through the waste, dragging out roll after roll of ruined cloth. He sank to his knees amid the sodden heap and wept. 'You bloody idiots! What will I do? My whole business. All my cloth. Ruined. What will I tell my wife?'

Knepp sank down to his heels and put his head in his hands. He couldn't bear it. The sight of that grown man weeping like a child. He imagined the man's wife coming home to this scene of destruction. It could so easily have been Bird.

Something in him cracked. He found tears seeping from his eyes. 'Just the smoke,' he said to himself, scrubbing them away.

Relief swamped him in a wave. His business was safe. His horses were safe.

But somehow in seeing that man's pain at the loss of his house, he felt like he'd lost his own.

CHAPTER 41

Stefan hung his leather bag that Bird had given him over his shoulder and carried the large holdall with the Jesuit History through the bustling town of Romford towards the docks at Tilbury. The sight of the people going about their everyday business brought a lump to his throat. London was destroyed. Life there would never be the same again. How could a whole city deserve such a disaster? Plague, war, and now a fire from hell. And he was stuck with these other two lame ducks. He glanced back to see the Frenchman, Robert, and his black companion dutifully following behind him.

He paused to wait for them. They looked foot-sore already, she looking at the ground to hide her black face, and he with his peculiar limp. How had he become leader of this little group? Because he was armed, that's why. And because he was the only Englishman amongst them. He hoped to board a ship to France, but anywhere would suffice so long as he was off English soil. There were Catholic sympathisers in Ireland too, or Spain. In fact, everywhere else but England.

When they neared the docks, he could see that the quay was blocked by a barricade, and armed men were stopping passengers who wanted to embark.

He stopped and turned to Livvy. 'Damn. There's a blockade. It looks mighty suspicious, two men travelling together, and us with no carriage and so little baggage.'

'Will they stop us?' she said. 'What now?'

'They might. All men coming from London will be under suspicion,' he said.

'I can't go back,' she said.

'Just pause here,' he said to the others. 'I have an idea.'

As well as a set of breeches, he hadn't been able to resist the blue costume that Anne Marshall had worn as Mrs Day in *The Committee*. He remembered Bird's words – that he was better than Anne. And besides, nobody would miss it. On impulse, he'd bundled the costume into his bag.

Stefan and Livvy hurried behind a wall. When the party moved on again, there were two women and one man.

'I'm your wife, and you just let me do the speaking,' Stefan said to Robert. 'Pretend to have a cold. Livvy is Hannah, our maid. We haven't come from London, but Romford, and we are going overnight to France. Our luggage is already aboard if they ask. Got it?'

Robert blinked, but seemed to have understood. Livvy took hold of his hand and squeezed it.

Stefan detached Robert's hand from Livvy's. 'She's my maid, so no touching, all right?'

Robert's face reddened. He saw them exchange looks.

Stefan wished he could have kept the gun. Trouble was, there was nowhere to keep it now he was dressed as a woman, so he'd given it to Robert to put in his belt. He hoped he'd be careful with it. He'd told him it was ready-primed, but he didn't look like a man much used to handling a pistol.

They approached a booth where tickets were being sold for the passage. 'Two, and one below for my maid,' Stefan said in an imperious voice.

The ticket seller loosened his dirty neckerchief, but barely looked up. 'Where you come from and where you going?'

'Romford, Tilbury to Calais.'

'How many?'

'Three.' Stefan raised his voice a register. 'My husband, myself and my maid.'

Robert coughed into his handkerchief.

'He's lost his voice,' Stefan said. 'First a cold in the head, then the chest.'

The ticket seller barely paid Stefan any attention. Women's conversation was of no account.

'Name?'

Stefan swallowed. 'Mr and Mrs . . .' He cast frantically in his head for a name. 'Mrs Day.' Stefan handed over the fares from the purse and took the three tickets, two for a cabin, and one for the servant's deck. They'd have to argue that one out later.

'Stroll, don't rush. And act natural,' Stefan said.

They approached the barricade. Two men examined their tickets and looked the party over. One was a tall swarthy man with a pointed beard and narrow set eyes, the other heavier, but with broad shoulders and muscled neck. Both looked rough men, in the pay of someone more important.

Livvy kept her head down, and stayed behind Stefan, but the men kept staring at her.

'Three of you, is it?' The tall man asked.

'That's right,' Stefan said.

'Luggage?'

'It's a short stay, sir, and my man sent the luggage ahead.'

'That your maidservant?'

'Hannah, yes.' Stefan tried to be casual.

'Step forward then, Hannah. Let's look at you.'

Livvy had no choice but to step forward. She stood like a statue in a way that showed she'd done it before; been subjected to such scrutiny.

The man with the beard addressed Robert. 'I'm afraid we've to keep your maidservant here, sir. We've a list of people we've to stop embarking. Black maids is top of the list.'

'But why?' Stefan asked in a voice of outrage. 'Hannah has done nothing wrong and has been with my family five years. I can't travel with no maidservant.'

'Well you'll have to, Madam, because she's under arrest.'

'Why? What's she supposed to have done?' Stefan said.

'Suspicion of fire-raising in London.'

'But we haven't been to London. We came from Romford.'

'I care nothing for that. All I know is, our orders are that black women stay. Now move along.'

Stefan took a gold coin from his purse. 'I need my maid. What's it worth to you?' he asked.

The man exchanged a glance with his beefy companion. 'More than that.'

Stefan took out another two coins, hoping it didn't make them seem desperate.

'That'll do nicely.' The man pocketed the coins and let them through. Stefan didn't like the way they stared after them.

The tender for the bigger ship they could see in the bay was preparing for departure, and the queue of people to get aboard was just a trickle. Stefan took Robert's arm. 'Hurry!' he whispered, picking up his skirts. His damn boots, they'd give him away. He dropped his skirts again.

They were just setting foot on the gangplank when the pikes and muskets of armed men reared above the crowd. They were moving swiftly towards them along the quay.

Bastards. They'd taken the money and betrayed them anyway.

'Quick! Get on board,' he said, shoving Robert ahead.

His feet gained traction on the boards of the gangplank. Nearly there.

A shout. Stefan froze. The men were running towards them. If he was caught, it would be the end. Dressed as someone else and carrying a forbidden Jesuit tract. As these thoughts flashed through him, he saw Robert push Livvy up the gangplank past him and into the knot of people ahead of them.

Then Robert started to descend.

'What are you doing?' Stefan said, grasping his sleeve to pull him back.

But Robert shook him off. He was shouting in French and trying to go the opposite way, against the last few families embarking.

What the hell was he doing? Crazy Frenchman! He was drawing everyone's attention.

'Be quiet, you fool!' Stefan said.

But he wouldn't. *'Vive La France!'* he yelled. 'Death to London!' He whipped the loaded gun from his belt and fired it off into the air.

The guards clustered like ants at the bottom of the gangplank.

'It was me,' Robert yelled. 'I am the French man. I fired the city of London. It break in flames, whoosh!'

Startled passengers cowered away from him as he pushed his way back down, waving the gun. Stefan gasped Livvy's arm and dragged her on board.

'What's he saying? What's going on?' she said.

'He's turned crazy. He says he started the fire.'
Another shot, and shouts from below.

'What?' Livvy tried to go back, but Stefan held her tight.

Robert was flailing his arms and shouting. 'Death to London! I confess all. I am the man!'

By now he was submerged under a sea of men in helmets. Arms lifted muskets high and brought them pounding down. When the soldiers stood back up it was to drag Robert's dead weight away along the quay. Nobody paid the tender any attention. A gaggle of spectators followed the senseless body, jeering and shouting.

The gangplank was coming up, nobody could go down it.

'No!' Livvy tore at elbows, trying to get through the crush but the tender was already moving. 'Stop!' she cried, 'I want to get off!'

But the oarsmen were already rowing. Stefan saw her stagger as the boat moved, and a woman angrily pulled her down into a seat. The quay drifted past as if the whole landscape was moving.

He saw her reaching hand fall to her side, and her shoulders turn rigid. She made her way back to him with a face naked with pain. 'Why did he do that?' Her eyes were dry but her lips trembled as she asked.

'So we could get away, I think. He saw they wouldn't let you go, and made a diversion.'

'That's what I thought.' Her voice wavered, 'What will they do to him?'

'Interrogate him. But if he didn't do it, they'll find no evidence against him.'

'He didn't do it.'

'Then he's nothing to fear.' Stefan said this, but he knew it to be a lie.

The way Livvy stared back at him left him in no doubt that she knew it too.

When the tender got to the ship, they climbed aboard without speaking.

He leaned on the rail and watched the grey sludge of water pass. Next to him Livvy was silent, but her hands gripped the rail watching England recede from view. Finally, she spoke. 'I couldn't go back,' she said. 'I am a bad person. He does this for me, but I couldn't go back. I don't want to see England ever again.'

'Where do you come from?' Stefan asked.

'Holland,' she whispered.

'Sheesh.' So that was it. Not only was she black, but Dutch. No wonder she was running away.

"What will I do without him?' The voice was so quiet he hardly heard it.

Stefan turned and gazed at the heaving expanse of water so she wouldn't see his wet eyes.

'Excuse me, Madam, but shall I take your bags below?' A barefooted boy stood before him.

He looked down at the boy, with his trusting, questioning gaze, and in that moment had a spark of realisation. He wasn't Stefan anymore. He was a woman. There was no reason why he should not continue to be one. Nobody in France knew him.

He had no ties. London was gone, burned to the ground. His whole past was gone. There was no need to cling to anything anymore, even the memory of his father.

The boy was still waiting. Stefan pointed to the meagre bags, and he heaved them up.

'Name?' he asked.

'Mrs Day,' Stefan said.

The lad scurried off.

He realised that all those years he'd not been studying to play a part, but studying to be himself. Phoenixes could rise from the ashes. He drew the papers from his bag, the carefully copied sheets of the Jesuit History, and held them up to take one last look. He pressed his lips to them in a kiss and cast them into the water.

'What was that?' Livvy asked.

'My past,' he said. 'Life is so short. I've decided to live it.'

She gave him an assessing look. 'Do you still need a servant, Mrs Day?'

'No,' he said. 'But I think I shall need a friend.'

CHAPTER 42

Bird left Mrs Knepp at Knepp's brother's house. James was surprisingly like Knepp, but a greyer, older version. One of the servants had to push him in a wheeled chair because his legs had not healed properly from his fall. He was horrified to hear of the fate of London, and wanted a first-hand account, but Bird was brief and made the excuse that Knepp would be waiting for her at home. Mrs Knepp insisted on keeping Anis with her, so James offered to keep the cart and loan her a driver, and his manservant, Bennett, along with a more comfortable carriage for the journey home.

When Bird and Bennett arrived at the coffee-house that evening, Grinstead had gone. She was hardly surprised, as she had never seriously expected him to wait. Though anxious to get home, they had given the city a wide berth, driving around the perimeter of the walls, for smoke still festooned what was left of the buildings, and even at a distance she could see the burning remnants of tar-barrel factories, smouldering houses, and the tanneries still spitting blue flames.

Bennett seemed unable to believe the sheer scale of the disaster. His mouth was open so often Bird feared it would stay that way. He kept repeating, 'Saints alive, saints alive.'

They drove past the theatre and Bird made the driver stop for a few moments so she could read a notice on the door.

No performances until further notice, God save the King.

Underneath someone had scrawled, *Burn in hell, heathen whores.*

'Drive on,' she said. 'Hurry.'

The horses lurched into motion. Would she ever have the chance to play on the stage again? There'd be no paying audience if Londoners had lost their houses and all their belongings. She had held the dream in her grasp, but now it was gone. It was elusive, like something from another, invisible realm. Her reality was here, in the blackened ruins crunching under the carriage wheels. Her mouth was dry. What if Knepp's Yard had gone the way of Viner's?

'I can't believe it,' Bird said, as they drove up. Knepp's Yard was still standing, though the fire had got half-way up the street. West Smithfield was ragged, but her house was intact, though the windows and walls were blackened with soot, and the smell of scorch intense.

She controlled the urge to cry by stuffing her forearm against her mouth.

The wind had dropped and the smoke billowed

away from them towards the ruined city, but the gates were locked, and a bedraggled welter of customers stood, sat or lounged outside. Probably camping out, in the hope of getting transport out of London.

When they drove up there was an immediate clamour. "When can this carriage be made ready,' asked a florid, elderly man, holding out a weighty purse of coins.

Bird shook her head, and yelled through the gate for Nipper. After a few attempts to get his attention over the hubbub, he opened the gate to let them squeeze by, immediately closing it after them. As soon as she drew up, Knepp appeared, his eyes locked on hers.

'Thank God,' he said, holding out an arm for her to grasp as she descended. 'I was worried for you on the road. Where's Grinstead?'

'I don't know. Your brother lent me Bennett instead.'

'My mother?'

'Safe with James in Romford,' she said.

'Nipper, see that the driver and Mr Bennett get a decent meal at the tavern, and look to the horses.'

It was only then she saw the bandages on his hands. 'What happened to your hands?'

'We pulled down the houses, but the wood was already hot, and some of the nails ripped my palms.'

'What about the horses?'

'All safe. It's a miracle. So much of London

burned. Tens of thousands of houses, and ours survives.'

Just at that moment there was a shouting and commotion at the gate. 'What now?' Knepp headed for the gate. By the time he got there, the portly figure of Ted Viner had forced his way in, followed by the parish constable. Viner sported a purple bruise to the forehead and a cut to the cheek that was dark with dried blood.

Viner marched straight up to Knepp. 'Bastard. You stole my horses.'

His arrogant manner was like a red rag to Knepp. 'Stole? They'd have been burned alive. You abandoned them to the fire.'

The tension between the two men tightened.

'Well, I want them back.'

'You should have thought of saving them yourself. I reckon because I was the one who saved them from the fire, they're mine now. What say you, Constable?'

Well now . . .' The constable, a burly bruiser in black, sucked on his teeth, unwilling to pronounce a verdict.

'Blaggard. They're mine.'

'Then why did you leave them to burn?' Bird asked, trying to defuse the situation.

Viner ignored her. 'I feared for my life, you bastard.'

'You feared for your gold, more like,' Knepp said. 'You're not fit to be in charge of livestock.'

'They're mine, and I demand them back.'

'Stop with your demands. A bit of politeness costs nothing. And besides, you're a wealthy man. Your gold can buy more,' Knepp said. 'Now leave us in peace.'

'I have no gold!' Viner shouted, his face blotched red. 'I have nothing. Nothing, d'you hear me? My house is burned to the ground. My wife has gone, God knows where. Highway thieves stole my sword, robbed me of my coach, my gold, everything. Soon as I was out of the city walls they set upon me with pistols and knives. I spent the night shivering in a ditch. My sons never made it out of the city either. Their carriage was overturned at the gate, beset by a mob who thought they might be foreigners. They await me at Ludgate in only the clothes they stand in. I tell you, I have nothing. And you would deny me my horses?'

Knepp's mouth tightened. He cast Bird an uncertain glance; one that clearly asked for her opinion. She nodded back to him.

'Nipper,' Knepp called, 'fetch out three of the new horses. The riding mounts.' He turned back to Viner. 'You never treated me fair, but I'll do what's right. Fair's fair. Half each. You take three, I keep three. But on one condition. I don't want to see you in this yard ever again.'

Viner puffed himself up, and his fists shot up, but the constable stepped in front of him. 'That's a gentlemanly offer, Mr Viner. I'd take it if I were you. There's trouble and grief enough in the city without you adding to it.'

514

'Gentlemanly? It's a swindle,' he said. But the constable cast him an icy look and he shut his mouth.

A few moments later Nipper opened the gates and Viner trailed out, the three horses in tow behind him.

They watched him go, standing side by side.

'I'm glad we never have to set eyes on him again,' Bird said.

'Poor man. I felt sorry for him. Imagine, all those years of work, gone. It could have been me, losing this place.'

'Don't feel sorry for him,' she said. 'He treated Livvy like a slave not a servant. No servant should ever have to live in fear of her life.'

'I used to want to kill him,' he said. 'Now I just feel nothing but pity. I've been a fool. I hung onto bitterness all these years. I thought I could prove to Arabella I was a better man than Ted Viner.'

'It wouldn't take much to be a better man than Viner.'

'No. I hated everyone and everything. I didn't dare care for anyone, least of all myself.'

She reached her hand out to brush a sooty particle from his coat. 'You were young, and you'd lost your father too. Your mother told me.'

He searched her eyes. 'She told you about my father?'

'Yes. Before Roly was born.'

His eyes grew glassy. 'I wanted to be a good father. To be the father to Roly that I never had.

I still miss him. Roly, I mean. Even though he was here for so short a time. I tried everything, you know, to bring him back. I couldn't bear it that I'd let him down; my only son. I felt so helpless.'

'I know. It's with me every day, too. Whenever I see another woman's child.'

'We only had him a few days, but in that time I saw my future. That I could be the father I always wanted myself, that even if my own life never amounted to anything; that all the pain – all of it – would be worth it, to make a golden future for him.'

She put both arms around his waist and pulled him to her.

'I'm sorry, Bird,' he said.

'What for?'

He didn't answer, but his face grew serious. Finally he spoke. 'Not being the man I should have been.'

They stood still, holding each other a moment before he said, 'Let's go indoors. Nipper will deal with the customers. My hands are in no fit state to do any labouring, and there's a bruise the size of a saddle on my shoulder.'

He tucked her arm into his good one, and they walked over to the house leaning on one another.

So this is what it is, to be married, Bird thought. To lean on each other in times of hardship and know the other will always be there. A comforting quietness fell over her.

In the house she opened the windows to let out the smell of smoke. Though the evening was drawing in, she did not want to light a fire. It seemed disrespectful somehow. She fetched a shawl, and they made do with a flickering candelabra on the table. She confessed to taking Livvy and Hubert to Romford, and that she'd left Grinstead at the coffee-house.

For a change, Knepp did not interrupt her. When she'd done, he took hold of her hand. 'I see I need to get to know my wife. She seems to be quite ungovernable.' But his eyes were warm with jesting.

'Tell me about the fire, and what happened to your hand.'

So he began, and they talked until darkness fell. She redressed his hands and when she returned from the still-room with a tankard of ale, he was already asleep over the table, his face cushioned on one elbow.

She placed the tankard down gently, so as not to wake him. His neck was grimed with soot, but instead of revulsion, a surge of affection made her place a hand on his springy hair. He shifted and sat up, his eyes bleary.

'You need sleep, Christopher,' she said. 'Fire-fighting is tiring. If you give me your clothes, I'll put them to steep so you have clean for tomorrow.'

'No need,' he said. 'I should go and check on the yard.'

'Nipper will deal with it. You can take one night's rest, surely. Tomorrow will be worse, when we see what the fire has wrought to our trade. Save your strength; you'll need it.'

He nodded and she watched as he hauled his way up the stairs, legs trembling with effort.

When he was settled, she took his clothes in a pail and went out to the yard pump. She worked the handle up and down, but no water came.

'No water, Mistress,' Nipper yelled. 'London's nearly dry. We can't lock up yet, 'cause we're having to fetch water from the Fleet for the horses. Right foul it is, too.'

She glanced over to the gate where a queue of people still waited in the dark under the heavy blanket of smoke which obliterated the stars and rendered the rest of London invisible. A commotion amongst those at the gate.

'Get to the back of the queue,' she heard someone shout.

'We were here first!'

The figures by the gate became more agitated, and she could see raised fists and hear the thump as someone fell.

'Nipper,' she yelled, 'they're fighting by the gate.'

He ran over amid yells and protestations. From within the mob two tattered figures emerged. A plump woman dressed only in a smock nightdress and shawl, crept forward, crab-like, a toddler balanced on her hip, and a small boy limping alongside. Just behind her, a man of solid girth, again half-dressed, with no hat and feet black and

518

bleeding, dropped to his knees. 'Thank God,' he said, kissing the ground.

'Yes?' she said. 'We're closed. If you want transport, you'll have to queue with the rest.'

The man stood. 'Don't you know me?' he asked.

The voice instantly took her back. Back to the words, 'up and coming.' Her father.

She was so shocked at the state he was in, no words would come.

'You have to help us,' Dorcas said, in a voice cracked with smoke. 'We lost everything. There was no time; we couldn't save even a button.' Her mouth crumpled and she buried her head in the toddler's shoulder.

'Horsey!' The child pointed at the stable door where a horse was watching them with pricked ears.

'Hello, Henry,' she said. The child dodged behind his mother, surprised she should know his name. 'And who's this?' Bird said, reaching out a finger to the wide-eyed toddler.

'Bethsaby,' her father said. 'It's thanks to her we're alive at all. She woke us with her coughing and crying. We never thought it would move so fast.'

'What do you want from me, Father?' she asked, although she knew. But she needed him to say it.

'Our house is destroyed. The furniture, our possessions, every small thing. Things I never valued before, like Henry's christening shawl, and your first pair of shoes when you were Bethsaby's age. I took no account of them before, but now they're gone . . . my whole past is gone. I should have looked at it all more closely. I never really saw it. I never saw . . . anything. And now it's too late.'

'Please, Mary Elizabeth,' Dorcas said. 'If you have room, may we stay the night with you? For the children's sake.'

'*He* has to ask,' she said, raising her eyes to her father.

'Dorcas is right,' he said sadly. 'There's nowhere else except the street.'

'Ask, Father.'

He wriggled as if the words were stuck, until they suddenly came in a great rush. 'Mary Elizabeth, please. I know we haven't . . . I mean, I know I haven't been the best father. I was selfish and couldn't see what was right before me. But now I see what's important. And having Bethsaby reminded me of you, of how you were when a babe, and I tried to cut you from my mind, but these last months, you've been in my head like a festering wound.'

'Then why didn't you come?'

'Pride. And shame. Because I knew I'd treated you badly.'

His eyes showed her what she wanted to see. She stepped forward to embrace him. He clung to her like a man who could not drink in enough. Over his shoulder, she saw Dorcas wipe a tear away with a rough swipe of her hand, and Henry peep out from behind her.

'Come in then, all of you,' she said, pulling on his sleeve.

He paused her by refusing to go forward. 'Is it . . . will he be easy with us, your husband? It won't make trouble for you?'

'No. He's soft as butter, my husband. The fire has changed us all. I wager he will want what I want. Now come within, and I'll see what I can do to make us all comfortable.'

She didn't know if it was true, but surely they had suffered enough. Whatever sins Londoners had committed, no good would come of not being neighbourly now.

CHAPTER 43

K nepp sat in the kitchen where his mother used to sit, leaning back in the chair and massaging his temples. He was exhausted; the seething anger he had nursed for most of his life had been doused by the fire. He found himself empty, and flummoxed by the loss of his customers, all their trades suddenly wiped out. Of course, there were still many who were waiting to leave, having seen that London was a burned-out ruin, and there'd be no-one left to sell or hawk their wares to.

He picked up the new *London Gazette* to see another woodcut of burning buildings, so he set it aside. London was in hiatus, waiting for the next disaster to fall, and afraid to rise from the ruins. The yard was running on half its staff, and Grinstead had sent a letter to say the air was so noxious in London, he would not be returning.

In desperation, he had asked Mary Elizabeth to take on the accounting. None of his stablehands could read a single letter. She told him that morning, in no uncertain terms, that Grinstead had left it a sorry mess, with no payments at all for the last six months. He had leant over the desk to look at the open ledger and seen she was right. She always seemed to be right, these days. The image of her dragging the horses from Viner's yard would not leave him. Her strong, determined face, even with the flames towering behind her. Her refusal to give up. He'd let her go in there, where she could have been killed.

How could he not have seen her properly before? It was as if he'd been walking in a fog half his life.

He'd better check the news, see if they'd found out the cause of the fire. He thumbed open the printed paper to see a name he recognised. Robert Hubert. Wasn't that the man who had run from Viner's the night the constable came? The man who was sweet on their maidservant, Livvy?

It couldn't be. This Robert Hubert had confessed that he did '*with malicious intent rouse the fire which lately destroyed the Citie, by tossing a fireball through the open window of Farriner's bakehouse.*' What was more, the tract claimed, he did it because he was a French spy in service of the Pope.

It couldn't be him. Not that crumpled little man.

He read it again. Impossible. Yet this was certainly the same man. What would make him do such a foul thing?

He toyed with the idea of keeping it from Mary Elizabeth, because he knew it would hurt her, that a friend of hers was responsible for this tragedy. But he knew she'd find out soon enough. The name of the person responsible for the fire would be all over London by now. And Mary Elizabeth's father, who'd lost everything, would be just one of those wanting the Frenchman's head on a spike, no doubt. With heavy tread, Knepp crossed the yard and went upstairs to the office.

'Bad news,' he said, laying it before her. 'Is this the French watchmaker who is Livvy's friend?'

Mary Elizabeth scanned the page, and he saw her inhale sharply. 'Who wrote this? It's nonsense,' she said.

'I can't see how it can be. He's confessed to it.'

'Under duress,' she said, thumping it down on the table. 'I daresay the rack would make a man confess to most anything. They need a scapegoat, and a French Catholic is exactly the sort of man they seek.'

'They must believe him guilty, or they—'

'He didn't do it,' she insisted. 'It was probably a loose coal, or a candle, same as always. They must have forced him to a confession.'

Knepp suspected she was right. For such a serious offence Hubert would surely hang, and he could see she knew it by the pallor of her cheeks and the expression in her eyes.

'Does it say anything about Livvy?'

'Nothing,' Knepp said. 'And that's mighty strange, for a blackamoor maid would surely make a good story.'

She took it up again and leafed through the pages. 'I left them with Stefan at Romford, so what happened? Why are they not together?'

524

'There's no indication in the paper about where he was taken, or when.'

'Where are they holding him?'

'They brought him from Romford to Southwark, it says, over the river. It's about the only gaol in the city left standing.'

'Then we must go and find out what's happened to Livvy.'

'Don't even think of it,' he said. 'They'd think us accomplices. It will be tantamount to hanging yourself. If he's a traitor it will be dangerous to be his friends.'

'But someone must speak out for him. I know he's innocent. Nothing he said on the journey made me think he had anything to do with any plot.'

'Have a care. The mood is volatile in the city. The people are like whipped dogs, ready to snap and snarl. They fear invasion by the Dutch or the French, and many claim that the calamities in these past years are because we harbour Popish men against God's law. It would be madness to seem to be the Frenchman's friend. I absolutely forbid it.'

She pursed her lips and rubbed a forefinger over the paper. After a moment's silence, she said, 'Maybe you are right.'

A deep unease made him snatch the paper away. She had capitulated too easily. He was beginning to know his wife, and also to see that when she decided to do something nobody would be able to stop her.

'You are not to go anywhere near Southwark,' he said. 'Do I make myself plain?'

'Yes, husband.'

He stood a few more moments, watching her as she dipped the quill into the ink and applied the nib to the ledger. Her meekness was unusual. Damn her. He couldn't put her under lock and key. He thought of Arabella, how she had turned crazed from living with Viner. The thought of her brought only pity, and a determination. He refused to be another Viner. He had wasted enough time hurting people and making enemies. But he feared Mary Elizabeth would disobey him, and short of force, what could he do? He had vowed to be less controlling, but now this.

He put a hand to her shoulder. 'If it means so much to you, I will go.'

She turned, and held out her arms to him. And in their warm circle, he suddenly felt he could do anything.

Later that afternoon Knepp took a gig, with Nipper driving. He stopped to ask a news vendor if he knew which prison in Southwark Hubert was held in. The rumour was that Hubert, who was of intense interest to everybody, was housed in the King's Bench. From other broadsheets he already knew that prisoners were kept in two houses known as the Angel and the Crane, the former giving its name to Angel Place, which bounded it on the south.

It was a day with a sharp nip in the air, and a damp fogginess that only made the sour smell of burning more acute. He couldn't get used to the look of London with all its familiar landmarks gone. London Bridge had one side torched completely to a heap of cinders, the other still standing as if nothing was amiss.

Nipper dropped him just over the bridge in Southwark. Knepp told him to return in an hour. With no houses left, the population of London seethed in the open air. The south bank of the river swarmed with refugees; they hung in ragged droves around the arched gates of St Augustine's Priory, and more loitered in makeshift tents in the grounds of St Thomas's Hospital. At the tables outside the Tabard Inn, men slumped over their elbows, soot-stained and insensible with ale.

With trepidation he approached the prison, a stone building converted from two houses. High barred windows loomed over a high wall and the stench from it was palpable, even from this distance. Two armed men were at the gate, but the head warder, a hefty lump of a man with an untidy beard, was easily bribed.

'I hope they hang the bastard,' he said. 'My lodgings went up with the rest of Watling Street. What's he done to you?'

'My father-in-law's a lawyer,' Knepp said. 'Joshua Carpenter. I'm to interview Mr Hubert on his behalf. To establish whether he's guilty or innocent.'

'He's guilty, right enough. He's confessed. Don't need more talk, if you ask me.'

'Nevertheless,' Knepp said, using his father-in-law's pompous tone, 'we must make sure. We wouldn't want to hang the wrong man.'

The warder's face grew grim. 'Who did you say you were?'

'Son-in-law of Joshua Carpenter, lawyer.'

'Aye, I've heard of him. Papers?'

'Burned in the fire. His house was on Lombard Street.'

The warder's face slackened with relief. 'You'll find something to nail on him, then. He's down below, away from prying eyes.'

The warder summoned two more burly individuals. 'End door,' the warder said, fishing a bunch of keys from his pocket. 'And Hodges, take a table and chair down for the gent. Just one chair.'

The warder called Hodges went to drag a folding table from an office, and the other man carried the chair down the stairs into the cellar area where a row of five identical doors greeted them. Each was of black iron with a single grilled window. The reflections of wall-sconces glowed dully in their metal surfaces.

He followed in the warders' wake, feet skidding on slimy flagstones. The cell was scarcely big enough for the huddled man crouching in the corner, let alone a table and chair, and Hubert showed no sign of moving. He kept his face to the wall, although Knepp could see his back rise and fall with his breath.

'A quarter hour, no more,' Hodges said, after the table and chair had been thrust inside. 'We'll wait at the top of the stairs. It stinks down here.'

The men's footsteps receded down the corridor.

'M'sieur Hubert?' He crouched down to try to see his face. 'It's Mr Knepp. Livvy's employer.'

No answer.

He tried again. 'My father-in-law might be able to help you. He's a lawyer.' He didn't know if this was true. Mary Elizabeth's father had never impressed him up to now.

Hubert stayed hunched over, and spoke as if to the wall in a voice hoarse and desperate. 'The lawyer, he is no use to me. They will hang me anyway because they need a man to blame. So go. My life is over.'

'What happened?' he asked softly. 'Where's Livvy?'

A clank of chain against metal and Hubert moved around to face him. A black bruise and swelling contorted his face. His hands were like lumps of meat, the fingers a swollen mass of blood and bruising. 'She got away. On the boat to France with Stefan. It was about to leave when they caught up with her. They were looking for a black woman. Someone needed to make trouble while the boat left, so I push her on board and make as much trouble as I can. I invent accomplices and make up mighty lies, to give them time to get onto French soil.'

'Stefan is with her?'

'I hope. I hope they stay together. The English sailors, they killed her family. Burned them to death at Terschelling in Holland. If no-one confess, they will see she had reason for vengeance. If I die, then blame is over. England will forget her.'

'You'd take the blame? When you know it to be false?'

'At first, I think it is possible for me to confess, to give her time to flee, and then say afterward it's false. I write to my friend Captain Peterson – ask him to tell them, I was still at sea when it started. To tell them I was in Sweden, not France. But now I realise even if he tells them that, they won't listen. They hear what they want to hear.'

'I don't understand. Who is Captain Peterson?'

'A friend to my father. He often takes me on his merchant vessel to France. But even if he speaks for me, I've woven such lies that I cannot myself fathom what is true. They break my fingers with a hammer to make me speak. No use for mending watches now.'

Knepp stared at his ruined hands. A lump came to his throat. 'They did this?'

'They'd do worse; if there was worse to do. So I am worth nothing now. But I don't care, if it keeps Livvy safe. She has the best heart of any person I know. She has had such sorrow.' He turned his face away as his eyes shone wet.

'But without you, where will she go in France?'

'Her brother, he is still a slave in Bordeaux. A slave! That men can use other men so. It disgusts me. I guess she will go to find him.'

'Let us help you, M'sieur Hubert. We can overturn this, try to make them see you didn't do it.'

'And if they didn't hang me, who would they look for?'

Knepp shook his head. M'sieur Hubert's sad blue eyes met his. *Livvy. That's who they'd look for. The black woman the constable was searching for, who said she'd burn down the city.*

'Hasn't she had enough pain?' Hubert asked.

A noise of a shot above and shouting. Running feet in the corridor and the clank of keys.

'Out!' the warder from upstairs appeared at the door. 'Quick! There's a mob outside after his blood.'

Knepp found himself harried out of the cell, and the warder pushed the key back in the locks and turned each one with a clank.

'Who broke M'sieur Hubert's hands?' Knepp asked, grabbing the warder by the shoulder.

'Bludworth's orders,' he said. 'Now move, sir,' he said, drawing his pistol. He pushed Knepp up the stairs, but they were too late; as soon as they were in the entrance hall, a crash, and splinters of glass and wood burst inwards from the windows.

'Out the back way,' the warder said, grabbing a bell from a stand near the door. Moments later the deafening warning clang rang out.

Men in the dark doublets of warders appeared from every doorway.

'Break out?' one of them asked, loading his pistol. 'Which section?'

'No. Men after Hubert's blood. They're breaking in.'

'Then let 'em. I'd like to see the weasel hung, drawn and quartered.'

'And so would the whole of London. Our job's to make sure he gets a public hanging, so every man-jack who lost his house can watch him squirm. Get this man out of here.'

Knepp was forced at pistol-point to a dark door into what once must have been the kitchen and servant's quarters, but was now a series of shelf-lined offices. Within a few moments he was shoved outside and the door slammed behind him followed by the scrape of bolts.

'Where's the French bastard being kept?' A woman with bad teeth, and the air of a snarling dog, grabbed his arm. Knepp was hemmed in before he'd taken two steps. The crowd was six deep, their expressions spoiling for a fight. He gave a quick glance at his surroundings; he was at the back, in a yard surrounded by a six-foot high wall. No way out or exit here.

'Who are you?' a man asked, thrusting a dagger at his shirt. He was wearing a tanner's apron, and Knepp's guess was he was from one of the tanneries that had gone up by Swan Stairs.

'Just a visitor,' he said.

'You weren't visiting *him*, were you?'

'No. A debtor. John Jones.' The first name he could think of.

'You didn't see where they're keeping him, this Frenchman?'

'No. But I believe somewhere on the first floor.' God help the man. Hadn't he suffered enough?

Shots from the front of the building made the crowd turn and run in that direction.

Knepp took his chance and ran with them. By the time they got to the front the mob had completely overwhelmed the gaol. He was in time to see the chief warder dragged out to the front. Two men had him by the arms whilst a third tried to take the keys from his belt.

Knepp took his chance and fled through the front gate. In the distance he heard shots and the crash of glass. He paused against the wall of St Augustine's to compose himself. He wiped his forehead, and his hands stung with the sweat from his brow. He looked down at his hands; still sore and blistered from the fire. Then he thought of Hubert's hands and angry tears sprang to his eyes. Bludworth was intent on foisting the blame for the disaster somewhere else, even if it meant torturing someone to do it.

'Sir! Over here!' Nipper was there, drawing the carriage up alongside.

Knepp stared at it a moment, unwilling to move.

He would have to tell Mary Elizabeth what he knew, and it would hurt her. He had disappointed her so often, and now he was to do it again.

'Sir?' Nipper called.

'I'm coming,' Knepp said.

Bird paced the downstairs chamber. She was glad that her father and Dorcas were out; he had gone to see if he could stake out his plot for rebuilding. Though what with, she had no idea, as the goldsmith he traded with, and who had the keeping of all his gold, had gone up in smoke too. Bethsaby was sleeping in a box by the window, and in the corner an absorbed Henry played with a pile of building bricks, constructing towers and then flattening them. Would that London could be rebuilt so easily.

She went to the window for the umpteenth time. She should have gone with her husband. He'd been away far too long, and a nagging unease would not let her rest. When the carriage finally clattered back into the yard, she ran out to greet it, but she could see by the way he avoided her eyes that it was not going to be good news.

'Come within,' he said.

She followed him, surprised to see his hands were shaking as he placed his hat on the table. He took a deep breath. 'Oh God, that place,' he said. 'We can't save him.' Tears leaked from his eyes.

Immediately she went to him, but he stood and turned, wiping his eyes on the ends of his neckerchief.

'Tell me,' she said.

'Take Henry outside to help Nipper,' he said.

She shepherded the boy out, and when she returned Knepp was more composed. He told her everything.

'They'll hang him then,' she said, sitting down opposite him at the table.

'He is as set on it as they are.'

'Oh, Knepp.' She reached to cover his hand with hers.

October 1666

The damp ruins of St Sepulchre's church were deserted except for Bird and Knepp. Most of London had taken the day off to go to the hanging at Tyburn, some three miles away. Knepp had closed the yard, unwilling to drive ghoulish spectators to the site of the gallows.

Someone had cleared the rubble from the church, but the scorched, chequered floor remained under wet soot marked with the scratch of a broom. Behind them, the church tower was still standing, and one blackened crumbling wall with a single arched window empty of glass. Through it, the grey blanket of cloud obscured the autumn sun.

Bird and Knepp stood arm-in-arm remembering. The last time they'd been here was to bury Roly, and both were seeing again the tiny coffin as it lay before the altar. Today, the absence of altar and pulpit seemed right, somehow.

Distant bells, mournful. Three sonorous clangs.

Bird felt Knepp's grasp on her arm tighten.

Three o'clock. The time Robert was to hang.

They bowed their heads.

The cries of the crowd were too far away for them to hear, but close by, from a jutting rafter, a blackbird began to sing.

In the quiet the pure notes were like holy rain.

He would be at peace. *Peace*. It suddenly seemed like such a precious word.

A few moments later, Knepp turned to her. 'Do you feel old?'

'I suppose I feel surprised. Surprised that I am here, still breathing, after all that has beset us these last months. But old? Yes, I know what you mean.'

He steered her past the rubble. 'I feel as if I have lived six lifetimes, not just one.'

'Grief does that, I think.'

'The London I used to know is gone.'

'It will rise again. We can re-build it. A fine new city that will welcome good men like Robert and women like Livvy, wherever they come from.'

He paused and turned her into his embrace. 'You see good in everything.' He smoothed a strand of hair from her brow. 'I remember when you first came to me, you were so pretty, and so determined to change everything for the better, but I, ugly old fool that I was, dug in my heels and forbade you.'

'Well you'll not stop me now, Christopher Knepp. Seems to me, the best thing for grief is to be busy, and let it take its own sweet course.'

'Happen so, my sweet Bird. And to share it.' He kissed her on the forehead. 'I missed your vitality after Roly died.'

'I had no hunger for life then. But now, I see how blessed we are.'

'You'll be back at rehearsal tomorrow then?'

'Unless you need me to clean harness.'

He looked sharply, but seeing her grin, began to laugh. His laugh was deep and full and shook him so hard he had to double over.

'What's so funny?' she said.

'Life,' he said, wiping his eyes. 'Life.'

CHAPTER 44

The King's Playhouse, March 1667

Bird's heart beat strongly under her bodice. The king was in the audience and had taken a particular interest in this play, since he had apparently given Dryden the whole idea. Her palms were sweating with nerves.

'Good luck' she whispered, as Nell rushed out onto the stage, clad like a boy in breeches for the second Prologue. Nell strode straight to the edge of the stage, and confided in an intimate stage whisper,

> *'And now I am sent again to speak the rest.*
> *And bow to every great and noble wit—'*

Nell already had them in the palm of her hand. How did she do it? The child was like a spark, lighting up everything around her. Bird glanced to the Royal Box. There was James, the Duke of York, looking mighty amused to see the king's face so pink with humour, his eyes fixed on Nell's antics.

When Nell was done, the prologue was met with catcalls and rousing applause, and Nell swept offstage with a little jig. In the back of the pit Bird spotted her old friend Samuel Pepys. No longer a stranger, it was reassuring to see his familiar bright-eyed figure in his usual spot. He was whispering to Elisabeth, who kept flashing her eyes at the king's party, a bag of sweetmeats on her lap.

Now. Bird took a deep breath. No time to think more; the drums and trumpets sounded from behind the painted cloth, and Bird strode purposefully onstage. She embraced Charles Hart, who was playing her brother, firmly.

'*Dear Asteria!*' he said.

She raised her voice so those at the back could hear.

'*My dear brother! Welcome; a thousand welcomes: Methinks this year you've been absent was so tedious! I hope you have made a pleasant voyage, and brought your good humour back again to Court.*'

As she rounded, she caught sight of Knepp, sitting proudly in the middle of the stalls, flanked by her father, whose expression was one of frank disbelief. It gave her a shiver of amusement. Dorcas, she guessed, would be somewhere at the back, taking care of Henry and Bethsaby.

They were all here. The sight of them, instead of embarrassing her, filled her with confidence. She was alight. Nobody could touch her here on the stage. In this other-world she was subject to different laws. She could be a different person entirely, one of no fixed personality. Although she was their family, up here they could not ever possess her. Up here was freedom.

She spoke her lines as if she truly were Asteria, the queen's scheming maid. The stage disappeared, and only the Sicilian Court remained; no longer a painted picture, but a real inhabited place, hot with noon-day sun. And when it came to her song, a song of unrequited love, she knew the pain of it, the same pain she'd felt for Samuel Pepys. What a foolish young thing she had been.

'I feed a flame within, which so torments me
That it both pains my heart, and yet contents me:
'Tis such a pleasing smart, and I so love it,
That I had rather die, then once remove it.'

Even as she sung of the sting of it, she knew it to be gone, used as fuel in this; her art. As she took a bow with a flourish, the thought came that perhaps there could be great art only where there was pain.

The applause went on, like a rush of wind through her hair. Dazed, she looked out into the blur of faces. To her delight Knepp was standing, his hands raised above his head in applause, and her father was clapping like a demon, fit to skin his hands.

She glanced further back to see Samuel Pepys and Elisabeth exchanging a jest between them. From here, the pair looked like characters in a play, and it struck her that she was unsure which was the more real; this side of the curtain, or that. As the applause swelled, she watched the Pepyses take their cue and clap with the rest. She curtseyed again, and as she came to standing, saw the king smiling down at her with his blessing.

At the end of the play, Anne Marshall came to her and said, 'You were good, tonight.'

'Thank you,' Bird said. 'So were you.'

'No. I mean, you shone. You played as if it really mattered,' Anne said.

'It does matter. It's never just an entertainment, is it?'

Anne smiled. 'So you have learnt what the theatre really is. A way of us seeing more clearly who we are.' She took Bird's arm. 'They're calling for us. Shall we take another bow?'

HISTORICAL NOTES

Pepys's Diary

S amuel Pepys is the author of the most famous
and best-loved diary in the English language.
Born the son of a tailor, Pepys was a self-
made man who rose up the ranks to become one
of the foremost citizens in Restoration London,
and his diary provides a fly-on-the-wall view of
life in the seventeenth century. His daily entries
combine coverage of major crises, such as the
Plague and the Great Fire of London, with political events, gossip, and intimate details of his many
affairs. It tells us what people ate, how they relaxed
(Pepys was a great musician and theatre-goer),
how they spent their money, and all the minutiae
of daily life. The importance of the diary to our
knowledge of the era cannot be over-estimated.

Pepys began his entries on New Year's Day 1660
using Thomas Shelton's shorthand, a method he
probably used in his work-life for speed. He wrote
with a quill pen in standard notebooks of 282
pages, with hand-ruled margins in red ink. The
diary at first looks like impenetrable code – all

squiggles and dots with only the occasional recognisable word. Perhaps Pepys also used this 'code' for privacy; for he certainly would not have wanted his wife to read about his extra-marital affairs!

Pepys was Clerk to the Navy, which in the era of sail, when wars were fought at sea, meant he had enormous responsibility for the supplying of ships with everything from ship's biscuits to cannon. He was a man who was held in great respect by the king, Charles II, and moved in scientific and intellectual circles as well as patronising the arts. He continued his diary for a little over nine years, to May 31st 1669, when he had trouble with his eyesight, and regrettably, stopped writing it.

Fortunately for posterity, Pepys left his diary to Magdalene College, Cambridge, where he had been a scholar, and his whole library can be seen there too – some three thousand books, still on the original shelves Pepys commissioned for the purpose.

Several of my novels have been set in the seventeenth century, and for all of them I have used Pepys' diary as an integral part of my research. In the process, I became fascinated by the women who appear as vague figures in the background, between the lines, always overshadowed by Pepys' ebullient presence. Mrs Pepys is referred to by Pepys only as 'my wife' and not by her name, so as a sort of revenge, I started to imagine what the women in the diary might be doing, when he was so to speak 'out of the room'. The first novel *Pleasing Mr Pepys* was told from the point of view of his wife and maidservant, but there are plenty of other notable women in his diary – as Pepys ruefully confesses; 'Musique and women I cannot but give way to.' I chose Bess Bagwell for the second book because it has always been a mystery why her husband seemed to encourage her affair with Pepys. And this book centres around the singer and actress Elizabeth Knepp, one of Pepys' great friends in the theatre.

ELIZABETH KNEPP
(KNEP OR KNIPP)

Elizabeth Knepp (sometimes known as Mary Knepp) was born Elizabeth Carpenter and records show she married Christopher Knepp, whom Pepys calls a 'jockey' but was probably a horse dealer or horse hirer, at Knightsbridge in 1659. I took the liberty of giving her the nickname 'Bird' in the novel as it seemed to suit her, and there are so many other Elizabeths in Pepys' diary. Mrs Pepys is also an Elisabeth, and I had already used most of the diminutives for characters in the other two novels.

There are 108 references to Mrs Knepp in Pepys' diary. Actresses in those days were always known as 'Mrs' whether they were single or married. In the seventeenth century, status was always conferred on a woman by the man. Thus Pepys always refers to his wife Elisabeth as 'my wife'. Although this seems in our ears to diminish her, in fact this is not an insult; it was designed to confer on her a status not accorded to his servants who were referred to as Dolly, or Deb, or Jane. The theatre was the one place where this did not hold sway

– female actors were always called 'Mrs' as a mark of respect.

Pepys first met Elizabeth Knepp on 6 December 1665; and he described her as 'pretty enough, but the most excellent, mad-humoured thing, and sings the noblest that I ever heard in my life.' Christopher Knepp, on the other hand, is described as, 'an ill, melancholy, jealous-looking fellow'. Scholars disagree on the full extent of Mrs Knepp's relationship with Pepys; but certainly some of our knowledge of the seventeenth-century theatre, including the career of Nell Gwynne, comes from Pepys' diary.

Pepys had an absolute passion for the theatre, and used to try to resist attending by fining himself, putting money in a poor box if he broke his vow to keep away. Nothing worked, and his diary for 1666-68 is full of references to the theatre and particularly to Mrs Knepp, including mentions of their amorous flirtations, and passages about how much he enjoyed their musical evenings and especially her singing. My impression from the diary is that they genuinely liked each other, and this was one of the things that attracted me to writing about her.

The professional actress was a new phenomenon in the 1660s. Up until the seventeenth century, women had no reflections of themselves in entertainment; all female roles were played by boys. The first female on the English stage was Margaret 'Peg' Hughes, who played Desdemona in a production of *Othello* in 1660. Only two months before, the role had been played by a boy, and the thought of this upheaval in the theatre led me to create the character of Stefan. Being an actress in this era was a way of both gaining and losing power – a woman was able to behave on stage in a powerful way, but also women were still seen as commodities; an attraction or novelty to please those that mattered at the time, i.e men.

Beauty was a woman's currency in the early theatre, and in life in general. A frank and unflattering assessment of women's looks was commonplace; their 'assets' as if it was a calculation – a checklist of features: how straight the nose, how even the teeth, how pale the complexion. In the theatre a good pair of legs was essential as in many roles the women played boys to show their legs. For a woman to reveal her legs, usually hidden beneath skirts, was considered extremely daring, and this is why so many 'cross-dressing' roles were written in this period. These were called 'breeches' roles. Voyeuristic? Certainly, but being a 'player' was a way for a woman to counter invisibility, and to have a voice denied her in any other public sphere. And a degree of freedom must have been felt by these women as they played assertive men's roles – the reverse of what had been the status quo before.

The idea of sleeping your way to the top in the entertainment industry was commonplace in the seventeenth-century theatre. An example is Mrs

Barry, who was 'procured' by the rake Rochester at fifteen years of age and then moulded (like Eliza Doolittle in *My Fair Lady*) to be an actress. At the onset of acting as a career for women, beauty was a necessity, it was supposed that acting skills could be taught and were less important for women than for men. Rochester's letters to Mrs Barry give us an insight into both his training of her and the progress of their sexual liaison. Ironically, Mrs Barry was then most famous for her tragic parts depicting an innocent maiden.

In this period the theatre was one of the few ways for women to transcend social boundaries. Through Pepys' diaries we can witness Nell Gwynne, rising through society from bawd's daughter to mistress of a king. Evidence shows Nell Gwynne certainly had a mind of her own and used her position on stage to advance herself, and of course now she has achieved some sort of national status. In Pepys' diary, Elizabeth Knepp is invited to musical soirées with Pepys and his civil-servant friends. Being in the theatre conferred a 'celebrity' status not available to other women, and just as today, celebrities were sought out by the upper echelons of society.

The theatre, even then, was a reflection of society. Pepys went to the theatre, not only to see plays, but to be seen. Only recently has the convention of the fourth wall between the stage and audience arisen, and at the beginning of women's life in the theatre, there was constant badinage across the divide between stage and audience with an emphasis on wit and banter on both sides. Scenes on stage echoed or parodied scenes at court, and Charles II was a rake of a king.

The women in the plays by Sheridan, Etheredge and Wycherly (for example, Lady Gimcrack and Mrs Figgup) were imitations of the rich women attending the play. Actresses of the time impersonated women who were almost always of a higher class than themselves, but in doing so, acquired the gloss of the characters they portrayed. In her theatrical life, Elizabeth Knepp made her debut in the title role of Jonson's *Epicene* on 1 June 1664. (She was also cast as Lucetta in Killigrew's 1664 planned production of his *Thomaso*, with an all-female cast, which was cancelled before completion.)

She played major and minor roles in a range of productions of the 1660s and 1670s, including the famous role of Lady Fidget in Wycherley's *The Country Wife* at Drury Lane in 1675. Beyond the scope of my novel, she is thought to have been a mistress of Sir Charles Sedley, who was a notorious rake and libertine, part of the 'Merry Gang' gang of courtiers which included the Earl of Rochester and Lord Buckhurst. In the late 1670s she became the mistress of actor Joseph Haines, a comedian, song-and-dance man, and eccentric.

Elizabeth Knepp probably provided Pepys with backstage gossip and inside insights into a world he was avid to know more about. She supplied him with the theatrical and social gossip of the day, and took part in evening entertainments alongside him, as an equal, when the theatres were closed down for the plague.

Many women's theatrical careers were cut short by pregnancy. Mrs Knepp had at least two children we know of, the first being a son born in June 1666. Pepys refers to her pregnancy in the diary, because he was asked to be a godparent, but then dismisses the child's death in a single line. The infant mortality rate was approximately twelve to thirteen percent of live births. Childhood diseases, such as scarlatina (scarlet fever), whooping cough, smallpox, and pneumonia killed thirty percent of England's children before they reached adulthood. The dangers of childbirth for women of this era, when there was so little effective medical help, cannot be overestimated.

Elizabeth Knepp died during the birth of the second child, which was stillborn, in 1681.

THE REAL AND FICTIONAL
CHARACTERS IN
ENTERTAINING MR PEPYS

All the major characters in the novel exist in Pepys' diary, and can be found in its pages if you look them up. Nell Gwynne, seen in this novel as she began her career, eventually found fame as an actress and mistress to the King, despite her humble beginnings as the daughter of a bawd in Coal Yard Alley. Pepys mentions her often in his diary, although he is not always complimentary;

'there saw *The Indian Emperour*; where I find Nell come again, which I am glad of; but was most infinitely displeased with her being put to act the Emperour's daughter; which is a great and serious part, which she do most basely.'

The watchmaker Robert Hubert was only twenty-six when he was executed following his false confession of starting the Great Fire of London. His initial confession stated that he started the fire at Westminster, but when he learnt it started in Pudding Lane he changed his story, and claimed he threw a fireball through the window of the bakery. The only difficulty with this was that the bakery had no windows. A Swede called Petersen also attested Hubert was still off-shore on his ship when the fire started.

Nobody understands why Robert Hubert insisted on making such false confession, and his subsequent testimony was so convoluted that most believed him to be crazy but entirely innocent. I have invented freely around his story, suggesting a fictional reason for his behaviour. Pepys discusses Hubert's confession in his diary and says, 'Yet the fellow, who, though a mopish besotted fellow, did not speak like a madman, did swear that he did fire it.'

After Hubert was executed, such was the intensity of feeling against him that his body was torn to pieces by an angry mob. After the need for a scapegoat for the disaster had died down, the cause of the fire was attributed to a probable spark from the bakery; a tragic accident that was fuelled by the dry weather and a strong wind.

Mrs Knepp (Christopher's mother), Stefan, and Livvy are all invented. Pepys tells us in his diary he employs a 'blackmore' cook, and people of colour were more common in this period than one would surmise from our dominant history. But I had serious misgivings about including Stefan and Livvy in the story, because of issues around race, sexuality and sensitivity to my invented material. But the characters came to life and stuck in my mind and wouldn't let go, and so began a lot of painstaking research and soul-searching about what was, or wasn't, appropriate for these characters, given my own background, the needs of the plot, and also the attitudes of today versus the attitudes of the time of Pepys' diary.

Likewise, views on morality, domestic violence and sexual conduct have moved on since Pepys's day. What was considered perfectly acceptable in the seventeenth century is totally unacceptable now, and we must seek to understand seventeenth-century attitudes and behaviour as a product of the time. Whether or not I have successfully picked my way across this quagmire of abuse versus the historical mores of the time is something I hope my readers will discuss between themselves.